PRETTY PERFECT

LANA SKY

Pretty Perfect
By Lana Sky

Copyright © 2017 by Lana Sky

Editing by Gemma Fisk Editing Services, Katrina Crane, Mickey Reed
Proofreading and Formatting by Charity Chimni

ACKNOWLEDGMENTS

A special thanks to everyone who supported me during the many, many drafts and edits of this story, including Kat and Gemma who tirelessly worked to whip this idea into shape, as well as Jilly who suffered a million different versions of it. Thanks to Mickey, who helped to take this draft to the next level, and a very emphatic thank you to Michelle Quinn whose patience knows no bounds. Last but certainly not least, thank you Charity Chimni for giving this story the final polish.

Please keep in mind that this story includes dark, graphic, and explicit content matter that is not suitable for readers under the age of 18—or for readers who are uncomfortable with the following subject matter: age-gap relationships, explicit sex, mentions of substance abuse, and graphic depictions of violence.

ACT 1

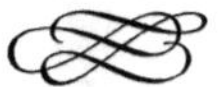

CHAPTER 1

The perfect fake smile required only two ingredients—glossy pink lipstick and pearly white teeth. From the outside, I looked charming, even while my lifelong dream drifted further out of reach.

Acting at its finest.

"Thank you for auditioning, Ms. DeSotto," the casting director told me in a rush. I think his name was Fred—or whatever he'd blurted at the start of this hasty call. "You have beautiful form, but we've decided to go in another direction with this production."

And there it was. I wasn't supposed to argue. For instance, if my lines were so beautiful, then why didn't I get the lead? A background role? Anything? My therapist would encourage me to find a positive in this situation. "The wrong direction" was a new excuse from the typical list, at least.

This could have been progress.

Or rock bottom.

"I appreciate the opportunity," I croaked when I finally found my voice. "Thank you for even considering—" The dial tone interrupted my well-rehearsed spiel. *Thank you for considering me for such an opportunity, blah blah blah.*

They remembered my name; that had to count for something. Rather than just written off, I had been artfully rejected, the truth sweetened with a little bit of sugar and personalized for dramatic effect. *You are a beautiful dancer, whatever your name is… But you aren't good enough.*

On the bright side, I couldn't even remember what that audition had been for. A ballet company? A local production? Either way, it was the third rejection in as many days, and I felt fine. Peachy, in fact.

"You're setting yourself up for failure, sweetie," my mother warned in her typical chiding tone as I tucked my cell phone into my bag.

She'd eavesdropped, of course. Not that it wasn't hard to from across the table. Crammed together in the dining room of a small café, we were both failing to hide our secrets. Like the fact that the "tea" she was drinking was really spiked with vodka—a lot, considering how long she savored her next sip. Like always, I pretended not to notice the flask sticking out of her bag and dug a tissue from my pocket to dab at my nose with. It was running again, but one peek at the napkin revealed that it wasn't bleeding.

Thank God for small miracles.

"I thought you were done with all that nonsense?" Mom watched me with a raised eyebrow.

"Am I…what?" Oops. My inner actress floundered, forgetting her lines for a split second. Caught off guard, I rubbed my nose again, checking for dust while fighting to maintain my cheerful grin.

"Ballet," Mom said. "I thought you gave that up. Your dad said you enrolled in some college courses. It's about time you moved on from that, sweetie."

Oh. It was the typical argument. Why couldn't I just grow up, bleach my hair blonde, and catch a man like she had?

"I'm not trying to be mean, sweetie," Mom added while patting her lips with a napkin. As always, an insult hidden between the lines, staining the air like the red lipstick coating the rim of her glass. *You should just accept your place, sweetie; you aren't a good enough dancer, sweetie.*

Her doubt was why I needed my therapist and my trusted "feelings" journal—to help me accept the flaws she loved to point out. I wasn't perfect. I spun too quickly. My feet sometimes pigeon-toed. There was always room for improvement. I simply had to accept that. She was supposed to help me in that endeavor, but maybe those mimosas made her too maudlin to remember her part in the "Saving Anya" crusade.

"I know," I said, playing my role anyway. My watch revealed that only five minutes remained in this scene. Five more minutes that I had to pretend.

"Hmph." Mom prodded her uneaten salmon fillet with a steak knife. "Perhaps it's time you outgrew dance anyway. I mean, you're already twenty, dear."

She made it sound as simple as putting away tattered coloring books. Or, in her case, ending a ten-year marriage and waiting only six months before slipping a brand-new rock onto that cherished ring finger. Mature people threw away old toys, dreams, and families like raggedy baby dolls.

Just like she had.

"Yeah, I guess…"

"I mean, look at Jake." She smiled for real, turning the head of every man in the room. "His mother says that he heard from an NFL scout already…" She paused as if waiting for me to fill in the gaps of information. I didn't. "Anyway, he needs your support now, sweetie. I know ballet used to mean a lot to you, but now, you have a future to worry about."

A future… I should have just let her criticize me in silence —like usual—but I've only been mended for just a few short months. Bad habits are hard to break.

"It's so nice to know that you dragged me to all those years of ballet lessons just to placate me and not because you might have *actually* believed in me." Oh dear. Snarky voice, sharp inflection.

"Anya, please don't do this." Mom sighed. "Not now."

Oops. Selfish Anya had shown her unwelcome face, resorting to what the therapist had deemed "hostile negativity." The truth was simply nontherapeutic—like the fact that Jake and I had broken up six months ago, and he could have been playing football in China for all I knew. One had to always "consider how your words might affect those around you. Try not to dwell on the negatives."

In other words, lie. My mother was the master of the art form.

"I d-do believe in you, Anya," she insisted, though her voice lacked any conviction. "I only meant…"

"I know. It's okay." I flashed my teeth, reassembling my charming mask. "I'll just try harder next time."

"Right!" she agreed. "That's what I meant, darling." Mothering was so much easier for her if someone fed her the right lines. Act. Scene. Our play was back on schedule, and the audience was none the wiser. "Next time, sweetie."

She patted me lovingly on the forearm, and I stood while she started on her second drink. There were only five other patrons in the café besides us. All of them were far too busy putting on their own strained façades to notice me slipping a ratty canvas bag over my shoulder, despite how it clashed with my designer outfit.

"Oh, and, Anya, sweetie?" Mom called as I pushed my chair under the table. "You might want to pick up some allergy relief stuff if you need it. You've been sniffling all day. The weather is a nightmare this time of year…right?" Her tone straddled that fragile line between hope and fear as I followed her gaze to the wad of used napkins piled beside my soup bowl.

"That's okay." I ran a hand underneath my nose just to be sure. "I'm fine."

On my way to the main doors, a cheerful waitress urged me to come again even though she served me here at least once a month. Mother then piped up from our customary table, loud enough for everyone else to hear and marvel at how close we were. "Same time next week, sweetie!"

"Like always!" I bolted from the café without a backward glance.

The luncheons were her way of bonding after the divorce—or, more importantly, her way of making sure my father and I couldn't bond *too* much, and she had a direct line of gossip into the goings-on of the DeSotto household. It made her feel better for having dumped me there.

Nine years later, the fear that I might ask to live with her instead of him was one of the myriads of reasons why her meals consisted of liquor. If I caught her sober, she might have to pretend that she cared. *Dwelling on the past, Anya,* my therapist would warn. *Focus only on the present.* Like racing to the bus stop before the driver pulled away from the curb.

The best tactic, per the good doctor, was to ignore *everything*—just not the old way. No handfuls of narcotics to swallow down the misery. The music blaring from my headphones was enough to separate me from the rest of the world because music was better than any high. The therapist said that too. And it worked—sort of. Rather than my mother's latest drama, my thoughts consisted of nothing but Tchaikovsky and an array of choreography so intricate that I couldn't afford to miss a single step.

"One flaw snaps the chain," Remsky liked to quip.

I repeated his mantra as I departed the bus ten minutes later and caught the train to the heart of downtown. Just my luck, the doors of the theater were already closed by the time I reached them, and the faint hint of Chopin drifted from beyond like an ominous warning.

"Shit."

I slipped around the side of the building, shouldered open a fire exit, and hurried down the dimly lit hallway that led backstage. The other dancers were already warming up. No barre work today, but straight into center work, which left me with no chance of hiding within the shadows of the studio.

Double shit.

Remsky shot me a death glare from his perch at the end of the stage while I skulked past. With gleaming silver hair and black sweats starched to the nines, he resembled an orderly in some clinical psych ward, ready to snap at any infraction. "Later," he mouthed.

Dreading the next few hours already, I entered the dressing room and changed into my leotard. Using an exposed pipe as a makeshift barre, I warmed up, hitting all the important joints—legs, knees, toes, ankles. My calves were burning by the time I reentered the auditorium and attempted to slip unnoticed amongst the cluster of dancers grouped near the front of the gallery.

"Hey!" A hand tapped my shoulder. "Incoming. Nosebleed."

A telltale warmth dripped down my upper lip. Thankfully, whoever had pointed it out was already in the process of shoving a napkin into my hand.

"Maybe you should sit out this round?" the do-gooder wondered.

I flashed my patented smile and dabbed away every trace of blood. "I'm fine." Better than fine. I didn't even feel the need to compare the way I filled out my leotard to Chloe, the bulimic whose straps threatened to slip from her waiflike shoulders. According to my therapist, that kind of thinking led to a dark place.

I eyed the stage instead, trying to decipher the routine being practiced. A blonde attempted a pirouette—turns today?—while Remsky berated her in a mixture of English and Russian. Spotting me, despite my hiding place, he frowned again and tapped the end of his walking stick against the floor.

"Tardiness is unacceptable, Anya."

I flinched, though it was a mild insult coming from Remsky. He was probably saving his worst for later.

Turning his attention to the rest of the class, he bellowed, "Group one, to the stage," and I was forgotten.

The warm-up group scattered. In their place, five new dancers filed onto the stage and performed to the tune of cheerful music while Remsky insulted mistakes and issued corrections. This was the instruction we all paid thousands for. Victor Remsky didn't believe in adding sugar to soften rejection. In his eyes, a lesson wasn't a very good one unless someone broke down in tears during it. Preferably twice.

"Sloppy feet!" he snarled, the first of his usual complaints. "Poor posture! Pathetic technique! I am not impressed! Next."

Once the second group had limped, panting, into the gallery, he called the next. Far too soon, there were only five dancers left, one of them me.

"Final group!"

I hurried from the wings and took the spot farthest from Remsky's perch. When the music began, I attempted to lose myself in the same role we'd been rehearsing all week—a variation Remsky had composed himself, with complex, repetitive motions designed to test endurance.

Like a hawk, the instructor paced the line, searching for the slightest flaw, and it wasn't long before he attacked his first victim.

"Timing, Katja!" Remsky scolded as she finished the first pirouette a full count behind. "Remember to watch your *timing*! Pretty feet! Posture! Are you a barn animal or a dancer?"

Eventually, his commentary trailed off as we fell into a well-rehearsed recitation of the steps. It almost seemed mechanical—a row of perfect, robotic music box dolls performing in sync. *Saute, arabesque, plié.* My muscles were throbbing beneath a thin layer of sweat by the time Remsky cracked his cane, commanding us into the finale, a fluttering motion of the arms, and a bow.

I breathed heavily, holding every limb in place, while Remsky began his customary slow stroll of the stage—something he did at the end of every lesson. For what felt like an eternity, he lingered three dancers down, trailed by the sound of his cane scraping the floor and the advice he spat out at random intervals.

"Too slow..."

"Too fast..."

"Sloppy posture..."

"If only your punctuality were as reliable as your technique, Anya." The acidic compliment accompanied the dry fingers that gripped my shoulder seconds later, easing me upright. "Don't be late again. I expect more from *all* of you," he barked once his scathing individual assessments were completed. "Rehearsal is done. For now. However... Cassandra, Katja, Anya. You will stay behind."

Damn. There went my plan to fly under the radar until the end of class. God only knew what kind of tirade Remsky had in store—not that I was worried.

Besides, Cassandra, a petite dancer with red hair, and Katja, the willowy blonde, didn't seem to have a clue why they'd been singled out, either. The three of us could only stand there awkwardly, sweating beneath the stage lights, as everyone else flitted off into the shadows.

"Now," Remsky began, commanding our attention. "I will warn you. I didn't select you because you are either the best or the worst in my class. I believe that each one of you might learn something from this experience."

"What experience?" Katja demanded, twirling a strand of golden hair around her finger.

Her outburst earned a withering glare from Remsky—not that I blamed her because I had the exact same question running through my head. Remsky's learning opportunities tended to resemble the average person's general concept of torture.

"A chance to prove your passion, Katja." The way Remsky's Russian accent thickened over the words made them seem more like a threat than anything else. "It's an *opportunity* for you all. An old friend of mine is visiting the theater today, and he just so happens to be scouting for an upcoming performance."

It was a suspicious coincidence—made even more suspicious by the fact that Remsky had no friends, at least none he had ever introduced at rehearsals. Even odder, he had picked only three dancers out of twenty-five to showcase in this supposed audition. Make that two wispy, thin ingénues. And me.

"Of?" Katja pressed.

Remsky shot her a death glare.

To her credit, the blonde only shifted onto the balls of her feet before contritely batting her eyelashes. "*Sir.*"

"*Giselle,*" Remsky continued. "This friend is affiliated with a company in London that is considering new talent for their—"

"London?" The outburst came from Cassandra. Her freckled nose twitched, her green eyes comically wide. "The role is in *London?*"

"If you were to be considered," Remsky snarled over her. "But I did not select you three purely based upon talent. Some of you…"

I didn't miss the way his unnerving gaze settled over me.

"Some of you could simply *learn* from this experience."

"They're here now?" Katja hungrily scanned the empty rows, already shifting into first position. "Are they—"

"They've arrived, yes," Remsky admitted icily. "You will be seen one by one. Katja, since you seem so eager, you may go first."

It was a punishment disguised as a favor. By being first, Katja wouldn't have an opportunity to recover from the rehearsal—and I wouldn't look at that as an advantage. That was old Anya's way of thinking—competitive, petty, selfish. Regardless, the blonde squared her shoulders, her eyes narrowed.

Together, Cassandra and I hustled into the wings. Once I escaped the glare of the stage lights, Remsky's offer sank in. A role in a local production—*anything*, really—had been my goal for months, but this…

"London," Cassandra whispered seemingly to herself. "London."

Without saying anything else, she launched into a frenzied warm-up while I settled into my own routine. *London.* The word reverberated in my mind, drowning out the sounds of pointe shoes scraping the floorboards and the flex of muscle.

London.

First position.

London.

Plié.

"Anya?"

I froze midstep and looked up. The stage lights were dimmed. I didn't see Cassandra anywhere, and Remsky stood nearby, sandwiched between the velvet stage curtain and the brick wall behind it.

"Are you ready?"

I blinked, staggering out of fifth position. "Wh-what?"

"Are you *ready*?"

"Yes." *No.* I wasn't ready, and once I'd crept onto the center of the stage in Remsky's shadow, my nervous swallow proved it.

Three strangers sat in the third row. Shadows obscured any defining features, reducing them to monsters perched on red velvet. Waiting to judge. Waiting to reject. Waiting to swallow me whole.

"The final dancer," Remsky announced before exiting stage left.

In his wake, the music began, and I rushed to perform the opening steps.

No dwelling on the negatives. Like how I found it nearly impossible to sink into that coveted zone where nothing else mattered but moving. I skimmed the surface instead, distracted by reality. It was bad luck to watch your audience, Remsky always said. My punishment came swiftly; one of the figures leaned toward another and whispered. Both shook their heads.

Finally, the first man raised his hand. "Enough."

I hadn't even gone another step before the music died altogether.

"We've seen enough."

"I...I'm sorry?" I shifted onto the heel of one slipper, my right arm still gracefully extended.

"I said we've seen enough," the man repeated.

His accent threw me off. British? I couldn't make a face out to go along with the gruff baritone, and it was a full minute of awkward silence before I realized he'd dismissed me. Just like that.

"Victor," he continued before I could move. "The other two. May we see them again?"

"Of course," Remsky replied, suddenly appearing by my side. "Would you like them to dance together or individually?"

"Together."

They debated the logistics while I stood there like an unwanted speck of dust on an otherwise pristine stage. Proper etiquette called for me to silently make my exit. God knew I had done it countless times before.

In slow motion, I processed Remsky rushing from the stage while shouting for Cassandra and Katja to return. The strangers shifted in their seats, prepared to judge between the two of them, yet there I remained, frozen in place.

"What did I do wrong?"

Four pairs of eyes honed in on me. *Uh-oh*. For the second time that day, I had said the wrong line and forgotten to play my unassuming role. In the grand scheme of things, the reasons for my rejection didn't matter. The usual nitpicks were that my hair wasn't the right color, I was too short, and I didn't smile enough. But, constrained in their pointe shoes, my toes throbbed with the knowledge that I had struck each technical element perfectly. In some alternate universe, that had to count for something.

"Can… May I please ask where I made a mistake—"

"Anya." Remsky's blistering scorn seared my skin from across the theater. "*Please* clear the stage."

The please was for show. I was embarrassing him, and for the next few rehearsals—probably for the rest of my career—he would never let me forget it. The old, selfish Anya was rearing her ugly head once again. It was wrong to compare yourself to another dancer—arrogant, even. But Katja had sloppy footwork. Cassandra's turns were always one beat too slow.

"Was there a flaw in my technique?" I scanned the blank faces for any hint of the truth, even though I already knew.

I just wanted the bastards to say it. Katja was beautiful, with a body that more than made up for any sloppy technique. Cassandra was willowy and graceful despite her limited stage presence. And I…

I was Anya DeSotto, the aging ballerina who couldn't even get a callback from a community theater production. Their silence said what they wouldn't out loud. *You aren't worth the effort.* Only after drilling that into my skull could I take a step toward the wings, mustering what little pride I had left to mutter, "Thank you for your time."

"Stay."

Just as the command echoed in the silence, one of the visitors stood and began to pick his way down the row. He was hunched over, moving awkwardly, and I didn't understand why until he finally cleared the aisle and a long device shot out in front of him to aid every step. A cane—and, unlike Remsky's, it didn't seem to be for show.

It took him a full five minutes to mount the stairs to the stage. By then, the lights fell over him, illuminating a head of black hair, and shock flooded my system. I'd expected someone young or maybe wizened like Remsky.

This man was…stone. Salt-and-pepper stubble covered his square jaw, which clenched as he observed me, starting with my head and roving downward. Shadows distorted part of his face, rendering his expression impossible to read—though, on second thought, the lines twisting the flesh around his left eye never wavered. Jagged and silver, they caught the light and threw it back at me like polished glass. *Scars maybe?*

Seconds passed before I realized I was staring. My cheeks burned as I jerked my gaze down to the rest of his body in an attempt to seem like a decent human being. A broad chest and shoulders strained the confines of his coat. Compared to his bulk, that cane seemed more like a toothpick supporting a statue. Paces away from me, he finally spoke.

"Play the music." His gruff baritone clashed with the soft notes filtering through the speakers on cue.

When I looked up, a cold gaze waited for me. Too mean. My therapist wouldn't like him. "Positive" people didn't have eyes like that, composed of fathomless ebony irises that shielded all emotion.

"Dance again," he commanded.

I swallowed down a question—why? Switching to my dominant foot, I raised my arm and lifted my left leg. Movement flickered in my peripheral vision, but before I could turn…

Thwack!

Pain exploded through my calf, but I caught my balance on the heel of my right foot while both arms flew up to shield my head.

At first, I thought he'd hit me with something until I remembered that it wasn't that unusual for old plaster to fall from the ceiling every now and again. In Remsky's thinking, the show went on unless someone lost consciousness or hemorrhaged. Thankfully, that didn't seem to be the case when I inspected my leg and saw no blood.

"I'm okay—"

"Not straight enough."

"Huh?"

The grunted assessment brought my attention to the stranger who brandished his cane at his side. His expression was stony, not panicked like someone standing beneath a crumbling ceiling might be. But, then again, there were no large chunks of plaster anywhere. Pain radiated down my leg while my brain struggled to connect the dots. *He didn't actually…*

"Keep moving."

Moving. It seemed to be the only course of action that made sense. As long as I kept moving, I didn't have to rationalize this. I didn't have to think about anything other than the usual list of reminders racing through my brain—*chin up, neck elongated, balance, balance…*

"Faster!" A harsher voice cut into the drone. "Straighten your spine!"

I caught the motion of a stick of wood flying out to strike my hip before a fresh burst of pain joined the rest.

"Sloppy," the man snarled. "Keep moving."

I didn't react in time, and a blow cracked off my knee. When the cane flashed again, I limped out of his reach, breaking character for the third time that day.

"What are you doing?"

"Focus on yourself." Heavy footsteps hunted me down. "Never falter!"

What felt like another strike to my hip had me gritting my teeth against a sound.

"*Never* hesitate."

A second hit struck my upper thigh.

"You have decent technique. But technique is not everything."

The rasp of my own erratic breathing edged his words out. *Not everything.*

I didn't know how long I stood there with my leg outstretched. My body refused to obey the commands my brain issued it. *Move. Stay! Go.* I could only stare as the man made his way off stage.

"Your nose is bleeding," he said as if in afterthought—but the glance he directed at my trembling fingers made me curl them into fists to keep from reaching up.

"Anya..." Something other than anger tainted Remsky's voice.

Pity?

I managed to race toward the wings before he caught up, swiping at my upper lip. My legs stung. My hip smarted. It used the last of my pride to keep my head held high as I ducked past the curtain. No dwelling on the negatives. No dwelling... The advice played through my mind like a mantra as the darkness of the backstage corridor enveloped me. Rather than stop by the dressing room, I kept going down the narrow hall that led deeper into the theater. Then through the emergency exit that opened to the parking lot.

An icy burst of winter air hit me like a slap as I dashed between two parked cars and headed through the alley leading to the main road. I tried to ignore the curious stares following me while I ran in nothing more than a navy leotard and thin tights.

That was how I coped. I ignored everything. I ran.

M y father's wife let me into the house without finding it odd that I didn't have my keys, my coat, or even proper shoes—not that she glanced up from the nine-year-old spouting Girl Scout facts at her side to pay me much attention. Ignorance was bliss, after all. Carrie had mastered the art of not dwelling on the negatives in her life.

The biggest one was named Anya.

"Your dinner is on the table," she called before drifting into the living room, where a cheerful woman on the television was explaining how to bake the perfect cake.

"Thanks." I stuck around just long enough to peel off my slippers. Then I attempted to hobble up the stairs, and I made it halfway before the pain registered. *Shit.* A glance at my feet revealed the damage—blisters were already forming over tenderized skin. I would be lucky if I hadn't ruined my shoes after the added wear and tear—just another expense to add to the growing tally. I needed new uniforms, and Remsky's renewal fees were due next month…

Money woes took a back seat to the pain ripping through my chest, however. *"You need to learn to cope,"* my therapist liked to coach. *"You need to develop healthy coping mechanisms, Anya.*" In his clinical, professional view, crying was one of said healthy coping mechanisms. My body seemed to agree. The moment I slammed my bedroom door shut, ruffling the worn poster of Anna Pavlova taped to the back, my vision started to blur, and I swiped at my eyes with the back of my hand.

Focus. Focus... I locked my door and tugged at the handle. Once. Twice. *Monster proof,* the twelve-year-old part of me declared. Only then could I actually focus on anything else. Biting my lower lip hard enough to taste blood, I peeled my leotard off and tossed it into the laundry basket in my bathroom. Then I climbed into the shower stall.

An impenetrable fortress of running water succeeded in blocking out everything but the words echoing in my mind —not my therapist's "empowering" mantras, for once. Another voice now filled the void.

You have decent technique.

But technique is not everything.

Not everything.

Apparently, sloppy form but a body like Katja Sorenson's *was* everything. I laughed into the shower spray, hating the bitter thought almost as much as I hated the fact that it was probably true.

Talent meant nothing.

I would never succeed because...

Don't dwell on the negatives, Anya, my therapist would scold. No, you simply scribbled in a journal and wished the pain away while reciting, "I am good enough," before a mirror as your parents lurked nearby, pleased as punch to know you were whole again—or that you appeared to be, anyway. You couldn't let the dark secrets slip, after all.

And I knew the best way to keep the act up. *No dwelling.* I gritted my teeth and reached for a bottle of shampoo at the corner of the stall. Then I ripped off the lid. It was hollow inside, containing just a single packet of white powder. I did my best to rake a line onto the dry rim of the bathtub. One sniff, two...

The pain stopped.

The monsters in my head got a little quieter.

I floated farther away.

No dwelling on the negatives.

CHAPTER 2

"Carrie told me you didn't have your key last night." Dad laid the accusation down the moment I dug into my yogurt.

I summoned my inner actress. It was eight-fifteen—ten minutes earlier than the time he usually wandered from the master bedroom upstairs. He probably hadn't slept, though neither had I. I hadn't compiled my daily script for that day, either.

"I left my bag in Jake's car," I lied after a slightly-too-long pause. "He brought me home last night." Not bad for improvisation, overall. It sounded plausible enough.

"Hmph," my father grunted as he headed for the coffee maker and poured himself a cup. He took a sip while gazing out the window that overlooked the covered pool and built-in Jacuzzi in the backyard.

Both had collected dust for the past two years. Only silly, idle people bought recreational toys with the intent to actually *use* them. Successful people stockpiled fun like the cars in a luxury showroom. You could look, but you couldn't dare touch.

"How was class?" Dad wondered over his shoulder, almost as if remembering that I was there.

I shoved another glob of yogurt into my mouth to hide my sigh. My lie had been eaten up with little notice. Just like always.

"Fine," I said, already prepared with a carefully rehearsed answer. "We're dissecting Chaucer in literature. *The Canterbury Tales*. I really like how—"

"That's great, honey." Dad took another measured sip of coffee while his gaze drifted over the entire kitchen—the marble countertops, the center island, and the breathtaking view of the hillside Carrie had insisted on during their house-hunting phase.

The sprawling McMansion itself was utter perfection, minus me seated on a stool.

"So, what do your grades look like this semester?" Dad asked.

I coughed, unintentionally spraying yogurt everywhere as I scrambled for an answer. "Mostly A's," I croaked after a sip of water, my eyes streaming. "And a few B's. Maybe a C."

"A C? Try to get it up," Dad advised, a note of authority seeping into his voice. He handed me a napkin for the mess. "You're too smart to settle for anything mediocre."

Of course not. I downed the rest of my water rather than answer. Then I stood and reached for the coat lying on the stool beside me.

"Well, I've gotta run. Don't want to be late for class." I smiled and held my arms at my sides, ready to participate in an impromptu wooden hug should the occasion call for it. It was a customary diversion, but my heart sped up a tad too fast. I sniffed. Last night's buzz was wearing off, my armor cracking.

"Sure thing." Dad nodded, making no move to hug me. I guess his customary show of affection wasn't in this scene. "I'll see you tonight," he said instead.

I folded my arms. Smiled again. "Sure."

After pitching my yogurt, I sidestepped a minefield of toys on my way through the foyer, where I slipped out the front door without so much as a goodbye.

I walked to the studio and saved time by cutting through alleys. Two Advil, three pairs of socks, and a mound of Band-Aids didn't make a dent in the agony pulsing through my feet. My last little helper hid inside an old tube of lipstick in my dance bag, and without my headphones to drown out the hustle and bustle of the city, the pain felt twice as distracting—along with dread and some good, old-fashioned shame that had my stomach twisting into knots as I approached the theater's entrance.

I was early, meaning I could grab my bag from the dressing room and change without catching notice. I didn't take a hit, though. Not yet. The halls were still empty by the time I found a distant spot at the back of the upstairs studio and began warming up at the barre, stone-cold "clean," as the therapist called it. A map of sinewy muscle and sore joints became my universe as I stretched my aching toes and focused on tuning in to every muscle. Legs first. Then arms, back, shoulders…

It wasn't until I finally paused, twenty minutes in, that I noticed Remsky watching me from the doorway.

"I canceled rehearsals for today," he said cautiously. "Katja will need to learn the role of Giselle."

"Oh." I looked down at the barre to hide whatever emotion might have crossed my face. A smug grin because I'd correctly guessed Katja as the chosen dancer? Or… disappointment? Rather than pick one, I settled my feet into first position and cleared my throat. Might as well address the elephant in the room. "I'm sorry for yesterday."

"You should be," Remsky scoffed without a shred of sympathy. "I expect better from you."

"I know… Thank you for the opportunity—"

"Don't thank me."

Something in his tone made me recall his words from yesterday. "You wanted some of us to learn something. Is that why you picked me?" I honestly didn't know if I wanted to hear a yes or no.

For once, the instructor didn't respond with a bellowed insult or sarcastic correction. "As I said," he quietly reiterated, "you all had something to learn from the experience."

Something to learn. *Technique is not everything, Anya...*

"Come," Remsky commanded, sounding like his usual self. "Katja will be here soon, and Monique called in sick. I need someone to assist." It was the polite way of requesting slave labor.

I hesitated for only a second before following him down to the lower level anyway. The theater was empty. After changing into my tennis shoes, I swept the stage, and I was in the middle of clearing the trash from the aisles by the time Katja arrived.

She appeared from backstage wearing a white costume, with her hair coiled into a neat bun and a thousand-watt smile that outshone the stage lights. The moment she saw me standing in Remsky's shadow, she looked at him, a blonde eyebrow raised.

True to form, he didn't dignify her with a response. "Warm up," he barked while mounting the stage steps. "You have a lot to learn, and with your disgraceful technique, you'll need all the time you can get."

From that moment on, Remsky berated her through a hasty warm-up, while I slipped into the shadows and watched from the sidelines.

The variation opened the first act when the young Giselle danced before her village. Delicate footwork and complicated spins composed most of the routine. The events of yesterday aside, it was obvious to see why Katja had been picked for the role. She pranced and played the part of a charming peasant girl, never breaking character even as Remsky raked her over the coals for sloppy footwork.

"Again!"

Almost two hours later, Remsky's corrections dwindled to his usual pet peeves—*more graceful! Graceful!*—and Katja learned the gist of the routine. Only when Remsky snapped me out of my stupor by shouting for water did I realize someone else was watching the rehearsal from the opposite side of the theater.

"Ah, Revend," Remsky called, noticing the figure at the same moment I did. "What do you think?"

"I cannot speak for Simon."

Something in me flinched at the sound of that voice. I could easily picture the face—harsh, as if chiseled from stone—to go along with it.

"Oh, that is correct." Remsky nodded. "Where is he, if I may ask?"

The hulking silhouette shrugged. "He was called away on business and sent me in his place."

Was Simon the one with the connections to the London ballet? Though, if he was, what did that make the man creeping closer to the circle of light spilling from the stage?

A dark coat and scarf made him appear even more intimidating than he had the day before. His face seemed designed to siphon all emotion from his expression, like a well-practiced shield hiding the thoughts within. It almost made him look predatory. A raptor circling the pretty little swan dancers like Katja were trained to emulate. To prove me wrong, his gaze swept over her once before settling on the velvet stage curtains as if they held his interest more than the petite blonde.

"I have seen enough," he declared on a sigh.

Of his lackluster surroundings or of Katja's dancing? I couldn't tell.

"All right." For once, Remsky seemed cowed. "We'll end the rehearsal here," he added.

I bit my lip to keep from gasping out loud. Typically, learning a new routine lasted well into the night.

"You are dismissed." Remsky headed for the edge of the stage, lowering his voice, so I caught only the tail end of what he said to the other man next. "How are you feeling…"

"Thank God," Katja muttered while he was out of earshot. She took her cue to escape from the stage.

I followed her, the lesser of two evils. It wasn't long before I thoroughly regretted that decision, though, when I entered the dressing room, and she turned to size me up.

"What are you doing here?"

"I didn't get the memo." I slipped past her and took a seat at the vanity which just so happened to be on the other end of the room. "Congratulations, by the way. You looked beautiful."

"Thank you." Placated by the compliment, Katja turned her attention to her reflection and began unpinning her hair from its coiled bun.

I watched her in the mirror in front of me, hating the thoughts that snuck into my head. She filled out her costume in a way I could only dream of—and not without the aid of plenty of socks shoved into discreet places, either.

"I really can't believe it," she murmured dreamily. "Everything's happening so fast."

My teeth descended into my lower lip to trap any impulsive reply. Fast. Her life was moving *fast*, while mine was ten paces behind the starting line—but I wasn't dwelling.

"So, when do you leave?"

"I'm only being *considered* for a chance to audition," she admitted. "The real one is tomorrow, and if I don't make it through...well, there definitely won't be any London."

"Oh." A chance to audition? It sounded so cryptic. In fact, why would anyone from a prestigious theater scout for talent in Buckley, Connecticut, home of the world's best pot pie?

"I'm sorry, by the way," Katja added before I could come up with an answer to my own question. "About what happened yesterday… That was harsh—"

"It was nothing," I lied, watching my mouth move over the mirror's surface. My inner actress was on fire today, even without her magical powder. No one could tell she was just reading her lines. I decided to spring for an encore by spitting out more of the perfect-girl script. "It was nice to hear an honest critique."

"Yeah. Honest," Katja replied with a wince. "Though, on the bright side, not many dancers can say they've had their work critiqued by Revend Marcus."

A frown tugged on my strained smile. "Who?"

"You've never heard of him?" Her tone made it sound synonymous with *you don't know how to breathe?*

I twisted around to face her, straddling the back of my wooden chair. Asking about a violent stranger who'd left bruises I could still feel aching beneath my sweatpants seemed like the definition of negative dwelling. Some part of me just couldn't resist the allure of a mystery, though.

"Who is he?"

"Only one of the most well-known ballet instructors on the European scene!"

Europe. The stranger's accent made sense now. So did his unorthodox training techniques, I realized, rubbing my sore thigh. At least this was something new—I had never been rejected internationally before.

"Or…he *was*," Katja added. She wrinkled her nose as if the thought of the past made her want to sneeze. "He disappeared a few years ago. I wouldn't have recognized him if it wasn't for the scars."

"What happened to him?" I asked, picturing the faint white lines that marred the left side of his face.

"Some kind of accident. I forget the details." Katja brushed the dark topic off with a flick of her nails and freed the rest of her curls.

"Remsky seems to know him," I said, picturing the way he'd abruptly ended the lesson; I had never seen him defer to anyone.

"They used to dance together, I think," Katja replied. "They were in the same company—though Remsky was just a member of the corps, while Revend was a principal dancer. Still, it was *something*. Why else do you think anyone would waste money learning in such a dump?" She eyed the peeling wallpaper behind her vanity and frowned.

I didn't answer. Regardless of his résumé, Remsky had been the only instructor within ten miles willing to take me on as a student. I hadn't considered what sort of career he'd had before teaching.

"Gotta run," Katja called before grabbing her bag from the floor and slinging it over her shoulder. "I'll see you around."

"Yeah, see ya," I managed to reply, but by then, she was already long gone.

CHAPTER 3

Canceled rehearsals meant a day of freedom for everyone else. In my case, "freedom" resulted in wasted time and yet another fib to add to the heap. I was supposed to be in English literature class until five. It was a terrible lie, but it kept Dad happy, and happy daddies wrote big, fat checks.

My only course of action was to stay out of his sight and lie low. Thankfully, the theater was deserted by noon, and Remsky had tasked me to close for the night. As I stood in the center of the stage, the chore felt more like a godsend.

There was a peaceful serenity about the place when Remsky wasn't hurling insults across it. Traces of its history showed in the faded cream paint and the worn upholstery. Actresses had gotten their starts there once and dancers their "big breaks." Some days, there even seemed to be enough magic left to rub off on me. All I had to do was squint to catch a glimpse of it lurking within the rafters.

Facing the empty rows of seats, I turned both feet out, entering first position. I began my usual exercises, if only to make use of a few hours of empty rehearsal space—at least in the beginning.

I wasn't exactly sure when a few pliés shifted into something else. With no one there to preen for, I lost the customary fake smile, ditched the perfect posture, and attacked every movement ten times harder than usual.

Perfect. Perfect. It was a silent mantra as my pointe shoes struck the stage with each step in the variation. Dancers spent their whole lives striving for perfection. The most flawless technique. The best artistry. But how much did that matter in the end if you didn't have the perfect body, the perfect face, or the perfect stage presence? That was ambition for you. The crumbling walls with their faded paint perfectly summed my potential up—*past its prime.* Bracing my weight with an outstretched foot, I bowed.

Well, there you go, I apologized to my imaginary audience who were yawning in their seats. *Anya DeSotto will never be perfect. So much for fucking trying.* I bowed again. *Thank you, thank you…*

A trickle of alarm raced down my spine, though I wasn't quite sure what sound gave him away first. When I finally caught sight of that hulking shape watching me in the same spot he'd observed Katja from, I was already scurrying backward toward the wings.

"Sorry! I didn't know anyone was—"

"Come back." Pure authority laced his tone.

I paid Remsky to verbally abuse me under the guise of training, but even he didn't affect me in the same way. My palms felt slick, my cheeks on fire.

"I...shouldn't even be using the stage," I insisted as Revend Marcus continued to advance. "I'm just closing up."

With every step he took, I found myself instinctively inching backward until I couldn't see his face clearly beyond the glare of the stage lights. The sound of his cane hitting the floor trailed off when I assumed he reached the front of the gallery.

"Keep dancing."

"I was just warming up. I—"

"Dance."

Wood struck wood, and I lurched onto the tips of my toes, a Pavlov dog trained to the thwack of an instructor's cane.

"B-but—"

"Begin."

The steps of Remsky's variation—a dance I had performed a thousand times—vanished from my memory. I could only hesitantly dangle my right foot in the air. Just like that, I was four again, lost within a sea of toddlers while the teacher attempted to show us body movements that didn't seem humanly possible. Revend wasn't as patient as Mrs. Appleby, however.

"*Dance.*" A dare tainted the command.

Remembering the sting of his cane, I rose on pointe and began another variation, feeling my cheeks heat up. I had to rely only on memory to guide the footwork. Katja tended to spike her routines with extra flounces and flirtatious smiles, which made it harder to distinguish what belonged to the core role of Giselle and what was just the showboating of a preening blonde.

"Again." The order came before my feet had even settled in the final position.

Without complaint, I performed the variation from the beginning, and the demand came even sooner.

"Again."

And *again.*

Again…

"I can't." Dizzy, I staggered out of what had to be the millionth pirouette. My legs felt disconnected from my body, my muscles jelly. "I can't—"

"Again." His voice could have been a recording someone had left on repeat to torture me. Only his silhouette, looming over the front row, disproved that theory. He stood unwaveringly. Unmoving. Like stone.

"I *can't.*"

"You can't?" His voice alone affected me in a way one of Remsky's glares never could.

I was frozen in place as he ascended the steps with the aid of his cane and approached me from stage left.

"You *will.*"

Without the glow of the stage lights shielding his face, I was forced to meet his gaze directly. A few adjectives trickled across my mind to describe the haunting irises—*dark, fathomless, cold.* I had never met someone so openly…negative.

"Dance."

I flinched as his arm swung out, the end of his cane pointing toward my sloppily placed feet.

"From the beginning."

"Why?" Gritting my teeth, I shifted into third position when he didn't bother to answer me. My arm trembled as it formed an arch, my fake smile slipping. I missed the first count. Then the next.

"You dance with too much tension."

Warmth ghosted the side of my throat—*too* warm to be the building's heat. Before I could turn to see the source, something fell over my shoulders, guiding them into perfect alignment. His hands?

"Face forward. Don't look down."

Thick fingers entered my peripheral vision to prop my chin up.

"*Breathe.*"

But he was too close, sucking up every bit of air I fought to drag into my lungs. Before I could adjust, another command grated against my eardrum.

"En pointe."

With my gaze on the tattered chairs in the front row, I carefully rose onto the toes of my right foot.

"Arabesque."

Exhaling through my core, I lifted my left leg and extended it behind me, only to feel an unfamiliar touch against my thigh.

"Wait." I started to turn. "What are you doing—"

"Higher."

Heavy fingers cinched my calf, snapping my fragile thread of control. I fell onto the flats of both feet, but his grip tightened until I had no choice but to rise onto pointe again or trip. Once I'd complied, he raised the leg even higher, far past Remsky's standard.

"You were arrogant enough to assume your technique to be flawless," Revend grunted before releasing his grip. "Hold."

A hysterical laugh bubbled inside my stomach and threatened to break free. This had to be some kind of sick joke. A plot devised by Remsky to ensure I never embarrassed him again. *Bad Anya.* Any minute, the man behind me would pat my head because I'd suffered through my punishment and let me lick my wounds in peace.

He didn't, and the seconds stretched into eons. During that time, my arms became lead weights. My foot went numb. God only knew how I managed to stay upright.

But I did. Then a second longer…

"First position."

I gratefully lowered my leg—only, somewhere within the transition to first, I wound up on my hands and knees. Breakfast was a bad, *bad* idea, clawing its way up my throat to land on the floor with a splash.

"Do you want to know what holds you back?" Revend Marcus wondered above me, his voice carrying across the theater, over the sound of my gagging. "It isn't your technique. It isn't even your artistry." He waited while I wiped at my mouth with the back of my hand before delivering the finishing blow. "You lack passion."

"What?" I directed the question at the puddle of puke slowly spreading across the floor before me, too exhausted to look up.

Passion?

"It's what enables you to dance the same variation seven times in a row with little change in your facial expression," he explained. "You hoard emotion in favor of honing your technique. The tradeoff is that you seem too robotic."

Robotic. Robotic. It should have been a compliment—my therapist certainly would have seen it that way. Robots were what little girls were trained to be. Robots got praised.

Those with faulty wiring and negative traits had accidents and needed to be reprogrammed.

"You want to learn how to land a role?" Revend Marcus wondered before I could ask the question myself. "Then stand up. First position."

You can't, my body told me in varying levels of pain. My legs were cramping, my toes on fire. Air held the consistency of pudding, clinging to the insides of my lungs.

Somehow, I managed to climb to my feet anyway. The world seesawed left and right while a Revend-shaped blur mocked every move I made.

"Again. Forget the technique!" he barked when I struggled to lift my leg. "You dance with this." He jabbed a finger toward my face.

"How?" Oops. My voice came out too loud. A shout. "Why are you even telling me this? Shouldn't you be helping *Katja* improve?"

"This isn't to help you improve."

"Then what—"

He slammed his cane against the floor to cut me off and bellowed that damn word. "Again!"

I took two graceless steps backward. So he wanted me to dance without thinking, did he? Well, this was it—a watered-down version of Giselle's variation. Without my technique, I had nothing, just a bunch of negative traits bounding across the stage.

"You're angry." It was a strange observation—especially considering that he didn't seem annoyed by it. "Good," he said. "Use it from now on...*instead* of anything else."

I tripped over my own feet, caught off guard. Use my anger? Didn't he mean suppress? I couldn't recover before the tip of his cane connected with my hip once. Twice.

"Ow!" The cry slipped out, but I bit my lip and flubbed my way through the rest of the steps. The fake smile was gone. I stopped preening. Stopped pretending. Stopped fucking trying to emulate Katja Sorenson.

I just wanted the pain to stop.

I wanted Remsky to tell me himself that he thought I was a failure rather than line me up before the firing squad. I wanted my father to look at me for once and see the web of lies I was too exhausted to spin anymore. I wanted...

"That's enough."

I couldn't stop moving, held together only by gravity and the emotions leaking from me like dissolving glue. Spin after spin, I drifted all the way to the edge of the stage, where the empty seats in the gallery loomed below. One false step...and I would fall off. Maybe I should have. Anything to end this nightmare and wake up again.

But, after my last fall, I couldn't afford any more cracks.

Shifting my balance, I managed to collapse inches away from the edge at the last possible second. Too fast. I lost my balance, fell, and hit the back of my head on the stage.

Crack! My vision blinked out like the faulty light bulb flickering in the ceiling. Revend Marcus merely watched. I could feel him there, devouring the residue of my anger and frustration, feeding on them both.

When he'd gotten enough, he shuffled into the wings, the stab of his cane marking each step, leaving me sprawled out on the stage like a broken marionette. Only God knew how long I lay there until a flicker of movement made me look up.

A gnarled hand loomed above me, dangling a white napkin between two fingers.

"Here."

Numb, I scrambled to reach for it and wiped at the worst of the sweat slicking my forehead. My eyes sought out Revend as I crumbled the used tissue into a ball. "T-Thank you…"

The words barely left my mouth before he was gone again.

Shouting jolted me awake. Stomping. Heavy footsteps marched past my bedroom door before fading near my father and Carrie's bedroom.

Glass broke, and a woman yelled, "Fine then, Andrew! Just leave!"

Seconds later, a door slammed, quickly followed by a child's high-pitched cry.

It'd become a familiar scene ever since I moved in, a break in the act. *We interrupt your regularly scheduled programming...*

At least the pain distracted me from the soap opera playing out beyond my bedroom walls. My comforter was crushing my legs. The thin sheets felt like glass against my arms. My stepsister's shrieks were scrambling my brain.

With some well-timed fidgeting, I managed to roll off the mattress and land on the floor, but it took five minutes of trying to remember which muscles controlled what before I could even attempt to climb to my feet.

"Anya?" There was a delicate tap on my door. "You in there?"

"Yeah," I rasped, recognizing Carrie's voice. "Class was... canceled today."

"Oh."

A second later, I heard Carrie pad back down the hall, most likely on a mission to quiet a wailing preteen, and I struggled to maneuver my legs into a pair of sweats.

The sky was overcast beyond my window, and the dark clouds on the horizon threatened rain—overall a bad morning for a run. I almost considered sleeping in, but if I didn't work the stiffness out of my muscles, I could be out of commission for the rest of the week. And a missed rehearsal would be a *bad* thing.

I still hadn't decided by the time I limped into the hallway —where the screaming echoed ten times louder—and descended the stairs, heading outside.

It was colder than I'd feared. My warm-up sweats were no match, and each breath painted the air white as I struggled to jog down the sidewalk. At least I was moving.

The pain dulled a little as I navigated my typical route around my father's scenic neighborhood and the small park on the outskirts of it. On a usual day, it was a fifteen-minute run, tops. This time, I didn't make it back to the house until nearly an hour later.

Carrie was in the kitchen when I hobbled inside, flipping a grilled cheese sandwich in a frying pan, while Taylor played with a decapitated doll at her feet. Neither acknowledged my presence longer than it took to realize I wasn't a burglar. *Merely Anya. Don't mind her. She's just a part of the custom wallpaper.*

"There was a phone call for you," Carrie said, cutting her gaze in my direction for what had to be the first time this week. "A man. He left a number. It's on the fridge."

"H-huh?" I froze halfway to the staircase. This wasn't a part of the script. "A phone call?"

"Yep."

I couldn't risk prodding for more details. Remsky knew better than to call my home number, and I didn't know anyone else who would bother, especially at ten in the morning. I had no choice but to return to the kitchen and program the number into my cell before heading up to my bedroom. The dial tone chimed four times before someone picked up.

"Revend."

I froze with my hand on the doorknob, gripping it so tightly that my knuckles whitened.

"How… How did you get my number?" Only when the words were out of my mouth did I realize just how rude they sounded. Not that I found the strength to take them back, my therapist be damned. Obviously, he'd gotten my contact information from Remsky.

The bigger question was why.

"Do you want to prove your worth?" His ominous tone alone made my room seem darker despite the grayish daylight streaming in through the window.

"What do you mean?" I managed to croak as my throat tightened.

"Come to this address," he said, rattling off a street in the nearby city of Glendale. "Be there by five, ready to perform. *Ready.* If you don't show up, I'll assume that you've made peace with your failings."

Before I could reply, he hung up, and I was left grappling for the edge of my mattress.

"Be there by five."

A glance at my clock revealed that it was already inching toward eleven. Glendale was at least an hour's cab ride away. Logistics aside, my body ached at the mere thought of rising on pointe, even though I stood and crossed over to my dance bag anyway. It was worse than I feared. My shoes were worn in places, the soles nearly black from their trek through the city. In two days, I had done more damage than six months' worth of Remsky's rehearsals.

But even their battered state couldn't stop me from dancing if I really wanted to. *"Do you want to prove your worth?"*

Absently, my thumb traced the frayed edges of a flesh-colored ribbon before I set it aside and scanned the length of my room. It used to be an office. My twin bed was squished against the wall, and the single window overlooked the roof of the garage. To make it "homey," my father had painted the walls blue with leftover paint fished from whatever supplies the interior designer had left in the basement after they'd moved in.

"Your favorite color, kiddo," he'd boasted, apparently having forgotten my lifelong love of green.

Nothing was really mine apart from the faded poster taped to the back of the door.

Do you want to prove your worth? Anna Pavlova wondered, her hands tucked under her chin, both feet perfectly pointed. A dare lingered behind her charming expression. *Prove yourself.*

My auditions were always cut short before I ever had the chance to prove anything to anyone.

Did I even *want* to anymore?

Either way, Revend Marcus left me with no choice. Luckily, I had the cab company on speed dial.

CHAPTER 4

Unlike quaint little Buckley, Glendale resembled a giant chessboard upon which my opponent was only one move away from declaring checkmate. I shivered when the cab driver brought me to the heart of the borough —the cross between a financial district and a bohemian one exploding with chic cafés. All in all, the setting served to make me feel even more like a minuscule pawn in Revend's grip.

I sat with the meter still running for nearly ten minutes and contemplated just leaving. My therapist certainly would agree. I wasn't supposed to be there. The drab, gray atmosphere wasn't "uplifting" or "positive." *Negative* was the very definition of it. I came close to telling the driver to turn around. But then I pictured *him*, with narrowed eyes and a taunting expression.

Giving up, Anya?

Hell no. I pushed the cab door open —fifty bucks lighter— and climbed out onto a street slick with ice. What little remained of the daylight was trapped behind the towering buildings, making it seem degrees colder than it really was. I shivered and examined the crumpled slip of paper clutched in my fist. The address scrawled across it led me farther down the block, toward a gray building slightly smaller than the rest. A sign had been taped to a pair of glass doors.

Roria Auditions—use the side door!

Weird. Revend hadn't given me a company name—or really any clue of what I was supposed to do there—but there didn't seem to be anything else of significance around. Following the instruction, I circled around to a fire exit that had been propped open with a brick and discovered a narrow hallway lined with burgundy wallpaper. An arrow taped near the entrance guided me into a larger room.

This venue was leagues above Remsky's decrepit little theater, that was for sure. Pale yellow walls and three French-style windows overlooked a small courtyard. Spread out amongst a row of metal folding chairs sat several restless women in crisp leotards, their hair coiled into perfect buns. I ran a hand over my own hair, tallying up the differences I wasn't supposed to. No loose pieces. No bent bobby pins. Before them was a long table where a woman who appeared to be in charge was shuffling papers.

Spotting me from across the room, she cleared her throat. "Number?"

"I...I, um." I froze, still holding Revend's note. "I was just told to come here—"

"Name?" the woman demanded. She was all crisp efficiency, dressed like a stopwatch with a white blouse and a black minute-hand-shaped tie pointing toward the stack of papers before her.

"Anya—"

"DeSotto?" She scanned the topmost paper on her stack, chewing on her lower lip. "Cutting it rather close, aren't you?"

"Excuse me?"

"You're last. Number forty-seven. You can change back there." She pointed a manicured finger to a hallway near the back of the room. "Then have a seat. You'll warm up when your group is called."

Warm up?

As if anticipating the question, the woman picked a pen up and began scribbling, her posture alone warning me against speaking anymore. With nothing left to do, I scurried away and found a dressing room at the hall's end. After changing into my leotard, I fished a tube of lipstick from my bag and approached the mirror. My fingers shook over the metallic surface. All I had to do was twist the cap off and fish out the tiny plastic baggie inside. One row would be all I needed. Just one...

I tightened my grip over the cap and caught sight of my reflection, those empty, blue eyes.

"Be ready to perform," Revend had dared me. *Ready.* It was like he knew—though he couldn't. Even my parents were oblivious. Screw him.

I tossed the lipstick tube into my bag and returned to the main room. A familiar voice rang out before I even took a step over the threshold.

"DeSotto!" the woman at the desk called. "You had some holes in your paperwork. Fill them out."

"P-paperwork?"

I accepted the folder she'd shoved in my direction and took a seat on the nearest chair. Inside the burgundy file was a stack of papers, and taped to the first one was a yellow sticky note with a taunt scrawled on it. *Use your anger— nothing else.*

Frowning, I peeled it off and scanned the words printed beneath it—an audition form. Someone had already filled in my name, my address, and my phone number. Only a few personal details were missing—but I narrowed my eyes once I saw what occupied the space where the applicant was meant to name their audition piece—*Giselle ACT 1, female variation.*

Was this his idea of a sick joke? Sign me up for an audition and make me dance a role I'd lost?

If he wanted to play that twisted game, then I would play back even harder. I shook the unease off and scanned the papers again. *The Roria Ballet* headed the documents, printed in gleaming script. I had never heard of it, though that didn't mean much; plenty of companies roamed the country searching for new talent.

Still…

Revend Marcus' aura tainted everything. The golden wallpaper took on a sinister edge. The dancers beside me were more specter than human, watching me, waiting for me to fail. My gaze darted to my dance bag. Five minutes alone was all it would take to regain control…

Are you scared, Anya? I considered tossing everything in the trash and storming out. If only I could ignore the mountain of lies piling up behind me just as easily. Lately, even the negatives were starting to seem like positives. I wasn't in any position to turn an audition down, though a sick attempt at revenge it might have been. Even if the other dancers looked like figures plucked right from a music box. Even if I didn't have a chance in hell.

Those were still pretty decent odds, in my case.

I shook my head to refocus. There was a pen sticking out of the opposite sleeve of the folder. Before I could change my mind, I took it and signed my name on the back of the audition slip—*neatly*, so that the differences in handwriting were suspiciously apparent. Then I returned everything, minus the yellow note, to the woman at the desk.

She sniffed, shuffled the documents, and then set them aside. "Here you are," she said, handing me a square tag that read *47* in block numbers. "The other groups are finishing up now. It won't be long."

"Not long" translated into roughly two hours. The entire time, I sat on a hard metal folding chair, watching the clock. Tick. Tock. Time seemed stuck, and I had no choice but to observe the other dancers—their clothes, their posture, their perfect, shiny hair. Just when I thought the wait might stretch into another hour, a door opened on the right-hand side of the room, drawing everyone's attention.

"Dancers forty through forty-seven," a man's voice called from beyond it. "You may now warm up."

I stood and followed the others, walking past the woman at the desk and down another narrow hall. This one opened onto a wider, rectangular room with a row of mirrors at one end and a barre at the other.

With little fanfare, the other seven dancers stripped their slippers and donned their pointe shoes before spreading out to warm up. They were soldiers in a familiar war, too busy battling their own routines to even notice each other. Or that was the trick, at least; they *pretended* not to notice.

I still caught several pointed looks at my feet as I rose on relevé while choking down a gasp of pain. So was the cost of "good" technique—faking a pretty smile as two blisters tore apart the moment I stretched my toes into an arch. The mirror's surface was an unforgiving portrait of me—the girl in the black leotard, two inches shorter than everyone else, who clung to the barre for dear life despite her perfectly-turned-out feet.

Revend Marcus wanted me to use my anger. What about desperation? It weighed me down, this teasing whisper at the back of my mind wondering what the hell I was doing. There? Dancing? Trying? Nothing I did drowned it out.

Barely five minutes into the warm-up, a door at the other end of the room opened, and a man walked in. A simple white shirt and black pants dispelled the idea of him being just another dancer.

"Welcome," he greeted warmly as we all froze, some midstep. "We'll take the first dancer now. Forty?"

Number forty, a lovely brunette, approached him with her head held confidently high. The door closed behind them, shielding off the unknown and…

Everything fell back into motion as if it had only been on pause. Bodies swayed and contorted. Feet were stretched beyond the average person's imagination. I soldiered through it all, trying to clear my head. *Focus, Anya.*

Common sense urged me to run. It wasn't like I honestly had a shot anyway. Numbers forty-three and forty-five were pretty much identical to the girls who beat me for every other part.

"Forty-five?"

I hadn't even noticed the last four dancers leaving, but there were only two of us left now. Aware of that fact, forty-six shot me a wary glance. She pirouetted. Paused. Pirouetted again. Every movement was flawless with her feet delicately pointed. When the blond man came for her, she tossed me a warm, "Good luck," over her shoulder.

Bitch.

The moment the door closed behind her, I glared at my reflection, searching for that prized technique I always touted. I couldn't see a hint of it anymore, and my brain recycled the same old excuse.

I'm tired.

I'm tired.

I'm tired?

Looking at my face, I couldn't tell. Strange, because I had never cared before yesterday. Good robot girls weren't supposed to portray anything other than a smile, reassuring the world that they weren't about to break. I got an A-plus on that front. My symmetrical grin showed teeth, but my eyes were expressionless.

I tried lifting my lips at the corners, but the woman staring back looked empty.

I lifted those corners a little higher and flashed more teeth.

She could have been dead.

Approaching the mirror, I let the fake smile fall, the muscles around my mouth aching in its absence. How long had it been glued in place? The twenty minutes of the warm-up? Since I'd walked into the building? My entire life?

I didn't recognize the girl staring back at me without it. Her blue eyes blazed, her black hair a messy knot straining against the confines of bobby pins. She unconsciously favored one foot while resting the other on its heel so that its throbbing toes couldn't contact the floor. She looked sloppy. *Now*, she looked tired.

"Use your anger, Anya," I scolded, watching wooden lips move on the surface of the glass.

A scowl replaced my pretty smile and transformed my face. My eyes seemed a little darker, my mouth a little wider. So very negative.

Without taking my gaze off the mirror, I stood back and began to perform my variation—only I wasn't Giselle happily greeting her village. I was the girl forced to pretend so damn well that no one really noticed that her charming grin was just a mask, that her graceful movements disguised aching, battered limbs. Blood stained the inside of her pretty pink slippers, but she just couldn't seem to stop fucking spinning...

"Number forty-seven?"

The blond man's pleasant voice was the equivalent of someone dumping ice water over my head. Without a word, I warily followed him through the door he'd come from.

Beyond it was another mazelike hallway and, at the very end, a room even larger than the warm-up area. Five people were sitting at a long table near the far wall. The rest of the floor had been cleared, presumably so that every dancer had enough space to audition. How many perfect pirouettes and ideal bodies had pranced before I did?

A man near the center of the table read my name off a slip of paper before him. "DeSotto?"

"Yes?"

"Did you bring music?"

"M-music?" My stomach fell to the floor and shattered. *Check and mate*, Revend's voice taunted through my conscience. Haha, very funny. Only a sadist would send someone into an audition without preparing them. "No."

There was a smattering of muttered conversation. Before I could make out a single word, the man in the center shrugged.

"Will you be able to dance without it?"

"I…I think so."

"Good. You may begin."

Begin. It almost seemed like a taunt. *Begin, Anya. Our red pens are at the ready. Show us your best before we send you on your way.*

I took my time settling into the starting position before facing them again. My gaze drifted to the wall behind them, allowing their faces to blur into the background, as I pranced forward, striving to make every movement slow and graceful. Pretty—not that it took much effort. Hell, it was such a pretentious dance. Beautiful Giselle putting on a show for the villagers who were secretly hoping she'd fall flat on her face.

Giselle with her beaming smile and lovely pliés. I bet she hated everyone on the inside. Hated having to pretend. Hated being adored for living a lie behind her smiling façade.

Like her, I tried to play the part. I tried to bite the pain back and stifle it with false smiles and graceful arm movements.

But I wasn't as good a liar as she was; somewhere halfway through, my mask began to slip. The judges' table disappeared, and in its place stood Revend Marcus. His black eyes traced my form, honing in on every flaw. *You're robotic*, he told me, slamming his cane against the floor as I dutifully turned on pointe. *Emotionless! Fake! Use your anger...*

The longer I danced, the less anything else seemed to matter. It wasn't a routine anymore. It was war.

Pointe shoes were my weapon. Motion was my armor. As long as I kept moving, nothing could touch me. At least not until I finally came to a stop, panting on the tips of my toes.

"Thank you, Miss DeSotto."

I glanced up and found that the judges' table had reappeared. The people seated there watched me with impassive expressions as they shuffled their paperwork. Someone coughed.

"You can leave your number on the table and join the rest of your group in the main lobby."

The man in the center pointed toward the exit, where the blond man was already waiting to usher me into the first room I'd entered. The other seven dancers in my group were back in their original seats, each pretending, once again, that the rest of us didn't exist. I could sense them watching me as I fetched my bag from the dressing room and took one of the metal chairs at the very back of the room. How had I done? Any better than they had? Any worse?

They wouldn't dare ask, though apparently only one dancer would be chosen from each group—or at least that's what I discerned from the whispered conversation of two girls nearby who dared to break the rules by speaking.

Only one dancer from the eight would get a callback. To where? I had no clue. I had almost gathered up the nerve to ask when a group of people began to file through the door I'd come from and, as if on cue, everyone lurched to their feet.

"Thank you all for coming," the man with the ponytail said, spearheading the group of judges.

Their neat smiles and warm expressions didn't fool me. I waited for someone to call number forty-five already and get it over with. I was late for dinner. If Dad or Carrie happened to glance at one of the corners, they might notice I wasn't there.

"You all danced beautifully. However, we would like to have a word with number forty—"

I shouldered my bag and started to head for the side exit.

"—seven—DeSotto, Anya."

I froze. The other dancers stared, struggling to hide their disappointment. They did that naughty habit we weren't supposed to give in to—*compare.* What did my wiry, compact frame hold that their slender ones didn't? Inquiring minds wanted to know.

"Ms. DeSotto?"

Almost in slow motion, I headed to the front of the room, past the other dancers fleeing for the exit. Once I'd reached him, the blond man handed me an envelope.

"You were marvelous," he said before turning away and following the other judges back down that narrow hall.

My robot brain couldn't comprehend. The words hadn't sounded like carefully rehearsed lines. I think he even meant them. And I could only stand there with a white envelope clenched in my fist and no clue of what to do next.

CHAPTER 5

The fairytale moment ended the second I left the theater and the freezing night air hit me like a slap. Ironically, it didn't snap some sense into me. I never threw that envelope in the trash and forgot about Revend Marcus like I should have.

I just…drifted.

Up above, charcoal-colored clouds threatened to bring another storm, but even they couldn't disrupt this surreal feeling of peace. It felt like I was trapped within a snow globe, anxiously waiting for it to be shaken up or smashed to pieces. A rude awakening lurked beyond this imaginary glass—nothing ever went my way for long.

Right on cue, I noticed the first crack in the façade—a black limousine idling alongside the curb halfway up the block. Just as I drew even with it, the door to the back seat opened, and a man's voice beckoned from within.

"Get in." He sounded gruff. Negative, too. Almost like the big, bad wolf from a particular fable.

Ironically, my jacket was red, with the envelope in my hand serving as the figurative basket of goodies.

"Who… Who are you?" I wondered, playing my part—but that accent was unmistakable. My fingers tightened over the strap of my shoulder bag while I scanned the deserted block. In a matter of minutes, the other dancers had disappeared into cars or through alleyways, leaving no witnesses.

"Get in," the figure in the limo said without elaborating.

I kept walking, focusing on the brightly lit avenue a few blocks ahead. With every step, the vehicle trailed closely behind. Seconds later, the order came again. I guessed this wolf was growing impatient with his robotic lamb.

"You know damn well who I am. Get in."

I imagined the expression of the man lurking behind tinted glass—narrowed eyes and an ice-cold frown. A full minute passed before I finally choked out a response. "Why should I?"

"I know where you live, if you recall." Only his bored sigh kept the words from seeming like a threat.

"Fine." I slowed my pace but didn't stop. "What do you want?"

The door opened wider, and the distinct stench of smoke drifted out to greet me.

"Get in."

Two blocks were all that stood between me and the safety of the main street. I only had to keep going and never look back.

"Otherwise," the voice continued, "I would have to assume that you are afraid, and I do not waste my time on *cowards*."

I froze midstep. My therapist would probably tell me that being a coward in this situation was a *good* thing. *Focus only on the positives, Anya.* There was nothing positive about getting inside that limo.

But it wasn't like I had an abundance of those positive traits lying around. Two impulsive steps brought me to the curb, and when I reached the open door, I hesitated only a second before climbing inside.

The interior was spacious, with leather seats framing a minibar built into the vehicle's right side. The last time I'd been in a limo was the night of senior prom with Jake, and I only had a vague memory of suffocating in my dress while he and his friends had taken turns mooning passing cars through the sunroof.

Revend Marcus sat across from me, partially illuminated by the cigar he held between two fingers. The moment our gazes connected, he exhaled a plume of spicy smoke into the air between us.

"This could be considered kidnapping," I croaked even though the limo had yet to pull away from the curb.

Rather than launch into the reason why he'd hunted me down in the first place, he reached for the door on his end. A split second later, an ominous click sounded—the locks activating.

"Now, it could," he agreed. "And I hope you have them mention in the police report that you willingly entered the vehicle."

I bit my lower lip again, drawing blood. No matter how fiercely my heart pounded, I didn't feel the urge to scream and throw myself at the door. At least not yet. Maybe it was his expression again? He looked so damn...bored. My therapist would have had a field day, charging him five hundred dollars a session to wash his negativity away.

"What do you want?"

"What *could* I want from a childish upstart with terrible posture?"

Ouch. He knew just where to strike to get a reaction out of me.

Despite myself, I sat a little straighter and tried again. "How did you get my number?"

"Victor," he replied, using Remsky's first name. "Once I mentioned the girl with poor artistry, he knew exactly who I meant."

It didn't seem like a lie, which only led to a more obvious question. "Why would you ask about me?"

He took an inhale of his cigar before nodding at my lap toward the envelope. Without being prompted, I peeled it open and withdrew the slip of paper inside it. My eyes strained. Even in the semidarkness, it wasn't that hard to make out the gist of the printed words.

We are pleased to inform you...

A formal callback. My first one in...well, ever. Something tightened inside my chest, making it harder to breathe. Was that pride? I'd almost forgotten what it felt like.

"Well?" Revend demanded. The glow from the lit end of his cigar reflected off his eyes, making them smolder and leaving no mistake. Whatever this meant...he was behind it. The genuine curiosity that I thought lurked within his expression was obviously a trick of the light.

"Well." I flexed my fingers and deliberately crumbled the paper into a ball. "If I'm so terrible, then why did you sign me up for an audition?"

He frowned at my tone. "If you're so terrible, why show up for said audition?"

"I'm twenty," I said without addressing his argument. "An adult—not a 'teenager'—which is good news for you, seeing as how you gave away my personal information without parental consent."

"Twenty." He grunted the word on a huff of cigar smoke that drifted toward my face.

I blinked, my eyes watering.

"You don't look a day older than fifteen."

I crossed my arms over my nonexistent chest. Age was a touchy subject in a world where an unrealistic body type was not only ideal but necessary. Robot dolls could only possess so many curves before they tumbled off their pedestal, after all.

"And you're the creepy stranger who just coerced me into your limo." My breath caught. The gravity of the situation was harder to ignore once said out loud. Regaining my senses, I reached for the door handle, allowing my thumb to toy with the lever. Something wouldn't let me push on it, no matter how much I wanted to.

"Twenty," Revend Marcus repeated, rolling his cigar between his fingertips. "Quite the age to be without a company."

A million sneaky questions lurked within that one statement. I did my best to ignore them, only to fail after exactly five seconds. "It's also quite the age to be kidnapped—"

"And once again," Revend interjected, "we arrive at the fact that *you* were the one who entered a vehicle with a man old enough to be your father."

"Forty?" I guessed, surprisingly curious.

The gray in his hair supported that theory, but his stern features almost seemed ageless—especially the jagged scars around his left eye. A faint silver, they shone in the dim lighting like ridiculously expensive jewelry. Daring you to look while at the same time warning you to look away.

"Old enough to assume that you were much younger than twenty." His hand drifted to the door on his end again, and the locks clicked open. "Leave," he prompted. "I wouldn't want to inconvenience a busy *woman* such as yourself."

Something kept me from taking advantage of the sudden exit. Maybe it was his expression? He still looked so…*bored.*

I pulled my hand from the handle. "So, what now? I did it. I went through your audition. Not everyone thinks I don't have talent."

"I never said you didn't have talent," he countered swiftly. "I said you were *stifled*. Even talent cannot make up for what passion lacks."

"You don't even know me—"

"Then you should have no trouble proving yourself." The challenge came as he flicked his cigar into a silver tray on the seat beside him and then ground out the cinder once and for all, much like he seemed determined to do to my pride.

"How?"

He nodded toward the partition behind me that separated the back from the driver. A moment later, the limo lurched into motion, and I had to brace my hands on either side of me just to keep from pitching forward. My breath hitched in my chest at the mental image of my picture flashing across the six o'clock news under the headline, *Missing*.

"Now, this really could be considered kidnapping," I croaked.

The picture of poise, Revend inclined his head. "Shall I call the police?"

I had no doubt that he *would* do just that. And then promptly hand the phone to me, leaving me to come up with an explanation for this whole scenario. *Well, see, officer, I went to the strange address he gave me…*

Revend was waiting for my answer, but my silence said it all. With running no longer an option, the only course of action seemed to be keeping him talking.

"What makes you think that I want to or *should* prove anything to you?"

He remained silent, draped only in shadow and the odd bit of light reflected through the windows. The glow from a streetlamp sliced his face in two while the reddish tint of a passing car's taillights illuminated a single black iris.

I sat back when the silence grew unbearable and settled my bag on my lap like a makeshift shield. Two could play this game. "Is this a hobby of yours?" I asked breezily. "Signing people up for auditions without their consent?"

Revend stared out the window at the blurring buildings. Which was fine with me. As long as the limo kept moving, the gravity of the situation couldn't sink in. I wasn't alone with a stranger, my heart wasn't racing, and my clothes didn't reek of cigar smoke.

"What do you want?" I repeated when he didn't respond.

Surprising me, he nodded toward my closed fist. "Show me."

I had to force my fingers to open one by one, freeing the page from my grip. I handed it over to him and watched him read.

Once finished, he set the paper aside and met my gaze directly. "Two weeks." A dangerous dare colored his otherwise blank expression. "Will you go?"

I looked away and mulled the question over while toying with one of the straps on my bag.

"Is that a no?" He formed a steeple with his fingers and propped them beneath his chin. His hands were big. Silvery scars riddled the backs of them, similar to the ones around his left eye.

Which brought my attention right back to his face.

"Why should it matter?" I searched his expression for any hint of…anything.

I wasn't the only one good at suppressing emotion. Deciphering him was like considering a well—endless, frigid, and dark. Nothing broke the surface to greet me, and I was left leaning over the water's edge, dangerously close to falling in.

"You tell me," he challenged. "Have I wasted my time on you already?"

Wasting time. The threat preyed on the part of me used to shelling out money for "expert training" and opinions. The teachers. The doctors. The therapists. *Please don't waste our time, Anya.*

"I didn't ask for your help—"

"But you received it," he said over me. "So the question is… Will you continue to waste my time because I may have damaged your *pride*?"

"You didn't damage *anything*." I fiddled with my bag again, running my fingers along the surface as if flicking his doubts away. "And honestly, whether I go or not isn't really any of your damn business."

"Will you or won't you?" He didn't even seem irritated by the lack of respect. Just impatient.

Matching his mood, I snatched the notice up and scanned the details posted near the bottom. The audition was in Holly, more than two hours away from home.

"Maybe if I could cough up a hundred dollars in cab fees," I scoffed, oddly relieved that I had a believable reason to say no. The logistics were indisputable. He couldn't accuse me of being a coward now.

"That has nothing to do with this," Revend countered. "In fact, forget the money. I'll cover it."

I nearly choked. *Forget money.* It was like asking me to stop breathing—even for a second.

"Will you go?"

Touché. I could appreciate how he'd turned the tables. That didn't mean I had to admit it.

"Even if I *did*," I said, "it wouldn't matter, would it?"

Another round of perfect number forty-fives would fill the next stage, and I would be shown the door.

"You lack faith in yourself." His gaze honed in on my trembling fingers. Then, if I wasn't mistaken, he eyed my nose next. "At the same time, you lack restraint."

"So says the world-class ballet instructor." I watched his reflection in the window rather than face him directly.

"Hmph. World-class." A corner of his mouth twitched into something that could have been a smile on a normal person. "And what does that make you?" He glanced me over from head to toe and chuckled. "Certainly not someone worth the time of such an *esteemed* instructor—"

"Try me."

"How many pirouettes can you do without stopping?"

"Five." *Maybe,* in a decent pair of shoes. It sounded like a reasonable number to me, but Revend grunted out another coarse laugh.

"I would expect you to double that number," he said coldly. "As merely a starting point."

I shrugged in order to disguise the way I'd flinched. "What else?"

His gaze narrowed, prodding a little deeper than before. "Are you versed in the classical ballets?"

"Yes."

"Enough that you could perform a different role each night? Principal as well as corps?"

"Y-yes." My teeth snagged my lower lip, betraying the lie, but he never called me out on it. It was as if he knew that admitting my limits to myself was painful enough.

"Interesting." He sat forward, bracing his hands against the seat.

His gaze was too sharp, seeming to notice everything, and I didn't even know what to hide. My not-quite-concave stomach? The quarter-inch of jiggle on my thighs? Or maybe the scars on my wrists, carefully covered up with hair ties?

"What is?" I asked.

Abruptly, he snatched his cane up and tapped the end of it against the nearest window. A heartbeat later, the limo jerked to a stop somewhere along Glendale's main street.

"You may not care to waste my time," he said, "but I won't waste another moment of yours. It was a pleasure meeting with you, Ms. DeSotto. You can go."

I should have. In slow motion, I even reached for the door handle, fully intending to yank it open and throw myself out.

"Wait..." I swallowed hard, flicking my gaze over in his direction. "Just tell me why you helped me."

He shrugged again. "I do not give out charity."

"What does that even mean?"

"It *means*...decide. Do you want to remain mediocre and blaming the world for your failings or..."

"Or?" I croaked.

"*Or* do you want to learn?"

"But why do you even want to help me?"

"Goodnight, Ms. DeSotto—"

"Wait."

"Well?" He paused, facing the window.

"I... So, you'll help me?" It took twice as much effort to get the words out as sweat dribbled down the back of my neck.

He didn't reply, and it was a full minute before I realized why. Contrite girls groveled for a second chance.

"*Will* you help me? Please."

"Prove that you want my help." He lowered his cane but still kept it against his knee, within his reach. "Why do you dance?"

I couldn't hide my sigh of relief. Finally, a question I could actually answer. "Because I love it, and I—"

"Once again, you seem determined to waste my time," Revend snapped. "You're lying."

"I… What? No, I'm not—"

"I'll repeat the question," he said over me. "*Why* do you dance?"

The answer appeared in my brain like a worn commercial jingle I'd memorized the words to—the same one I'd been spouting in response to that question for sixteen years. My memories of dancing weren't tainted like the present, shining in my mind like the sequined costumes tucked at the back of my closet.

"I've wanted to be a ballerina since I was four," I admitted. "Dancing is all I think about. All I—"

"Why do you dance?" Once again, Revend wasn't following the same script I was.

"What do you mean? I just told you—"

"A lie." He slammed his hand against the leather seat. "Why. Do you. Dance?"

"I…"

His brutal tone shook a different answer loose, from that dark place that even my special "feelings" journal couldn't touch. The truth?

"I dance because…"

"Why?"

"Because I *have* to."

Something in his expression wavered, revealing that it wasn't quite the answer he'd expected. "Say it again."

"I dance because...I have t-to?" I couldn't resist making it a question. Did I even know the right answer?

"Why?" Revend prodded.

"I don't know—"

"I much prefer your honesty to the prissy act you put on," he declared on the cusp of a sigh.

"Huh?" I could only gape at him. "I...I'm sorry—"

"My patience is wearing thin, Ms. DeSotto. You dance because..."

"Because." I inhaled and ran a hand through the hair on the top of my head, ripping stray strands from the neat bun. A million half-assed replies flashed through my mind, but for some reason, I found myself uttering something not on that list. The truth? "When I dance, I don't have to...feel."

"Feel." A corner of his mouth lowered, casting a shadow over the bottom half of his face.

Was it a good answer? Bad? Looking at him, I couldn't tell. His expressions didn't follow the script I was used to.

"Feel what?" he asked.

"I don't know. Anything?" I bit my lower lip as if to hold the word in, but it broke free anyway. "I don't feel *anything.*"

My stomach curled into knots as I waited for his reaction.

A laugh?

A scoff?

For him to rap me over the head with his cane and warn me not to "dwell on the negatives"?

It wasn't until his mouth finally opened and a rush of air flooded my chest that I realized I'd been holding my breath all that time.

"MacMillian's *Romeo and Juliet.* Do you know it?"

I blinked, caught off guard. "Yes…" What dancer didn't?

"What days do you usually practice with Victor?"

"Sunday through Thursday," I blurted, once again blindsided by how expertly he could change the subject.

"Cancel them."

"What…what? I can't just cancel a week of lessons—"

"I will replace them."

"You?" An argument died at the back of my throat as Revend folded his hands over his lap.

"Tomorrow. Five o'clock," he said. "I will supply you with the address."

"T-tomorrow?"

"Yes," he snapped. "That is, if you have decided not to waste my time. Goodnight, Ms. DeSotto."

It was only then that I recognized the street we glided onto next—my father's. The familiarity made my stomach clench. The driver pulled into the driveway, and I scrambled out the moment the limo came to a stop. A frigid gust replaced the stifling heat of the interior, disrupting my hair and chasing the memory of him away.

Revend Marcus could have been entirely a figment of my imagination—if it weren't for the red flicker of the limo's taillights as it drove off.

CHAPTER 6

Stealth was the most important tool in a liar's arsenal. Following that rulebook, I eased the front door open as softly as I could.

"Anya?"

Shit. Any hope I had of sneaking upstairs unnoticed died the moment the voice rang out.

"Is that you?"

"Y-yes." I crossed the threshold and closed the door behind me, rattling the frosted glass built into the doorway. Only the light at the top of the stairs was lit, which forced me to make my way through shadow to follow the sound of the voice to the kitchen.

Dad was at the counter, his robe hanging open as he poured a glass of water from the tap. I'd caught him during one of his midnight breaks. I wasn't supposed to notice the beer can tossed in the trash or his bloodshot eyes. Shadows shielded most of his face, but I could tell even from the distance that he was mostly sober. For now.

"It's a little late isn't it?" he asked over his shoulder.

Thank God my pointe shoes were in my bag and my coat had been fastened over my leotard. The only clue as to where I'd really been was the tight bun straining my temples, and without thinking, I tugged on the elastic holding it together. Four bobby pins met their deaths against the floor with tiny, metallic pings.

"Yeah…um, studying just ran a little late. That's all." I flashed a smile while trapping the nearest bobby pin beneath the toe of my sneaker. "Sorry for not giving you a heads-up."

"Don't work too hard," he scolded without glancing up from the counter.

I knew why. His second beer can was hiding behind the coffee maker, waiting until I'd scurried out of sight to be poured into the mug in his hand.

"And I know that you're twenty and 'officially' an adult now, but try not to stay out too late, all right?"

"Sure thing!" I nodded and darted for the stairs.

"Wait—"

"Yes?" I noticed then that my clothes reeked of cigar smoke. With my luck, so had he.

"A package came for you," Dad said. "I left it on your bed."

"Oh…okay. Thanks."

Desperate to escape, I took the stairs two at a time and tore into my bedroom, locking the door behind me. Once I found the white box waiting on my bed, the fragile calm I felt during my meeting with Revend shattered. With the box balanced on my lap, I fell back onto the mattress and ripped the lid off.

I don't know what I'd expected. Cream for my bruises, maybe? Instead, a pair of ebony pointe shoes rested on a bed of tissue paper inside. They were obviously custom-made, tailored more finely than my old ones.

And expensive. That much was apparent from the fancy brand name embossed on the soles in golden thread. Almost numb with shock, I set them aside and then noticed the envelope at the bottom of the box, which contained a simple note.

Five. 1347 Haven Lane. You will wear these.

Damn. Revend's aura could taint even a simple piece of paper.

I let it fall back into the box as if I'd been burned by it before I cast a reluctant glance at my old shoes. They weren't completely dead just yet. I lifted one and grazed its sole with the pad of my thumb as if to convince myself of that fact. The padding was torn in some places, and the elastic securing the ribbons was starting to give way.

But the new pair was too bright in my small, plain room. Too clean. Too perfect. Too negative.

Chewing on my lower lip, I approached my closet without giving in to the urge to shove the new shoes back into their box. On the top shelf was a dusty shoebox, which I set on the floor. Inside it were a few haphazard tools for preparing new pointe shoes—none of which had been touched in an embarrassingly long time.

Before I could talk myself out of it, I picked one of the black slippers up and removed a coil of ribbon nestled inside it. It took me only ten minutes to cut the right length and sew the halves into the backs of each shoe, which I reinforced with elastic fished from my kit. I let the familiarity of the task drown out the voice at the back of my mind insisting that I shouldn't accept them.

But they were beautiful. Not only that, but fresh slippers promised a fresh start, fresh turns, and fresh potential. Impulsively, I peeled one of my socks off and bared a foot that was almost as battered as my old pointe shoes underneath. Band-Aids clung to open blisters. Purple bruises painted my toes.

"A dancer's most prized possession is his feet," Remsky liked to insist time and time again. "Cherish them. Worship them. Without them, you cannot eat."

Aware of that advice, I cradled my heel in my palm, feeling the ache of a thousand practices that had resulted in layers of callused skin. If a dancer's passion could be judged by their feet alone, then Revend Marcus didn't know a damn thing.

Though he did know my shoe size.

The slipper perfectly hugged the arch of my foot. The toe felt heavy, weighed down by the box meant to support my weight when on pointe, but apart from that, they felt…

Almost as perfect as my old ones.

I stood and experimentally flexed my left foot, hating how the shoe conformed to every curve. Shoes were such an intimate part of a dancer's arsenal. It would have been more acceptable for him to have guessed my bra size or ordered a custom pair of underwear.

I could have returned a pair of underwear.

I knew I *should* return these. There was no way I would show up the next day anyway. Why should I? Revend Marcus was a stranger—a thought which brought my attention to the closed laptop on my desk. All in all, the damn thing took only a few minutes to boot up. When I finally typed a single name into the search engine, I expected maybe one accurate post hidden amongst hundreds. Instead, I found thousands.

Katja hadn't embellished her story for once. Revend Marcus owned several theaters across Europe—in addition to a storied career. *Romeo and Juliet. Carmen. Don Quixote. Giselle.* In his prime, he had starred in them all, having retired only twelve years ago.

That was all I needed to know. In theory. Curiosity took over, though, and I found myself scrolling down to learn more about him than I'd meant to. He was forty-four and had been supposedly married twice but widowed once. I couldn't find the result of his last marriage—the one that Katja claimed had resulted in his scars. Not that I cared once I caught sight of what several articles claimed was the crowning achievement of Revend Marcus' legacy—a certain international ballet company currently scouting for new talent in North America.

The Roria.

The address Revend had given me led to a part of town far beyond my father's sparkling new development and the cozy condominium my mother lived in. It might as well have been in another universe. There, the old brownstones reeked of high class and old money— at least on the surface. Underneath it all was this odd, grim atmosphere that made me subconsciously clutch my bag a little tighter.

Though it could have been the apprehension talking. Every time I tried to picture what a "lesson" with Revend might entail, I could only come up with vague scenarios. Like being beaten with that cane, for one. Still, I couldn't seem to turn back.

It wasn't that hard to find his address in the end—the last house on a street that loomed over the rest of the city. Nearly three stories tall, it had been built in the Gothic style, with sprawling gardens on either side of it, both overrun. In fact, that word summed up the entire property.

Weeds poked through cracks in the path leading to the

front door, while an icy wind tossed candy wrappers and garbage across the unkempt lawn. When I reached the front door, it opened a fraction of an inch before I could touch it.

"H-hello?"

I jumped as a steady thudding sound came from inside the house instead of a reply. Footsteps? They receded deeper inside—my cue to enter, I assumed. I tiptoed over the threshold and allowed the door to close behind me.

Waning daylight filtering in through a nearby window illuminated a narrow foyer bathed in shadow. I blinked as my eyes adjusted. The layout seemed relatively simple. A grand staircase straight ahead led to an upper level, while two elegant archways on either side opened up to other areas of the house. The peeling wallpaper and dusty floors betrayed that the place hadn't been inhabited in a long while, but it didn't scream *lair of a madman*, either.

Speaking of which, there was no one else in sight.

"Hello?" I called again, unnerved by just how far my voice seemed to echo. "Mr. Marcus—"

"Do they fit?"

I followed the gruff voice across the foyer and into a rectangular room. The floors were marble, enclosed by cream walls, and a row of floor-to-ceiling windows overlooked a neglected garden. It was such an odd mixture of beauty and decay, so different from what I'd expected. Anywhere else, it would have seemed like the typical rehearsal studio, if an old one. At least it wasn't a dungeon.

"The shoes."

A glance over my shoulder revealed Revend lurking on the other end of the room.

He nodded curtly toward my feet. "Do they fit?"

"Y-yes." I shrugged my bag from my shoulder, using it as a makeshift barrier despite the yards of space already between us.

Without his heavy coat, I almost didn't recognize him. Instead, he was wearing a dark shirt and pants that emphasized the muscle coiled in both arms.

"They fit...okay," I stammered while tearing my gaze up to his face.

"Okay?" His eyes flashed with suspicion. "Let me see."

I backed over to a chair placed along the far wall—conveniently as far from him as the space would allow. I never took my gaze from him for even a second as I fished the black pointe shoes from my bag, kicked my sneakers off, and crammed my feet into the slippers without taking the usual care. Even still...

They felt damn near perfect. A few hours of practice would have them fully broken in.

"Change," Revend snapped, apparently satisfied with the fit as well. "There's a room in the back. You have five minutes."

I followed his instruction and found a narrow bathroom at the hall's very end. I'd barely closed the door before a harsh rap rattled the frame.

"Wear this."

The door opened wider, and something flew through the gap before it slammed shut again—a box that landed open at my feet. Inside was a complete warm-up outfit. It wasn't my typical style, just a pale pink leotard and a sheer ivory skirt meant to be secured by a length of white ribbon.

Of course, everything was in my size.

My hesitation to accept them lasted all of five seconds once I'd glanced over the spare warm-up leotard I'd brought with me—a gray cotton one that had a few holes around the hemline.

The new one fit perfectly, flattening my stomach and concealing unsightly flab. I looked *almost* like the ballerina dolls every other dancer seemed to resemble. If only my smile were real and not painted. The emptiness behind my glassy eyes refused to fade no matter how many expressions I tried on like masks—happy, sad, and terrified.

Robotic! an imaginary Revend snarled.

When I finally left the bathroom and entered the larger rehearsal room, his real voice berated me from the center of it. "About time. Warm up."

A chandelier hanging from the ceiling was already lit, flooding the room with orange light—as well as illuminating several distinct fixtures. He owned his own piano, tucked into the corner. There was also a metal dance barre, about six feet long, placed near the wall before me. Behind it was an even longer mirror stretching nearly all the way up to the ceiling. My reflection mocked me from it, wearing a sheer skirt that hung crookedly around my waist.

Revend frowned at the sight, though who could blame him? How in the hell was he supposed to transform this robot into a real girl?

"Warm up," he barked, gesturing to the barre.

He never gave me any direction, so I began my usual exercises, focusing on each core muscle group one at a time. Legs. Arms. Back.

The mirror threw his reactions in my face, making them impossible to ignore. The frown when I lifted one leg over the barre. The way it grew more pronounced when I started to work on the second. How, with every plié, his narrowed gaze scanned my face for emotion.

"Look at me."

I wasn't brave enough to mention that I had never stopped. When I glanced over my shoulder, I found that his *real* expression wasn't any warmer than the reflection.

"We will do the *pas de deux* from the balcony scene in *Romeo and Juliet*," he said. "I will only rehearse the partner work minus the lifts, but you need to know the full routine."

The full routine. One that just so happened to include an infamous kiss at the end. Sizing Revend up, I couldn't tell if he planned on rehearsing that part too.

"Why?" I asked.

"Why?" His eyes narrowed into slits. "Did you even read the instructions for the next round of auditions?"

I bit my lip rather than admitting my lack of preparation out loud. *Two weeks*. Only then did it sink in just how little time that was to prepare.

"Get into the starting position."

I stiffened as Revend appeared behind me. Before I could react, his hand captured my waist.

"En pointe," he commanded as his fingers flexed possessively. "Now, begin."

What was that saying? *Third time's the charm.* It fit there almost, considering that I had danced the role of Juliet only twice before in my junior year of a performance arts academy in the city. I had been an understudy at first, only to be thrust into the lead role when the principal dancer got sick off bad sushi. The reviews in the community newspaper read something along the lines of, *Beautiful production but stiff female lead*—an opinion Revend seemed to second.

"Don't tense," he hissed. His hands went to my shoulders, correcting my posture with precise nudges. "You're stifling your own motion."

"I don't—"

"You *don't* speak. You dance."

Dance. I used the command as an excuse to move away from him, but I could never escape my own reflection. The woman performing a series of light steps alongside me was no Juliet. Maybe just a jilted member of the corps shoved onto the very back of the stage as a nameless extra—*servant number one.*

"Stop!" Revend snarled halfway through the variation. Tearing a hand through his hair, he retreated to the other end of the room.

For the first time, I realized he didn't have his cane. It leaned against the chair in the corner.

"You're a young girl," he bellowed, his voice reverberating through the walls. "You're in love. Passionate. Show me."

How did people show passion outside of forced luncheons and silent dinners? Maybe this damn ballet held the answer; the act began with Juliet rushing excitedly to meet her Romeo. One count passed. Then another as I hesitated on the balls of my feet.

I didn't recall Romeo having graying hair.

"You're thinking like a *child* and not a dancer," Revend scolded as if reading my mind. "All that matters is maintaining the illusion. Make me believe it!"

I launched into the steps without giving myself the chance to believe in anything—to regret having shown up at this lesson. I was Juliet, prancing across the marble to meet the man she'd admired from afar. Juliet, rising on pointe to pirouette in her lover's arms…

And I was Anya in the arms of Revend Marcus, who seized my waist mid-spin and marshaled me over to the mirror.

"Look! Watch your face," he hissed against my ear. "Your heart is racing. Your body is tense. But what do you *see?*"

Negative traits stood out in stark contrast, impossible to overlook. I only saw someone in over her head, dressed in a pretty uniform that highlighted the blank, unnatural expression on her face.

Feel?

Robots couldn't feel.

"Forget the dance." He captured my head with his hands, raking his fingers through that perfect bun at the nape of my neck. "Only feel." His thumb brushed the corner of my mouth as if to give me a sensation to study.

When I flinched, the nail grazed my lip. My chin. Lower…

"Ignore the source. Focus on the feeling and take what you need from it to create your own illusion."

What I needed?

Maybe for him to stop touching me. My own family didn't touch me. They looked. They watched. Monitored. Pitied. Hugs were for real girls; robots simply needed daily programming. The firmer Revend's fingers dug into my hip, the more my insides twisted, struggling to register every sensation. *Too warm. Too hard. Everywhere.*

"S-stop—"

"No." He muscled in even closer. My back struck his chest, his right thigh caging my hip. "Ignore *everything* but what you need to craft your illusion."

Easier said than done. Only his tone kept my heart from racing. He sounded cold, like a professor attempting to show an ignorant student the folly of her ways. Even the way he touched me held purpose. His nearness forced my spine to lengthen. His hands urged my feet to turn out further, my toes perfectly pointed.

"Become Juliet," he grunted before standing back. "Move."

I raised my arms and turned out my left foot. *I'm Juliet. I'm...*

"Dead!" Revend hissed. "You're already dead before an ounce of poison even touches your lips."

Staring into the empty, blue eyes watching me from the mirror's surface, I had to agree with him. I didn't even recognize the woman he was taunting. Why did she seem so damn cold?

"Begin again," Revend snapped, but I lifted my arms only for him to swat them down. "Try again. Move. *Feel*, Anya."

He made it sound so damn easy. *Feel.* But how could I with no lines to recite? No fake smile to wear for show? No daddies to lie to or mommies to placate?

No script.

Feel. My support foot wobbled as I rose on relevé. Any attempt to flow into the next step was met with a nudge to raise my shoulders, a shout to extend my neck, a heavy hand striking my thigh when I didn't move quickly enough, gracefully enough, perfectly enough.

Again.

And again.

And *again*.

"No, no, no!" The more furious Revend became, the deeper his voice lowered. He was growling, each word revving in his throat. "Pathetic!"

"This isn't fair. You're not even letting me dance—"

"You're not trying!"

I wasn't prepared when he lunged, shoving me forward. I had to brace my hands against the mirror or crash into it.

"What the hell was that for?" My expression watched me fearfully, my nose barely an inch from the glass. If he'd been even a tiny bit aggressive, I'd have had a reason to leave.

But he looked more frustrated than I did.

"*You* are holding yourself back. Again," he said. "Forget the pretty smiles and the charming flourishes. You are a puppet...on *my* string."

I shivered, my fingers flexing against the glass as he approached me from behind.

"Show me what I want to see."

What he wanted to see?

That was the million-dollar question. I was an expert at showing the world what—or who—they wanted me to be. Perfect little Anya, always striving for success. Meeting her mother for weekly luncheons and giving her dreams up at her father's behest.

Dancing is a dead end, they said. *Go to college. Get a job. Be* something.

But the only something they ever seemed to notice was whatever cardboard cutout they wanted her to be that day. If she failed, it was straight to the clinic or a therapist to rub any flaws out and fix her faulty mechanics.

I excelled at pretending…

Or so I'd thought. Only then did I finally realize that no one had ever looked closely enough to see the obvious flaws in my mask.

No one but him.

"Close your eyes."

I obeyed, shutting him out.

"Listen to me with this." He nudged my spine, urging it into perfect alignment. "Respond. Don't think. Feel."

I squeezed my eyes shut tighter, attempting to ignore everything else. *You're Juliet,* I insisted, pressing my palms flat against the mirror as if some of its unyielding strength might seep into me.

I'm Juliet. I'm…

"Move!" He didn't say another word, even as he led me into the first step and then shoved forward into a pirouette.

It felt like I spun for ages until two hands seized my waist and guided me into an arabesque. Just as my balance began to waver, he let me go, and I continued to dance the routine without daring to open my eyes.

It was so much safer if I couldn't see his face.

I'd always hated the *Romeo and Juliet pas de deux.* It was too intimate. Too intricate. Too much trust to place in your partner not to screw up.

Revend, apparently, had no faith in me. I could sense him standing there in the center of the room while I pranced around. *Pirouette, arabesque. Pirouette, arabesque.* After one last delicate variation, I was supposed to return lovingly to my Romeo and clutch his outstretched arm to my chest…

My eyes opened, and I found Revend much closer than I'd thought, but he never offered his hand as I flitted toward him on the tips of my toes. He gave me nothing to feed off of but a grunted command.

"Dance!"

I snatched for his fingers and regretted it instantly. Despite the cane, despite the gray streaking his hair, even despite his apparent age, strength emanated from his palm. I could feel it in the callused knuckles that tensed as I brought his hand against the center of my rib cage and held it there for half a count.

Feel.

My heart was beating—pounding, surging. It didn't let up when I released him and flounced away to spin before the windows while he watched me perform, unamused.

When I attempted to flit past him, he snatched my arm, yanking me against his chest. "What. Do. I. Have. To. Do?"

His free hand seized my upper thigh, forcing it against him until we stood parallel, while his foot kicked mine farther apart. There was no subtle correction to my posture. Just nearness. Overwhelming heat.

I tried to pull away. He pulled me back, wrenching on my arm.

"Move with me." He stepped forward, bringing his thigh flush against my hip.

Too close...too close! Fire sparked, searing the inside of my veins, spreading up and down... Everywhere. Too much. Too fast.

I tried to breathe.

I *tried* to ignore him.

Dance.

Feel.

"Stiff," he hissed in disgust, pulling back enough to allow me to breathe again. "Have you ever been in love?"

"W-what?" I couldn't ignore the mocking note embedded in his voice. Teenage girls fell in love every other day. Even robot girls. "That's none of your business—"

"I'll take that as a no, then." If anything, he sounded disappointed. *Tsk. Tsk.*

I couldn't even feel silly emotions like a normal girl. How hopeless.

Another question came as I attempted to run through the variation without his input.

"Have you ever fucked?"

One foot wavered in the air, my eyes widening before I could attempt to disguise my shock. "That's none of your business, either," I croaked. "It doesn't matter."

"Of course it matters," Revend insisted, but his voice was softer. A low, raspy baritone, it sank into my skin and irritated the parts of me his fingers could never reach. "Dance is physical. Attraction is physical. Trying to convey one without the other is impossible. Or, in your case, the root of your mediocrity."

I flinched at the word choice and took a step toward the mirror. A wide-eyed Anya watched me from behind the glass. How pathetic. The corner of her mouth was twisted, but even I didn't have a clue why. Was she disgusted? Intrigued?

"I thought you were going to help me improve my *dancing*," I gritted out. "Not give me abridged sex ed—"

"Sex is physical," Revend said over me. The sound of approaching footsteps preceded the warmth that crept through the back of my leotard. "And fucking is pretentious, like this dance. It's two bodies desperately trying to meld while ignoring the physical limitations."

I struggled to swallow, painfully aware of him behind me. Everyone always touted the so-called *pretentious* romance featured in *Romeo and Juliet*. In two seconds, Revend had degraded that undying love to two people simply trying to "fuck" across a stage.

"I'm not sure that MacMillian would appreciate his work being so…bluntly analyzed," I countered.

"If you understand fucking, then the passion in this variation should be easy for you to convey," Revend said, unconcerned by the flush creeping into my cheeks. "However, I have to say that, for such an adept liar, I am disappointed at how poorly you play pretend."

Adept liar. "What…what do you mean?" I asked innocently.

He grunted and pointedly eyed my nose. "You know what I mean."

My hand absently swiped at my upper lip. "H-how is this supposed to help me to be Juliet?" I demanded, meeting the gaze of his reflection rather than turning to face him directly.

"You stop trying," he said. "You react. You act. You *feel* the emotion you need to convey. Now, do it again."

His hand settled on my shoulder without warning, eating through what little composure I had left. I tried to ignore him by entering first position before transitioning carefully into fifth, but his touch never withdrew. I still heard his voice in my head. *Feel. Fuck. Feel.*

When I moved, he followed, throwing me off-balance. For once, he wasn't trying to unnerve me; he was simply playing the role of Romeo.

But I wasn't Juliet.

"I can't do this." I staggered away from him, my heart in my throat.

"Try again."

"I said I can't—"

"Try!" He grabbed my arm and pulled me in close. Alarm ran down my spine. I lashed out blindly. My fingers caught his hand and flexed, the nails grazing his flesh. "Damn!" He recoiled from me, clutching his hand to his chest.

I panicked.

Run!

I snatched my bag up before racing out into the foyer, leaving my sneakers behind. My hands clawed at the front door, wrenching it open, and then I stumbled down the front stoop and across the lawn just as raindrops fell.

I only had enough sense of mind to stop near the bottom of the hill and take my pointe shoes off before they could become soaked. Then I wrapped them within the skirt and walked the rest of the way barefoot.

*P*ride carried me to the center of town before I collapsed onto a soaked bench outside of a McDonald's, a completely random destination—or so I tried to tell myself. No dwelling on the negatives, after all.

Thankfully, the storm had died down to just a smattering of raindrops, but my hopes of making it home on my own shattered more by the second. My legs were cramping, my muscles dissolving to the consistency of jelly. It took the last bit of energy I had left to fish my jacket from my bag and slip it on.

Even in all of my months of training with Remsky, I had never pushed myself so hard. Never *thought* I could be pushed so far. I had to bite my lip to keep from whimpering. From screaming.

"You need to feel," Revend had hissed, but he was wrong. Emotions were dangerous, and feeling could be impossible when you needed a lever just to turn it *off*.

One lesson with him and it was like the floodgates opened. Everything from the past week came back, one thing after the other, beating me down and leaving me breathless.

You.

Are.

Hopeless.

So hopeless that I could only get a callback if the audition were handed to me on a silver platter. So hopeless that some washed-up dancer in his forties had to take pity on me. So hopeless…

Gritting my teeth, I hunched over, raking my fingers through my hair. *Don't think like that.*

My hands were shaking, my lips were shredded beneath my teeth, and I hated the way I scanned the block, searching for someone who might be lurking in a nearby alley.

I'd lied to myself. This wasn't a random destination. I knew every inch of this corner of town, on the "wrong" side of the tracks—and in the opposite direction of my father's house. I knew this damn bench…and they knew my face.

Thankfully, the rain seemed to have driven everyone inside. But not for long…

Move. I tried to stand only to wind up crouched over the damp pavement, clinging to the edge of the bench. My heart hammered in my chest as a rickety car sputtered past, spraying water in its wake, dousing me beneath the splash.

Call someone.

I dug through my bag for my cell, my fingers shaking as I scrambled through the numbers in the directory. *Dad?* No. *Carrie?* No. *Mom?* I cycled all the way down to the very last contact and hesitated, my thumb hovering over the screen.

Shit. Footsteps came from the alley, and desperation made me finally hit the call button. Not even ten minutes later, a battered blue Mustang pulled up alongside the curb. The driver's side window lowered, revealing a familiar face sporting a grin I couldn't muster the energy to return.

"You rang?"

Without responding, I gathered my bag up and managed to hobble around to the car's other side. I opened the door and had to stifle a frown. It even smelled the same—like sweat a mint-scented air freshener vainly tried to cut through. Had he even cleaned it during these past six months? Was that old bag of fast food still tucked, forgotten on the back seat? I collapsed onto the passenger's seat without asking and squeezed my eyes shut against the migraine aching behind my temples.

"Rough day?" Jake asked. His joking laughter contrasted so sharply with Revend's growls that it made my head spin. In a good way? Bad way? I couldn't tell relief from revulsion at this point. "You look soaked, Ann. Tell me you weren't out walking in this shit."

I didn't answer. It was so much easier to slump against the window and press my forehead against the glass. Jake already knew my address, so there was no need to say anything else. At least in old, selfish Anya's world.

He was frowning, though, in that brooding way he only did when hurt. Tomorrow, I might feel guilty, but when the Mustang pulled into my father's driveway, I poured all of my energy into grabbing my bag with one hand and the door handle with the other.

"Thank you—"

The sound of the automatic locks engaging cut me off.

"Six months, Anya." Jake faced straight ahead with his jaw clenched, and his hands braced against the steering wheel. "No phone call. No e-mails. No texts. Then a request out of the blue to give you a 'ride,' which I'm surprised to realize was actually just a ride."

"I'm sorry."

"No," he said harshly. "*I'm* the one who's sorry. I thought you were different, you know? Everyone warned me, but I didn't listen. *'Not Anya. She's not an ice queen. She's not some frigid bitch who would break up after a fucking year with no damn explanation—'*"

"Can we *please* not do this?" I sounded pathetic.

Jake just grunted, but a second later the locks disengaged. "You look like shit."

I glanced up, assuming the words had been some delayed insult after a rather amicable breakup. Instead, his eyes were on my trembling hands.

"Damn, Anya. Are you okay? What the hell are you wearing anyway—"

"I'm fine." I wrenched on the door handle, effectively proving the opposite when I nearly fell out of the car.

My head swam. It felt like I was drowning, submerged beneath gallons of exhaustion and pain. The driver's side door opened and footsteps approached my side, but I couldn't find the strength to move when someone slipped their arm around my shoulders and hauled me to my feet.

"No." My head lolled against a firm chest despite my protest. "I can walk on my—"

"You look like hell," Jake said over me. His breath smelled like bubblegum, not peppermint. "At least let me help you to the front door."

I needed the help.

Revend Marcus had drained me of everything—even the sense of decency to feel ashamed for using someone as damn earnest as Jake. He was right; I owed him more than a random phone call in the middle of the night. He had dated me despite the whispered rumors. And I, of course, had proved every last one to be true by insisting on a break a week after his declaration of the dreaded L-word.

I was an ice-cold bitch who didn't even deserve to be hauled up the front walkway.

"Thank you," I managed to croak when we finally reached the front door. I braced one hand against it while the other slid into my bag to fish for my keys.

"Don't worry about it." Jake let me go and took a step back, but I could sense him hesitating. And I was terrified that he would try to continue the one-sided conversation from the car. *Our breakup. This phone call. Where he picked me up.* "Anya—"

Something else drew my attention; the lock turned before I could even close my fingers around my keys.

"Shit!" I pushed back and somehow managed to balance upright just as the door opened.

"Another late-night study session?" my father inquired. He stood sandwiched in the doorway, still wearing his work shirt, the tie partially undone.

I doubted he'd had time to grab his nightly sip of "water" yet. His eyes weren't bloodshot at least.

"I hope this won't be a regular thing," he said.

I couldn't speak—not that I had the chance to once he caught sight of Jake.

"Hey! It's been a while!" Smiling, he stepped forward to shake Jake's hand while I stood there praying that I could melt into a puddle.

Please. If only the plea could have been transmitted telepathically. *Don't say it. Don't say it.*

"How's it going? You two should ace that test the way you've been studying."

"S-sir?" Jake glanced at me.

I could only shake my head.

Damn it.

Oblivious, my father continued. "What's it been? Every night this week?"

"Yeah… You know Anya," Jake chimed in after an awkward pause. "Always striving to be the best."

My father laughed. "Just be sure not to overdo it, okay?"

"Sure thing, Mr. DeSotto. I'll see you around, Anya…"

"Bye."

"Don't be a stranger, eh, Jake?"

I could only stand there, hugging myself as my father cheerfully waved Jake off. He waited until the Mustang had finally pulled out of the driveway before he headed inside.

"What's it been now for you guys?" He wondered from over his shoulder. "Almost two years?"

"Yeah," I rasped. "Almost."

Thankfully, Carrie called to him from the living room, and I was no longer the focus of his attention—it wasn't like he noticed that I wore only a dance skirt and no shoes anyway.

It felt like it took ages for me to limp up the stairs while the sounds of a lighthearted television comedy drifted from the living room. The moment I entered my room, I locked the door, tossed my bag into a corner, and climbed onto my bed without bothering to pull the comforter back.

Sleep came in twos.

First, my body went blissfully numb.

Then I lost consciousness amid the memory of a single bellowed word that began a nightmare.

Feel!

CHAPTER 7

How strange was it that a simple *smell* could seem comforting when all the coke or medication in the world didn't help? When the "feelings" journal became pages filled with lies and the cravings you weren't supposed to experience anymore returned in full force.

Breathing in the moldy aroma of Remsky's theater, I almost felt the pride I used to feel—*before* I'd started to snort a different substance up my nose. Back when I'd known that, as long as I kept practicing, I could "make it" one day.

Back before a voice in my head had started whispering that it was all a lie. The doubt was even easier to chase away once I laced my old pointe shoes on, tying the frayed ribbons tight. My therapist would praise my actions. I was starting over today. Out with the new, in with the old.

Remsky's crumbling studio above the theater was the perfect place to forge that start. The walls didn't echo with the clack of a cane. The mirrors there didn't lie. Beneath the faulty ceiling, I was pretty, perfect Anya once again—at least until a familiar shadow appeared in the doorway and ruined everything.

"This is a surprise, Anya," Remsky said softly.

I turned to face him. "Was practice canceled again today?"

"No. What are you doing here?"

"What do you mean?" I faced the wall, bracing my hands against the barre as I sank into a plié. As long as I kept moving, I didn't have to decipher the hesitant frown tugging at his mouth. I would only focus on the positives. Like my stretches, the sun shining through the arched windows, and…

"I thought you were training elsewhere, so why are you here?"

I fell to the flats of my feet. "Oh."

Revend must have told him about training me because I hadn't gathered up the nerve, though I suspected Remsky had known about the offer even before I had.

"Oh, that. It didn't work out." I switched positions to support my left side and started the exercises over from the beginning.

He remained silent for exactly four more pliés, eight breaths, and one dreaded realization. "Anya…"

"You don't have to say it." Rising into first position, I kept my gaze on the peeling gray wallpaper ahead of me while my peace splintered. Cracked. My next words were the hammer, delivering the blow Remsky seemed too hesitant to inflict. "You're dropping me."

It wasn't that much of a shock—go figure. Remsky didn't let his best students go without a fight. In this economy, he rarely let *any* of his students go without a fight. Just me. Just robot Anya, the hopeless student even the ruthless Victor Remsky pitied too much to cut loose.

"You sent me into that 'audition' on purpose." Only then could I put the pieces together, and just like that, Remsky's past words were all reduced to nothing more than sugar disguising the poison everyone else had no trouble shoving down my throat. "You *knew* that Revend would tear me apart."

"I *hoped*"—he stressed the word—"that you would learn something from the experience. I—"

"Learn something?" I blinked back the burning sensation that had crept behind my eyes. "I *learned*…that, for the past year and a half, you've been taking my money while pretending that I might improve."

"That's not the case—"

"Isn't it?"

When I turned to face him, my stern mentor seemed at a loss for words for once. Gone was the harsh expression that usually clouded his eyes; all that was left was pity.

"So, I guess this is it, then?" A year and a half of training had come to this. I had been such an idiot not to realize it sooner… Or maybe I had? Maybe lying to myself had just made it easier to keep lying to everyone else.

"I knew that Revend could help you where I cannot," Remsky said, shrugging his shoulders.

"Can't?" I echoed. "Or *won't?*"

You're projecting, Anya, my therapist would warn. *Seeing things that aren't there. Jumping to conclusions.* It was "mean" to doubt the motives of those around you, after all. For instance, with the help of many pricey therapy sessions, I'd come to the realization that my parents really did love me very much. Their inability to spout off those three words I rarely heard was all in my imagination.

Maybe Remsky's deliberate lies were all my destructive, cynical imagination as well, attempting to throw a tantrum. Be the victim. Blame. Hate.

Maybe it hurt a little less to give in and project my anger onto him anyway.

"Pretty feet, Anya. Perfect posture, Anya," I parroted, mocking his crisp accent. "All you had to do was tell me the truth—'You're *hopeless*, Anya!'"

Remsky didn't say a word in his defense. Instead, he took a step forward, his arm outstretched—to *comfort* me.

"Don't touch me." I snatched away from the barre and pushed past him before he could call me back.

Not that he ever did.

The halls remained silent as I grabbed my spare dance bag from the dressing room and slipped out a side door without looking back.

✿

Ten minutes of knocking and no response. No sign of life lurked beyond the darkened windows, either. No hint of Revend pacing behind the glass. Just silence.

To stall, I pressed my back against the closed door and sank to my knees. Before me, the wind wreaked havoc on the overgrown weeds—a perfect visual to match how I felt inside. Hopeless.

I wasn't sure how much time had passed before a black limousine finally approached the front gate, and a man emerged from the back seat. He started up the front path with the aid of a cane, his eyes like black holes threatening to swallow me whole.

"If you are here about your belongings," he said after spotting me, "I've already had them delivered to your home—"

"I want another chance." I could only get the words out while staring down at his boots rather than his face.

"No." When he came close enough, he used the end of his cane to nudge me sideways, clearing a path to the door. "I told you that the moment you walked out of that door, I wouldn't allow you back in."

Rejected again. I hadn't expected anything less. Still, it hurt, being written off twice in one day. Remsky's expression haunted me as I inhaled and released the air in a rush.

"Please—"

"Don't. Do not grovel." Scowling, Revend fished a key from his pocket and inserted it into the lock. "I suggest you leave before you make an even bigger fool of yourself, Ms. DeSotto." He pushed his way past me and slammed the door in his wake.

I should have taken his advice. Instead, my head fell back against the door, and I found myself uttering three words I never thought could sting so much.

"You were right."

The door remained shut, but something told me he was still there, lurking on the other side of it.

"You were *right*, Revend. That's what you want to hear, isn't it? Remsky dropped me from his studio. Though I'm sure you already knew that. I have nowhere else to train. I get it now. I'm…I'm too stiff…too robotic, and I…I'm not good enough."

Eons seemed to pass before I heard the sound of heavy footsteps inside the house. Seconds later, his voice came, muffled from behind the wood.

"The door is unlocked—"

I stood and grasped the handle. It turned easily, but no sooner did I take a step over the threshold than Revend's snarl reached me from what sounded like the rehearsal room.

"Think," he warned. "I won't have you waste my time again."

Think. How desperate was I, really? Even the shadows flickering across the floor seemed to wave me off. *Run.*

"Think quickly—"

Rather than answer, I closed the door behind me—*without* thinking for once—and followed the sound of his voice across the foyer. Today, the rehearsal room was lit only by the daylight flooding in through the windows, which created shadows that draped the floor.

"Remove your shoes," Revend commanded from the center of the room.

If my decision had surprised him, I couldn't tell from looking at his face alone. He was still frowning, still unconvinced.

"But don't bother with the slippers if you've brought any."

I wasn't brave enough to ask why. Instead, I picked a spot along the wall and sank down to take my spare sneakers off one by one. Once finished, I flexed my bare toes against the floor, observing the bruises and the blisters in the light.

"I don't have a leotard," I admitted without looking up. I guess it made no sense to come to him without the proper attire anyway—whether he took me on again or not. A pair of jeans and an oversized T-shirt had been meant to reinforce an inevitable future without dance…

And I just felt suffocated. Go figure.

"It doesn't matter."

When Revend beckoned me forward with a sharp jerk of his chin, I wasn't sure what to expect. To stall for time, I took my jacket first off and threw it down beside my shoes. My teeth were chattering within seconds—it felt even colder inside the house than it had outside.

Revend, however, seemed unfazed. His own coat had been slung over the surface of a piano tucked into the corner, leaving him only in a gray, short-sleeved shirt. My eyes automatically traced the muscle coiled in his bare forearms. He wasn't much older than my father, but years of stress and cocktail parties had erased any trace of the once star quarterback from the latter's body.

In comparison, Revend's limbs seemed designed to crush. Mold. Shape. Destroy.

"I wasn't aware that we were on *your* timeframe, Ms. DeSotto," he snapped.

I hurried to the center of the room only to be abruptly spun around to face the mirror. Before I could question, he tossed his cane aside and then cinched my hips in his hands, trapping me in place.

"Tell me what you see."

"I see…myself," I admitted. Just Anya. So damn thin. Pale. Pathetic. I looked like the child he'd accused me of being before, with NEW YORK written across my chest in blocky, black letters—the old souvenir was the only shirt I owned that didn't, in some way, relate to dance.

"For now," Revend agreed.

A shiver racked my spine as his stubble grazed my throat with every word.

"But if you are serious about your training," he said, "then prove it to me."

"How?"

"Break the wall you've built up." He withdrew, leaving me in a puddle of overcast daylight. "First position."

I glanced over my shoulder and found him watching me. With one look, he measured me up, divided me into equal parts, and mixed them all together again.

"You could have told me that you owned the Roria ballet company," I blurted out before he had the chance to bark another command.

His expression hardened even more. "I wasn't under the impression that I was obligated to explain anything about myself or my business ventures to a child. First position."

With a sigh, I placed my heels together and turned both knees out on cue.

"Now, raise your arms."

He circled my position faster than he should have been able to. I had to physically bite a gasp back when he seized my waist from behind. One of his hands flattened against my hip, the fingers fanning out along my stomach.

"W-what are you doing?" My heart hammered against my rib cage.

Before real panic could set in, he withdrew after correcting my posture.

"Arabesque," he said.

Performing the technique distracted me from the heat lingering over my skin—at least until he cinched my right leg and wrenched it higher without warning.

"W-wait—" I bit my lip so hard that I tasted blood, but I didn't pull away.

Almost as if taunting me, he tightened his grip. "Does it bother you when I touch you?" he wondered, his breath hot on my neck.

"Yes." Keeping my balance took too much focus to waste any on lying.

"You create a wall." The words accompanied the touch on my shoulders that shoved them lower, into perfect alignment. "Between yourself and the world."

I didn't respond—not that I could when he caught my chin next, lifting it. I inhaled without meaning to, dragging his scent into my lungs. He smelled like peppermint, and not the soothing, grandmotherly scent that tended to permeate my grandparents' home. Revend was all pepper and mint, burning the inside of my nostrils and leaving me no choice but to breathe him in.

"You claim not to be able to feel when you dance…and therein lies your problem." He cradled my jaw in the palm of his hand, holding my gaze. "A dancer's emotion is the most important weapon in their arsenal," he told me. "Without it, there is no connection to the role, and you can only hope to be mediocre, at best." The hand withdrew, and he turned away. "First position."

Already panting, I faced forward.

"Your first lesson," Revend began behind me, "is to break down that wall."

"How?"

His answer came in the form of his fingers harshly cinching the back of my shirt in a fist, drawing the fabric taut. The outline of my ribs was visible, sculpting a nonexistent chest. Their jagged edges aimed toward my heart, illustrating the words he hissed next.

"You *feel*." He shoved me so that I staggered three steps forward. "Perform your variation—not Giselle. Dance the one from the theater."

"R-Remsky's piece?" I reluctantly outstretched my right leg when he didn't answer. My right arm followed a second later, fluttering into an arch meant to curve above my head.

"Straighter." His finger tapped my shoulder. "Keep your head up. Don't look down!"

The tap became an impatient strike. Pain flared for a second, but his frustrated grunt cut deeper.

"Forget the movement. What do you feel?"

Feel? My right arm lowered. When my therapist asked me that same question, I knew what to say. *I feel happy. I feel secure. Calm. Cherished. Needed. Wanted.* All of those magic words to keep me from being locked up and numbed with medication. With Revend doing the asking, the answer wasn't so certain.

"I...I don't know. It's just a routine—"

"Not true." His hand settled around my neck, the callused fingers clenching just tightly enough to make me fall silent. "Everything has a purpose. An emotion. Finding it is the duty of a dancer."

I swallowed hard as each word registered. Once again, he was shredding the carefully crafted script I lived by. *Emotions are dangerous*, my therapist would warn. Negative. *They make pills to keep them mellow and manageable. Would you like a prescription?*

Revend simply wanted an answer.

"How?" I asked.

"You find something. Here." His hand cupped my waist again, sliding around to my stomach. "You find it, and you use it...*here.*" His foot nudged mine, jarring me backward against his chest.

"H-how?" I hated myself for flinching. For breathing too fast. For not moving away.

This should have been no different than a session with Remsky or any other instructor. But Revend didn't toe the same boundary those other men had. He didn't coddle the cracked China doll like my parents or "teach" me lessons like everyone else.

Any attempt to put space between us was met with harsh retribution; he moved even closer, swallowing the gap between our bodies. With every frantic breath, his scent filled me further, creating a prison more restraining than the physical touch.

"Straighten your spine. Then continue." He stood back and watched while I attempted the first difficult variation in footwork.

Not even five seconds later, pain exploded through my calf, and I staggered, fighting to keep my balance.

"Too slow." He had his cane again. The tip of it flashed through the air, taunting me as I pranced across the marble. "Your face! Watch your face."

I spun…and he was there. *Thwack!* Another blow resonated through my hip.

"Forget the technique," Revend snarled when I hobbled away from him. "Move. Feel."

"What?" Apart from *irritated*, I didn't know what the hell he expected from me.

As if reading my mind, he grabbed my arm and wrenched me around to face the wall. "The stage is in here," he growled against the nape of my neck.

I felt his lips there… Wet and warm and dangerous, grazing a jutting vertebrae.

"You perform it here." His thumb raked my cheek. "Show me."

It was harder to ignore the negatives with him so close. They taunted me, a weakling shadow flung against the wall beneath the hulking shape his body cast.

"How?" I asked.

His lips moved again. "You *know* how."

"I wouldn't be asking if I did—" I tried to step away only to find myself yanked back.

"Do what you did that day in the theater when you thought no one was watching. What did you feel then?"

I shook my head. "I didn't feel anything—"

"And now?" His hand returned to my waist, sensing my flaws through fabric.

"I-I *feel* uncomfortable."

His grip shifted to fully encircle my thigh. A second later, two of his fingers vengefully dug into the muscle, taunting me.

"Are you afraid?" He made it sound like such a harmless question. *Is the sky blue?*

"No… Yes. I-I mean…"

"Good." He let me go so suddenly that I tripped over my own feet. "Maybe now you'll move like a living creature. *Use the emotion, Anya. Dance.*"

I couldn't keep my eyes from drifting over to the doorway. Maybe my therapist was right.

"Leave if you want," Revend dared me, following my gaze. "But know that the minute you walk through that door…you won't be coming back again, Anya DeSotto. And know that, if you choose to stay, you will endure whatever I have in store, and you will be grateful that I'm wasting my time on you."

"Why are you?" I tossed back. "Why even have me audition for the Roria if you are the director—"

"Perhaps…because I hoped that others might see something in you that I didn't," he admitted. "Now, you have to *prove* to me that you deserve the second chance my colleagues awarded you."

How pathetic was it that I wanted another answer? *Because I took pity on you,* maybe. It would have been easier to ignore charity.

"How?" I asked.

He gestured to the empty floor with a wave of his hand. "Prove to me that you are more than just a blank expression with pretty feet."

"I don't have to prove anything to you."

Yes, I do.

Ignoring him wouldn't make the truth any easier to swallow. He'd opted to forgo the customary dose of sugar, leaving me to swallow nothing but straight poison. *You're not good enough.*

"Make your choice."

My choice.

How long had it been since I'd truly been presented with one?

Seconds had stretched into minutes by the time I realized I didn't really *have* a choice after all. Facing forward, I swung my left arm up and rose onto relevé. My shadow mocked me as I performed each step—apparently not well enough.

"Show me emotion!" Revend blew past me.

I glanced over my shoulder just in time to catch sight of the door creaking on its hinges.

"You claimed you were afraid," he accused. "Show me through this." He jabbed a finger at his face, and the dark expression etched there before slamming the door shut. "Move!"

As I pirouetted in the opposite direction, Remsky's many past corrections chose that minute to cycle through my brain, driving me forward. *Be light! Be graceful! Like a bird, Anya! Like a bird!* I felt more like that damn creature he'd pushed us to emulate than ever—trapped in a gilded cage while the cat rattled the bars.

"Empty," Revend hissed.

I couldn't see his face as I spun, untouchable.

But the moment I came to a stop, he was already there. He snatched at my shoulder, snagging the sleeve of my shirt. Too hard. Cotton tore, and the sensation of cold air ghosted my collar. I could only stand there, grasping at my arm, as a single desperate thought ricocheted off the inside of my skull.

He didn't.

He didn't.

He wouldn't.

"What are you doing?" I clasped the front of my shirt, staggering back. It felt too loose. "What's wrong with you?"

"What am I doing?" he wondered, sounding completely unfazed. "From your expression, one would never be able to tell…" He raised his hand, swinging it in my direction, and nodded when I flinched. "Ah, now, I see it." When his hand did touch me, it shoved me toward the center of the room. "The hint of *some* life. You shouldn't have to pretend now. *Show* me your fear."

Show him? The room was spinning. My lungs heaved, but I couldn't breathe.

"You're crazy."

"Am I?" He sounded farther away, on the other end of the room now. "You are nothing more than a puppet. Meant only to display whatever the audience demands, whether it be an innocent princess, or a witch, or a swan. You are molded by their desires, and you reflect what they want you to be. However…"

The hiss of his cane scraping the marble trailed him as he advanced on my position again.

"It's not enough to have perfect motion. Good technique is not enough." His shadow flickered over the floor in front of me. Then he was beside me. Behind me. "Your duty is to make them *feel*. You create a fantasy so real that they have no choice but to believe it's real. Make me feel something."

Feel? I didn't know which emotion to focus on first. The fear that grew with every second his breath basted my throat? Or the shame that swamped me at the thought of running? Almost two years after graduating from the academy without a position at a company and I hadn't given up yet.

"Look at me."

I turned, meeting his gaze for only a second. His eyes were glacial, daring me to make my choice.

Suddenly breathless, I settled both feet against the hard floor. *Feel.* With nothing but the thrum of my own pulse to guide me, I rose on tiptoe and began the first part of the variation.

"Faster!" Revend snarled as I spun across the floor. "Keep your chin up!"

My chin up. Head up. Shoulders up. *Pirouette. Arabesque...* Mid-step, I froze, my leg still outstretched, my eyes transfixed by the sight of someone watching from the window.

"What are you doing?" Revend bellowed, sounding miles away. "Move!"

Couldn't he see her? The intruder was standing directly across from me with both arms raised as if to ward off an attack—though she didn't seem afraid. Hell, a statue could have portrayed more expression than her face did.

Nothing changed, even as I fell out of relevé and her shoulders slumped in response. Confused, I crept forward to brace both hands against the surface of the glass while she mimicked me step for step. No warmth emanated from her. Just ice. How the hell could someone be so cold?

"You need to forget about control," Revend hissed.

That's when the woman's expression began to show some hint of life. Her blue eyes widened, and she shifted a little closer to the window as if hoping to lift it open and slip inside. Or out...

"You need to lose it."

A hand appeared over the woman's shoulder, calling attention to the fact that one of her sleeves was torn—a weakness the offending hand seemed willing to exploit when it seized the material and twisted the rent cotton. The woman's lips flew apart without a sound, and only then did I realize she was afraid.

"Try again," Revend commanded against my ear. "This time…pretend that your expression is the only thing holding me at bay."

At bay from what? I couldn't make myself ask. *You don't want to know,* the woman in the window seemed to warn me. Real emotion transformed her face, stretching all the way down to the trembling corners of her mouth. It didn't make her any prettier. Or taller. Just more…alive.

"Begin."

The hand withdrew from her shoulder just as I felt thick fingers press against my lower back, nudging me toward the room's center. I turned away from the window and rose on tiptoe, struggling to remember the correct order of the remaining steps. A pirouette…and then what came next?

He must have memorized the routine, because he was always a step ahead, placing his hands on my shoulders to force them into alignment when I did a bit of footwork, wrenching my leg even higher during the arabesque.

Every twist. Every turn. Every step. He was always there. Pushing me harder. Faster. I twirled dizzily, vaguely aware of the room spinning out of control. Darkness descended, feeding those hungry shadows until I was draped beneath them and there was no one there to see me break.

It started slowly. My vision blurred. Those perfect lines every dancer strived to achieve wavered around the edges. My focus was consumed by the harsh fingers fanning out along my rib cage, claiming any part of me they could reach. Testing me. When he came too close to the sensitive flesh beneath my breast, my balance faltered.

I failed. "S-stop—"

"Not with words." The offending touch traveled up to my jaw, forcing my chin upright. "You're a puppet, remember? Show me what I want to see."

There was no hope of ignoring him. He was everywhere. Fingers digging into the flesh of my thigh. His hand yanking on the waistband of my jeans until they started to inch down my hips.

One inch.

Two.

I shoved his fingers away. "Stop! I-I can't focus—"

He was there to block me in before I could even think to run. "Good. Stop *thinking*." His breath hit me full in the face while his hands went to either side of my head as if to grind his words into my skull. "Just move. Feel me here and ignore everything else. Move!"

He matched me step for step while I danced on the tips of my toes. Faster. Better. Harder. More. I panted my way through the finale, bowing low with him at my back.

When I rose again, I faced the window. The voyeuristic woman had vanished, and someone new had taken her place—a waif with wild, dark hair straining at the confines of a once neat bun. She looked fragile. Like the wind whipping through the barren lawn might scatter her into pieces.

She looked…real.

Something wet glinted on her cheek, and she swiped at it with her finger. Almost in shock, she mouthed a single word to herself.

Tears.

"Better," Revend Marcus declared behind me, sounding almost satisfied for once. "And *now*…you can warm up."

CHAPTER 8

"No! Get up, Anya."

The shout came as I curled into a ball while a blunt object struck the floor near my head to emphasize each wasted second. *Thwack! Thwack! Thwack!*

"I won't tell you again."

I sucked in a breath; it wasn't an idle threat. Whereas Victor Remsky specialized in verbal torture, Revend Marcus was a cruel sadist. He showed no mercy, making me hold a movement until my muscles burned, pushing me to the brink when my own body quit following my commands.

Yet he still wanted *more.*

"Fine, then," he growled, turning on his heel. "Give up—"

"Wait," I managed to gasp out before he could take a single step. "Just…wait."

He stood there while I braced one quivering hand against the floor and tried to push myself upright. I didn't even move an inch before pitching onto my side.

"Hmph." Revend's disgust was a palpable blow to my ribs. Or was that his actual foot nudging me sideways? The command he barked out gave me a clue. "Roll over."

Like a boneless rag doll, I let him manipulate my body until I was on my back. Frowning, he stared down at me without a shred of sympathy.

"When's the last time you've seen a masseuse? You shouldn't be this stiff after only a few hours," he accused.

A few hours. I choked an ironic snort down, even though the root of his question wasn't all that funny. It was stupid to train the way I did without regular physio, but I could barely scrape together the fees for Remsky's lessons out of what my father gave me for each "semester."

"They're expensive," I finally admitted out loud.

His scoff revealed just what he thought about that excuse. "Lie back."

Suddenly, the air shifted, and I craned my neck and found Revend sinking down on one knee. With a grace I hadn't expected, he set his cane aside and caught my ankle in his free hand before I could react, pushing my thigh flush against my abdomen.

"I'll give you the number of a physiotherapist," he said while slowly extending my leg again, stretching my hamstrings out. "The cost will factor into the price of my lessons."

"Price?" I choked out.

"As you might recall," he reminded as his fingers dug into the base of my calf to massage the muscle, "I don't offer charity."

Of course not. I'd always intended to pay him—though, now, the prospect of shelling out money for...this was beginning to sink in.

If he was a sadist, then that made me an even bigger masochist—no better than those buttoned-up businessmen who paid prostitutes to spank them to get off. You *had* to like pain in order to survive just a simple conversation with him. Every word was a knife honed to sink deep and inflict critical damage.

"What do you pay Victor?" he demanded. "Whatever it is, cut it in half. This week will be on a trial basis. At least until I decide whether or not to continue."

Until *he* decided?

I honestly wasn't sure if I would even come back. My body ached with the consequences of my stupid decision to stay. I would never be able to perform Remsky's variation the same way again. Before I could make my mind up, Revend seized my heel.

"W-wait..." I couldn't bite a groan back. Nothing he'd done until now had made me feel as vulnerable. He might as well have held my *soul* in the palm of his hand.

"You're in shape, at least," he grunted, ignoring my discomfort as he wrenched my foot flat. "You have strength in your feet." He flexed my foot into an arch, pressing his thumb along the tops of my blistered toes. "But it is foolish to dance without regular physio unless you desire an injury."

He released me, and I didn't realize I'd been holding my breath until icy air slowly trickled back into my lungs—only to rush out again when he took the opposite ankle and repeated the motion. My nails scraped the marble at my sides, my teeth skewering my lower lip with every second that passed.

Once he'd finished stretching the foot, he held it captive, sliding his grip down to the heel again. "It bothers you even when I touch you in this way…" He made the observation sound harmless, but his expression revealed curiosity more than anything.

Don't dwell on the negatives. Taking my therapist's advice for once, I pretended to not hear him in favor of admiring the beautiful, if semi-faded, crown molding that edged the entire room—delicate roses sculpted into the wood.

"Isn't the answer obvious?" Revend continued after a moment of silence as his grip slowly inched up my leg. "You're an old man who I don't know," he said, parroting an American accent. "Keeping me captive in his home."

I glanced up, and his expression almost could have been called smug.

"Your face reveals more when you're too exhausted to filter your emotions."

Did it? I shivered as he set my foot on the floor and then reached for my hand to haul me upright.

"Were you ever injured?"

He didn't seem to realize he'd set a grenade off. The script was in flames, and my poor inner actress floundered, unsure of which line to spout off next.

"N-not recently," I said without looking up. My last debilitating fracture had put me out of commission for six months—which, back then, had seemed like the end of the world. Ironically, I *almost* wished I'd had an injury now, something to explain my lack of progress in nearly a year and a half. Something other than "the clinic" and "my therapist" and "my faults."

"Interesting."

I flinched before I even noticed the heavy hand that had fallen over my shoulder.

"Whatever it is, you'll need to overcome it. The next stage in the audition will feature the full *pas de deux*, unlike how we've practiced it."

"You mean partner work?" My voice sounded wooden. Oddly enough, the thought of dancing with someone other than him felt way more daunting than it should have.

"Yes. Partner work. Including the lifts." Revend stood, leaning heavily on his cane for support.

With his back to me, I couldn't see his face, but that made the impact of his words sting twice as much.

"No one wants a dancer in the *corps de ballet* who doesn't at least have the potential of accepting a principal role. You are to be a puppet, remember?" He turned and drilled his gaze into mine. "Every puppet needs to dance prettily on a string while controlled by a master—or at least maintain the illusion."

Control. Master. The word choice recalled his unorthodox teaching methods and made the bruises on my legs decide to throb at full force.

"That's a misogynistic approach."

"Misogynistic."

I couldn't tell from his tone whether or not he was irritated by my retort or just reinforcing it as fact.

The next second, his hand appeared before me. "Get up."

I let him yank me to my feet and winced in anticipation of the pain. Surprisingly, the impromptu massage seemed to have helped. I experimentally flexed my bare toes against the floor and *didn't* want to scream in pain.

"Be here tomorrow by one," Revend said as he headed for the foyer. Over his shoulder, he added, "We will rehearse the balcony scene again."

He opened the door without waiting to see my reaction. Only then did I realize how late it was. Sometime in the three-hour-hell of our lesson, Revend had managed to switch on the worn chandelier that was missing two light bulbs in the center of the room. Beyond the windows, the sky was a sheet of ebony. Rain hammered against the roof, and a sudden strike of lightning shook the structure to its core.

All that time, a storm raged around us.

"I'll pay for a new outfit."

It wasn't until he nodded to my chest that I remembered... With a lump in my throat, I reached up, fingering the loose sleeve of my shirt. Thankfully, the material was too tight to reveal anything more than a few inches of skin.

"Thank you," I croaked. As my therapist had suggested, I would try to look on the bright side. My current warm-up clothes consisted of the same ratty sweats and three leotards I'd worn for the past year. I couldn't afford to turn a replacement set down.

"You should practice in a skirt anyway," Revend scolded while I approached my bag. "Every rehearsal. Every moment should prepare you for the stage. Here."

He held something out to me—small, round, and wrapped in tissue paper. The moment the bundle settled against my palm, I knew what it was. A peek beneath the packaging confirmed my suspicion—a new pair of pointe shoes, white ones.

"Thanks." I shoved the bundle into my bag and then pulled my sneakers on. I slipped into my jacket next, yanking the zipper up to my throat.

Revend didn't say a word as I passed him and headed for the front door. Fresh bruises throbbed when I reached for the handle and pulled it open to face a sheet of rain lashing the front stoop.

Common sense told me to stay and wait the storm out. I didn't have the money for a cab, and the last thing I needed was to tramp across town in wet shoes.

However, pride won out. I left and silently closed the door.

CHAPTER 9

White shoes were beautiful, meant only to last for one performance—never for practice. They were so easy to taint. But their purity didn't matter to Revend. The moment I showed up at his house, he made me lace up, warm up, and dance. Despite what he'd said the night before, we didn't rehearse the full *pas de deux*, and I was too relieved to wonder why.

Instead, almost as if to make up for it, he led me through grueling exercise after grueling exercise in everything from the most basic of steps to the most complicated. There wasn't a muscle he didn't stretch. A bone he didn't test. A ligament he didn't push until the breaking point.

And I *broke* at the mercy of his cane.

A tap to my hip. A strike to my knee. Eventually, he allowed me, "Five minutes!" for a break, and I had to lean against the wall just to stay upright. When he returned, I was tasked to perform Remsky's variation.

"Faster, Anya!" Revend snarled, punctuating each word by harshly clapping his hands.

A second earlier, I'd been *'Too fast! Stop rushing! Too harsh!'* Now, he wanted, "Softer! You're light as a bird. Do. Not. Drag. Your. Feet!"

Thwack!

Spin.

Thwack!

Sweat dripped down my back, gluing my leotard to my body by the time Revend finally stalked off in disgust.

"Enough," he bellowed from the foyer. "Rest. While you're at it, contemplate the future of a dancer who performs with the grace of a stampeding buffalo."

I slumped to the floor, my back against the mirror, trying and failing to silence a groan as my feet pulsed. A few blisters had torn, I suspected, though I kept my gaze on the window ahead rather than look for myself. The sun was shining for once, but it seemed wasted over the dying flowerbeds that stretched to a wrought-iron gate at the other end of the property.

I didn't know how long I'd been sitting there before a water bottle appeared under my nose.

"Drink."

I flicked my gaze up and found stern features pulled into a scowl. I hadn't even heard Revend return. Perhaps because he wasn't using his cane? On the palm of his other hand balanced a plate adorned with slices of fruit.

"Eat," he snapped, placing it on the floor beside me. "Though you should incorporate more protein into your diet to preserve what very little muscle you have."

Too tired to argue, I snatched an apple slice up and nibbled while he crossed the room and faced me. Today, he was wearing a white shirt and slacks. Unbrushed hair, oddly enough, made him seem even more menacing than usual.

"Tomorrow you will be here at seven," he said. "And *yes*, I mean in the morning."

My stomach sank as I dropped my half-eaten apple slice back onto the plate. "I can't."

Unsurprisingly, his expression darkened, minimizing the golden sunlight filtering in behind him. "Can't?"

"I spend Sunday mornings with my mother. If I skip one of her luncheons, she'll inflict more misery upon me than a million *pas de deux* rehearsals."

It wasn't until I heard the words out loud that I realized they might have been misconstrued as a joke.

"Fine." Revend drew the single syllable out without picking my alibi apart, for once. "You will come after, and we will just have to double your workload."

I nodded while my feet throbbed as if to spite me. Could I even survive a double workload? Thankfully, Revend changed the subject before I could settle on the obvious answer.

"Have you taken any thought to arrange your transportation for Monday?"

I blinked. "M-Monday?"

He reached into his pocket and withdrew a folded slip of paper. "One would hope that your dedication would mirror your preparation," he admonished while stomping just close enough to shove the page in my direction.

I took it and warily unfolded it, revealing the details for the next stage in the Roria auditions—a week-long affair composed of four days of rehearsals and then one grouped audition.

Oh. I fought to keep my expression blank. The stakes were higher than any other audition up until now. *Now*, I had something to lose. Pressure to live up to. Not only that, but I had Revend to answer to if I dared to fail.

Still, before I could even focus on the rest, I had the simple logistics to worry about, considering that the town where the auditions would be held, Holly, was two hours away from Buckley by car.

"I…I'll call a cab." The lie was pointless. He knew I didn't even have enough money to scrape together for bus fare.

"Be here two hours before the listed time," Revend said.

"Thank you—"

"Don't thank me. *Prove* to me that I'm not wasting my money or my time."

At the mention of money, I glanced at the shoes on my feet. Despite the pain inflicted from the rehearsal, the slippers fit more intimately than the black ones. Together, both pairs must have cost him over a hundred dollars. Maybe more.

"I'm paying everything back," I blurted out.

We both knew it was a lie. Rather than respond, Revend waited until I'd half-heartedly nibbled at a few more pieces of fruit. Then he pulled away from the wall and headed out into the foyer.

"We're done for today." His voice drifted back to me as I stood and followed him, wincing with every step. "Be here tomorrow ready to rehearse—" He broke off suddenly. The next second, he lunged in my direction. "Get down!"

A violent sound reverberated off the walls the moment his hands struck my shoulders. Breathless, I stared up, dazed, at the ceiling. A layer of paint had started to peel in places, revealing the harsh wood underneath, much like the expression of the man scrambling to his feet above me. His dark eyes weren't narrowed for once, instead flashing an emotion I never would have thought could be found on his face. *Fear?*

"Stay down," Revend hissed, already limping in the direction of the front door.

I had no idea what made me pull myself upright and brace one hand against the wall. Stupidity? My head throbbed. A cold wind ruffled my hair as I blinked to make sense of the scene before me.

Everything sparkled…adorned by the countless shards of glass that littered the floor of the foyer. It must have belonged to the window that now sported jagged edges forming a circular gash. Beyond it, I could make out someone racing across the lawn to climb into a car parked against the curb. I caught a flash of dark hair but nothing solid enough to form a decent description. I struggled to read the license plate—anything—but then Revend's silhouette flickered from the corner of my eye, consuming my attention.

"Get back."

From over his shoulder, I could make out an object lying at his feet. A stone from the lawn? Wrapped around it was a square piece of paper with something written in the center, which I couldn't decipher. The image printed above the words was a little clearer. A black swan with its wings outstretched.

"I said get back!" Revend snapped when I took a step closer to read it. "Or at least make yourself useful!" He impatiently flexed his hand.

I raced to grab his cane. When I returned, he snatched it from me and used it to rise to his feet.

"Should… Should we call the police?" I barely heard myself speak above the deafening thrum of my heartbeat. *Don't panic.* I tried to be useful by scanning the floor for any visible evidence that could be mentioned in a police report. Only a clump of dirt seemed out of place, beside the glass, and the stone—but whatever had been strapped to it was gone.

"No," Revend said without bothering to glance in my direction. His hand lowered to his side, tucking something into his pocket. "But you need to leave. Now."

"My dad knows the police chief," I stammered.

Typical crime in Buckley amounted to pranks performed by teenagers on Halloween. Not this. If Revend had moved just a second faster…

"I can call him—"

"I told you to *leave*."

I bit my lip against a protest. "Fine." Squaring my shoulders, I turned to the rehearsal room.

Crunch! Pain shot up my left leg without warning. I hopped backward and managed to collapse on one of the steps of the staircase. Cradling my foot in both hands, I inspected the sole of my pointe shoe. Sure enough, a glittering piece of glass stuck out from the canvas amid a growing red stain.

"Don't touch it," Revend commanded before stalking past me.

"It's nothing," I bit out. But I didn't move as he hobbled down the hallway, past the stairs.

A few minutes later, he returned holding a length of gauze in one hand and a pair of tweezers in the other. "Show me," he grunted, snatching my foot up when I didn't move quickly enough.

"W-wait…" I sucked in air. Held it. Tried to remember how to breathe when he didn't let go.

His hands were too damn big. Too warm.

"Don't move," he warned while manipulating the tweezers in one hand as the other held my foot captive.

It took him two seconds to pry the glass loose. Blood welled from the cut left behind, but he smothered the mess with a wad of gauze before a single drop could hit the floor. Then he wrenched the pointe shoe off and assessed the bare heel underneath.

"It's not deep," he said finally, tracing the shallow wound with the tip of his finger. "But"—he hesitated—"you can rest it tomorrow if you feel the need to."

"No." I shook my head, gritting my teeth. The Roria auditions began in two days. Tomorrow was the last chance I had to practice. "I'll be fine."

Nonetheless, I winced when he applied a bit of pressure and then secured the gauze to my heel with a longer strip. He should have let me go after that—I didn't dare drag my foot away. But, for a minute that felt more like an eternity, he held it, his thumb firm against my heel, distracting me from the pain. From breathing. From everything.

It was funny how he could make me feel numb yet painfully aware at the same time. Almost like a high—but different. Harsher. Around him, I felt frozen enough to ignore the way my fingers shook as glass sparkled around us yet painfully in tune with his presence. Like how something hitched in my throat when his thumb drifted too close to my sensitive heel before he finally let me go.

"Get your stuff," he said. With the aid of his cane, he stood.

I slipped past him, limping to avoid putting pressure on the wound. After I threw my jacket on and gingerly slipped into my sneakers, I found Revend in the doorway, wearing his coat. A pair of car keys glinted in his free hand.

"Come on."

I froze, resting my weight on the sole of my uninjured foot. "You… You're taking me home?" A million more stones could have crashed through the window, and the shock still wouldn't have come close to what I felt right then.

Rather than respond, he jerked his head, indicating for me to follow as he marched back into the foyer and through the front door.

I was surprised to find that it wasn't quite as cold outside, despite a gray, overcast sky that spit droplets of rain onto my forehead. The garage was a few yards behind the house. It seemed just as neglected as the rest of the property, but inside, gleaming amongst a cloud of floating dust, was a black vehicle that I suspected was worth more than my father's flashy new sports car.

"Get in," Revend grunted as he climbed into the driver's seat.

I slipped around to the passenger's side. The tan leather interior squeaked beneath my weight as I closed the door after me.

Ten minutes later, he pulled up in front of my father's house without any need for direction. His intimate knowledge of my life was unnerving. Confusing.

Even Remsky had never driven me home, no matter how grueling the lesson. I didn't know how to react. What to say. I grappled to find *something*.

"Thank—"

"Tomorrow," Revend said over me. His gaze was on the gaudy McMansion at the end of the driveway, and his overall expression could politely be deemed unimpressed.

Unwilling to stall, I grabbed my bag and scrambled from the car. "Tomorrow."

I expected him to drive off the moment I headed up the driveway. But he didn't… Not until I'd finally turned the doorknob and slipped inside did his car pull away.

"*A*nd then do you know what she said? She said, 'The Kate Spades are on the left, but please do *not* touch my Louboutins!'"

Mom giggled at what was apparently a joke while I contemplated reaching across the table to sneak a sip of her "water." I'd caved earlier that morning the first time that week—and, already, my buzz was wearing off. My good-girl routine was wearing thin. Something had to give.

My sanity, or the charade? Every passing second held a Russian roulette of consequences, not that Mom noticed.

She had insisted on spending the morning shopping. Again. The therapist had suggested outings to the park or maybe a movie. Nice, quiet, intimate places where we could figure out how to reconnect the fractured puzzle pieces of our "valuable mother-daughter bond."

But my mother had never been good with words, and taking me to the mall meant she got to use that tiny square of plastic in lieu of conversation. With every sweater, skirt, and blouse, she could build my confidence up just as easily as she filled my wardrobe. *Cha-ching!* In my mother's language, that meant *I love you, Anya.*

As a result, the side of our table was barricaded by a mound of shopping bags—each one loaded with pretty, charming outfits I would never wear beyond the walls of this café.

"Anya?"

I glanced over and found Mom anxiously swirling a finger around the rim of her glass.

"Are you okay, darling?"

"Fine," I said. I had fished my Perfect Daughter script from the recesses of my mind. I still knew all of my lines—but my time with Revend had smeared the ink. I couldn't remember the actions meant to go along with the words. I cautiously tried a smile. "I had fun today."

"You did?" Surprisingly, she didn't seem very convinced. "You seem a little…" She searched for the right word, and when she couldn't find one, she settled for taking a sip of her vodka. "Antsy," she declared a moment later, smacking her lips. "You seem antsy, dear. Is something wrong?"

"Not at all."

Everything was wrong.

Our "lunch" was stretching nearly two hours past the usual time. I tried to play my part and primp and preen like a good, perfect daughter, but Revend was waiting. Knowing that made the seconds feel like eons. My good-girl charm was rotting away around my skeleton as I struggled to keep fucking smiling.

"Do you have somewhere else you need to be?" my mother wondered. "Maybe you and your father had something planned…"

"Of course not!"

Dad's idea of bonding was the one day a month when he wrote me a check to fund my education. It was tax-deductible as well as conducive to my emotional well-being, and we never even had to exchange a single word.

"I just… I need to go to the bathroom." I grabbed my bag and made a break for the back of the café before she could get a word in edgewise.

I barreled past an old woman powdering her face at the counter and then squeezed into a narrow stall. I pawed my searching fingers through my bag until I found my lipstick tube, and then I wrenched the cap off. I poured the rest of my magic powder in a single line on my palm and used a straw from my earlier milkshake to make it disappear. *Tada.* I was good old Anya again, ready to face my mother and her crippling small talk.

She was all smiles when I reappeared, my slip-ups forgotten.

"I'm ready for dessert," I said with a beaming grin.

"Oh, yes!" She tossed me a menu and cheerfully went back to regaling me with stories about the other housewives she associated with in the condominium. In her own words, they were all just threatened by her—what with her being barely thirty-eight and newly married to such a successful entrepreneur.

I knew the real reason why rumors flared wherever my mother went. She was charming, pretty, and utterly dependent on the validation of other people in order to believe it. Without constant reassurance that she *was* charming and beautiful, the vodka-flavored waters became candy-coated pills. Like mother, like daughter, I suppose.

The moment she laid a heel through the gates of some wealthy community, the soccer moms instinctively knew to lock their husbands up and ostracize the beautiful, buxom blonde. She'd tear their charming lives apart without really meaning to.

My mother wasn't the only destructive figure in my life at the moment. I fingered the menu while picturing Revend's reaction if I never showed up for the lesson. He would be furious. Dark eyes. Terse frown. His voice might even dip to that dangerously low octave. *Do not waste my time, Anya.* In a way, he was ironically similar to my mother—demanding the sole attention of whoever they graced with their magnanimous presence.

"Anya? Is everything all right?"

I flipped the menu over. "Yes. Why?"

"You're…frowning."

"Huh?" I caught sight of my reflection on the surface of a polished soup spoon.

She was right; the customary smile had slipped. Left in its place was an expression I had never truly studied on my own face before. The sad part was that I didn't even know how to describe it. Was I sad? Angry? All of the above?

"Is everything okay?"

"Fine…" I snatched the menu up again and scanned the options. "I was just thinking of what to order."

"Okay."

Her frown told me that she didn't believe the lie. But questions tended to lead to messy answers, and my mother had never cleaned anything in her life. Once again, her magic credit card was the answer, so she talked me into splitting a slice of "the most decadent" cake and I endured more mind-numbing stories until she finally announced that she had a hair appointment.

"Next Sunday, like always, sweetie!" Her voice ushered me from the café.

I couldn't even muster the strength to utter my customary line in return. I just waved.

CHAPTER 10

Not even an hour later, I stood on Revend's doorstep. My head was floating against an ebony sky as I struggled to make sense of the scene unfolding before me. The door was already open, but I didn't know why. Had I done it? I reached out for the doorknob, but before I could touch it, a man's voice drifted through the crack in the doorway.

"You need to protect yourself," he warned.

Wait... I knew that thick Russian accent, though my brain couldn't come up with a name fast enough.

"From what?" a second man replied. His voice was deep. Unsettling. Familiar, as well.

"You know *what*. If Camille—"

"Don't say her name."

"If *she*," the first man quickly amended, "followed you all the way to North America, you can be sure that she's planning one of her sick little games. You need to hire security, Revend. Protection. You should—"

"I know what I should do. I should let her play."

"You can't be serious! You have to stop this before—"

"I said let her play," Revend growled. "She's already driven us to another continent to recruit. The Roria's name is worthless in Europe. Whatever game she has in mind, she's already won. I have nothing left for her to take."

"Nothing…except your life."

A scoff reverberated off the walls of the hall. "Really, Victor—"

"Don't ignore this, Revend."

"It was only a broken window."

"It was only a broken window *this* time, but you and I both know what that woman is capable of, and you have the scars to prove it. Come with me. We can—"

"No."

"Revend—"

"*Enough.*" The familiar thwack of a cane striking the floor abruptly ended the conversation.

Seconds later, the door swung open further and I barely managed to scramble out of reach.

"Anya?"

I blinked, struggling to take in the graying-blond hair of the man lurking in the doorway. Remsky? He stood there awkwardly, still wearing his teaching attire.

"What are you doing here—"

"Goodnight, Victor," Revend spoke up from the foyer.

With a wary glance in my direction, Remsky hurried past me. "Take care," he called over his shoulder. "*Both* of you."

Maybe I should have mustered up something polite to say, but I could only watch him go while turning his words over in my mind. Who was Camille? What did Revend need protection from? Though, on second thought, that part was obvious. A stone hadn't thrown *itself* through the foyer window.

Just then, the door opened even wider, shedding the orange light from inside at my feet. Revend's fingers clutched the edge of it; his knuckles stark white—he held it that tightly.

"It's you," he rasped.

Uh-oh. Five seconds and I'd already managed to piss him off. His tone alone made me feel like a child caught eavesdropping on the adult's conversation. I'd heard something I shouldn't have.

"Get in."

I obeyed and took my time scanning the entryway to distract myself from the ominous feeling building in my stomach. He had been busy. The glass had been swept from the floor, and a piece of plywood had been nailed over the broken window. Only a streak of mud near the staircase remained—but suffocating tension still laced the air. Or maybe it was just the hostility in Revend's glare that had me so uneasy.

"You're late," he huffed before slamming the door shut.

I wasn't the only one who'd had a previous engagement. Tonight, he was wearing a gray shirt and a pair of dark pants that matched the dangerous hue coloring his eyes.

"Are you going to waste my time all night?" he demanded before marching into the rehearsal room.

"I'm not late," I blurted out. I was still five minutes early—in my robot brain, that counted for something. Time was money, after all, charged for by the hour at some therapist's discretion.

"You didn't come ready to dance," Revend pointed out. "Therefore, you are late." His eyes skimmed over my outfit in disgust.

Oops. The "trendy" sweater was tighter than any leotard, and the neat skirt lacked any leggings underneath to hide my exposed legs. Tugging on the hem didn't salvage my appearance any.

Revend tore his gaze away with a scoff. "Unless you had something else in mind."

I flinched. Even coming from him, that was harsh.

"Is this a bad time—"

"You have five seconds to change," he said over me.

I swallowed my questions and hurried into the bathroom to dress in a gray leotard. When I finally joined Revend, he didn't seem any calmer. His shoulders were tense, his jaw clenched, his eyes distant yet sharp. They were the same subtle changes I saw in my father when his nightly "sip" of beer turned into ten cans and a shot of whiskey from the mahogany liquor cabinet.

"See anything interesting?" he demanded once he caught me staring.

"Um, is this a bad time?" I was only stating the obvious. That conversation at his door had given me a clue. Something about a woman. A *dangerous* woman…

"Eavesdropping now, Anya?" Revend wondered, derailing my train of thought.

All comparisons to a maudlin drunk evaporated. His expression wasn't guilt-ridden and tormented like my father's. Just ice cold.

"No, I—"

"*What did you hear?*"

"N-nothing," I stammered, thrown off by the vitriol. "Just Remsky saying goodbye."

"Is that so?" His eyes honed in on mine, searching, probing.

Nearly a minute passed before I found the strength to look away.

It was *definitely* a bad time.

"I…I'll just practice at home tonight."

"No," Revend growled before I'd even made it halfway to the door. "You will *stay* or forfeit what little hope you have to train with me. Now, begin. Grand plié!"

Obediently, I bent my knees and sank low while keeping my back straight.

"Again." The butt of his cane tapped the marble inches from my feet.

For the next hour, the shout played like a broken record. I'd *plié* and *jeté* and *arabesque* before him, and each time, he'd demand a little more brusquely, "Again!"

His eyes weren't even trained on my feet or observing the posture of my legs. They roamed my face and scanned my body instead, searching. Hunting. What for, I wasn't sure.

"Again," he snarled as I pirouetted past. "Terrible! *Again*! Focus, Anya!"

Panting and dripping sweat, I balanced on the toes of one foot and extended the opposite leg only to earn a hiss of disgust issued near my ear.

"Pathetic! Do it again."

I lifted the leg higher, but he was there to swat it down.

"Terrible! That's enough. I changed my mind." He turned away. "We're done for the night."

"D-done?" I scrambled back into position. "Let me try again—"

"Again?" Brushing past me, Revend jabbed his thumb at the mirror, pinning my reflection beneath it like a bug he could squash. "Look at yourself! You. Are. Pathetic."

At this point, such an observation was like pointing out that the sky was blue. The woman staring back certainly looked pathetic. Her lips moved, though I didn't even recognize the breathless voice that came out of them.

"I'm *trying*—"

"You're trying!" Revend's fist impatiently struck the glass, rattling the frame. "That, Anya, is the problem. You shouldn't have to *try* to be graceful. You shouldn't have to *try* to be innocent! Watch me." One of his arms came around my waist, pressing into my stomach, forcing me against him. "Move *with* me."

He extended his right leg, creating a long, lean line with that half of his body.

"Stiff!" he hissed against my throat when I failed to master the same motion. "Bend." His supporting arm curved against my lower back, but I wasn't prepared when he wrenched my spine, deepening the curve and testing my limits. "Stiff."

He abruptly let me go, and I landed on my ass.

"Ow! What the hell?"

Ignoring me, Revend stalked to the other side of the room and glared out of one of the windows. "We're done here," he hissed. "Now, get out."

Like a kicked puppy, I could only stare at him, rubbing my side. Remsky could gently give up on me. My parents, with pity lunch dates and monetary bribes. None of their indifference had ever felt like this. Hurt like this.

"But it's only been an hour—"

"Long enough to determine that you are *hopeless*," Revend countered without even turning around. "You think I don't recognize the look in your eye? You're bloody high."

"I'm not," I countered, swiping at my nose.

He didn't even bother to argue.

"The audition is tomorrow." I hated the desperation that had crept into my voice. "We didn't even practice the *pas de deux*—"

"The *pas de deux*?" The windowpanes trembled as he pushed away from the wall and turned. In a heartbeat, he crossed over to me, seized my forearm, and wrenched me to my feet. "You can't even keep your balance," he snarled when I swayed and wobbled on my support foot. "This is just a silly little game to you now. A way to pass the time."

He stormed off while I just stood there, taunted by my own reflection. Robot Anya had lost her pretty smile again. Her eyes were narrowed, almost as mocking as his were. *Ready to give up?*

"I can try again," I said, though I wasn't sure if I spoke more to him or myself. "If you just *tell* me what you want from me—"

"What I want?"

Something heavy struck the floor behind me and clattered across it. I'd barely processed what it was—his cane—before Revend shoved me into the mirror. I went flying, forced to throw my hands out in front of me to soften the impact. My chin smacked off the glass. Hot. Sharp. Pain. My jaw was on fire, but I didn't even have time to process the sting.

"What I *want* is for you to realize the truth you seem too stubborn to grasp," Revend growled into my ear as he advanced.

My lungs seized. There was something terrifying about his face this close up. Not the anger, though. Just his disappointment.

"You're a child trying to convince yourself that you could ever be anything more," he said, his jaw clenching. "Give up, then, if you aren't willing to try. You are hopeless."

Repeat your mantra, Anya, my therapist would encourage in a moment like this. *You are good enough. Say it with me...*

But, when Revend finally withdrew, I couldn't move. The woman staring back at me in the mirror was a mess. She seemed to feel nothing, like the good doll everyone *but* he wanted her to be.

"If I'm so terrible, then why train me?" she asked—the million-dollar question, it seemed.

"Why did I take *pity* on you, you mean? You were the worst."

The stranger in the mirror frowned. "How?"

"You've just proven how."

"My technique is *good*." I sounded like a child trying to argue the validity of Santa Claus. "You said so yourself—"

"I lied. And your two left feet should attest to that fact."

I hated how quickly he could counter me. He didn't have to think. Hell, he almost made me miss that artfully applied dash of sugar.

"Then why did you take me on?"

"Why?" He shrugged, which I caught in the mirror's reflection. "Because Victor *begged* me to."

Remsky. Was I really surprised? "Victor" had even said it himself; he had pawned me off on Revend, like two bullies on a playground trading a broken, little doll. The same way my parents traded me back and forth, a little more desperately each time. *You fix it.*

"Why?"

"It doesn't matter."

"Yes, it does." *Uh-oh.* I was malfunctioning again. Unchecked, my robotic hand struck the mirror glass when he didn't answer quickly enough. "*Why?*"

Two seconds crawled past before I realized he was hesitating —and, unlike Remsky, when Revend hesitated, the whole world stopped spinning. Nothing dared move again until he exhaled.

"Victor thought…that I might be able to salvage what little talent you do have," he admitted, frowning. "But he was wrong."

Wrong. My eyes slid shut. When I opened them again, the unfamiliar expression from earlier was back, cracking my perfect mask. In two seconds, Revend had stripped my shiny, glossy veneer away and revealed the irreparable damage underneath. This robot was defective, destined to be smashed down for scrap. At least she didn't have to wear her fake smile anymore.

"I'm terrible," I said, delivering my own dose of honest poison without any pity or disdain or guilt. Just the bitter truth. "All this time…everyone just didn't want to say it."

"You have potential. Unfortunately, you are *passionless*," Revend corrected, stressing the word. "How can you expect to improve when you put nothing into your performance?" He approached me again, crossing his arms over his chest. "You need to use this anger. This pain. Prove to me that you can feel it."

Feel. But my therapist claimed that that was a bad thing. Feelings needed to be scribbled down, locked into the fiber of notebook paper, and shoved into a desk drawer.

"How?"

"Stop thinking."

I shivered as he hooked a thumb beneath the strap of my leotard, fingering the gray elastic.

"Stop worrying about how you look or seem to anyone else. Just *feel*."

Soft fabric kissed my skin as he dragged the strap down my shoulder. Lower. Too low… The underside of my breast had popped out of the material by the time I realized I should have pushed him off.

I didn't.

I couldn't.

While I was frozen in place, he took hold of the other strap and wrenched *both* down my shoulders, allowing a cold burst of air to replace the skin-tight fabric. At that moment, it felt like being on stage, in front of a million people who never looked up from their paper programs. Modesty wasn't even worth feeling. Before I knew it, I was left standing there with my arms crossed protectively over my chest.

And not even a fake smile could make it all better.

"You will dance the same *pas de deux*," Revend explained as he manipulated my body where he wanted it. There was nothing sexual in his touch—a tap on my calf to make me shift to the right, a nudge on my shoulders to urge them to straighten. "You already know the steps in here."

I flinched as he cupped the palm of his hand over my forehead, simultaneously forcing my chin upright.

"Now, you only need to bring them to life."

Life? My nails dug into my shoulders as he reclaimed my waist with both hands, grazing the bare flesh.

"Move."

I stumbled into place, watching our reflection. He towered over me, his chest hard against my back. I could feel every variation of the palm flat against my spine. The calluses at the base...

Everything.

It was impossible to breathe without testing his grip and forcing the nails just a fraction of an inch deeper into my skin, his words just a tad deeper into my skull, his presence into my soul...

"Don't tense." The warning came as he guided a fluid turn. "Extend your arms."

A million different reasons to resist ran through my mind, but with my eyes closed, it was so much easier to pretend, as he insisted, that this was all an illusion—he wasn't real. I opened them slowly only to have that fragile lie shatter the moment his gaze bored into my own, its intensity barely tempered by the mirror glass.

"Focus!"

I lurched onto tiptoe, stretching my arms out behind me.

"Keep moving! *Fluidity*, don't force it."

I pushed off with my toes at the same time he lifted, guiding me into an arabesque. My arm rose a second too late, but for once, he didn't call me out on the hesitation. He didn't say much of anything other than, "Keep your back straight. Elongate your neck!"

By then, I was already flush against him, at the mercy of every vibration rumbling through his chest. Physiology betrayed me; my nipples hardened, teasing the cotton of his shirt.

"No." Revend's hand was like an anchor on my shoulder, pinning me in place before I even realized I was starting to pull away. "Ignore it," he demanded, stepping even closer.

"Wait…" My hands flew up to his chest. I was desperate to preserve what little space there was left between us. One inch…a half an inch…a centimeter. Nothing.

"The *movement*," Revend insisted. "Focus on the movement. Ignore everything else."

Like the voices in my head, maybe? *You don't know him. You can't do this. You're hopeless.*

Revend was louder than them all, growling into my ear. "I said keep moving. Use what you are feeling to anchor your movements. Don't hesitate."

He was unforgiving stone against me—forcing me to work twice as hard to close the required distance. I couldn't keep up with the pace he'd set, and the whole time, the face staring back at me in the reflection showed nothing but the same empty expression.

"Enough." Halfway through, he wrenched me around to face the mirror again.

I tried to shield my exposed breasts, but he swatted them down.

"No." As if to punish me, he pinned my arms at my sides while his gaze raked me over from head to toe.

There was no escaping it. I was half-naked in his grip. Sallow, pale, gawky little Anya.

"Don't resist the insecurity," Revend snapped while my teeth began to shred my lower lip. His eyes settled on my heaving chest, and I hated myself for almost wishing that he would look at me like he wanted something more than…*more.* Even this still wasn't enough. "Embrace this," he told me, his breath basting that tender spot between my shoulder blades. "Feel it, and turn it into something else."

"In… Into what?"

He scoffed as if the answer were obvious. "Passion."

He wanted passion. I couldn't get past the shock of his hands on my skin, branding his name into the muscle underneath.

"Ignore your body's responses to me," Revend insisted as if it were really that simple. "You're supposed to be in love. Feel it." His hands slid beneath my arms, ghosting my torso. "Don't resist," he said. "Use the reaction to fuel the emotion you need to convey. Show me."

His past corrections raced through my thoughts. *You're in love! Show me! Feel!* But my body was numb. Dance? I couldn't even breathe. This robot dancer's control panel was fried, her metal limbs forever frozen in place.

"Again," he growled when I faltered. "Focus. Watch your expression."

I took a step, and he seized my chin, forcing me to face him directly.

"Give me *something,* or we're done," he warned, black irises boring deep into mine. "There are no more second chances."

Give him something. My gaze was hollowed out when he let me go to face the mirror again. *Feel,* I thought, trying to contort my face into showing…something.

Anything.

When I raised my arms, Revend raked his fingers down the flat of my stomach as if to remind me of my assignment. *Feel.* We started the variation over again—way too close to display any true technique. I just mimed the motions like a Juliet doll glued to an unyielding base, and he was the shadow determined to swallow me whole.

You're in love...

With every pirouette, Revend was there. He caught me and roughly let me go. Pushed me harder, faster... and then there came this terrifying point when I could only feed off his heat, too exhausted to feel modesty anymore. One brush of his fingers became the jab from a white-hot poker. My skin was paper. He was all fire, setting the air between us ablaze as he advanced regardless of which step I hastened to conquer.

Can you feel me, Anya? He was everywhere—even in my head, goading me onward when I lost track of the count.

Move, move, move.

Feel, feel, feel.

Give. Me. More.

Desperate to deliver, I arched, pranced, and spun until the steps finally dwindled to nothing. The stage I had been performing on my entire life became a black hole, devouring me without a trace. There was no count anymore or a pretty list of techniques to master. There was just endless silence and the solid, searing heat smoldering in the center of it all, melting my robot parts down to nothing more than scrap metal.

Give me something!

I had nothing left. Somewhere in the process, the woman in the mirror became a stranger, her dark eyes far away as she danced fluidly in the arms of a hulking figure.

Wait. I didn't move like that.

I *couldn't* move like that...

I sought out Revend's gaze as he circled my position, searching for reassurance, though I wasn't sure what I needed or even hoped for.

A growled correction?

A bellowed insult?

A shove into the mirror's glass?

I wanted something. I received nothing—for once, Revend was stingy with his reactions. He merely watched. He waited. Like Romeo and his poison, Revend possessed his own destructive weapon of choice—*feeling.* There was no course of action left but to flatten myself against him, mimicking his ideal Juliet—a ruined puppet in the hands of a monster who liked to break his toys.

How did such a creature show love? I relaxed my hands to start with, testing the give of the muscle underneath. A steady heartbeat caught me off guard. He wasn't like Jake.

But my time with him was the only script I had to pull from.

What reactions would he want from me? A simpering look? A gasp? Or maybe for me to shift closer and press my breasts up against him? Maybe he wanted me to flex my hip against his thigh and grind my need into his skin? Sane, normal people seemed to be so *needy* for affection. To touch. Be touched. Felt. Claimed. Devoured.

Jake liked it when I pressed my lips into his throat. Revend didn't.

"That's enough." He shoved me away one beat too early, and I was left to find my balance. "We're done."

"N-no! Wait…" *Pull away,* a part of me warned as my hands scrambled for purchase over his forearms. "I-I can do this, please—"

"I said we're done." His pulse thrummed beneath my palms as if in a warning. *Get back. Back. Back.*

I couldn't understand why. Then I took a step closer and —*bingo!* Something nudged my hip, firm and unmistakable. Just like prom night all those months ago, when slow-dancing with Jake had left him more breathless than usual. So eager to head upstairs to the stupid suite he'd rented.

"Come on, baby. Let me show you how much you mean to me…"

He had considered *that* romantic—lying back on a used and abused mattress while he pawed me out of some ridiculously expensive gown my mother had bought. The whole time, I had stared up at the ceiling, willing myself to feel something.

Do anything.

Ironically, when he'd finally groaned that he loved me into my neck and fallen asleep partially on top of me, I just remembered thinking, *What a nice room.*

In stark contrast, Revend didn't act as if sex were the only thing in the world that mattered. He glared instead. He tried to pull away—because neither of us could ignore the elephant in the room.

Describe it, my therapist would encourage. *List out exactly what triggered this reaction.*

Well, for starters, he was aroused. Now. With *me*.

"We're done for tonight," Revend insisted, still trying to disentangle his limbs from mine. "Now, go—"

I dug my nails into his shirt and nearly tugged it down his shoulder to keep him from moving. "D-dancing is like fucking." I expected him to look guilty to have had those words thrown back in his face. Embarrassed?

If anything, he looked even colder. "Stop it—"

"Do you make all of your protégés dance around fucking naked?"

Of course, he did. Why else would he attempt to "mentor" someone like me? My fingers scrambled to cover what little of me they could, but it wasn't enough.

"God, I'm so stupid—"

"Don't flatter yourself." Revend jerked out of reach. "Dance is physical," he insisted. His grip on my arm held me back. "I cannot help my body's *physical* reaction any more than you can help your sloppy foot placement."

That blunt honesty caught me off guard, and I found myself shuffling the feet in question. "So, you would react this way to any dancer?"

His jaw clenched, effectively wiping all trace of emotion from his face. "Of course."

But I was the only one pressed against him *now*. With my body aching after his brutal rehearsal, it was a stupid, selfish victory. He could push me to the brink, but *I* had made him lose control. Even for a second.

"I said we're done for tonight." His grip on my arm slacked, but he didn't make the first move, even as his body continued to betray him.

Apparently, I had missed a lot more than just a bulge in his jeans. I finally glanced down and caught the way his chest rose and fell with every breath. Too fast. Labored. As if flicking through a slideshow, I recalled every past moment. Every glance. Every bellowed "again." Was I overreacting? Or did they all add up to one insane conclusion?

"Was watching me dance naked your real payment?" I asked, the words hitching in my throat. "Did you get your jollies and, now, you regret taking me on—"

"I said stop it, Anya." He turned his back to me, shrugging his shoulder as if repelling a fly. "Don't be so childish."

"Then tell me the truth." For once, my voice was almost as harsh as his was—enough to stop him in his tracks. Though maybe I should have let him go.

Everything he'd promised was splintering around me like glass, and it hurt to realize just how much faith I'd had in that fragile web of hope he'd woven. *Feel, Anya. Dance, Anya. It's possible to be more than just a robot.*

Liar, liar. He'd put my fibs to shame.

"You said it yourself—I'm *terrible*. So then why are you wasting your time, unless it's because all you want is—"

"The truth?" In two steps, he was in front of me, seizing my chin in one hand so that he could throw his next words directly in my face. "The *truth* is that you're so dead inside you couldn't portray a real emotion without me beating it out of you. The art to any dancer's performance isn't looking pretty, Anya. It's feeling. *Moving.* Conveying emotion. And you would be minced meat before I could even get you halfway there."

I winced as his fingers briefly clenched, setting every nerve on fire before he let go. In a way, I knew he was right.

"And let's not be ridiculous," he spat as if to hammer the point home. "Before you even consider the fact that I might be attracted to you, realize that I would rather fuck the wall. At least then I might have a chance of it responding to me."

"F-fuck you." My cheeks flamed, but it didn't negate the impact of those two words coming out of my mouth. Perfect little Anya didn't curse out loud. She didn't inhale brokenly, fighting to keep control because a stranger had the nerve to point out what everyone else in the world already knew.

You're not good enough.

Revend didn't even seem shocked by the response, either. He shrugged, his expression merciless, those eyes jet black. "If only you could," he tossed back. "But that might require portraying some *emotion* on your part—"

"Then try me." The words flew out of my mouth before I realized just what I was asking. "If you're such the expert, then stop yelling and show me what you fucking want me to—"

"Fine." He surged forward to close the space between us.

Before I could recoil, one of his hands caught my waist.

"Dance," he snarled, sounding miles away.

He made it seem so simple while every cell in my body grappled with how to react. *Panic. Don't panic. Keep breathing.* In the end, I just exhaled and shifted closer, taking stock of him all at once—thick limbs, steel frame, and a pulse that hammered like a battering ram.

"From the beginning," he bit out.

I didn't even know where to start.

Gone were the pretty movements and lovely variations done on pointe. All that remained was the harsh slide of skin over skin. Heat.

"You need to feel," Revend urged, ghosting his fingers along my side. "Quit thinking about the movements. Just let your body react. Give me *something...*"

Something. One of my hands traced the side of his neck, slowly, slowly… Almost on its own, it settled against his shoulder blade. The other drifted down to where he clutched my waist, my fingers hesitantly settling over his. Allowing my eyes to shut, I used the motion of his body to decipher what came next rather than any count. Just sinew and bone intertwined with my own.

Left.

Right.

Turn.

Halfway through, my eyes flew open, and I saw our reflection for the first time. Though that couldn't possibly be us…

That woman with the messy, black bun and heavy-lidded eyes wasn't the cold, lifeless Anya DeSotto I knew. The broad-shouldered man hunched over her from behind wasn't Revend Marcus. Only the color of their skin gave them any distinction—they were entwined that closely together. Their slow, grinding motion wasn't ballet. It was…

Intimate. Too intimate.

My face heated, matching the blush that crept into the woman on the mirror's cheeks. That wasn't us. Me. It couldn't be. As if sensing the doubt, Revend chased my gaze over the mirror's surface and held it. *Oh, yes it is.*

Without warning, he spun me around, his hands traveling up to my shoulders in a hesitant stroke. I let him touch me.

I let him feel, desperate to copy whatever sensation his fingers sought. In a heartbeat, we were chest to chest, smothering every ounce of air between us.

His forehead glistened beneath a sheen of sweat. Strands of loose hair stuck to my skin as my messy bun came undone while I sought his eyes out. The moment our gazes met, I knew better than to remain so close. I knew…but I couldn't move.

"*Now*, you seem to realize that this isn't a game," Revend started. "This isn't…"

He shifted, and whatever jutted into my belly finished that thought for him—*him*, still pulsing between us. My mother used to utter this terrible cliché with a giggle whenever she hugged her guests at parties and thought their wives weren't listening. *Is that a gun in your pocket, or are you just happy to see me, Mr. Johnson?*

But Revend didn't simper once caught red-handed like the poor men subjected to my mother's flirting. He glowered. He commanded.

"Keep dancing."

There wasn't much left *to* dance, though I moved robotically anyway, allowing him to set the pace. We were nearing the end of the routine. Without the lifts, all that remained was the final embrace. The infamous kiss.

Before I could reconcile that, Revend spun me so hard that it was a scramble to stay upright. I braced one hand against his chest. At the same time, he lowered his head, his lips grazing my temple, my forehead. Impatient. Demanding.

"And this is where you fail," he rasped against my earlobe, but I knew what he really meant. *Checkmate.* "Pretending is the duty of a performer. Without that passion, you will never succeed." Once again, he pushed me back. "We're done for tonight—"

He hadn't even finished talking before we were nose to nose. For the first time in my life, I didn't think. I just *felt* the unyielding marble beneath my feet. Felt the pounding surge of my blood as I rose on tiptoe, grasping his shoulders for leverage.

Felt his mouth against mine.

It should have been a peck. My answer to his dare.

But my mouth slipped, melding with his.

Lips parted.

Tongue escaped.

I honestly never meant to kiss him.

He tasted like cigar smoke and bitterness. And maybe… sweet, too. Musk mingled with a faint hint of fruit. *Wine?* His lips flexed against mine before I could home in on the exact makeup, and then he flooded my taste buds like poison. Deep down, I knew it wasn't right. The wet heat of his lips parting purely out of reflex. His teeth threatening to serrate my tongue. I should have been running. Instead, my toes were curling in their shoes, my fingers fisting further in his shirt as I struggled to get closer. Closer...

Feel.

But he was way too much to decipher all at once. Every surge of his mouth against mine overwhelmed my robotic body. Coarse stubble grazed my chin—a sensation so different from kissing Jake. Bad? Good? I couldn't tell.

Kissing Revend was like downing an entire bottle of oxy all over again. Every. Last. Pill. The high was so damn intense that I lost myself, and it felt good to fall again, if only for a second.

Maybe desperation was why my hand slid down between us. Why I touched him at all. But, when my fingers met steel pulsing through denim, I couldn't seem to pull away. My poor internal actress had lost herself among the many masks she wore to play pretend. All that was left was improvisation.

"What the hell are you doing?" Ripping his mouth from mine, Revend snatched my wrist.

Pain shot through my arm as bones compacted beneath his grip. I thought he might have broken them if my fingers hadn't instinctively clenched.

All at once, he filled my palm, terrifying me. Sparking curiosity. A part of me knew how to touch him, sliding my thumb around the rigid shape.

What was I doing? My own brazenness terrified the hell out of me. *Almost* as much as the way his expression changed. His dark gaze fluttered up to the ceiling, glaring at the crumbling tiles. But he didn't look angry. His jaw went slack around a harsh exhale, even as he continued to shove me off.

"*Stop*," he said. "Fuck…"

A rush of emotion I struggled to decipher flooded my veins. Fear? Confusion? And something else…

Something that made me feel like I was the puppet master for five seconds. Which was wrong. Bad. For once, the unshakeable Revend swayed on his feet—because of me.

Maybe that was why I didn't pull my hand away.

Why he was looking at me for the first time like I wasn't just a mistake to erase. Like I mattered. Like I meant something.

Even though I didn't want him. Want this…

I didn't.

Though I didn't remember tugging on the latch of his pants, either—but *my* hands were sliding beneath the denim a second later, touching him in a way I'd never felt the urge to explore Jake. His pulse surged through taut flesh. Hot, visceral, and violent. It felt like I held his beating heart in the palm of my hand. All of him…and I didn't know whether to crush him or just keep feeling.

"Anya!" Nails dug into my shoulders. "Stop!"

I didn't. I couldn't. My fingers coiled as if disconnected from my body. From common sense. Touching. Stroking. Needing more. Wanting…

"Anya!" He shoved me.

I staggered backward. My head struck glass. Ricocheted off it. Stars flared and died behind my eyelids, and then I was floating, suspended only by trembling feet.

He was there, right when I would have lost my balance, to pin me flat against the mirror with the weight of his body. Face-to-face with him, I waited for the barrage of insults that I knew was coming. Slut! Idiot! Fool! Instead, I only felt the impatient brush of fingertips assault the bare skin beneath my collarbone. My breasts. Lower…

I gulped for air, paralyzed by the sensations that shot through me one right after the other. *Rough. Raw. Heat.* My therapist would push me to describe them. *How does this make you feel, Anya?*

The answer seemed inescapable as his fingers clenched. What did I feel? Not bad things…

"W-wait," I heard myself gasp when those creeping fingers stilled. His heat electrified my mechanical parts—without it, I couldn't breathe. "I-I don't… I want—"

"No." A callused thumb returned to my shoulder, drifting down. "You don't."

But I didn't pull away. Neither did he. I didn't resist when he came closer, either, seizing the back of my skull with one hand, fisting his fingers through my hair. Our lips met, his forehead connecting with mine—openmouthed, messy.

Only then did I realize that his free hand had lowered between us—so damn slowly that it was almost as if he didn't even know he was doing it. A nail grazed my hip. Lower. Two fingers hesitated against my upper thigh, coaxing my legs into parting. Every cell prickled with the creeping sensation of his touch. Higher. *Higher.*

The first bit of contact was just that—he touched, sliding a thumb along that taboo part of me. The second was harder, probing, forcing me to admit that this was real. Before I could adjust, he pushed a finger inside me, crushing me simultaneously with his weight. The sharp pinch was unexpected—even his fingers were too big. I yelped, smothering the sound against the cotton of his shirt, but for some reason, I couldn't understand; I didn't pull away. Didn't resist. Didn't scream.

I moaned.

Feel, Anya.

He was everywhere, invading me in a way Jake never had. The scent of his sweat filled my nostrils. His words were in my head, tearing me down—then building me up again. Each breath he took reverberated off the mirror, searing my skin, harsh and unsteady as his hand withdrew.

As if from miles away, I heard the snap of a clasp being undone. The delicate crunch of fabric. Felt the unmistakable slick of bare, hot skin along my inner thigh.

The shadow in the mirror showed me what he was doing. This dark piece of my soul didn't even care—was ravenous for the destruction.

Two breaths were my only chance to regain any shred of sanity. Two measly, pathetic gulps of air before my legs were wrenched apart and a heavier body was between them. My hands gripped his shoulders, my chest heaving, each breath exhausting. Then he was sliding into me with a grunt.

Deep.

Hard.

Rough.

With Jake, there had been some pain. With Revend, there were a million different agonies. My body was tearing. My brain was splitting. My head—everything forced to reconcile him *everywhere*, all at once.

It didn't hurt. I just *felt*…

Everywhere.

One thrust and I was shaking. When he withdrew, I didn't think I could take all of him again. He was too deep, too big, too much—but still, some part of me craved more, more, *more*. It was sick. I was infected by him. Revend was in my conscience, demolishing every little barrier I'd ever erected and smashing whatever secrets had been carefully locked beyond them.

I couldn't shut him out. Maybe a part of me didn't really want to.

He used his height advantage to his benefit, flexing his legs at the knees to fuel each powerful surge, driving me higher on the tips of my toes. Inch by inch, until I had to curl one leg around his waist while my other foot dangled a hairsbreadth from the floor. Harder. Faster. *Deeper.* I was gulping for air. Clutching his shoulders, my fingers scrambling for purchase against the muscle coiled beneath his shirt. His breath basted my shoulder. His free hand caught my thigh, clenching tight, grinding his presence into me deeper than his cane could ever reach.

Pleasure came in jolting little bursts—something I hadn't learned to expect from my previous trysts. I was already so close…so close to feeling that feeling I could only achieve on my own when I felt bored enough to try. Like my lungs were on fire. Like nothing in the world mattered more than feeding the itchy hunger taking residence in my skin. I needed…

More. And my act took on a life of its own. I moaned louder. Dug my nails in harder. Writhed. Reacted… But, once again, Revend didn't respond the way he should have.

His entire body tensed when I started to arch my back, driving him deeper. Everything slowed down, and a single word replaced the mindless rush—something I couldn't decipher growled hotly against my ear. Or maybe I could understand, but the word was far too dangerous. *Stop.*

Without warning, he pulled back. Too fast. I winced, slamming back into reality with the shock of my feet hitting the cold floor. Clutching at the mirror, Revend sank heavily on one knee. I could only stare as his hand flew out, snatching up a piece of gray fabric from the floor—my leotard. I had watched Jake "take care of business" on his own enough to recognize the way he caught himself in a wad of fabric, stroking up and down. Faster. Faster…

I couldn't seem to look anywhere else.

The sound that revved in his throat was almost like that of a car engine coming to life. His shoulders tensed. Another smothered groan caught the air—deeper, as his hand manipulated the fabric in hard, firm strokes. Seconds later, actual words rasped from his throat.

"Get…out." He stood, tossing the remains of my leotard aside. "Now."

Hefting his pants back in place, he limped to the doorway, favoring his right side. Before he could cross the threshold, his last words drifted back to me.

"This…was a mistake."

ACT 2

CHAPTER 11

After Mom left, Dad used to claim that a little soap and water could fix any mistake. Unrequited crushes. Bad recitals. Juice stains on leotards. Before Carrie and his second daughter-doll had come packaged in their pretty little box, at least. *Just a little soap and water, Ann.*

It was "single father" logic, according to my therapist—the desperate belief that a simple solution could fix any and all problems like some universal Band-Aid. But it didn't help me then. I was lathered up in body wash, but the roar of the shower spray couldn't drown out the four words circling the inside of my skull.

"This was a mistake."

Mistake.

Mistake...

"Anya?" A knock rattled the bathroom door. "It's late."

I recognized Carrie's voice, slurred and half-asleep.

"Do you mind cutting it short?"

"Yeah…sure." I reached for the faucet and shut it off. Without the rush of running water to smother them, Revend's final words echoed ten times louder. *Get out!*

I tried slapping my hands over my ears, but it did little to drown him out. If anything, the shouts ricocheted off the inside of my skull. I wound up scrambling out of the shower just to escape him, dripping wet.

Every single muscle throbbed despite the punishing layer of steam that blurred my surroundings as I hunted for a towel. Or maybe that was just my pride throbbing? The inside of my legs? My stupid brain succumbing to the undiagnosed aneurysm I must have been suffering from?

Focus, my therapist would demand. *Arrange your thoughts, Anya. What do you feel?* Shock, mostly.

What the hell had happened?

What the hell had I *let* happen?

Had…had I wanted it to happen?

A pained sound escaped my throat as I stumbled to the counter and braced my hands over the surface of it. My wide-eyed reflection watched my every move. I was bleeding. The corner of my lip was split—just a tiny nick in the skin that could have been inflicted by someone's raking teeth. A single line of red painted my chin, adding a splash of color to an otherwise sallow complexion. The ghostly robot had come back to life, still sporting her fatal injuries, but I didn't even recognize her.

How funny. Revend had wanted me to *feel* something. But, now, I felt *everything,* only I was too exhausted to decipher what each emotion churning through my veins meant. *Fear? Confusion?* The most terrifying realization of all was—None of them seemed remotely close to regret.

Not yet, anyway.

"Night," Carrie called, still at the door.

I waited until the sound of her footsteps trailed off before I crept back into my bedroom without bothering to turn the lights on. It was easier to get dressed that way if I couldn't see the bruises. The blisters. The cuts. The blood.

Shaking, I finally climbed into bed. My legs hurt. My back ached. My head throbbed—or so I tried to tell myself.

The truth was that the only real pain I felt as I settled my head against the pillow and squeezed my eyes shut was the sting of four stupid words that shouldn't have mattered.

"This was a mistake."

The moment the sky lightened, I got up, crammed my feet into my sneakers, and went for a run. A long one. When I returned to the house, I slipped in through the back door and nearly ran over someone waiting on the other side of it.

"Shit!" Carrie cursed as she staggered back, spilling coffee over her silk pajama bottoms. She glanced up, her eyes narrowing once she'd taken in my sweaty appearance. "Anya? What are you doing out so early—"

"Just went for a run," I blurted while pushing past her before she could see my face.

In the polished basin of the stainless-steel sink, I could easily make out my reflection—messy bun, bloodshot eyes, the tiny droplets of moisture that still seeped out of them. To distract myself, I snatched a glass from the row drying along the counter and filled it with water from the tap. Closing my eyes, I drained it while Carrie shut the back door and approached me in her fuzzy slippers.

"Another package came for you," she mumbled around a yawn, which explained why she was out of bed before noon. "Can't you have them only come in the afternoon or something? What are you ordering anyway?"

"Schoolbooks." Setting the empty glass aside, I braced both hands flat against the countertop and exhaled. "Just stuff for school…"

"It's a little late in the semester for that, isn't it?" After tossing her empty mug into the sink, Carrie padded back out into the hallway without waiting for an answer—saving me the trouble of having to come up with a convincing lie. "By the way," she called from what sounded like the top of the stairs, "I left the package in front of your door."

I waited until I heard her drift into the room she shared with my father. The door closed. Hushed voices came a second later, a byproduct of the walls being so paper-thin.

"You should do something about her, Andrew. Midnight showers and early morning runs? Don't you think that's kind of suspicious?"

My father's grunted reply could have been real or imagined. "Don't go there. I trust Anya."

I didn't know how long I stood there, leaning against the counter for balance. When I finally crested the top of the staircase, the house had gone silent again, and sure enough, a white box barred the way to my bedroom door.

Once inside the safety of my bedroom, I opened it and discovered a note, its message simple and blunt. *Don't waste my time.* Beneath it were leotards, four of them—pure white, beige, gray, and black. Underneath the stack were packages of tights in matching colors and another pair of shoes nestled in tissue paper—a plain, pretty pink.

It took nearly a full hour of searching before I realized that my very last spare leotard had been left ripped to pieces on Revend's floor, which left me no choice but to wear one of the new ones.

He could make me give in that much.

But he couldn't make me wear the shoes.

CHAPTER 12

$\mathcal{I}$ reached Revend's with only five minutes to spare before his deadline. Was his offer still even on the table? A man was leaning against a car parked in the driveway, smoking a cigarette. As I came closer, he turned to face me.

"Ah, Ms. DeSotto? Right on time. I'll be your chauffeur for today." He laughed as he tossed the cigarette to the ground and stamped the cinder out. "Are you ready?"

An answer welled up behind my tongue. *No.* I swallowed it down and climbed into the back seat anyway. Moments later, the car drifted down the highway while I attempted to reassemble my broken robot programming. *Follow the script, Anya. Follow the script. Think, Anya. Focus, Anya. Breathe, Anya.*

All of that seemed impossible when Revend was in my head, infecting any thought that didn't contain him. I couldn't escape. His touch. His scent. The inescapable feeling of his body against mine.

Only a sick person would dwell on something so...*wrong*.

However, the two-hour drive to Holly seemed to last two million years while I tried not to remember. I was exhausted by the end, and it was a struggle to keep my eyes open as I hurried out onto the curb and approached the theater listed on the audition forms.

Named the Chirstmark, it was three times the size of Remsky's small venue. A gleaming marquee overhead advertised the names of several upcoming ballets—*Swan Lake*, *The Nutcracker*, and *Don Quixote*. A front patio of gray marble led visitors to the entrance.

Shadows obscured most of an enormous lobby, which was decorated in soft shades of crimson and gold. Two other women, both sporting dance totes, lingered near the main doors, seeming just as lost as I was. I joined them, lurking on the outskirts of the room as time slowly inched toward the official start of the rehearsals.

Ten minutes later, two more women skittishly approached the theater's entrance, followed by six men who came grouped like a pack of wolves and sized us up from the other end of the lobby. *Partner work,* Revend's voice echoed inside my head while I inspected them all, fidgeting with the strap of my bag.

To pass the time, I assembled the dancers into perfect hypothetical matches. The willowy blonde leaning against the wall would be with her equally-as-tall, blond counterpart from the male side. The nervous redhead chewing on her bottom lip with the almost arrogant brunette who glanced over the women with a permanent half smile.

And I would be with…

Well, that was the trick question. I was the anomaly, drifting in the background, too insubstantial to fit in anywhere. I didn't even notice when another figure appeared until they spoke.

"You will be grouped into pairs," the pale woman wearing reading glasses announced. "This way."

We followed her down a narrow hall and into a spacious studio with yellow daylight streaming in through artistically placed windows. Two parallel rows of mirrors displayed us from all angles. The pretty, statuesque, and strong. The small, thin, and weak.

What a collection.

"I'm Rebecca," the woman announced with a heavy sigh that jarred the wire frames resting on the bridge of her nose. "Please change into the proper attire, and we'll warm up. Slippers for now, please." She directed the women to a dressing room on the right side of the studio, while the men filed out on the left.

Once inside, each girl instinctively took an empty spot at a vanity and unpacked her materials. There was an art to displaying your perfectly polished pointe shoes in just the right light, stripping down to reveal your toned body, and laying out the makeup carefully selected to help you appear flawless.

Intimidation at its finest.

My inner actress was out of practice in that arena. In Revend's white leotard, I felt sallow. My hair was a mess that refused to be pinned in place. I almost regretted that I'd left the new pair of shoes behind as I fingered the stained laces of my old ones.

The other girls glanced me over before turning away in search of the real competition. They were all young and fresh out of their respective academies, eager to embark on the path that they just *knew* would catapult them to stardom as the principal dancer of some prestigious ballet.

They were ready.

I was tired.

Once we all filed back into the main room, Rebecca grouped us by sex only to frown when she finally observed us together. "One of you is missing…"

As if the words were her cue, a woman burst through the door to the studio, her arm raised to ward off any wrath directed her way. "I'm so sorry! Traffic was awful. I'm coming from nearly three hours away and I—"

She broke off, noticing me at the back of the women's group at the same time I recognized her—blonde hair, green eyes... Rather than meet her gaze directly, I stared straight ahead as if riveted by a pristine section of the wall.

But just because I couldn't see her didn't mean I couldn't still sense Katja's confusion as she hurried forward. It mirrored my own—though I shouldn't have been so surprised. Revend only owned one company, after all.

"All right." Rebecca sighed again and gestured to the women's dressing rooms. "Change, please. You'll have to catch up. Our schedule is too tight to risk running behind."

While Katja rushed off, the rest of us began to warm up at the barre, alternating male and female. There, a few simple stretches served to separate the exceptional from the average. Those slender girls able to make their raised legs touch their ears with little effort. The men who could hold a grand plié for several solid minutes without flinching. Those who could barely manage to turn their feet out during simple exercises.

The practice dragged after that while we paraded like horses before a disinterested audience—Rebecca—to see which two might play well together. In the end, most of the pairings turned out exactly how I'd predicted. Beauty with the handsome. Strong with the wiry. Graceful with the charming.

The only surprise match was my own—a shy blond named Caleb who towered over me and didn't seem to know where to place his hands. For what felt like hours, we were led, step by step, through the *pas de deux*—ignoring the lifts to focus on the movement. Caleb, though hesitant, was a strong, reliable dancer. He carefully supported my technique, guided my spins without forcing. He was patient.

And, together, we made the worst pair.

It was my fault. All of that time rehearsing with Revend had amounted to nothing. My technique was laughable. I could barely keep track of Rebecca's steady count, distracted by my own heartbeat. It sped up each time my brain decided to interpret a brush of Caleb's fingers as a cruel reminder.

This dance is pretentious, Anya.

Fucking is pretentious, Anya.

You fucked him, Anya.

My leotard wasn't the only thing that had been left shredded on Revend's floor, and it seemed that dignity couldn't be hand-delivered in a little, white box.

When the rehearsal finally ended, I was too exhausted to change. Instead, I grabbed my bag from the vanity and ducked out of the theater before a curious Katja could corner me.

Outside, the sky was already dark. Traffic was thick, but a familiar black car resisted the flow to wait for me along the curb.

Once again, the driver wasn't Revend.

Not that it mattered at all.

The next three days, and the next three rehearsals played out the same way.

Every morning, I woke up early and jogged to Revend's. From there, the driver—whose name I learned was Huey—dutifully drove me to the theater in Holly. For the next eight hours, I rehearsed with Caleb, seeming to crush his spirits a little more each day, and I was always the first to leave at the end of every session, avoiding Katja.

Wash. Rinse. Repeat.

By the fourth day, I had made peace with the fact that I didn't have a shot in hell of making it into the next round. Poor Caleb seemed forced to reconcile that as the other couples flitted and flounced across the floor, deep within their roles of Romeo and Juliet. He could only keep the act up for so long, and the night before the official auditions, his good-natured façade finally slipped.

The workout was harsher than any before it. Even Rebecca—who, unlike Remsky, was more inclined to dramatically sigh to voice her displeasure rather than sling insults—was unusually on edge.

"It's the final night," she reminded, her monotone voice cracking around the edges. "Please, try to"—her gaze found me as I staggered against Caleb after a relatively simple variation, and she braced one hand against her temple—"do your best."

My best was a sloppy arabesque and then a bourrée sequence that sent me crashing into another dancer.

"Sorry!" I struggled to find my balance, feeling like a pigeon trapped in a cage with larger, stronger, *beautiful* swans. A pigeon with broken wings, who wore sweatpants when everyone else flitted around in skirts that displayed their bare, perfect legs.

"It's okay," Caleb reassured me while hooking one of his hands around my forearm. "Let's try it again. From the second lift."

Squaring my shoulders, I faced him from the opposite end of the studio. Out of the corner of my eye, I saw five other Juliets easily falling in love and five other Romeos confessing their undying devotion, taunting me with their feather-light steps.

When I rushed over to him, Caleb gracefully caught my shoulders and lifted me while I arched my back and tried to seem weightless. That time, I cleared the ground.

"Yes," Caleb said under his breath.

Could it be possible that we might make it through a rehearsal without being held up by one of my mistakes? I almost believed so until the door opened, bringing in a burst of cool air and a smell I'd have known anywhere. My gaze was on the ceiling when my nostrils caught that dangerous spice, and the world snapped in half.

"Anya! Shit!"

My steadying arm on Caleb's shoulder slipped, and I plunged downward. He had to paw at my hip just to keep me from hitting the floor.

"Watch your concentration, Anya," Rebecca called out as I struggled to catch my balance, but the advice seemed halfhearted.

The truth was painfully obvious, and the expressions of the four figures who had entered the room didn't let me escape those three words I couldn't seem to outrun. *Not good enough.*

They were wearing suits, cold expressions, and vacant eyes. In a single line, they approached Rebecca, led by a man who barely spared a glance in my direction.

"Can we see a run-through?" he muttered.

"Oh…of c-course, Mr. Marcus." Rebecca scanned the room until she spotted a graceful couple in the corner. "Sarah and Mark, will you—"

"No," the man interjected. He turned as if searching the dancers on his own, but I wasn't surprised when his finger jabbed in my direction a second later, followed by a command that set every cell in my body on edge. "Make them dance it *again.*"

"Oh…um, all right," Rebecca stammered. "Anya and Caleb. Can you give us a…another brief run-through?"

"Sure." Poor Caleb was still smiling as he took my hand and manually steered me to an empty part of the studio. "Just focus," he told me before stepping back to mark the first section of partner work.

Focus. I inhaled, unable to ignore the gazes of the four figures grouped along the nearest wall. Make that one figure. Fire spilled from his black eyes, igniting the floor. The room narrowed down to nothing but my body and his. Ice and an inferno. Darkness and…emptiness.

Had he been able to forget any of it? Jealousy twisted my insides at the possibility that he had when I *hadn't.* I couldn't.

"Anya."

I jumped and looked up.

Caleb flicked his fingers in my direction and mouthed a single plea. "Move."

Rising on pointe, I pranced across the room and nearly smacked Caleb in the face during the first series of pirouettes. Like a professional, he powered through, but any hope we had at recapturing that previous flow had shattered.

Revend had shattered it.

I could almost hear him snarling inside my head. *Pathetic! Sloppy! Robotic! Feel, Anya!* My gaze found him without meaning to, drifting his way during every turn. Every step.

Each time, I found nothing. When it came time for the lift, I approached Caleb from the wrong direction, and he couldn't even risk lifting me in the air.

"Again." The grunted command came before my foot had even hit the floor.

I froze, half leaning against Caleb for balance.

"Come on," he urged, pulling back just enough for us to mark the lift again. "Just focus."

Focus. There was that damn word again. It sounded so easy in theory. In practice, however, Revend consumed my focus. Every cell in my body was attuned to his presence— paralyzed by it.

Feel, Anya. Give me something, Anya.

"Anya!"

I wasn't sure if the prompt had come from Caleb or someone else, but I hurried forward, completely off-center. Caleb had to jerk out of the way before I crashed into his chest.

"That's enough." The words preceded the thud of a cane striking the floor in disappointment.

The three strangers followed their leader out of the studio, taking all the air with them, and I was left with nothing but shame to drag into my lungs.

A nervous Rebecca could only pace the room in their absence, tearing a hand through her hair, before she ended the rehearsal altogether—just as darkness blotted out all trace of daylight beyond the windows.

Just like that, I knew what true rock bottom was—that hollow place where your own failure meant nothing. When a stranger's indifference mattered more than the dreams you could feel slowly slipping right through your fingers.

And you didn't know *why*.

By the time I'd managed to change into my street clothes, the theater was nearly empty. Sighing, I started for the entrance, slipping my bag over my shoulder—only to freeze the moment I heard someone speak.

"Shit," a man hissed into a cell phone while leaning against the wall of the deserted lobby. Caleb, I realized, still wearing his practice leotard, his hair slicked back with sweat. "All this shit for nothing," he croaked. "I'm never going to get a second look with my fucking partner."

I hurried past before he could see me. Outside of the theater, the cool night air offered little relief as guilt hammered me down, flattening the ruins Revend had left behind. Failing myself was one thing, but sabotaging another dancer's dreams was a new footnote in the Anya DeSotto legacy. Maybe, next to me, the judges would see Caleb in an even better light…

Or maybe the smart thing to do would have been to just give up and let him dance alone. I was hopeless anyway.

"Change of plans." The words came from Huey as I settled into the back seat of the car idling alongside the curb.

My hand stilled over the strap of my seatbelt. "Is something wrong?"

He didn't respond before pulling into the thick of traffic—but rather than head toward the highway, like usual, he took a right a few blocks down from the theater. Minutes later, he came to a stop before the gilded façade of a hotel named The Blackbelle.

"He's on the tenth floor," Huey announced while stoically facing forward. "Room ten seventeen."

"Who?" I asked even though the identity of the figure wasn't that much of a mystery.

"Goodnight, Miss," Huey said firmly. What he *didn't* say resonated in my ears ten times louder. *Good luck. You'll need it.*

My chest tightened as I warily stepped onto the curb and slipped through the hotel's glass doors. Running wasn't even an option. Like a good doll, I was resigned to my fate as I took the elevator to the tenth floor, numb with every step. Then I traveled down a pristine hallway toward the door at the very end. As if on cue, it flew open before I could even raise my hand to knock.

A scowling giant stood behind it. After a sufficiently intimidating second, he stood aside to allow me into a suite that seemed worth more per night than one of my father's car payments. I was too exhausted to play my role anymore, so I shrugged my bag off and just faced the wall.

"Yes?" I directed the question toward the rest of the elegant suite.

However, the velveteen sofa was unamused. The crystal coffee table was disinterested. The gleaming windows, revealing a breathtaking view of the city, were unimpressed.

Revend was furious.

"Give me a reason." His tone stung like the blow from a whip, glancing off the walls and grazing my sweat-soaked skin. "Just one reason why you would spit on my generosity and make a mockery of *my* company."

I swallowed hard. Courtesy of Rebecca, I suspected that word of my performance all week had gotten back to him, and I couldn't escape this stupid sense of guilt. He didn't have to say it—What little chance I might have had, I'd already thrown away.

That didn't mean I had to admit it.

"I never asked for your help—"

"You accepted it," he threw back.

A broken sound that might have been a laugh tore from my lips. "You didn't give me much of a choice—"

"Do not let some brief error in judgment break your resolve," Revend hissed over me, cutting right to the chase. "Be stronger than that."

Stronger. The word triggered something raw and ugly festering beneath my skin. *You need to be strong, Anya,* my therapist always encouraged. *Think about the feelings of others. Put yourself in their shoes. Be strong.*

"You're one to talk—" I broke off as his hand fell over my shoulder, the fingers clenching tight.

"Don't do this, Anya," he warned.

"Don't *what?*"

He was imitating my therapist again. *Don't do this Anya. Don't dwell on the negatives, Anya. Don't think, Anya. Don't feel.* What wasn't I supposed to do this time? Throw his own "mistake" in his face? I hadn't been the only one to make a "brief error in judgment" that night, after all...

"Don't be *childish*," Revend scolded, wrenching his hand away as if trying to prevent any naughty emotions from seeping through his fingers. "More importantly, don't be a *fool*, Anya."

"Whatever." I headed for the door, desperate to put space between us. Inches. Yards. Miles. "You don't have to worry about dealing with my *childish* antics anymore," I told him over my shoulder. "Because I quit—"

"No." He surprised me by yanking me back. *Hard.*

My entire arm stung beneath the force of his grip, and I staggered across the room, forced to cling to the back of the velvet chaise for balance. In an instant, his heat surrounded me, caging me in further with every inch he gained. *One step. Two.* I had to brace my weight with both hands just to obey his earlier command. *Be strong.*

"You…you can't make me dance for you—"

"Oh, can't I?" His tone lowered as he advanced another step. "Don't you remember? You lost the ability to quit the moment you came crawling back to me with your tail between your legs."

That was one way to put it.

"Well, my tail may have been between my legs," I spat back. "But so were *you*."

It was the wrong thing to say, so openly *negative*. I bit my lip, but it was too late to take the words back. God, I wanted to.

Revend looked like I'd hit him before the anger set in and his eyes flashed a lethal shade of obsidian. "Don't—"

"Do you mind keeping it down?"

The sound of a door opening somewhere down the hall forced us both to realize that the door to his own suite was still open. Our voices were too loud. *"So were you"* had echoed off the walls.

"Excuse us." Revend pulled away from me and marched forward to close the door with a deceptively quiet click that didn't match the ferocity burning in his gaze when he faced me again. One of his hands tugged on the hem of his shirt, smoothing the wrinkles out, while the other raked through his hair, disrupting the raven strands. "What happened was nothing more than a *mistake*," he began, sounding composed once more. "Say it."

When I didn't speak, he surged forward, and I staggered back, unintentionally knocking a vase off a nearby end table. It smashed into pieces, resembling my resolve, as my shoulders struck the wall a heartbeat later. In mere seconds, he had me blocked within the corner near the windows with no escape in sight.

"Say it, Anya." He caught my chin in his palm, forcing me to meet his gaze. The more his grip tightened, the faster my pulse raced, until it threatened to drown out every word he said. "'It was a mistake, Revend.' Say it."

Without a shred of mercy, his fingers dug into my jaw until I finally pried my lips apart.

"It…it was a mistake, Revend—"

"Agreed." He roughly tilted my head to the side, allowing his next whispered words to drip directly into my ear. "'It meant nothing, Revend.' Say it."

My lips moved woodenly, my voice robotic. "It meant n-nothing," I told the wall.

"'I'm not stupid enough to throw away what little chance at a future I have, Revend.'"

"I'm not stupid…"

Whether intentionally or by accident, his thumb drifted to the corner of my mouth, and my breath hitched in my throat. He was too close. Too warm. I was shivering, my teeth threatening to chatter, and I hadn't even noticed until he touched me. Until his heat seared the insides of my lungs and prickled along my skin.

I knew I shouldn't feel that way. I tried to moisten my dry lips with a discreet flick of my tongue, only his eyes caught the motion, and he let me go as if I'd caught fire. Thrown off-balance, I had to catch myself against the wall, jarring a floor lamp that swayed and threw erratic shadows over every nearby surface.

"Get out," he told me.

I didn't move.

When seconds had passed, Revend merely glowered, his hands fisting into his pockets, his shoulders tense. Like a predator, he shot his gaze to my throat as if searching for the most vulnerable area to attack.

"You're quite libidinous, aren't you?"

The insult struck a bull's-eye, setting my cheeks aflame. *Libidinous—slut.*

"You're attractive enough, so what is it? Does your father not love you? So what? You chase all the boys around your playground, desperate for any hint of attention?"

I knew what he was implying. Daddy issues. Loose morals. Whore. Why else would I come onto a grown man more than twice my age?

Why else, Anya?

"Do you have a thing for *children*, Revend?" I threw back, hitting below the belt with the one insult that I knew would affect him.

Bingo. He grimaced, his jaw clenching—but the reaction didn't satisfy me the way I'd thought it would.

"Get out," he spat, jerking his shoulder in the direction of the door. "I've humored you long enough—"

"I should have known that your *prodigies* didn't last very long." God, I didn't even know where the venom was coming from, but it was there, lacing the words like poison and spilling out before I could swallow it back down. "Is that how a washed-up old man gets laid?"

"Enough," Revend snarled when he seemed to regain control of his voice. He sounded too soft. Damn near calm.

After all, we couldn't make the neighbors any more suspicious, now could we?

But, while they could hear the puppet master berating his doll in the next room over, they couldn't see. Before I could react, his hands fell over my shoulders, yanking me forward.

"Watch yourself, *child*," he hissed. His accent had hardened, lacing each word with acid.

"The same way you *watched* me?" I managed to match his tone, but my voice cracked. My eyes burned as I peered deep into his and saw nothing but shadow. "Or...was that just part of the *illusion*?"

The words had barely left my throat before I found myself drawn even closer to him, his fingers clenching the fabric of my shirt, our faces inches apart. Close enough to drown beneath the scent of peppermint before he shoved me back again and scoffed.

"I should have known better than to take on a fool well past her prime," he said, sounding so weary, like the quintessential professor stuck rehabilitating a problem student.

Tsk. Tsk. She failed every test. Botched every lesson. Really, there was nothing left to do but salvage his reputation by throwing her away.

"You shouldn't have taken me on," I echoed.

I didn't even notice that he'd moved until he had me pinned flat against the glass. There was fragile security in feeling the cool surface at my back in contrast to his heat. Just enough pressure would shatter it, but it still felt so much steadier than he did.

"Maybe you had it all planned," I croaked before he could deliver another disparaging "lesson." "Make the desperate ballerina think she had a chance, and then get your jollies before yanking the rug out from under her—"

"Stop."

I flinched as his hand met the wall inches from my right cheek.

"Don't you ever…*ever* question my intentions again."

Questioning. He made it sound so much worse than fucking him. He was the puppet master. I was the doll. His mistakes resulted in my tiny, hairline scratches—but how dare I question?

"Don't you ever touch me again," I countered—a good enough tit for tat.

Before he could say anything else, I pushed away from him and managed to snatch my bag from the floor. My vision blurred for some reason, and I could only stumble in the direction I assumed the door was in. The moment my fingers caught the curve of the handle, I thought I was safe.

As if it would be that easy to walk away.

"Wait. You insinuate that I've taken advantage of my other dancers—but what about you? Has Victor—"

Like a true puppeteer, he knew how to pull the right strings.

I spun around. "N-no. Of course not."

Revend didn't seem convinced. His eyes ruthlessly raked me over from the tips of my toes to the top of my head. "That's how you really paid him, isn't it?" he accused. "I wondered why he seemed so damn invested in *one* dancer—"

"Stop it! Just stop it." I clutched either side of my head as if to smash his disgusting allegations out. *Lalala, I can't hear you.* "I've never slept with my dance instructor."

But then what did that make him? He scowled as if he were wondering that very same thing.

And neither of us had an answer for that.

I turned for the door again, struggling to reassemble my perfect robot armor. "I'm sorry for wasting your time, but—"

"You're lying."

"Do you want me to *prove* it to you?" At that point, the consequences meant nothing as I faced him, hooked a hand beneath the waistband of my pants, and yanked them down just far enough to reveal my inner thigh—and the reason why I'd worn cumbersome sweats to practice all week.

It was almost funny how the worst marks on my body hadn't been left by his cane. Four days later, an ugly, greenish bruise still discolored the skin. If he looked closely enough, he'd find the scabbed-over nicks left by groping nails.

Four days later, *his* mark was still there.

"You're the only person over thirty I've 'fucked'," I blurted, oddly satisfied by the way he flinched. "And that includes the little boys on my playground."

His silence terrified me more than anything he could have said. My pulse quickened when he settled for just holding my gaze, and I glared back without flinching. *Romeo and Juliet* had been cast aside, and we had both taken up new roles. Who the hell was I now? Why did she frighten me so much more than the empty waif from the mirror?

We stood there for what felt like an eternity before his gaze settled over the bruise again. I didn't know what reaction I'd expected, but this wasn't it.

In the end, I was the one who finally gathered up the nerve to speak. "Maybe you were wrong. Maybe…maybe I was just too good of a liar."

Wrenching my pants back up, I turned my back on him and fumbled for the door. I was trapped in the lion's cage, inches from the only exit. Already, the monster's breath fanned the back of my neck.

And I *still* wasn't prepared when he seized my arm from behind.

I found myself pressed against the door. His hands pinned my shoulders to the hard surface. His breath seared my chin. His eyes were too fucking dark, mercilessly probing my own. I thought about calling for help, but any shred of resistance disintegrated the moment his lips crashed into mine.

It was a test, I think. The same way someone might taunt a child who claimed to have a sweet tooth with an overload of sugar. You flooded their system. Taught them a lesson. Gave them a bad tummy ache and they learned to eat veggies.

But the joke was on Revend; his kiss made me feel *something*—a dark, twisted feeling fed by every hungry press of his mouth. Every delicious tendril of heat licking at my skin. The deep-seated knowledge that this was wrong.

My sweet tooth was overloaded, but I couldn't pull away. I couldn't stop myself from matching every probing stroke of his tongue, clutching his shoulders for stability. He ripped his mouth from mine but didn't back away. Before I even had the chance to catch my breath, he yanked on the hem of my shirt, wrenching it up and over my head. I let him.

A callused hand dipped beneath my bra a heartbeat later to graze my breast, and I lurched toward his touch. *Craved* it. The sudden shift in weight threw him off-balance. He stumbled, dragging me along by my waist.

Then, somehow, we were against the wall. The side of an end table. The back of the chaise—still kissing. Devouring. Consuming.

Drowning.

I was faintly aware of something soft giving way beneath my back as Revend's weight pinned me down, crushing the air from my lungs only to have it replaced by the heat he breathed into me. In and out...

Looking up, I didn't recognize the man above me. His gaze swallowed every ounce of light as he fisted both hands in my sweats and yanked them down my legs before I could decide if I wanted him to stop.

Maybe I didn't.

Not even as his gaze returned to the ugly bruise on my thigh. His finger flicked out to trace the purplish mark and followed the line of my hip down, down...

All at once, the atmosphere shifted. The storm clouds that I figured had been gathering around us since that morning swelled overhead, threatening to break. As if sensing them as well, Revend hesitated. Then he merely thumbed the swell of my right breast with his other hand, never breaking eye contact.

My teeth descended into my bottom lip as my nipple reacted to the contact while admonishments chanted through my skull. *Wrong, wrong, wrong.*

What was that he'd said about choices? That they led to mistakes? Well, he *chose* to touch me, sliding a hand beneath my waist, and I chose to spread my legs. When we released a joint exhale, I knew we both consciously made the decision to jump.

And it was *wrong.*

Regardless, my underwear disappeared seconds later. As the crumpled cotton hit the floor, he unbuttoned his pants and pulled his erection free. Dazed, I eyed the blunt tip, startled by the white bead of moisture already slipping free.

There was no escaping it; every inch of hard, flushed flesh was because of me. While I was still sore from the first time, my body seemed inexplicably hungry for the second—even though it was insanity to want this, to want him.

Who are you, Anya?

My right foot twitched, my toes impatiently digging into the upholstery, as I forgot the answer to that question. Beneath us, the cushions shifted when Revend hovered over me, his weight pinning me down, his heat intoxicating. I spread my legs wider, hooking one over the closest armrest, as I arched my hips up to meet him.

And then he was plunging deep, deep where I couldn't even begin to shut him out.

I didn't *want* to.

The pain of accepting him serrated me like shards of broken glass, electrifying dead nerves and bringing them back to life. Through the gaping wounds, a million emotions bled into my veins as he withdrew—then forced his way back in, stretching me to accommodate his size. Every. Last. Inch of him.

I couldn't get over the harsh beauty of the way he moved. He wasn't horny and unsteady—just...invincible. Fluid muscle coiled and released, dancing beneath his skin, driving us closer and then farther apart. In and out. I almost didn't know where to look. His eyes were too dark. His scars caught the light.

Desperate to focus on *something*, I noticed the gray streaking the stubble on his chin. A broken laugh tore from my throat at a sudden, hysterical thought—*He's so old, Anya.* The sound quickly deepened into a moan when he withdrew, the searing friction setting me on fire. Then he pushed into me yet again as his nails bit into my skin, urging me to match every firm, desperate stroke.

Again.

And *again.*

Slick with sweat, my legs caught his waist, my hips arching up to get even closer, to feel him even deeper. Before our gazes could make contact again, his hand tore through my hair and wrenched my head back while callused fingers possessively fanned out against my spine. Then he continued to move. Harder, harder, slower, *slower.*

It was too much tension, friction, fire. *Everything.*

I gasped for air, terrified of being consumed by it all. By him.

"Rev—" My nails raked down his arm urging him to stop. Or maybe begging him for more?

Hell, I didn't know.

Revend only heeded Revend, regardless. He picked the pace up when *his* breath hitched and mine had already devolved into gasps. I could only feel what he wanted me to feel, wherever he touched my body in stingy, rough grapples for leverage. He seemed determined to renew every mark, grinding his presence into my skin so that I'd still feel him tomorrow. For days after. An eternity.

When I tried to touch him in return, he retaliated by seizing my wrists and pinning them flat against the back of the couch, still thrusting. Still in control. But there was one thing he *couldn't* control. It started out so subtly that I almost didn't feel it beneath every other punishing sensation

—heat spreading up from between my legs, down along my spine. Like brush fire, it crept into every pore, surging, growing, consuming.

Then he lunged for one last thrust, and my entire body came apart at the seams.

Jesus. Christ. I couldn't breathe.

I didn't *care*.

Nothing mattered as long as he remained against me, inside me, possessing me while I broke into a million tiny pieces. Amid the height of the destruction, his lips brushed my ear, and I heard him rasp two harsh syllables.

"Fuck. *Fuck*."

The rawness ignited something inside me, and I was convulsing around him, crying out broken, wordless nonsense at the ceiling. When my voice started to echo off the walls, his hand fell over my lips, sealing them shut—and then I bit them, tasting blood, too out of control to stay silent.

The whole time, he continued to thrust. Faster. Harder. *Deeper*. Just when I thought he couldn't claim me any further, he *did*. Buried inside me, he threw his head back as an ugly sound tore from his throat. Heat flooded through my body, and I was tumbling inside myself too quickly to stop.

My vision blurred around the edges as his body collapsed on top of mine. And then we slid off the precarious edge of the sofa and onto the floor. Breathless peace lasted for only a second before he stiffened and jerked away.

I'd barely recovered my bearings by the time he made it halfway across the room, pretending as though this second mistake hadn't happened.

Like I didn't exist.

"I'm on the pill." It was the only thing I could seem to say as Revend paced the length of the main room.

With enviable composure, he had already refastened his pants, while I sat on the edge of the couch, shrouded in a dark-blue afghan that didn't feel like a sufficient enough barrier against shame.

I felt plenty of it as I noticed my clothes scattered on the polished floor.

"It...it's okay," I repeated weakly, though I wasn't sure if I was trying to convince him or myself. "I'm on birth control."

Once again, Revend ignored me. Or maybe...he couldn't even hear me.

Like a caged animal, he swept from side to side, slightly favoring one leg. His left hand ruthlessly raked through his hair while the other grasped anything within reach. The back of a chair. An end table. When a knock sounded on the door, he used the wall for support to limp toward the entryway.

I didn't know what made me follow him on unsteady legs. Halfway across the room, I saw the door open and heard a male's voice inquire, "Is everything okay in here?"

"Everything's fine," Revend grunted.

"A few other guests reported a...disturbance," the visitor said.

I came close enough to make out parts of him from beyond Revend's shoulders—a navy-blue jacket with the hotel emblem on it and a gunmetal-gray walkie-talkie on his hip.

And, by "disturbance," of course, he meant the shouting.

"Everything's *fine*," Revend insisted in a voice so deep that it grated on the words.

"Really?" The security guard placed a hand on his flashlight. "Then would you mind if I had a look inside?"

There was this awful moment of anticipation when I thought Revend would slam the door in his face. Seemingly on the verge of that very action, he finally stood aside at the last minute so that the guard could see me there, wearing nothing more than a woolen blanket and a look of utter mortification.

"Oh." The guard's cheeks reddened. "Sorry to bother you... Are you okay, miss?"

I readjusted my blanket to cover my bare shoulders. "I'm fine—"

He was gone before I'd fully gotten the words out, and Revend slammed the door behind him. Then he turned, pressed his back against it, and cradled his face in the palms of his hands. I would have preferred that he shouted at me. Kicked me out. Kicked *me*. Seconds passed without him moving an inch until he resembled a statue more than ever.

Alone, I found myself drifting in the opposite direction, feeling oddly weightless. It didn't faze me at all to see that the coffee table had been knocked off-balance and the blue lampshade hung crookedly over the lightbulb. And the curtains were open, meaning that anyone with binoculars and good eyesight could have seen what had taken place from any one of the nearby buildings.

Reality couldn't touch me as I gingerly sidestepped my discarded, crumpled clothing and wandered down a narrow hall until I reached the master bathroom. I left my afghan in the doorway and approached the walk-in shower without bothering to close the door.

I turned the water on, grabbed a bottle of sample shampoo from the sink, and ducked beneath the spray. I was in the middle of lathering up when everything hit me like a punch to the chest, and I could only stand there, blinking into a cloud of steam and dripping liquid soap.

He hadn't used a condom.

I hadn't cared—maybe I still didn't.

That had me scrambling backward until my back hit the tiled wall, supporting my descent while I sank to my knees. A hysterical sound bubbled in the pit of my stomach and escaped through my mouth. Then I was half laughing, half crying into a washcloth, desperate to smother it.

I had never let Jake anywhere near me without protection. Despite my being on birth control, we'd never had sex without a condom. In fact, paranoid about how my career would end in the event of any "mistake," I hadn't even liked it when he'd finished inside me. Something he'd sensed and started to handle on his own after pulling out midway.

It hadn't been anything against him, I'd said. I'd been worried about my future. Like a perfect boyfriend, he had understood.

The thought made the tears flow harder, and the sobs come faster. I was drowning beneath a layer of terrycloth and soap. Too. Far. Gone. No hope of resurrection.

I could still feel Revend inside me, everywhere…everywhere.

There was no escaping it.

No escaping him.

Regret would have been understandable. Shame would have been acceptable. Anything but this greedy, reckless part of me that relished the fresh bruises his fingers had branded into my skin. *You don't regret it, do you?*

I didn't regret it.

With Jake, I'd been responsible.

With Revend, I felt like a whore.

And maybe I was.

CHAPTER 14

The shower spray had gone ice cold by the time I shut it off. A complimentary towel set hung on the rack beside the counter, and I wrapped one around myself before creeping, still dripping wet, into the main room.

I wasn't surprised that the blue afghan had been picked off the floor and slung over the back of the couch. My clothes were missing, too. With little effort, Revend had taken control. The only glaring flaw in his neat illusion was me, standing near the edge of the room while he faced the window.

He didn't speak at first.

Neither did I.

More could be said in the water dripping from my body and into the Persian carpet than words anyway. So I let the sound count the seconds. Drip, drop. Then one inhale. A ragged exhale. Two—mine and his, melding together.

"You can stay here tonight," Revend finally said, bracing one of his hands against the window glass, marring the view of the gleaming city below. "But don't make the mistake of reading into it any more than that." He glanced over his shoulder to meet my gaze. "What happened… It means *nothing*. Do you understand that? Say it."

Nothing. I *tried* to say it. I truly did, but my tongue wouldn't budge. My teeth clamped down, my lips sealing shut over the words.

"Nothing," Revend insisted as if my agreement on that fact didn't really matter. "I'm sure you've done this before enough times to know not to contact me. Tomorrow, you will be judged objectively. That's what you deserve. After that…our arrangement is over."

Without waiting for a reply, he turned and used his cane to spur his way to the door. It opened, he stormed out, and the door slammed behind him, and I found myself drifting across the room to a table in the corner sporting an elegant glass vase filled with beautiful roses. My finger twitched as it trailed along the smooth edge of the neck. I didn't mean to apply any pressure, but a second later, the vase wobbled on its base, and I watched it fall and shatter into countless chunks of glass that speckled the carpet.

Perfectly broken pieces.

I woke up partially wrapped in a damp duvet. Only after five minutes of blinking up at a darkened ceiling did I realize that someone was knocking… somewhere. The sound echoed like the remnants of a nightmare, kicking my heart into overdrive.

"Carrie?"

Groaning, I rolled over and nearly fell off the edge of the mattress. Reflex saved me as my leg instinctively shot out to brace my weight against the floor. It was only when my toes flexed—against hardwood and not carpet—that I realized I wasn't in my bedroom. In fact, the elegant furniture would have never been found within my father's house, considering it wasn't christened with juice stains left by a messy preteen. The pillowcase beneath my head felt like silk, and a scent other than cheap detergent wafted from the sheets; sweat and…peppermint.

I jolted upright as if electrocuted. At the same time, the series of knocks sounded again, and I stood without giving myself the time to put the pieces together. My head pounded. The inside of my mouth felt dry. Only after stumbling halfway down the hall did I even realize that I was naked.

A bed sheet made for the perfect makeshift covering when I finally approached the door. My heart raced as I pictured any one of the countless figures who could have been on the other side of it.

A security guard to kick me out? Revend himself demanding I leave?

It felt like an eternity before I finally wrestled the door open, only to find a smiling woman greeting me from the other end. A name tag clipped to her collar read *Kaycie*, and slung across her right arm were what appeared to be two clear garment bags. I only made out a blur of colored fabric before she shoved them both in my direction.

"Sorry to wake you!" she chirped. "But your father wanted to make sure that you received these as soon as possible."

My father? Without questioning, I took the clothing and watched as she skipped down the hall.

When I closed the door behind me, I observed the top garment in the dim daylight that filtered in through the windows. Carefully encased in the plastic was a dancing costume, fit for any Juliet. Layers of pale violet chiffon formed a delicate bodice and the flowing skirt that, I knew without even having to try it on, had been perfectly tailored to my size.

The second bag held my clothes from the night before, starched and clean. I unzipped that one and sniffed the cotton, heart in my throat. No peppermint.

Despite the hand delivery and the obvious expense of the costume, I knew that the gesture wasn't out of kindness. Every crafted bit of fabric was a challenge.

I'm still watching, so don't waste my time.

CHAPTER 15

I reached the theater a full hour before anyone else. By the time the first dancers trickled in, I was already deep within a grueling warm-up, glistening with sweat. Rebecca arrived not long after and broke us up by pair, each assigned to practice in another part of the theater for final run-throughs.

"This is it," she warned. "All that will factor into the final selections is your performance tonight. Nothing else."

I doubted she realized that those words of "encouragement" sounded more like a threat.

Nothing else echoed in my mind as Caleb and I were directed to a spacious room in the basement that was likely used for smaller rehearsal groups. A flickering fluorescent light hung from the ceiling, casting a harsh glow that seemed magnified by a mirror mounted on the entire back wall.

After we'd changed and settled in the center of the room,

Caleb barely looked me in the eye. A stern expression had replaced his usual charming smile, and his slumped posture screamed of defeat.

Taking a deep breath, I reached for his hand. "Look, I know I've been a mess these past few days—"

"You've been okay." He withdrew his hand from mine while still avoiding eye contact. A second later, he approached a CD player perched on a small table in the corner of the room and fished a CD out of a stack nearby.

"I *haven't*." I waited until he'd slipped the disc into the console and hit play. "But I want you to know that…I want this too."

It was more than that. I *needed* to prove myself—and not to Revend. I wanted to prove something to the waif in the mirror who haunted me, even now. *I'm not hopeless.*

"It might not be enough," I said quickly. "But I want you to know that I'm going to try."

Seconds passed. Then, for the first time that morning, Caleb cracked what might have been the hint of a smile. "I think we should spend less time talking and more time dancing." He took my hand again and led me to the center of the room as the opening notes of music swelled, depicting the moment Juliet noticed her admiring Romeo beneath her balcony.

Then we danced.

The final audition took place in the main auditorium of the theater—a sprawling complex of red velvet chairs all facing a grand stage. According to Rebecca, we would perform before the executive directors of the Roria—those four figures who had intruded on the final rehearsal. They would have the final decision, regardless of any progress made beforehand. One botched pirouette could cost someone their lifetime dream.

Every single one of us knew it. Our anxious footsteps echoed as we filed into the wings behind the main stage, ducking costumes racks of bright clothing and elaborate sets from past performances. They taunted me, their garish colors outlasting the shadows. *You will never be a part of this.*

As the hum from that morning's rehearsals dissipated from my muscles, I found myself wondering if Revend would be among that elite group of judges. I couldn't think of a reason why he wouldn't be. Then again, I couldn't think of a reason why he *would*.

Despite his perfectionist nature, Revend didn't seem to micromanage the inner workings of the Roria. I think he preferred to watch from the shadows, manipulating events to his liking without visibly affecting them—the ultimate puppet master wielding invisible strings. I felt the tug of them as I entered the female dressing room and took my place at the far end of the vanity.

All around me, the other girls carefully hung their costumes on a nearby clothing rack or over the back of a chair, fondling creations of silk and satin, while I shoved mine on the counter and hastily unzipped the bag.

I couldn't get it on fast enough—for all the wrong reasons. The gown was relatively simple—a skin-tight bodice that flared out into a billowing skirt that would allow my legs to move freely on stage. At first glance, it seemed almost painfully simple, lacking the bold flourishes of some of the other costumes. But the sheer quality of the fabric caught the eye. The bodice emphasized my figure, minimizing the harsh lines and drawing attention to my throat. From the right angle, one might get a far-too-intimate glimpse of my bare legs.

"Nice dress."

I used the pretense of adjusting my appearance to hide my reaction as someone came up beside me in a burst of flowery perfume.

"Where did you get it?" Katja wondered while I woodenly dragged a brush through my hair.

"Thrift shop," I lied.

Appearing beside mine, Katja's reflection looked perfect. Her costume was a simple one of white silk and lace meant to mimic a nightgown but designed with two daring slits down either side to allow her to maneuver better on stage. White ribbons streaked her hair, which had been plaited into an elegant coil at the top of her head. Expertly applied makeup highlighted her big, green eyes, and blush colored her cheeks. She looked every bit the youthful, innocent Juliet. In comparison, I resembled…

Someone hollow. Juliet's ghost, frozen in time.

After setting the brush down, I reached for a tube of lipstick and then swiped it along my lower lip, hoping that the color might help. It didn't. My wide eyes revealed the truth I wouldn't admit out loud.

I'm too tired. Too tired. Tired.

"So…" Katja prompted after clearing her throat. Her eyes sought mine out over the mirror's glass, and she shifted her body slightly to block my only escape route. "I was surprised to see you here."

I shrugged and began to scrape my hair into a ponytail, ruthlessly pulling the strands flat against my scalp. "I didn't really expect to be—"

"So, *why* are you?" A sweet smile tempered the acid barely concealed beneath her charming tone—the perfect mixture of sugar and spice.

Revend probably would have praised the equally vicious expression lighting her eyes. Katja, for one, didn't struggle to portray her emotions.

"Did Remsky somehow manage to sneak you in?"

I raised an eyebrow. "Why would he do that?"

"Oh, no reason." Katja broke the eye contact to admire her pink nails. "Other than the fact that you were always his favorite." Her tone carried a bitter mixture of jealousy and guilt.

She was so off base that I wanted to laugh, but the topic of Remsky did offer a convincing scapegoat.

"I think he just wanted to teach me another lesson." I reached for a bobby pin and jabbed it in so hard that it scraped my scalp. My left foot was throbbing from the earlier practice, and my stomach lurched at the thought of strapping my pointe shoes on. Worst of all, beneath the sheer fabric, I could still make out distinct blotches of colored skin. The bruises.

"Hmph." Katja didn't seem convinced. A second later, her smile returned. She still wasn't happy, but she wasn't threatened, either. "Good luck, Anya," she said warmly. One of her hands reassuringly squeezed my shoulder before she pranced off.

I wasn't stupid enough to mistake the gesture as a sign of friendship—more like one of careful calculation. She thought I was intimidated.

I was.

My fingers shook as I ran one hand down the side of my costume. It was too tight. Too restricting. Every inch of satin contained a dare. *Do not fail me, Anya. You can't do it, Anya. You're pretentious…*

"Five minutes!" Rebecca called as she raced through the dressing room brandishing a clipboard and shooing dancers out of her way. "Five minutes everyone!"

As I laced my pointe shoes on, my stomach clenched at the way the faded pink satin clashed with the pristine fabric of the costume. After this week's grueling rehearsals, I doubted they would last on stage. Already, the right one barely seemed capable of supporting me on pointe.

I almost felt bad for having left the new ones at home, shoved into the trash can beside my desk.

"Two minutes!"

After smoothing my hair one final time, I joined the rest of the girls in the main auditorium and took a seat in the first row of the gallery. Not long after, the men rejoined us and each pair scrambled to sit next to each other.

"You look nice," Caleb whispered, waving his hand toward my costume. He resembled the quintessential Romeo, wearing a long-sleeved shirt and matching tights.

I muttered a compliment in return, though I doubted he even heard me as Rebecca stood before us, commanding our attention.

One by one, each group was called to quickly mount the stage and block their routine to adjust to the assembled set —a large balcony formed of painted wood with a series of steps leading to the stage proper, where Romeo would appear.

"Do not stress about the time," Rebecca urged, apparently unaware of just how impossible a request it was. *It's only your entire career on the line. Don't stress.* "Sometimes, you might arrive at a new venue with hours to spare. Sometimes, sets are rearranged opening night. A Roria dancer must be prepared for anything."

When Caleb and I were called, I mounted the steps to the balcony and rehearsed my descent while he blocked his entrance from stage left. From the height, the entire theater stretched out before me, including the upper balcony, where I assumed the Roria executives would sit.

The imagery lingered as Caleb and I reclaimed our seats, leaving me feeling…

So damn hollow.

By the end of the night, six dancers would have their dreams shattered. Their careers stilted. The moment they'd dreamt about since prancing in ballet slippers as toddlers would be pushed even further out of reach—all because of a missed cue or a sloppy pirouette. Or because they simply weren't good enough.

Keep telling yourself that, a part of me hissed, threatening my precarious balance as I breathed in and out in an unsteady rhythm. I should have been mentally rehearsing my role or trying to recall the correct placement for each lift. I should have been focused or at least stoically calm, like Caleb. A part of me tried to insist those things, that I wanted this. I *needed* this. Yet reality sank in only as the lights finally died down, and the sound of nearby footsteps ushered the arrival of the executives. My nostrils flared, testing the air for a scent I was too chicken to even name inside my own head.

You're pathetic, Anya. So damn pathetic.

"The first group," Rebecca began, "will be Sarah McMahon and Mark Alloy. Then Gina Sorano and Terrance Lee. Katja Sorenson and Michael Kent…"

Caleb and I were to perform last—a damning placement despite the cliché saying of saving the best for last. In this case, the best performers would have the benefit of dancing before judges who weren't bored by the proceedings and eager to point out every flaw. The worst went last, when the winners had already been signed, sealed, and delivered.

Caleb's jaw clenched, so he knew it too. It killed him to have had his hopes dashed before we even went on stage. Because of *me.* I reached for his hand and gave it a squeeze as the first—and the most technically solid pair—took their places on stage.

Sarah McMahon was the redheaded dancer who flitted about with all the willowy grace of a besotted schoolgirl while the slightly taller Mark supported her lifts and displayed breathtaking artistry. Together, they made an ideal Romeo and Juliet. Their only stumbles were a shaky lift in the middle of the scene and a few sloppy movements of Mark's, but it didn't detract any from their performance.

The next two dancers weren't any less stellar. Following them, Katja and her partner botched one of the more difficult lifts, but they made up for it with an attraction that sizzled off the stage. Their kiss wasn't faked either.

However, for all of their skill, neither dance came close to a professional performance of the actual live ballet. After only a week of rehearsals, there was an understandable lack of polish. Most *pas de deux* partners rehearsed months—if not years—to build the level of trust and rapport needed to convey love on stage. Despite how well each dancer performed, they were still just two amateurs pantomiming exaggerated emotions they didn't really feel.

Dry, an unwelcome voice hissed in my thoughts, tinged with a heavy accent. *Passionless fucking.*

It was the kind of assessment I never would have made three weeks ago, when flawless technique had meant everything. Who cared if their expressions were rehearsed or if the female dancer was in love with her own reflection more than the boy she danced with?

Pretty lines and perfect feet—*that* was what mattered.

"You okay?" Caleb whispered to me.

I jumped in my seat as the opening bars of music began to play. The next group of dancers had already taken the stage, and I hadn't even noticed.

"Fine." My fingers kept toying with the skirt of my gown, twisting the fabric around and around until the threads strained. "I'm fine—"

As if on cue, a piece of satin tore, leaving a hole I couldn't disguise above my right thigh.

"DeSotto. Martin," Rebecca whispered from the end of the aisle. She jerked her head toward the stage. *Get ready.*

We were up next. Heart pounding, I stood and woodenly followed Caleb backstage to stand on deck.

The dancers before us tried their hardest, but their skill wasn't on par with the more fluid, stronger pairs. They faltered and missed choreography, eventually glossing over a lift altogether when it became apparent that they couldn't pull it off safely. By the time they finished, disappointment was etched on their faces despite the loving smiles as they leaned in for a quick, chaste kiss.

Rising from her seat, Rebecca checked their names off a list and announced the final dancers, loud enough for everyone to hear. "Anya DeSotto. Caleb Martin."

I hurried to my place at the top of the balcony, while Caleb waited slightly off stage. The music began. When I drifted forward, watching Caleb preen down below, I realized something I never understood until right then about Juliet.

She was a liar—the worst kind. Every shy smile and innocent glance were a silent plea only she could understand. *Feel something! You're in love!*

Romeo was just a scapegoat. Anyone would have sufficed as a buffer against the crippling feelings of shame that welled up whenever she tried to decipher her true feelings…

Like the fact that she knew that Romeo's uncle was watching the balcony proceedings from a hidden perch, searching for any crack in her façade. Daring her to reveal the truth.

You're in love…

When she hurried down the balcony steps to meet her lover in the dead of night, it was a last-ditch effort to convince herself that the discreet touches and the breathless moments meant *something*. Maybe that she didn't *need* destruction to feel alive. That she didn't crave the vicious rise and fall—that reckless high and the desolate crash that followed.

Only, the longer she danced, the harder the lies were to believe. Every pirouette unraveled the pretty picture she'd struggled to paint until she became desperate.

Give me something, she silently pleaded with every featherlight spin into Romeo's embrace. *Give me something. Give me something. Let this be real. Make this real.*

But he couldn't. And there came the painful moment when she was left panting on stage, realizing that her life *was* a stage. The audience was fooled, but she was the one forgetting the lines in an act she had never asked to be a part of.

Poor Juliet was a good liar. But she never could fool herself.

A hand fell on my shoulder, and I jumped, snapping back to the present. Caleb was closer now. We were at the very edge of stage left, already nearing the end of the variation—

right before the fated first kiss. I panted. He leaned in. I hesitated.

Caleb looked different now from those countless practice sessions. Rather than defeated and grim, his eyes were bright and I noticed their color for once—a metallic blue. Oblivious to the way I stiffened, he leaned in closer, bringing his jaw alongside mine and whispered something only I could hear.

"Let's go for it."

Juliet panicked. *No. Yes…*

There wasn't really a choice.

Romeo pulled back, meeting my gaze while I stared through him, my lips slightly parted in anticipation of his. He kissed me carefully, romantically wrapping an arm around my waist while being sure never to deepen the contact beyond just a chaste lip-touch.

That's all it was.

And, at that moment, Juliet could feel herself begin to crack. The illusion shattered. She felt nothing. And then she felt it all. A million lies crashed down around her, revealing what had always lurked beneath the fake reflection—a hulking figure with searing, black eyes, who scoffed at her pathetic attempts to make believe.

When Romeo pulled away, beaming with the hope of young love, she could only scurry back to the safety of the balcony and try to keep pretending.

CHAPTER 16

*L*ike the end of a distorted dream, Caleb and I were ushered off stage by only two words from Rebecca. "Thank you."

As the last dancers, we had nowhere left to go but the dressing rooms. I started to head toward the women's side, but Caleb surprised me with a quick, impromptu hug the moment we left the stage.

"God, you were fucking amazing!" he gushed into my shoulder, and he didn't seem to be lying for my benefit for once.

I mustered up a smile and tried to congratulate him as well, though I barely registered the words that came out of my mouth. They must have meant something, because he smiled back and walked off while I staggered into the dressing room, Then I tugged my costume off.

The air backstage had changed. Gone was the need to subtly intimidate. All that was left were furtive motions and pure exhaustion. The ones who hadn't done well avoided eye contact with anyone else and packed their belongings once and for all, while the ones who'd excelled held their heads high.

After shoving my costume back within its garment bag, I freed my hair from its ponytail and brushed it out. I managed to stall for nearly an hour. When I eventually drifted into the theater's lobby, only a janitor was left behind, already locking up for the night.

I didn't know what to expect when I started forward. For a Thursday night, traffic was relatively mild—but one car stubbornly idled alongside the curb. The headlights came to life as I crept closer, and I could make out a familiar figure seated in the driver's seat.

"Good evening," Huey greeted as I pulled the door open and settled onto the back seat.

There was no ominous detour this time. He drove straight to Buckley, and with every mile, something inside me hardened up. Froze over. Cracked. I was fractured ice by the time we finally arrived at my father's house.

"Same time tomorrow," Huey prompted.

"No." I unbuckled my seatbelt and stared down at my hands, pale even in the dark. "I won't need you to drive me tomorrow."

By then, the results of the auditions would be posted.

And I struggled to convince myself that I didn't care.

"All right, miss," Huey finally said.

The words he never spoke chased me up the driveway louder than the thunder that echoed in the distance. *I'll have to tell Revend.*

I opened the door to an ear-splitting sound. My first thought was that my step-sister was throwing another one of her temper tantrums. Then red lights blinked a few feet away—the alarm.

Shit.

I lunged for the console and typed in a series of numbers. The sound cut off a second later—but it was too late. The hall light flipped on, illuminating my father's silhouette at the top of the stairs.

"Anya?" he called out. "Do you have any idea what time it is?" He descended the steps two at a time and glared at me from the bottom one. His hair was tousled, and the blue robe thrown over his plain pajamas alluded to the fact that he had been in bed.

"S-sorry." I closed the door and flicked the lock one-handed.

"Sorry?" His eyes flashed. Upstairs, a Taylor whine was followed by a woman's muttered curse. "You might be twenty, Anya, but if you're going to live under my roof, you will respect the rules of this house."

Rules.

I bit it a nasty retort back and settled for groveling instead. "I'm sorry. Studying ran late…and then we went shopping after."

"Hmph. *Shopping,* huh?" He was implying something, but the suspicion left his gaze once he finally noticed the garment bag slung over my arm.

"Yeah," I insisted.

"What time did you leave?" he grunted. "We thought you were already in bed."

Already in bed. The statement twisted something inside me. I'd spent the night in Revend's hotel room. I hadn't been home in nearly two days. At the back of my mind, I had placated myself with some halfhearted lie that I would call and explain. But I hadn't.

And no one had noticed. Even worse, deep down…a part of me had known they never would.

"You were watching a movie," I croaked, blurting out the first lie I thought of. "Didn't you see me? I told you I was leaving."

"Oh?" Something that might have been guilt briefly crossed his expression. "I probably didn't hear you."

You never do. "That's okay." I shrugged and held the garment bag up so that he could clearly see the outfit inside it. "Do you like it? It's a sweater for class. A little plain, but I think it suits me."

The violet satin caught the light as his gaze brushed over it once. "It's nice, honey."

"Do you like the color?" I prodded with an irrational recklessness I couldn't fathom. After all, the first rule of lying was to know when to stop. *Stop, Anya.* "Yellow's in this season. It's a little short, though. Probably too thick."

"Lovely," he said, but his eyes were on the portrait of Carrie, Taylor, and himself that hung in the center of the hallway. "Suits your eyes."

"Yeah...I thought so too." I couldn't swallow past a sudden lump that threatened to choke me. *Focus, Anya. Just get upstairs.* "S-sorry for waking you."

He grumbled a reply I barely heard as I followed him up the steps with the costume tucked carefully over my arm. "Did you see the letter?" he asked before returning to his room. "Carrie put it on your dresser. It came while you were out running."

"Oh... Thanks."

I laid the costume over my bed when I entered my bedroom. Sure enough, there was an envelope on my dresser. It wasn't from Revend—and that realization sent equal mixtures of relief and anxiety shooting through me.

Instead, the return address scrawled in the left-hand corner was for one Victor Remsky.

Inside was a refund for a month's worth of prepaid lessons and scribbled on a piece of paper nestled amongst the bills was a simple message. *I have always believed in you, Anya.*

My fingers trembled as I crumbled the note and threw it away. Without bothering to count it, I shoved the money into my bag and then peeled my warm-up sweats off. Wearing nothing more than a bra and underwear, I climbed into bed and curled up beneath the duvet.

But I didn't sleep.

*M*orning came in bits and pieces, fighting back the shadows that had claimed the edges of my room. When it finally lightened, the sky was just a churning sea of gray beyond a sheet of frosted glass, too damn exhausted to even settle on a color.

Not that I had room to talk; I was just a ghost trapped within the shell of the person I used to be. Or at least who I *pretended* to be. Today, someone new gazed out from behind those blue eyes, daring me to describe her. Sad? Empty? Defeated?

I didn't know. She didn't offer up any answers as she dragged a brush through her hair and pulled a pair of gray sweats on. When she finally crept downstairs, the house was silent apart from the wind howling beyond the walls, and no one was there to identify her when she entered the kitchen.

Get a hold of yourself, Anya. I tried. After rummaging through the fridge for a carton of yogurt, I ate it woodenly, tasting nothing. I washed it down with water from the tap and tried to settle on a course of action. The Roria was officially out of the running. I would have to crawl back to Remsky, find a new instructor willing to take on a twenty-year-old student past her prime or...

Reenroll in school? Get a "real" job? Be all of those things I pretended to be?

A clear course of action hadn't formed in my mind by the time someone finally descended the stairs as tendrils of sunlight broke through the cloud cover.

"You're up early," my father tossed over his shoulder as he padded to the sink, bundled in his navy robe. "Do you have class today?"

It was Saturday.

"No," I said, swirling my spoon around the lukewarm remains of my yogurt. "Day off."

"It's nearing the end of the semester, isn't it? Just think," Dad mused while pouring himself a glass of water from the tap. He took a sip and then glanced at me over his shoulder, smiling for once. "In a few years, you'll graduate with a degree. You'll have a head start. Settle down into a career."

In other words, end up just like him with the perfect family. The perfect life. The perfect daughter who spouted off perfect, little lies.

"I'm sorry about last night," I said rather than respond to his fantasy.

"Just try to be more considerate. Carrie's trying to get Taylor on a schedule."

"I'm sorry."

"Don't let it happen again." He downed the rest of his water before setting the glass aside. "By the way, Jake came by looking for you the other day, though I guess you met up with him later to go shopping."

"Jake?" I struggled to master my trademark "Anya" expression. Perfect smile. Empty eyes. But the corner of my mouth wavered. I blinked too much. "He never mentioned it… Did he say what he wanted?"

"He said he had tried texting you?" There was a more probing question hidden beneath the obvious one. *Why aren't you answering your phone, Anya?*

"I lost my cell," I lied, dodging it.

If he found that suspicious, he didn't say so out loud. Instead, he crossed his arms and faced me while leaning against the counter. "What's going on with you two anyway?"

"Going on?" My fingers shook around my spoon, knocking the yogurt carton over. A few drops spilled onto the countertop, painting it a garish pink. "What do you mean?"

"I mean…have you two talked at all about a future after you graduate?"

A *future*. Marriage. Children. Family. The topics that made my skin itch and my throat close up.

"W-Why would we?" I stammered, forgetting the ruse I'd spent six months living. *Don't break character now.* "I mean…we might not even make it that far."

"Why not?" Dad challenged. "He's good for you."

"Good for me." I stared at a messy glob of yogurt, mulling the irony over. Just how had he reached that conclusion when I didn't even know what I wanted? Father's intuition, I guessed. "He's good for me," I echoed. Saying it out loud didn't help the statement sink in.

Jake was good…but *his* touch didn't linger over my skin the same way something rougher did. Something dangerous. Wrong.

"You okay, Anya?"

"F-fine." My heart racing, I stood up and swiped my hand across the counter to clean up as much yogurt as I could. Then I tossed the empty carton into the trash and headed for the back door while compiling a lie on the fly. "I'm going for a run."

"Anya, wait…"

I turned and found him watching me, his eyes narrowed and focused. It terrified me, that look. For once, he seemed to be staring directly at me.

"You know that I'm proud of you, don't you?"

Proud. That stupid word cut into me, slicing open old wounds that I knew deep down would never heal.

But the show must go on.

"Yes," I rasped, wrenching the sliding glass door open. "I know."

CHAPTER 17

I ran like hell. As long as I did, nothing else mattered. No one could touch me—at least not until a car swerved out of nowhere and forced me off the road.

Breathless, I staggered into a row of weeds, forced to notice the neighborhood I was in for the first time—a desolate stretch of sprawling, decrepit houses on a lonely expanse of the hill. My stomach sank as I turned back to the road and studied the car frozen in my wake. Before I could make a single move, the driver lowered the passenger's side window to issue a simple command.

"Get in."

I needed to leave. This early in the morning, no one was around to witness me climbing into a random vehicle. No one who might be able to hold me back.

Was that a good thing or bad?

Feeding off my hesitation, the driver wondered, "Are you afraid to be alone with me?"

I shivered at the underlying challenge. *Are you a coward, Anya?*

Without a word, I staggered forward and wrenched the car door open. Before common sense could reel me back, I settled into the passenger's seat and slammed the door behind me. "What do you want?"

Maintaining the silence, Revend drove down the road before turning into a vacant lot riddled with weeds and random bits of litter. "Here." He switched the car off and fished something from his pocket—a slip of paper he promptly dropped onto my lap.

It took me only a few minutes to decode what had been scrawled across the page—names, numbers, and a row of lines. A judge's score sheet. Every dancer had been awarded a possible ten points from each of the four judges, with the combined total being forty. The highest score belonged, unsurprisingly, to Sarah McMahon with thirty-five points. Then Katja Sorenson with thirty-two. Then...

My fingers shook as I spread the page out over my knee. I probably read the next line a million times before it sank in. In fourth place, among the women, was one Anya DeSotto with thirty points. Overall, I took the seventh spot, a realization that made my stomach clench into knots. Was that fear? Pride? Relief?

"I made it." The words sounded hollow out loud, so I said them again and tried to settle on one of those conflicting emotions. For the first time in what felt like a lifetime, I could breathe, if only for a second. Relief it was.

"Your score would have been the highest," Revend bit out as he slowly skimmed his gaze over me before flicking it away. "However, one of the judges elected to award you zero points."

Zero? "Which one?" I figured a part of me already knew the answer.

"Me."

"W-why?" I caught myself digging my nails into the armrest of my seat. One word had never sounded so dangerous.

"So that *you,* or anyone else for that matter, cannot minimize what you achieved on your own merits."

Despite the apparent compliment, a bitter note strained his voice. Or maybe I'd imagined it. To check, I peeked out of the corner of my eye, sneaking pieces of him. Dark shirt. Darker eyes. Silvery scars that stood out in contrast from how tightly he was clenching his jaw.

Swallowing hard, I faced the windshield again. "I thought you were going to be objective."

He didn't respond.

"What did you think?" I wondered, eyeing the naked trees up ahead.

"You were convincing."

Again, I couldn't shake this irrational sense that I had missed something. The air around us crackled with electricity. I would have given anything in the world to roll the window down and relieve some of the pressure—my fingers twitched to do just that—but I couldn't seem to move.

"Convincing," I echoed instead, blankly staring at the dashboard with the same intensity that he glared at the road. "But not perfect."

"Nothing is perfect."

We sat in silence before I gathered the nerve to reach into the pocket of my sweats and withdraw what I'd shoved inside it without ever really expecting to see him. The wad of Remsky's money landed on the console between us—a heavy, solid mass of paper secured by a single rubber band. Judging from the way Revend went rigid, it might as well have been a ticking time bomb.

"Take it," I croaked while he stared ahead, barely paying the bills a passing glance. "It's enough to cover your lessons."

He didn't move, and I was the one who combusted in the end.

Tick.

Tock.

Boom.

Without waiting for him to react, I wrenched the glove compartment open. I started to shove the money inside only to freeze once my eyes fell over something nestled against the car owner's manual.

Something silver. With a round base. A trigger. A narrow point…

Revend leaned over me and shoved the compartment shut before I truly processed just what I'd seen. Then he took the money from my trembling fingers only to toss it right back onto my lap.

"Keep it," he said gruffly. "Use it to buy a dress. There's a gala tonight to introduce the hopefuls to members of the company. You will attend."

"Why?" Oddly enough. I wasn't alarmed by the fact that he had a possibly loaded weapon in the car. Everything about him was a weapon—the most lethal one being a piece of paper containing my future scribbled on a list.

A second glance revealed that the edges were crumpled. Parts of it were even stained as if he had thrown it away first then fished it out of the trash after deciding to indulge in his mistake one last time.

"If you want to succeed as a dancer, then you need to network. I will not navigate that field for you," Revend said. He almost sounded convincing—only I knew what "networking," in this case, really meant—*Hitch your wagon to someone else. My time is limited.*

Dejectedly, I curled my fingers around the money and returned it to my pocket, where the bills weighed me down like a lead ball and chain. As if in slow motion, Revend reached for the gear shift, and his fingers were inches away from it when I decided to finally take his advice and stop pretending.

"I told Huey not to pick me up."

"I know," he grunted while wrenching the car into drive.

"You told me we were done."

That made him go still, with his foot hovering over the gas pedal. Two seconds later, the engine was back in park.

"I told you…not to waste my time," he said gruffly as if that explained everything.

It didn't. Not when I had been the good one and stayed away. I hadn't chased him down just to rub his nose in the aftermath. This wasn't fair. Him…*this* wasn't fair.

"You made it very clear that our arrangement…" I fished for the right word. "I wouldn't have tried to contact you," I settled on finally, and maybe just saying that out loud made it true. "We're done."

For once, he didn't echo that sentiment. Instead, the tension ratcheted up, sucking up all of the oxygen. *Bingo.* I'd unintentionally stumbled upon the real reason why he'd hunted me down at the crack of dawn—and it had nothing to do with some stupid score sheet. Go figure.

Did he want to hammer the point home? Make it sink in?

You're a slut. I'm a lecher. We made a mistake. Get over it.

"I get it, you know," I gritted out, shifting so that the money in my pocket pressed painfully against my hip. "I get it."

He didn't say anything. Not a word as he started to put the car back into drive. Nothing…and I found myself uttering the *one* thing that I knew would knock him off-balance out of pure spite.

"We had sex. *Twice.*" And there it was. Our naughty little secret, spoken out in the open. Unavoidable.

"We fucked," he corrected.

That word stung. Jake and I had always "made love"—even if it had been five-minute quickies in the back of his truck after football practice. Revend was right; what we had done was cruder. It was fucking. I just hated him for admitting it so freely. For scarring me with the truth like deliberate figurative cigarette burns.

"We fucked…"

Without a nasty retort on hand, Revend clutched the steering wheel, his knuckles turning pale. In a heartbeat, he transformed from stone into a dangerous animal locked within an impossibly small cage. And some reckless, stupid part of me wanted to poke my fingers through the bars. *Bite me already, you bastard.*

"Correction," he growled, unable to let the subject drop, either. "You threw yourself at me. I reacted. And each time meant *nothing*."

"Nothing," I agreed through gritted teeth. I even managed to nod. "Just a *reaction*. A mistake…" But I shied away from stating the obvious. *Then why are you here?*

My fingers fluttered to the inside of my thigh as if sensing the imprint of his hand still there, aching beneath the cotton.

It meant nothing.

"I won't play this game again," Revend hissed. His voice resonated in my bones, rattling that prized posture every ballerina strived to achieve. "I warned you not to let childish emotions cloud your judgment—"

"I'm not." The denial rang out startlingly clearly. Maybe I even meant it. Maybe I could have sex with a total stranger and have it not mean anything.

Because it didn't.

"Good." He reached for the steering wheel. "Then, as you yourself have pointed out, we're done—"

The sensation of my hand falling across his forearm made him go silent. He wasn't wearing a jacket despite how cold it was outside. My fingertips greedily flexed against the cotton of his gray shirt, sensing the strength coiled in the muscle underneath. *Feel me, Anya. Let go, Anya.*

I was sure he'd pull away. He didn't, and touching him somehow made it easier to finger the zipper of my jacket with my free hand and wrench it down. Chilly air tickled the flesh bared beneath the V-neckline of the T-shirt I was wearing. The cotton was so old—damn near see-through— that I was sure Revend had gotten an eyeful of what lay underneath before he finally shrugged me off so violently that my shoulder slammed into the passenger's side door.

"What the hell are you doing?" he demanded.

What was I doing?

I didn't respond right away. I *couldn't*. Not with him sitting there, pretending that he wasn't hungrily eyeing the contours of my body through the thin fabric. Somehow, that made it so much easier to wrench both arms from my jacket and toss it aside.

"Anya, stop it." His voice was a whip, but he never took his hands off the steering wheel to stop me himself. He never actually looked in my direction. I think he just interpreted the sound of my clothing striking the floor of the car to discern what was happening.

The click of my bra being undone. The hiss of my sweatpants sliding down my legs. My underwear next.

"If it doesn't mean anything, then prove it," I panted finally, kicking my panties off —though I didn't recognize the sound of my voice anymore.

A stranger was in my place, rising out of her seat, well aware of the fact that she was putting on a show for anyone who might pass by. Any potential Peeping Tom might as well have been in another universe. My focus was solely on Revend and the way his gaze traced the length of me while he tried to pretend like it wasn't.

"*Fuck* me again," I dared, my voice catching in my throat. "It should be easy, right? Just another notch in the belt, no strings attached."

God, more than anything, I wanted him to push me away. Shove me back into my seat. Throw me from the car. *Anything* but hold my gaze with an unwavering one of his own, daring me to close the space between us. *You won't.*

I *did*, hissing through my teeth as his warmth seeped into my skin. It was a precarious trip over the console to reach him. My right knee grazed his hip before I managed to balance it against the driver's side door while the other became wedged within a cup holder. Unsteady, I had to brace one hand against his shoulder to keep my balance, and it was like measuring the seismic activity of a volcano right before the eruption. He was so damn hard. So hot. Alive. Sweat gathered between my legs as his hand caught my inner thigh before I could lose my balance. Almost reluctantly, he pulled me closer, pinning my body between his and the steering wheel.

We didn't say a word as I settled against him, fitting easily on his lap despite the size difference. For once, I had the height advantage. I carefully traced the stubble on his jaw with my gaze while my hand drifted between us and began to tug on the zipper of his pants. Two pulls were all it took before the metal unraveled on its own. His lips twitched as if he might protest. Then, at the last minute, he shifted, allowing me to slide my fingers through his fly.

We exhaled in unison as solid flesh came alive beneath my fingertips. My thumb traced the outline of him first, and he reacted to me in a heartbeat, hardening even more until he strained against the partially undone zipper. Another hesitant brush and *pop!* The zipper head disappeared within the gap between the denim, freeing him completely.

One of my nails strayed to graze the sensitive tip, and a sigh tore from his lips, scorching my neck. *Harder.* I obeyed, squeezing until my knuckles popped and corded muscle strained the flesh along his neck. I wished that the contact would have made me feel dirty. I wished that this ache in my stomach hadn't tightened in response to the way he twitched against my palm.

I wished that I could have pulled away.

Instead, there was this painful moment of silence while I coaxed the head of his erection free and watched it strain toward me, already weeping tiny white beads of arousal. I blushed, my cheeks on fire, but I didn't know what made me slide my finger over one, gently smearing it over the smooth head of his cock. Carefully…carefully painting him with the evidence of his own lies.

In retaliation, his nails dug farther into my inner thigh, impatient. Demanding. *Now.*

Trembling, I held myself above him, hunched against the roof of the car and supported by my knees while he remained unmoving beneath me. Our gazes drifted, sneaking glimpses of each other without ever making contact. Tan skin. Dark eyes. Salt-and-pepper stubble.

I wondered how he saw me. Did I still look empty now?

Exhaling in a rush, I lowered myself onto him just as another crack of thunder rumbled in the distance. The moment he entered me, my head fell back, my eyelids fluttering. It wasn't like before. I controlled the pace, allowing him to stretch me deliberately slowly, slowly, slowly. The intoxicating rush swept through me, leaving me dizzy, and I slipped, taking him farther than I meant to.

A gasp broke loose at the way he stretched me. Tighter than the fit of a pointe shoe. *Perfect*, filling me up and overflowing through the tiny cracks I'd spent years trying to mask with lies and smiles. Another thrust and the cracks spread, splintering what little sanity I had left.

Good riddance.

I would have rather died than stop. Even though it was harder to move this way. Harder to pretend that there was any real space between us as my bare breasts met his chest and my nose settled in the crook of his shoulder, inhaling him with every frantic breath.

This means nothing, Anya.

Nothing.

Nothing!

So, why are you already close?

I squeezed my eyes shut as I rocked in an unsteady rhythm, unable to silence the moan that broke free as he started to meet each thrust. Too hard. Too *deep*.

When I slowed in a desperate attempt to regain control, Revend bucked, jolting my body into the steering wheel and blaring the horn. The sound made me jump—or maybe it was just the pain as nails succeeded in piercing the skin of my upper thigh, holding me in place as he began to thrust again. Faster. Amid the slide of flesh over flesh, a low sound teased the air, too guttural to be thunder. From the corner of my eye, I saw one of his hands fumble in the gap between the seat and the car door. A second later, the back of the chair lowered, pitching me forward.

Weightless, I flattened both hands against his bulk, scrambling for purchase, while his heartbeat hammered against my rib cage as if trying to communicate with mine alongside every stroke. *Can you feel me, Anya? Now?* One thrust later, he yanked out my hair tie, and the strands fell forward, hanging down between us.

Feel.

He let me pretend to hold the reins for one more sloppy thrust before taking hold of my waist and wrenching me along his length. First all the way in, and then nearly all of the way out. Then deeper. Deeper. Harder.

I clutched the back of the headrest, shaking and slick with sweat as his stubble scraped the side of my jaw. Every breath he took forced my chest to contract. In, out. Out. Out. *Out.*

I didn't know who initiated it, but somehow, his mouth was on mine. Easily, his tongue slipped between my lips, mimicking the part of him invading my body thrust after thrust. He nipped. I bit back harder. It was…too much. Too fast.

The only way to save myself was to push away and arch my back against the steering wheel. When my eyes opened, he was already looking up, forcing eye contact even while I hadn't been aware. Dark, his gaze held me captive as he invaded me in every possible way. He was in my body. In my head. Watching unashamed as I continued to crack into a million little pieces.

This means nothing.

My body was just a tool to sate his lust, pressed up against the steering wheel for leverage—and it was so much better this way. Impersonal. Indifferent. Gasping for air, I closed my eyes, waiting for the inevitable.

You can do this. Be nothing.

And I *could* have until two of his fingers found me above where we were joined.

"W-wait!" I tried to push his hand away, stiffening at the unfamiliar sensation of a heavy thumb maneuvering through my folds.

He retaliated by finding that part of me boys always snickered at when mentioned during anatomy. *Clit.* He caught the bundle of nerves beneath his thumb, rubbing. Stroking. Detonating.

My back bowed as my body jerked like a marionette on taut strings. In two seconds, I understood why stimulation of that ball of nerves was so damn vital.

With a harsh intimacy, he set me on fire. Made the car, the hard curve of the steering wheel pressing against my lower back, and the cold glass beneath my fingertips—everything —disintegrate. All of it was ashes crumbling around my flailing fingers, which were desperate to hold on to *something.*

His shoulders served that purpose. I held tight as my hips undulated, meeting each thrust with a frantic one of my own. His thumb was still flicking. The heat became all-consuming. Somewhere, miles away, the horn blared three more times, each one punctuated by a moan and a million unspoken connotations.

This.

Means.

Nothing.

Rain came down hard against the windshield as he pulled out of me, replacing his length with two fingers that were an insufficient substitute—not that it mattered. I was climaxing anyway. When the first wail broke from my throat, he stiffened, his erection twitching against my inner thigh. A heartbeat later, he forced himself back in, ripping a gasp from my throat.

It was too much.

I think…I could have survived being used.

I couldn't survive being *fucked* again.

I heard myself cry out again as my body clenched around him, thoughts dissipating while instinct took over. Then we were crashing and falling and trying to pretend that we could ever assemble ourselves again.

One second passed.

Two.

He was still pulsing inside me when I scrambled from his lap and snatched my clothes from the foot of the passenger's seat. With an urgency honed from years of quick dressing room changes, I pulled my sweats on, yanked my shirt on backward, shoved both feet into my sneakers, and pushed the car door open.

Rain struck my hair and glued loose strands to my forehead as I leaped out onto the damp earth. My knees were jelly, threatening to give out, and I clung to the hood of the car just to stay upright. Even then, I could still feel him inside me.

This means nothing.

The rain fell harder. A few yards away, a woman was walking her dog beneath the shield of a purple polka dot umbrella.

What had she seen?

What had she heard?

Why didn't I care?

The moment I found my breath again, I ran. Without looking back, I cut across the road and around the back of a decrepit, blue Victorian. Then I took the back way home.

I was shaking when I reached my father's house. Carrie and Taylor were gone, for once. *Went grocery shopping!* read the note stuck to the front of the fridge.

For all their indifference toward me, I didn't know how to be in that house alone. Wind lashed at the windows as rain smattered the glass. The walls tauntingly echoed every step I took, but the sound couldn't even drown the thoughts in my head out.

It didn't mean anything, Anya.

Nothing.

Nothing.

The words outlasted the rush of the shower spray and seeped through the terrycloth of the towel I dried myself off with.

In the end, desperation to hear *something* else made me dig my cell phone from my bag and dial one of the three numbers programmed into the contacts.

"Hello!" the voice on the other end chirped.

"Mom?" I rasped, my grip over the cell shaking. "It's Anya… Do you want to take me shopping?"

CHAPTER 18

Ten minutes before seven someone rang the doorbell and footsteps approached my room.

"Anya?" Dad knocked once before pulling my door open to stick his head through the gap. "There's someone here to see you." His tone was eerily level, containing the million other things he seemed unwilling to say.

Someone male.

An older male, Anya.

Someone who isn't Jake.

"He's one of my professors," I lied to the ceiling. "History of Dance."

"Oh." He frowned, trying to process the information. Was I lying? Why would I be? "Well…he's waiting for you outside."

After he'd closed the door, I padded over to my closet, where two dresses hung on either side of the double doors —both of which my mother had convinced me to buy with Revend's money. According to her logic, *"You need at least two options!"*

The first was a frilly, innocent pink sporting a matronly neckline, something a good, wholesome, hopeful ballerina might wear to impress a room full of executives. The other was a dark ruby red. Formed of silk, it was tailored close to the body and cut dangerously short. Something that same ballerina might have worn…

Never.

My fingers shook as I eased the fabric off the hanger and held it up against my body. Like always, my reflection taunted me. *Are you insane, Anya?* The red clashed with the paleness of my skin. It was painfully apparent that I didn't have much to fill out the low bust line with. If I wore a bra, the material would peek through instead. Not to mention that girls like me weren't sexy—we were disciplined. Positive.

And maybe picturing my therapist's reaction was what made me finally strip my clothes off and tug the ruby dress up over my hips.

I took my time, not wasting any effort on makeup to disguise the shadows underneath my eyes or the pallor of my skin. Instead, I piled my hair on top of my head and zipped the back of my dress using the mirror as a guide.

Before leaving my room, I paused only to slip on an old pair of black heels and a necklace.

My fingers trembled as I secured the clasp around my throat and the gaudy pendant settled against my collarbone. It was a silver heart-shaped charm Jake had gotten me for our sixth-month anniversary, one of those obnoxious ones with our initials engraved on the front. I had tried to return it after our breakup to no avail, but I didn't know why I slipped it on *now*, wielding the piece of metal like invincible armor. The untouchable Anya, guarded by an impenetrable heart.

When I finally descended the stairs, Carrie, Taylor, and my father were in the living room, laughing at a program on the television. I doubted they even noticed when I slipped through the front door and closed it behind me.

Overhead, the sky churned black with the threat of yet another storm. Like a storm cloud itself, Revend's car lurked in the driveway, right behind Carrie's minivan, and my heart picked up speed as I approached the passenger's side. My fingers grazed the handle—hesitating for a split second —before I finally climbed inside.

The weight of his presence hit me like a punch to the stomach. It didn't help any that the interior smelled like peppermint…and something else that mingled with the sharp scent of cleaner. Him. Me. Sex. I could picture him meticulously scrubbing away each droplet of sweat…of lust. But we were ingrained within the leather, and no amount of bleach would erase this last mistake.

He didn't greet me as I settled into the seat beside him. I didn't speak, either. Only the sound of tires crunching over gravel broke the silence as the car reversed out of the driveway.

Once again, the unspoken cues clearly spelled out what words never could. The way his nostrils flared in the semidarkness, catching my scent even as he glared in the opposite direction. The way my heart thumped when I noticed my green hair tie peeking out of a cup holder.

We were resolute in our deliberate attempts to ignore each other, and with every passing second, his nearness weighed me down further. I suffocated beneath every inch of muscle. His fingers clenched my nerves, rather than the steering wheel, twisting, manipulating until I was squirming in my seat, desperate for relief.

Oppressive, the tension lasted until we reached an elegant hotel only a few minutes outside of Buckley. The lights of a brilliant plaza threatened to blind me as Revend navigated a circular driveway before finally parking near a waiting valet.

"Wait five minutes," he grunted and then climbed out, snatching his cane from the back seat.

He lumbered toward the entrance while I unbuckled my seat belt. Unsteady on my heels, I could only linger in his wake like something unwanted tossed off the back of a cargo ship, left to eventually drift to the shore.

The icy air caressed my exposed skin. I hadn't brought my jacket, and the fabric of my dress was tissue-paper thin—

but the funny thing was…

I didn't *feel* cold. In fact, I couldn't feel anything at all.

Five minutes.

It felt like an eternity had passed by the time I entered a spacious lobby decorated with white marble and paneled walls. Jazz blared through unseen speakers, creating a deceptively soothing atmosphere that contrasted with the voice still echoing through my thoughts. *"Five minutes."*

"Good evening!" a beaming receptionist greeted me from behind a modern-style desk. "Can I help you, miss?"

I could only shake my head. The location of the gala wasn't hard to pinpoint anyway. A ballroom on the left was already brimming with elegantly dressed guests milling about, sampling wine from crystal flutes. *Welcome to the Roria* had been printed in flowing script on a banner propped on an easel near the entrance. One step over the threshold and I froze.

Seeing the makeup of the Roria in bits and pieces was one thing—but viewing it all spread out, composed of very real people in charge of a very real company, made it sink in. Revend might have taken pity on me, but it was comparable to a king taking pity on a pauper. Only an idiot would look the other way. Only an idiot would fuck it up.

This is your last chance, Anya. Focus on what matters.

I tried to. But the moment I took another step forward and caught sight of Revend from across the room, I forgot myself. He stood amongst a group of well-dressed men and women who I assumed were other key players in the company. Like a perfectly chiseled puzzle piece, he fit within the elegant scenery and didn't look my way once, reinforcing what he'd said that morning—*Network. Find someone new to take on your baggage. I'm done with you.*

I was invisible within a sea of unfamiliar faces and swishing silk, wearing a dress that rode up my thighs with every step. This unshakeable urge to do *something* itched at the back of my mind. When a waiter brushed past me carrying glasses of champagne balanced on a tray, I snatched one and hurried off before anyone could bring up the question of ID.

I downed the liquid in two seconds, barely registering the fact that I had never actually tasted alcohol before—apart from sampling my mother's wine back when she used to drag me along with her to fancy soirées. The brief rush of dizziness paired with the pride of feeling "mature" was nothing compared to this. *Desperation.* Right then, I almost understood why my mother preferred drinking to facing her problems. Maybe it should have been my poison of choice as well.

Two glasses later, my thoughts were fuzzy, and Revend Marcus was just a blur among many smeared faces and smudge-like suits. With his presence obscured, it was easier to focus on the supposed reason he had brought me there in the first place. *Network, Anya.* Squaring my shoulders, I set my empty glass on a nearby table and drifted around the edges of the ballroom, trying to pretend that I fit in.

Somewhere.

Maybe the alcove in the corner crowded with willowy figures who might have been dancers? Or the group of potential executives Rebecca was chatting to, looking at ease for once? Behind a nearby potted plant?

It was a futile search. Everywhere I went, I could still feel his eyes on the back of my neck—only, when I turned to look, he wasn't ever facing in my direction. We were in two different worlds. Two completely different universes, both connected only by a dirty little secret.

"You…you came."

I spun around and almost didn't recognize the man who'd greeted me until he spoke again.

"I…um, glad to see you."

"C-Caleb?"

His expression threw me off. Maybe because he wasn't even trying to smile for once. Shock made his eyes seem bluer than normal. I guessed I wasn't the only one surprised by my sudden luck.

"I wanted to invite you," he added, flashing a quick grin that didn't reach his eyes. "But I didn't get your number. Congratulations, by the way."

"Um, thanks. You too." It wasn't that hard to assume that he had made it to the next part of the auditions as well, though I felt a pinch of guilt anyway. I'd been so wrapped up in myself that I hadn't even bothered to check Revend's score sheet for his marks. Maybe that explained the awkward way he kept eyeing me as if waiting for something. A compliment? I tried my best to smile and improvise on the fly. "You deserve it."

Apparently, I'd missed the mark, because his strained grin faded.

"Thanks… Um, do you want to dance?" He gestured to the semi-crowded dance floor.

For the first time, I noticed the other hopeful dancers mingling with members of the Roria. Sarah. Mark. Near the corner of the ballroom, Katja was dressed to kill in an emerald-green gown. It shouldn't have, but the sight of her almost made me wish I'd chosen the frilly, pink dress instead. She was a beautiful peacock, effortlessly attracting attention, and I was just a wayward pigeon.

"Anya?" Caleb repeated, sounding miles away. "Want to dance?"

"S-sure," I stammered, but he was already leading me onto the dance floor.

I flinched as his hand slid around my waist, pulling me in closer—not that he noticed. He was his normal self again, too busy chattering on about the Roria, the *pas de deux*, and the next auditions. Distracted, I just nodded along while absently scanning the room.

Every few seconds, my gaze would stray to the same distant corner—to that same figure leaning heavily on a cane, his face expressionless. I wasn't the only one drawn to him.

There was something about the mysterious Revend Marcus that made everyone instinctively hover a few inches back, even as they continued to circle his position like flies. He was that damn magnetic. That untouchable.

"You okay?"

I glanced up at Caleb.

"F-fine."

"You're thinking about *him*, aren't you?"

My heart sank to the bottom of my heels while simultaneously picking up speed. Was it that damn obvious? "Who?"

"Him." He nodded to my throat.

I blankly followed his gaze, catching sight of silver. *Oh.* Jake's necklace. I'd almost forgotten that I had it on.

"Whoever gave you that," Caleb clarified while I fingered the delicate chain and considered ripping it off. "I'm assuming *he* was the reason why you struggled during rehearsals, huh?"

I shook my head and let my hand fall. "No…it's not like that—"

"Let me guess," he said, a playful tilt to his mouth. "At first, he wasn't happy with you dancing with another guy, but once he gave his permission"—again, he nodded to the stupid pendant—"you were able to kick ass."

I swallowed hard and flinched at the word choice. "No. It wasn't like that at all."

"Ha. Just ignore me, then," Caleb said with an apologetic shrug.

We danced for a moment longer before he nodded behind me and flashed a mischievous grin.

"Should we insinuate ourselves?"

I glanced over my shoulder and immediately wished I hadn't. Whether intentionally or not, Caleb had brought us closer to the group containing Revend. Unsurprisingly, Katja had already pounced on the most powerful figures in the room. She was the center of attention, laughing at something one of the other men had said, her head thrown back to display her pale throat. I wasn't sure if I was relieved or not to find Revend beside her, staring stoically at a wristwatch, his jaw clenched.

"Hello." Reaching around me, Caleb shook the hand of the nearest figure—an older man I recognized from the first round of auditions. "I'm Caleb Martin."

"Simon," the man replied, though I barely heard him.

My brain was too busy replaying a single image—*groping hands, sweat, moans.* It was only when Caleb nudged my shoulder that I realized the man had started to speak again and was smiling warmly at me. I struggled to smile back. Polite introductions went around, and one by one, the other executives spoke up.

"How are you?"

"Wonderful performance."

"Congratulations," greeted a familiar voice, cutting through the drone.

I blinked, and it took me a second to recognize the smiling man from the auditions.

"Nice meeting you, Anya. Good luck." He winked at me before drifting off to mingle around the rest of the room. In his wake followed a hulking figure who used a cane for balance and didn't even bother to introduce himself.

I didn't know how long I stood there, staring after him, before someone asked me to dance. Then I found myself waltzing with a man who complimented my audition performance, his face a blur of indistinguishable features. Broad smile. Cloying cologne. Shifting eyes that kept gazing at my dress's plunging neckline.

"So, what made you apply to dance for the Roria?" he wondered in a voice tinged with a lilting British accent.

I shrugged and struggled to muster a smile while the truth slithered across my mind. *A stranger forced me to.* "I've always wanted to travel to Europe," I blurted out loud. "And I would love to dance for such a renowned company."

For some reason, the man laughed, but the expression didn't reach his eyes at all. Instead, they drifted around the edges of the room as if searching for something…or someone. A second later, he leaned closer and used the pretense of tucking a piece of hair behind my ear to whisper, "Then you, my dear, have never actually heard of the Roria. Have you?"

Ice encased me from head to toe. I fumbled and nearly stepped on the stranger's foot. "W-what do you mean?" I felt like someone who'd taken a test only to realize they'd studied from the wrong book.

"I didn't mean to catch you off guard." The man smiled warmly. "I just meant… Tell me," he began, changing the subject. "Have you ever heard of the *Cygne Noir*?"

My knowledge of the French language extended to a vague idea of how to ask for cheese with my bread. So I shook my head. "No, I haven't."

"You will," the man declared with a certainty that made me shiver. "Especially if you continue to perform well. And… heed my words, miss. When the *Cygne* comes calling, it's better not to refuse—"

"May I cut in?"

That voice sank through my skin, resonating in my bones. A familiar heat prickled the back of my neck in warning. *Don't turn around.*

"Of course." Just as another song began, my current dance partner let me go and stood back, shooting me a wink. "If there is anyone you should meet, it is *this* man."

I knew instinctively that the newer hand over my shoulder wasn't like the others. It was too hard. Too hot. Already slick with sweat, I turned to face him as my hands traveled up to a pair of strong shoulders, sensing the coiled muscle underneath.

The man before me was stone, holding me rigidly. Reluctantly. A fringe of dark hair cast shadows over a sternly clenched jaw and a set of scars that glowed silver in the light of a nearby chandelier.

"I'm networking," I found myself blurting out when he didn't speak first.

If anything, his expression hardened as he forced me to step left. "So you are."

He woodenly steered me across the room while I staggered to keep up. It was funny how I only realized just how off-balance I really was when he was there, taunting me with unyielding strength and corrosive heat. A giggle broke loose before I could help it. So damn funny.

"You're drunk." The tone was a sobering blow. Within a heartbeat, his gaze was on my face, dark with disapproval. "Are you really that foolish?" The words he didn't say were even more scolding. *Unprofessional. Stupid. Desperate.*

"I-I'm not." To prove it, I took a step closer to him, straightening my spine. My feet moved clumsily, trying to match his steady pace. *One, two three. One, two three.*

In a way, ballroom dancing was so much simpler than ballet —yet twice as complicated at the same time. Allowing a partner to contort my body through numerous spins and lifts was one thing. But this...

I glanced at my feet, watching them struggle to match step with his. Struggle not to be crushed underneath his. Struggle not to trip.

"Keep your chin up," he scolded, seemingly unable to resist correcting my posture even outside of the rehearsal room.

I obeyed and held my breath while I scanned his jaw, searching for a crack. A twitch. Something to prove that my nearness affected him the same way his affected me.

I *was* affected. His scent filled me. My heart sped up to the rhythm of the music—to find any rhythm at all. And I almost craved the steady pulse of the count tapped out by an instructor's cane. That certainty of always knowing what came next. *One and two…three…*

"Well, are you?"

The fingers on my waist tightened their grip, straining the satin.

"What?"

"You said you were networking." He made it sound like an accusation.

"Yes."

"With who?" He skeptically raised an eyebrow. "Have you met Coleman, yet? Andronick Bellakov? Simon Guilles?"

The names struck me like blows, each one phrased like the questions on a pop quiz. *Are you doing your duty, Anya? Network. Sell yourself. I'm done with you.*

"I've met enough," I retorted.

He scoffed, his eyes darkening. "I'm sure you have."

"What is that supposed to mean?"

"Tell me," he began near my ear, his gruff tone contrasting with the sweet musical notes. "Who will you pick to be your next mentor?"

He cast a knowing glance at my cleavage, and my cheeks caught fire at the innuendo. *Who will you fuck next, Anya?*

I wrenched away from him, self-consciously tugging at the stupid hem of my dress. Someone coughed nearby. We were in the middle of the room, frozen solid amid a sea of swaying bodies. He stood too close. My face was red. A few confused looks were cast our way, threatening to shatter the illusion he'd set into motion by making me arrive after him.

"Goodnight, Mr. Marcus. It was nice meeting you," I croaked. Then I turned on my heel as my heart surged with the need to escape. *Run. Run. Run.*

His hand fell over my shoulder before I could even go a step. "Wait."

In a blur of shadow, he barreled between a waiter and an elderly couple, dragging me by my wrist out of the ballroom. Fighting to keep up, I registered the scenery of the lobby passing by in bits and pieces—white marble, gleaming glass. I assumed he'd head straight for the main doors—and shove me through them—but he changed direction at the last minute and dragged me down a deserted hallway.

"Where are we going?" I blurted out only to be pulled into a small room with a couch at one end and a row of magazines on a glass coffee table nearby.

Without a word, Revend followed me inside while I staggered forward to catch my balance.

"I'm not, you know," I said, transfixed by our reflection in a glass window that overlooked the dark streets outside.

He stood behind me, my unwavering shadow always lurking just out of reach.

"I'm not drunk." I wasn't—and that was the sad part.

Nearly painful sobriety made it easier to notice every inch of him. The scent wafting from his body, flooding my senses. The dark eyes impassively watching as I stood before him in a too-short dress with a neckline that displayed way too much.

I *wished* I were drunk.

"Do you enjoy sabotaging yourself?" Revend wondered, his voice harsh with derision, his black gaze hovering over my throat.

I was too busy swaying on my feet to wonder what I'd done wrong. "I'm not trying to."

"Really?" His gaze raked my reflection up and down before settling on my cleavage, communicating what even he was too tactful to say out loud.

"Simon seemed pretty nice," I said without really understanding why.

Revend's jaw clenched. His eyes flashed an unholy shade of black.

"Though that is why you brought me here, isn't it?" I asked. "So that I could find another mentor?"

"Simon has a weakness for *desperate* young girls," Revend replied coldly. "Why am I not surprised? At least, with you in that dress, he knows what to expect."

Anger coursed blindingly hot through my system—melting my brain along with any common sense.

"What? Too classy?" I croaked, hating the way my voice broke. "Yeah, that's right. We both know that you would prefer me to take it *off*." I shoved my hand down at my side, viciously snatching a handful of fabric. Before he could react, I wrenched it up, revealing the bare skin of my thigh, my hip, and the black panties underneath.

Maybe I wasn't so sober after all.

"Stop it." Surging forward, he caught my hand, keeping it from traveling any higher. But he didn't lower it, either.

Instead, my fingers remained trapped within his, pressed against my thigh. His breath set my shoulder on fire, his body heavy against my back. Oppressive.

This way, he had an even more intimate glimpse of just what the dressed showed off. So did the woman who walked past the window, bundled in a pretty pink coat. Her dark hair was coiled in a bun that grazed her neck as she glanced at the cell phone in her hand while her other was raised toward the street, beckoning a cab.

She almost looked like me. That perfect, collected person I used to be, eager to catch a ride home so she could bond with her parents over some crappy movie. The bright girl with an even brighter future and a loving boyfriend to text.

Not the train wreck who craved something...*someone* utterly wrong.

"Tell me to go away," I heard myself croak to the specter lurking behind me, almost pleading. "Tell me I'm a hopeless dancer. That I'm ugly. That you hate me. That I'm s-stupid —" My voice cracked.

The perfect not-Anya was still scanning the road, taunting me with all the things I would never be again.

"Tell me that it all meant nothing. That you aren't aroused right now. That you don't... Tell me you don't want me."

Revend said nothing.

Yards away, Not-Anya was smiling, unconcerned by the wind whipping strands of her hair from its neat coil. A stream of cars sped past, no cab in sight, but she didn't seem bothered. She didn't even seem aware of the two strangers watching her aptly from behind a sheet of glass.

My right hand was numb, still clenching a fistful of my dress. Revend's larger one still clasped it, keeping my fingers in place. His breath struck my earlobe. I didn't know how it happened, but suddenly *his* hands were creeping toward my inner thigh and then tugging my panties aside to slide underneath.

A broken sound tore from my lips, my breath fogging the glass and the sight of a glaring yellow cab that slowed before the woman on the street. My insides twisted, struggling to register the sensation brushing between my legs, slipping through the moisture already gathered there. Revend grunted, and my cheeks flamed as if my body's reaction to him were some terrible secret he'd just uncovered.

An old man gets you hot, Anya, a part of me hissed, throwing the crude language in my face. *Wet.*

I didn't even care. I *couldn't*, not when every inch of me felt heavy. My heart. My head. Even irrational parts of me were weighted down by his touch. That spot between my legs. My breasts. Heavy fingers drifted up my torso to cup the right one. I gasped, my back arching, as a million nerves seemed to gather in that one damn spot—and he seemed determined to stimulate every single one. Breathless, I panted against the glass, frozen in place as he shoved his hand entirely beneath the low neckline, cupping me fully. *This is wrong, Anya.*

My heart was in his palm, pulsing madly with every harsh stroke. Overwhelmed, I squeezed my eyes shut, blocking out the sight of my own face, my mouth open, my dress hiked up like I was some scandalous slut while Not-Anya sped off into oblivion. By then, he'd already slipped a finger inside me, and I couldn't feel anything but fire. He kept the penetration shallow as if aware of the ache that still lingered from that morning. My hips undulated anyway, chasing his touch, desperate for it in a way I had never been for anything else. Then his thumb caught my nipple, tugged, and I was gone.

Revend was a drug unto himself—only the high came too fast. Too high. And the crash...

It would desolate me.

"Spread your legs."

I almost didn't recognize the sound of his voice, bitten out on the back of my neck. When I didn't move quickly enough, he maneuvered me closer to the window himself and removed his hand from inside me to grasp my hips. My backside hit the front of his hips. Then I could hear his pants being undone, settling around his legs. A second later, he was dragging my panties down, and I was powerless to stop him.

"Look at me."

I obediently opened my eyes, meeting his gaze in the reflection spread over the glass. Dark power clashed within the irises. Beautiful. Dangerous. Like the eye of the storm about to obliterate me and there was nothing I could do but let myself be consumed. Then he grunted, guiding his erection between my legs while lifting my skirt, and I was lost to the sensation. Him. Me. Ice-cold glass. The knowledge that any other poor, innocent passerby could look right in and see me pinned and vulnerable.

He never broke eye contact, drilling into me physically and figuratively, and somehow, we managed not to make a single sound other than the slap of flesh on flesh—and even that was too damn loud.

I didn't know if it was the noise alone that drew someone to our distant corner, but passing footsteps slowed near the entrance of the room what felt like a million years later.

"Hello?" a woman called out, her voice laced with a drunken giggle. "Anyone in here?"

My entire body tensed as the unfamiliar voice cut through the inferno swamping me. Revend smothered a groan against my ear as the reaction pulled him deeper inside me. *Stay still.* His fingers were in my hair, his mouth against the back of my throat, but somehow, he managed to choke out a coherent response when I was far beyond words.

"I am."

"Oh, sorry!"

The stranger skipped off, and I was suffocating, trying to smother my moans against the glass. It was a bit like trying to trap a forest fire with your bare hands. Painful. Impossible. Hot.

Revend grunted again, and I felt his body stiffen on the verge of pulling out—the responsible thing to do. But something selfish and greedy made me buck against him before he could, and he finally came undone with a guttural sound that caught in his chest like the rev of a motorcycle engine.

Only God knew how he managed to hold me upright. Seconds later, he was the first one to pull away before we caught our breath, shoving himself back into his pants.

"I hope you've made your connections," he gritted out between clenched teeth, while I still clung to the window for balance.

Did that just happen? Could it have happened again?

Only belatedly did I realize what he'd said. "W-what?"

"Don't worry about cutting me loose," he added, adjusting his crisp suit jacket. "I've gotten my fill, and you've gotten what you've wanted. This was mutual. You never fooled me."

His fill?

"What... What are you talking about?" My cheek struck the glass, my eyes shutting against the sight of my own reflection. I looked so damn hungry even as he withdrew. Desperate. *Slut,* a part of me hissed.

"My driver will take you home," Revend added, his voice cutting through the shame. "You deserve that much."

Deserve? I opened my eyes and found him glowering, his face so damn expressionless that it made him seem hollow.

"What are you talking about?" I asked.

"Victor may have been one of your toys, but I've dealt enough with girls like you to know that it isn't worth the risk. Find another old fool to toy with."

Old fool. Toy. Girls like me. I pushed away from the glass, swaying on my feet, my panties still bunched around my ankles. "What the hell are you talking about?"

His gaze narrowed, cutting me down to nothing. "Drop the innocent act." He reached out and flicked the pendant dangling from my throat with the pad of his thumb. "You may have fooled *him* as well, but make no mistake. I've had my fun, and you're all but guaranteed a spot in the Roria. We're done."

He turned for the door, but I was still stuck somewhere in the middle of the conversation, too lost to ever catch up.

"W-what... I don't... What..."

"The final audition is next Friday," he said over me. "Show up or not. I don't care. Goodnight, Ms. DeSotto."

Then he was gone, and I could only stare at the doorway, still waiting for answers.

CHAPTER 19

Three days later, I stayed curled in bed as the day went on around me, too exhausted to move.

Think.

Care.

It was Monday, and I was still reliving *Friday*. Not the words, ironically enough—just the feeling, this bitter ache in the pit of my chest that wasn't quite painful but still there, nonetheless, pinching that delicate area between my heart and my spine. Maybe it even had a name.

Revend's vicious lies.

Revend's stupid ball of shame.

Revend.

I tried to tell myself that nothing he'd said mattered, but some part of me would scoff and betray that reassurance as a lie. Since the day I'd met him, for whatever reason, his words had *always* mattered in some way or the other.

Only he could break through my armor and pick at the holes that I'd thought had been patched up long ago. Only he could have me second-guessing every movement as if he'd turned my life into a giant faulty stage. Only he could make me feel so out of control.

Aren't you tired of it yet? Anna Pavlova wondered from her perch on the back of the door. *Aren't you tired? You know how easy it is to feel numb again,* she taunted. *You can make it all go away...*

A sudden knock rattled the door, causing the poster to sway, and Anna fell silent again.

"Anya?" Without waiting for a response, the door opened, and my father's head appeared in the gap.

In an instant, I knew that something was wrong. His hair looked mussed as if he'd spent the morning running his fingers through it. Dark circles lined his eyes, and apprehension swelled in my gut as his gaze met mine. Cold. Blue. Partially narrowed. The expression mirrored the razor edge in his voice.

"Can you come downstairs? We...we need to talk."

Talk.

"Huh?" I sat upright, clutching my thin, blue comforter for balance. "A-about what?"

His tone took me back nearly three years ago when he had uttered those words with that same quiet intensity. *We need to talk, Anya. We know, Anya. You have a problem, Anya.*

It could have been a coincidence. Regardless, my heart pounded, kicking up speed until I could barely hear the words he tossed at me next.

"Five minutes."

I had no choice but to scramble out from underneath my duvet and throw a sweatshirt on. *You're being paranoid,* I assured myself while I racked my mind for a clue—any slip in my façade these past three days.

I was positive there hadn't been any.

Despite Revend's accusations, I had stayed true to my routine. The fake smiles. The Sunday luncheon. The pretty, perfect clothes.

I'd played my part through all of it, never breaking character even while his words festered inside me. Fingers shaking, I reached up to feel my hair, as if the wayward curls slipping from my ponytail were the equivalent of parts of me breaking loose. *Again.* Had my mask cracked without my noticing? I was too terrified to creep into my bathroom to check.

Go talk, Anya, my poster of Anna Pavlova goaded, her mouth still split in that mocking smile. *Go lie.*

I was shivering by the time I finally gathered the nerve to head downstairs and into the kitchen. My father was standing at the center island, and Carrie was beside him. She was wearing a floral print sundress, her arms crossed over the lacy neckline like she was a beautiful princess enforcing the law of her dutiful general wearing his matching sweater set.

"It's time to tell us the truth," my father began, his gaze sweeping over my unkempt hair, my baggy sweats, and my sallow skin. "Tell me the truth. You're using again. Aren't you?"

By some miracle, I kept from laughing out loud. I'd always hated that stupid word. *Using.* It sounded so dirty. So selfish. Especially when paired with the simple fact that I had never used the pills.

They had *used* me.

"Answer me, Anya."

His tone battered the amusement down. He was serious; this wasn't a drill. *Mayday.*

I stared him in the eye and uttered the truth for the first time in six months. "N-no."

Only to have him laugh in my face.

"Are we really going through this again?" Disappointment laced his tone. *Tsk. Tsk.* His pretty, porcelain doll had fallen again. "Really, Anya?"

Carrie shook her head, blonde curls flying. *Really?*

"Where…where is this coming from?" I managed to rasp, squaring my shoulders. *You're in control, Anya.*

"I called the university," Dad explained, bracing both hands on top of the counter.

My heart stopped beating, leaving a deafening silence that made each word seem ten times louder. *Oh no.*

"I was proud of how hard you were working. I wanted to surprise you," he said. "So imagine my surprise when I learned that the only student by the name of Anya DeSotto had withdrawn six months ago."

Gritting my teeth, I stared at the floor and frantically counted each tile like the beat of some insanely complicated variation. *One, three, five, ten.* "It's not what you think—"

"Then where is the money, Anya?" A sharp sound echoed as if he'd slammed both hands down at once. *Thwack!* "That two grand that I give you at the start of every 'semester'? Where has it all gone?"

I opened my mouth, but the truth wouldn't come out. *Ballet.* The word had been tainted by Revend. In the end, I could only choke out, "It's not what you think."

"What I think?"

I glanced up just as he threw something I hadn't realized he'd been holding onto the counter. The envelope opened, spilling crisp, colored squares all over the marble.

"What the hell am I supposed to *think*, Anya?" he shouted, throwing his hands up. "If you needed the money, you should have fucking asked for it!" His voice shook, his face red. "If you needed the money, all you had to do was ask. You didn't have to—"

"Have to what?" This was about more than lying. More than the money and the fake classes.

Anxiety welled within me like unshed blood, but I never could have been prepared for the moment I crept closer to the counter and finally noticed what had been scattered over it.

Pictures.

There were four of them, a black car visible beyond a row of weeds. Two of the photos only revealed a blurry image of the figures who might have been inside the vehicle—but one was crystal clear—a woman straddling a hulking male figure. Only her profile was visible, but it was obvious that she wasn't wearing a top. Her black hair was unbound, and something about the shape of her face seemed eerily familiar.

Her nose resembled mine. Our heights were similar. Too similar.

All at once, the world crumbled under me, and I was left clinging to the counter, unable to breathe. I nudged the stack of photos with my fingers, causing them to scatter. Hidden among them was a note containing one neatly penned sentence.

Do you know what your daughter is doing?

My mind ran with the statement, twisting it. *Doing. Do you know what your daughter is doing? Who she's doing? What are you doing, Anya?*

Only God knew what conclusion my father and Carrie had reached—even in the photo, it was obvious that Revend was older. Bigger. Stronger. Untouchable. Then the answer came like a slap in the face. *If you needed the money, you should have fucking asked for it.*

They thought I was so desperate to get high that I'd do *anything* to use again. Maybe, in a way, I had been.

For a minute, I only saw Revend's face. That cold, callous look in his eye. *"I've dealt enough with girls like you to know that it isn't worth the risk."* Girls like me. Girls like the one in the photo. The girl sleeping with a stranger because he made her feel even more fucked up than pills ever could.

"Pack your stuff," my father spat, sounding miles away. "I already called Hope Bridge. You're checking in tonight."

Hope Bridge. The fancy rehab my mother could approve of, with its charming, cheery walls and casually dressed staff.

"Like hell I am." I didn't realize that the protest had come from me until my throat ached in its wake. By then, I had somehow managed to stand upright, leaning heavily against the counter for support.

"Oh, yes you *are*." The tone was so sharp that I rocked back on my heels as if struck. "It's either rehab, or you're out of this house. There won't be a second chance."

"I'm not seventeen anymore." It was a struggle to keep my voice level. The illusion wasn't shattered yet. The mask was clinging to my skin by a thread, and I couldn't reveal what hid underneath. *You're losing it, Anya. Just shut up.* But I couldn't. "You can't just clean me up like your dirty little mess and shove me away until some doctor with a bogus degree tells you I'm perfect again."

I had no idea where the words had come from. That venom—the inside of my mouth stung with it. Or maybe it was just the taste of my own blood? At some point in the past few minutes, I'd bitten my lip. Severed it, and the pain mingled with dregs of shock weighing me down. Suffocating me. Bit by bit, the illusion began to strain.

Crack. Crack. Crack.

Keep control, Anya. Stay in control.

"You're not seventeen, but you're still acting like a child," my father hissed. The lack of an accent was the only difference from the way Revend had said those same words, and I hated myself for noticing. Hated myself for flinching. "Face your problems for once, Anya," he snapped. "Pack your stuff, or *we* will pack it for you."

Face your problems. Coming from him, it could have been a twisted joke. I croaked out an unintelligible reply, and then I was laughing hysterically, unable to stop. The sound echoed brokenly off the walls. Tears streamed down my face, and both Dad and Carrie could only stare at me.

"'Face your problems, Anya,'" I managed to gasp out between cackles, clutching my stomach. "Like *you're* such the expert. You. Can't. Even. Look at *me*!"

Unless, of course, he was drunk and I was an available punching bag to take out his frustrations on. It started as a shove here or there. A slap or two. Always when Carrie was fast asleep. Sometimes, he told me why.

It was *my* fault Mom had left.

My fault Carrie was so stressed.

My fault…

My arms must have given out because I was face down on the counter. Shoulders heaving, I laughed and laughed while something inside me shattered, severing vital arteries and leaving me hemorrhaging emotion.

Feel, Anya! Revend had finally gotten his wish, only I didn't know what to make of it all. It was too much. Too fast, and there was no filter in sight.

Stay in control.

Control…

Fuck control.

"For twelve years, I've been invisible to you," someone mumbled, her voice high-pitched and childish. "You don't even know who I am…"

The stranger trailed off to a whisper. I doubted that anyone had even heard her apart from me. My father was speaking over her already, growling words I barely comprehended. Shouting. Threatening.

Rehab, Anya! Rehab! Someone else needs to fix you. I can't deal. Get out, get out, get out.

"Where the hell are you going?"

His words chased me up the stairs before I'd registered moving. Blindly, I staggered into my room, and for a few, desperate seconds, I could only stand there, trying to make sense of the space that had never really felt like mine. Those baby-blue cell walls. That stranger's bed with the matching duvet. That damn poster, mocking me with every breath escaping my chest.

You can turn it off, Anya, Anna reminded me. *You know you can. Such an easy way to turn it off.*

Turning away from her, I snatched my sneakers and shoved my feet into each one. Then I grabbed my bag. My jacket.

Move.

My father and Carrie were both waiting at the bottom of the stairs, their arms crossed, their expressions stern.

"This doesn't have to be a punishment, Anya," Dad insisted as I descended each step. "We love you."

Only Carrie didn't nod in agreement. Her gaze was beyond me, up the stairs, where Taylor was most likely being rudely awoken from a nap.

So this was love.

No wonder I couldn't remember having truly felt it for anyone before.

I kept moving past the bottom step, shrugging off the heavy hand that grabbed me. Hard. Bruised. Regardless, the front door opened easily, and in only three steps, I had cleared the stoop.

Then I ran.

Shouts chased me. The sound of a car door opening and closing echoed a second later. By then, I was already running, cutting through alleys.

And no one could touch me.

CHAPTER 20

That lonely bench outside of a McDonald's wasn't deserted. One sole occupant was braving the bitter cold—a man who lounged across the structure lengthwise with both feet propped on an armrest.

In my head, I'd always called him Sally Elias, though I think his real name was Ryan. Ryan Something-Italian. Ryan, the drug dealer.

I had never bothered to ask how the real Sally had known him. All I knew was that "Whatever you want, he'll get it." Two years ahead of me, the real Sally Elias had made it all look so easy. She could light up a room with one smile, even when she was hunched over in a bathroom stall, sticking the end of a toothbrush down her throat. She had been much better at the juggling act than I ever could be. According to rumors, she was starring in a New York ballet company these days, while I was standing on a street corner, back at square one.

For nearly five more minutes, I lingered on the curb, my hands stuffed into the pockets of my sweats. Slivers of sunlight kept the storm clouds at bay, though an icy wind still nipped at the skin bared above the collar of my jacket. I was shivering, but the man on the bench didn't seem affected. He was wearing only a baggy T-shirt and jeans against the elements, but judging from his body language, he might as well have been relaxing on some tropical beach. Only God knew what he was on today. Percocet? Just oxy? Cocaine? Whatever it was, I wanted some.

Anything to take me far, *far* away from here.

When he saw me—once I'd finally gathered the nerve to cross the intersection—his mouth split into a disarming smile that froze me to the core.

"No way... No fucking way." His husky voice lifted an octave, which caused a woman two blocks ahead to glance back. "The princess returns! I was wondering how long it would take. It's been about a month, huh?"

The way he looked at me made my skin crawl. Unsurprised. Gleeful.

It was funny. I'd composed some grand speech in my head to explain away why I was there. *It isn't what it looks like. It's for a friend. Not me.* In the end, I just managed to croak, "Do you have anything or not?"

My brusqueness amused him. He smiled wider, revealing two gold teeth. I could smell him even from a good three feet away. Beer. Sweat. Cigarette smoke. I tried to tell myself that it was better than peppermint.

"Step into my office," Sally Elias called, inclining his head toward a shadowy gap between two buildings.

After making sure the block was mostly deserted, I followed him, already fishing a wad of money from my pocket, my fingers slick with sweat.

You're pathetic, Anya, a disembodied voice taunted as I skirted a dumpster that reeked of old grease—though it didn't sound like me for once. An accent tainted the voice of this demon. *You're a fool.*

"All right, princess," Sally Elias began as he turned to face me. "I'll give you the welcome-back special." He withdrew a sandwich baggy of white pills from one of his grimy pockets.

Suddenly, the air in my lungs became heavy. My palms itched with anticipation, with dread. I almost didn't hear him speak.

"Ten milligrams each. Fifty for this whole batch."

Without bothering to count, I shoved the money into his hand and reached for the bag, but he pulled it out of reach at the last second.

"Uh huh. Not so fast…"

I flinched as those blue eyes raked me over from head to toe and eventually settled over my mouth. Like a snake's, his tongue slithered out to trace his bottom lip. Once. Twice.

"Don't think I forgot about last time," he warned. "Consider this a mere *delay* of the debt you owe."

Gritting my teeth, I snatched for the bag again, and he let me take it. Keeping my head held high, I turned on my heel and tried to pretend like I wasn't shaking on the inside. Like I wasn't splintering apart.

"Enjoy the high, princess," Sally Elias called out behind me. The words were spoken softly enough that no one else could overhear, but they chased me down the street regardless.

Enjoy the high.

I didn't knock. Instead, I slipped around the back of the house, feeling more like a wayward ghost than ever. In the waning twilight, the once-grand structure appeared painfully decrepit. Was that how *I* looked on the outside? Already crumbling in on myself, far too rotten to salvage?

The bitter cold snatched the air from my lungs. Frozen, the fingers of my right hand clenched a stupid sandwich baggie of pills, and I couldn't even bring myself to shove it out of sight. My body had already gone numb in anticipation of the high. I was fucking greedy for it but too scared to take the plunge.

I could only stare. From the outside looking in, the rehearsal room was a strange, cavernous space of white walls and polished marble. I could see my reflection in the mirror from there—a pale ghost, oddly expressionless as the world went on around her.

Stupid.

Pathetic.

Hopeless.

The sight of her made something hot bubble up inside my chest. Anger? Whatever it was gave me the strength to shove the pills into my pocket. Within seconds, I was already crouching down, snatching something from the ground to replace it. Something heavy. Wet. Its weight registered in my grip for barely an instant before it was hurtling through the air, connecting with a wall of glass.

Smash!

The sound was more violent than I could have ever expected. Glass went flying everywhere—jagged shards of it —threatening to serrate anything in their path. There was almost a cold beauty in it.

The echo taunted me as I shrugged my jacket off and wrapped it tight around my left arm. Clumsily, I used my shrouded elbow to knock out enough of the damaged windowpane to climb inside.

Once my feet hit the marble, I managed to stagger forward two more steps and then slumped to my knees. Before I could catch them, two drops of moisture slid down my chin and landed on the marble. One more. *Drip. Drop.* They wouldn't fucking stop falling until I was drowning in my own pain.

I couldn't bear to take out the one thing that could make it all go away. Though maybe *that* was why I'd gone there after all—to the one place and the one person who could compound my misery and justify that final trip over the edge…

Right on cue, heavy footsteps approached from the foyer, preceding the husky voice that called out, "Who's there?"

I hadn't expected the dangerous edge to his tone. The alarm. The anticipation of violence. I hadn't expected him to round the corner, either, brandishing an object that wasn't a cane.

I was riveted by a fathomless black hole encircled by a layer of glinting metal, the way his finger toyed with a trigger. Flick. Flick. In reality, he only aimed the pistol at my chest for a second before shoving it back into his pants.

"What the hell?" Furious, he swept his gaze over the shattered glass. Then over the broken window. Finally, over me, crouched amid the destruction, smearing blood all over the floor. "What have you done—"

"Why did you do it?" My voice came out thick, and the tears only fell harder. Hate melded with remnants of pain, surging hot and fierce through my skin. "Why?"

"What the hell are you talking about?" He frowned, his mouth a dark smudge on an otherwise unwavering surface.

"The pictures," I said.

He frowned again. "What—"

"Stop lying!" I shook my head, battling my own logic. He had sent the photos. Or at least paid someone to sneak around and take them. "Why would you do that?"

It took him two steps to reach me. In a blur of motion, he snatched my wrist, yanking me upright. "What," he growled, shaking me until I staggered, "are you talking about?"

"Like you don't know?" My fist connected with his chest once, twice—each time leaving a scarlet stain. "Why did you send the pictures?" Snot rolled down my face, mingling with the words. I swiped at my chin with the side of my free arm only to feel something even wetter coat my skin— metallic-scented warmth. *Blood?*

Before I could figure out from where, Revend spoke.

"What pictures?"

"Of us." *Us.*

The word seemed to trigger something, and suddenly, he looked…alive. His eyes widened. His fingers tightened their hold, pinching nerve and bone.

"In the car," I added, barely aware of the words coming out of my mouth. My attention was on his eyes, the way they flickered darker, obsidian, and then pure black. "When we…"

All at once, I was falling, curling in on myself. Revend was gone, and only the wind whipping through the broken window was there to listen to me sob brokenly, tossing the sound back at me on a violent echo. It felt like eons before the floor trembled with approaching footsteps and harsh fingers were snatching at my arm again.

"You cut yourself," a man hissed. "Let me see it."

"No." I flinched, shifting out of reach despite how my arm throbbed. I didn't even care—his touch stung worse. He was too hot. Searing.

"*Anya.*" That dangerously low octave resonated in my bones. "Give me your arm. You're bleeding—"

"Don't touch me."

Wham! He let the kit fall. I glanced up just as tweezers landed near the piano. A pair of scissors slid over near the doorway while an empty, plastic box landed open at Revend's feet.

"Clean yourself up," he snarled. "Then get the hell out."

He stalked off, disappearing through the doorway, and I couldn't move. Not even as pain belatedly began a slow creep up my elbow and then into my shoulder, threatening to shatter my numb shell piece by piece.

I didn't know how long I lay there. How long before the temperature plummeted around me and the sky turned the color of ink. How long before I managed to wrestle myself somewhat back into a shadow of who I tried to be.

It was ironic, really. A few cuts and bruises pulsed a sharp ache through my arms and my legs—but at the same time, I felt utterly numb without having swallowed a single pill.

Though that could have been because I was starting to lose all sensation in my fingers.

The fear of frostbite finally forced me to move, and I climbed unsteadily to my feet. Blood flowed through my frozen limbs like fire over ice, and I had to brace one hand against the wall just to stay upright. Blinking through the darkness, I staggered into the foyer and managed to pull the front door open.

I think I laughed out loud at the sight. On second thought, the sound could have been the wind gusting over snow that had come from nowhere to coat the walkway and continued to fall with a vengeance.

Riveted by the storm, I wavered on the threshold for way longer than I should have, still clutching the doorknob. Only an idiot would try walking home in this. As if to taunt me, a burst of icy wind threw a handful of snowflakes in my face—along with a dose of cold, hard reality. *Well, you certainly can't stay.*

Hours must have passed since I'd broken in—though I hadn't heard any movement come from inside the house since then. Maybe Revend really was a ghost after all, merely haunting the residence to torment me. The floorboards overhead squeaked, betraying the motion of footsteps.

The house was silent enough that he could have heard the door opening from above. It wasn't hard to picture him creeping toward one of the windows, making sure I left for good. Counting the seconds down, I drew a ragged breath in and weighed my options.

You can't stay, Anya.

You can't.

Don't.

In the end, I didn't know what made me close the door without crossing the threshold. Before I could regret it, I crept toward the staircase. Because I was a masochist, apparently—not even a brave one. With every single step, I hesitated.

Just leave.

Step.

Hide.

Step.

Run.

Step.

By the time I finally mounted the topmost one, it was too late to turn back. At least no one was there to block my path. Instead, a narrow hallway stretched from one end of the house to the other, encased in dark wallpaper and a few scattered windows. The only tangible light seeped out from underneath a closed door near the end of the hall—repelling me while beckoning me closer at the same time.

You can't stay…

I swallowed hard, what little remained of my pride going down as well. My heart hammered away as I approached the door, prepared to beg. Apologize. Plead?

I'd only gathered enough nerve to knock when the door flew open on its own, revealing Revend in the doorway. He was wearing that Baron coat again—though, in the semidarkness, he resembled a reaper more, stealing my breath away. When he saw me, his eyes widened, their irises ten shades darker than the shadows. An unreadable emotion flickered across his face as he took a step back, rattling the car keys dangling from his hand.

His throat jerked, but he said nothing.

I didn't, either.

The seconds ticked by like eons, both of us frozen in place. Eventually, the silence became unbearable. Without thinking through the consequences, I moved forward, slipping past him.

His heat was like a buffer between the cold emptiness of the rest of the house and what appeared to be the only sliver of life nestled inside it. The room itself was spacious, but it contained only a wooden dresser and a massive bed. A single lamp mounted on the wall cast that sole source of light, illuminating the peeling gray wallpaper.

My gaze drifted absently while I waited for Revend's reaction. Only, it never came, and I stood in the center of the room, consumed by the anticipation of what he would say. *Get the hell out?* Minutes passed, but there was no harsh admonishment—yet. No shout to leave.

It was coming. Restless, I found myself approaching the bed, distracted by a sense of morbid curiosity. The brown comforter stretched tight over the mattress, appeared to be undisturbed. Did he even sleep there?

I heard the metallic clink of his keys being set aside before I could fully explore that thought. The material crunch of his coat being shed. Then footsteps, heavy and aimless…

I sank onto the mattress, curling up on my side. *Any minute,* I told myself while I scanned the wall opposite the man guarding the doorway.

Any minute, he would kick me out.

Instead, the light shut off and steady footsteps advanced on the bed from the other side. I held my breath as the mattress squealed beneath the weight of someone heavier than I was. A harsh exhale caught the air, ruffling my hair, as someone else's body heat crept into my frozen skin—not close enough to touch.

But close enough to still burn.

I couldn't tell how much time passed before I finally fell asleep.

Morning came in a mocking burst of golden sunlight that painted my eyelids red. Groaning, I peeled them open to the view of a single window that overlooked a desolate lawn and a row of naked trees swaying in a fierce wind. A glistening blanket of snow painted everything white.

Untouchable.

I could have been Alice, deep within an unfamiliar wonderland—if it weren't for the scent filling me up with every breath. *Peppermint.*

Oh, God. Wincing, I shrugged a thick brown comforter off and shifted to the edge of a soft mattress. My arm stung, and I glanced down to find a dark-red row of three slender cuts above my elbow, all neatly sealed with clear butterfly bandages—only I didn't remember applying the first aid. Or placing my sneakers neatly on the wooden floor beside me.

I scrambled from the mattress and caught sight of my reflection in the mirror over the lone dresser.

That crazy girl—she wasn't me. Three shallow cuts marred the right side of her face as if I'd decided to mockingly recreate Revend's scars. My arms sported even more. Some were scabbed over, while others had been ripped open by movement and were bleeding shallowly. My hands were bruised. Blood stained my clothing.

I looked like the survivor of a train wreck, and the comparison had me snickering even as two beads of moisture slid from my bloodshot eyes. Anya DeSotto's crazy train had flipped the tracks a long time ago. At least I now resembled the twisted shell inside my skin.

When my reflection became unbearable to look at, I scanned the few objects placed on top of the dresser. One was an upright photograph, carefully framed. A smiling man with black hair had his arm thrown over the shoulders of a slender blonde, her hair elegantly coiled. Both figures were wearing elaborate costumes that I assumed were from a ballet. *Giselle?* The woman was wearing a thin, white gown that could have been the attire of a Willis, one of the tortured souls of scorned women who danced men to death in the second act. The man was obviously the lead male, wearing tights and a brown shirt. Written at the very bottom of the picture in neat script was *Revend and Vika.*

Vika. She made me remember the things about Revend I had chosen to forget—like the fact that he had been married. Hell, for all I knew, he still could have been. Was she one of them? His wives… Without thinking, I allowed my finger to trace the cool glass. The man in the photo didn't even look like Revend. The scars were absent. Gone was that ice-cold look in his eye. He *almost* seemed happy.

Confused, I turned my attention to a second photo frame— only this one rested facedown. A layer of dust caked my fingers as I lifted it to see the picture underneath, but the glass had been badly fractured, which obscured whatever it covered. I managed to make out the general shape of a woman's face before the back of my neck prickled with awareness.

"You're awake."

The quiet observation brought my attention to the doorway, where a hulking figure was standing just out of sight. Only the shadow stretching across the wall and the husky voice that incited something in my skin alluded to his presence. Bits of glass scattered as the picture slipped from my fingers and landed face down once again.

The sound of retreating footsteps was my only clue to follow, but when I finally crept out into the darkened hallway, it already seemed deserted. In two seconds, the sunlight had faded, replaced by a grayish overcast that threw wispy shadows over the walls.

My feet were numb in their socks. My breath painted the air white. I couldn't seem to stop shivering and had to hold the banister for balance as I tiptoed down the staircase. Up ahead, the square of plywood over the foyer window taunted me when paired with the closed door of the rehearsal room. Guilt churned my insides, and I couldn't keep myself from choking out, "I'm sorry."

Standing in the opposite doorway, Revend didn't say anything. He just moved woodenly through the archway, devoid of his cane for support. My heart hammered as I descended the final three steps of the staircase and followed him into a large room with a lit fireplace at one end. At one point, it might have been a rather elegant sitting room, only it now contained just a few obscure pieces of furniture. A chaise. A sofa. A few mismatched wooden chairs decorated in faded upholstery.

And Revend…

"I'm sorry," I blurted at his back again. "I don't know what I was thinking."

Silence. With all the grace of a living shadow, he grabbed a poker from the mantel and stoked the flames with brutal jabs.

"I'll pay for the damages," I found myself adding.

"How?" He tossed the word over his shoulder, daring me to come up with a logical reply.

"I'll find a way."

His expression revealed what he was too tactful to say out loud. *So you really are a slut. A lying slut. You accepted my charity and threw it away—even though I will never call it charity.*

"My parents kicked me out," I said before he could say as much out loud. "We had some stupid fight. I just need a place to…lie low…just for a while…"

What was I really asking? I didn't even know.

Revend frowned. "You can't stay here."

"I know that," I said quickly. My lips were so damn dry. I licked them, but they scraped at my tongue like broken glass. "But...I could just crash somewhere. I'd stay out of the way—"

"No." In a ripple of fluid muscle, he approached me from across the room and snatched something from his pocket. "You're not going anywhere until you stop lying to me."

I could only stare at the crumpled sandwich baggy of pills clutched in his fist. They looked so dangerous then. So fucking pathetic.

"I haven't taken any," I insisted, holding both hands up like the hostage in a robbery. *Not even one, honest.* But there was more to it, and the seconds passed in silence until I finally admitted the rest. "Yet..."

Revend's expression hardened.

"My parents want to send me to rehab," I blurted out. "They think I'm using again—"

"Are you?" He sounded so damn in control.

I hated him. Envied him.

Sucking in air, I met his gaze and forced myself to hold it. "No." One second passed as it seemed to ring true. Then four. Ten. "I'm not."

With a sound of disgust, he clenched the pills before letting them fall to the faded carpet. "Then explain why the hell you were carrying these."

"Yesterday was the first time in over a year that I even touched them."

"You're lying."

I was. My mouth opened, but in the end, I could only manage a whispered version of the truth. "I haven't touched them…but I've always had a stash hidden close by."

How pathetic was I? Daddy's little princess, sneaking pills right under his nose, hidden safely within his perfect dollhouse.

Revend's eyes flashed as he processed that. "Where?"

"M-my friend Anna has them," I said without bothering to elaborate.

Unsatisfied, he shook his head again, ruthlessly tearing a hand through his hair. "Give me one good reason why I shouldn't call the police."

Police. There was plenty he could have me charged with. Breaking and entering. Assault. Drug possession. The potential consequences crossed my mind, and the more serious they became, the less I cared.

"Call them," I croaked, turning on my heel and staggering for the doorway.

He let me toe the threshold before yanking me back by my shoulder. "Oh, no, you don't," he grunted while I stumbled back toward the center of the room. "You're going to—"

"What?" My voice was too loud. It echoed off the walls, reverberating in my fragile skin. *What are you going to do, Anya?* "You wanted me to feel," I snapped, though I wasn't sure if I was even talking to him anymore. "I'm *feeling* now. Are you happy? I've always felt everything…"

The room was spinning. Memories were drifting on the periphery of my consciousness, threatening to overwhelm me, and my chest heaved with the effort it took to push them out. Regain control. Forget. Ignore. Lie…

It was a family trait, after all. Lying. Ignoring. Denying. My parents had put the *sue* in suicide, using litigation to dish out blame as far as they could spread it. They'd tried to blame the school for my "mental collapse." The teachers. The grueling, demanding schedule of professional ballet.

Anyone but them.

Everyone but me.

You're using again, Anya. Aren't you?

"What are you doing?"

I barely heard Revend above a violent sound that exploded throughout the room seconds later. Another stone crashing through the window? I couldn't understand why I didn't care. Why my hands were stinging.

"Anya!"

The shout snapped me back to reality just in time to register the fact that I was shoving something across the room, heedless of the man standing in my way. A wooden chair toppled over halfway to the fireplace, and one of the legs broke off and rolled across the Persian carpet.

What are you doing, Anya? my father's voice demanded. *You've ruined everything.*

"Shut up!" Screaming, I kicked the wall, ignoring the pain that shot through my foot.

It wasn't enough to distract. It wasn't enough to push the memories away. It wasn't enough to keep me from cracking.

Perfect, Anya. Be perfect.

Pretty.

Smiling.

Happy.

Normal.

Sane.

Good. Bad. Feel this. Don't. Stop. Run. Scream. BREAK. CRY.

"Anya! Stop it!"

Those hands grabbed me again and spun me around…

And then I was suffocating. Revend was everywhere. His arms caged me in. His body was a stone slab pinning me to the wall. I couldn't breathe. I didn't *need* to. He held me up when my knees buckled. Didn't react when my forehead met his chest and my hands fisted in his shirt, shielding my face with the cotton.

He didn't flinch when I started to cry.

And he let me.

CHAPTER 21

$\mathcal{I}$ was semi-sane again by noon, having carefully assembled the crumbled pieces of me with masking tape and glue. Revend watched me from the sole surviving chair opposite the faded blue couch I was sitting on, and he waited in silence until the very last shard of Anya was gently shoved back into place.

The moment it was, he stood. "Get your shoes." Without giving me the chance to respond, he headed for the door.

I sat for a few seconds longer before heading upstairs to grab my sneakers and my coat. When I returned to the foyer, Revend was already there, holding his car keys in one hand. He inclined his head to the front door and then pulled it open while I descended the steps.

Instantly, a gust of icy wind snatched at my hair, numbing my cheeks. The snow had stopped falling, but everything left behind was coated beneath inches of crystalline white. Or *almost* everything. Sometime in the aftermath, someone had shoveled a path to the curb, where a black car waited alongside a road covered in slush.

Without a word, I followed Revend to the vehicle and climbed inside while he started the engine. I would have expected to find the town sleeping, slumbering beneath the blanket of snow—but everything was almost painfully alive. People were everywhere, shoveling, driving, racing, standing, *staring*. They saw me. They saw the man I was with. They assumed; they ignored; they struggled to put the pieces together.

I tried not to care and just focused on the road instead. It wasn't long before I recognized the path he was taking, and I wasn't surprised by the destination—a gaudy McMansion at the center of an upscale development. My stomach curled into knots, but it took me seconds to realize that both my father's and Carrie's cars were gone from the driveway. In all, the house seemed deserted.

Good.

The moment Revend put the car in park, I couldn't scramble out fast enough. The desperation to put distance between myself and the man behind the steering wheel outweighed any lingering shame I might have felt. For all I knew, staff from Hope Bridge could have been lurking inside, readying to stage an intervention, and I would have gladly let them take me away.

My fingers shook as I fished my keys from the pocket of my jacket and somehow managed to maneuver one into the door. It opened to silence—the alarm wasn't on, but there was no sound of the television blaring, either. The oppressive emptiness nearly pushed me right back out again; only something heavy was there to bar my path.

Someone.

"Where is your room?"

I sucked in air as a deep baritone reverberated down my spine. "Upstairs."

The hallway, with its bright-blue paint and neatly hung portraits, almost seemed like a stranger's. I was a trespasser, absent from every single one of the framed family photos featuring a perfect smiling family. If Revend noticed that fact, he didn't say anything during the trek up to my bedroom.

There was a note taped to my door. *Anya, we aren't mad. When you've calmed down, we can talk. Love, Dad and Carrie.*

I snatched at it, leaving a trail of clear masking tape against the wood, which I didn't bother peeling away. When I started to shove the note into my pocket, Revend surprised me by tugging it out of my hands. I watched him scan the neatly printed words. Then he folded it and slipped it into a breast pocket that must have been concealed inside the lining of his coat.

"Open the door."

My fingers trembled as I gripped the doorknob and twisted it open. His presence inside the house was disruptive, shattering the illusion that I might have lived there. My once modest bedroom had become a cell with baby-blue walls, minimalistic furniture, and a pile of shopping bags gathered in the corners. The only object I recognized as my own was the poster of Anna on the back of my door, smiling at me as I crept to the center of the room.

Revend followed me in, taking in everything with a hardened expression. "Do you have a satchel?"

Assuming he meant a suitcase, I crouched and dragged an old duffel from underneath my bed. Wordlessly, he took it and approached my dresser. My cheeks flamed as he opened a drawer containing a plain array of lace and cotton underwear.

I tried to take the duffel from him. "I can do it—"

He shrugged me off. "If you have anything else you'll need, I suggest you get it now."

Dizzy, I staggered into the bathroom and fished my toiletries from under the counter. The whole time, my own reflection taunted me. Who was that empty person who looked like she might scream or cry at any second? I didn't know whether to hug her or kick her as she snatched my toothbrush from the rack near the sink and turned back into my bedroom.

In a little under five minutes, Revend managed to pack my duffel. Alarmingly full, it rested on my bed, zipped up tight. Revend himself stood near the door, fixated on the poster hanging from the back of it before he entered the hall.

I lingered and found myself inching toward my desk and the small wastepaper basket beside it. From inside it, I retrieved two pairs of beautiful pointe shoes—one black and one pink. If Revend found that odd, he didn't say anything as I followed him with the duffel slung over one shoulder. My heart hammered in my chest with every step back through the perfect house, down the perfect driveway, and into the sinister black vehicle that didn't fit into the neighborhood.

I didn't realize I'd been holding my breath until Revend finally drove away with me in the passenger's seat.

"Where are we going?"

Unsurprisingly, he didn't respond.

My duffel rested on my lap, crushing me beneath the weight of years of perfect little lies. The clothes locked behind the zipper belonged to some other girl—not me. The remnants of her life were haunting me, chasing me down every block Revend drove. For the first time, I realized that my parents might give a damn if I didn't show up two nights in a row. I wished I'd felt guilty or even cared. It was almost too damn easy to sit there as Revend wove through indistinguishable streets, eventually leaving Buckley altogether.

What felt like hours later, I jolted into awareness as the car came to a stop. Blinking, I took in a blurred landscape beyond a splattering of fallen rain that painted the windshield gray. A massive building, its windows illuminated like diamonds, loomed to my right. Something about it seemed familiar, even before a grinning valet opened my door while holding a black umbrella.

"May I take your bag, Miss?"

I felt like a robot as I stiffly climbed out of the car and followed the valet through the doors of an exclusive hotel. Revend lingered in my wake, his gaze searing the back of my throat, demanding answers I wasn't sure I could ever really give. *Why are you so crazy, Anya? Why did you have to drag me down with you? Who are you, Anya?*

I was shivering when the valet finally set my bag at my feet, and Revend's hand fell over my shoulder, sparking a million tiny embers that had no business flaring to life.

"We'll take it from here," he said as if we were two perfectly normal people checking into a hotel.

Even though one of us was wearing day-old sweats and sporting multiple cuts and bruises. The man beside her was far too big. Together, they were mismatched. Abnormal.

Revend and I both might have been good at pretending, but lying could only get us so far. I waited as he snatched my duffel from the floor and limped toward the sleek reception desk, where two neatly groomed staff members watched us warily. I suspected they were torn between calling security and swiping the pristine credit card he'd pulled out of nowhere.

Then he said the magic words and all was well. "I would like a room."

Ten minutes later, I entered a spacious suite with Revend at my heels. He pushed the door open wide enough for him to be able to toss my duffel inside. Then he stood there, taking up the doorway until I gathered the nerve to meet his gaze.

"Stay here," he told me in a tone that left no room for argument. "You disappear, and I call the police. You contact anyone who might supply you with…" He danced around the word. *Drugs.* "I will call the police. Anything you need, the concierge will supply. I'll be back tomorrow." He turned to leave, but at the last second, he tossed over his shoulder, "If you're not here…"

The door slammed in his wake—though I wasn't sure if he had closed it or I had.

Alone, I scanned the suite, taking in the expensive, plush furniture and the breathtaking view. A sudden realization hit me like a bullet to the chest—It was that same hotel near the Chirstmark. Nearly identical to *that* room.

That fact didn't make it any easier to strip my clothes off and crawl underneath the duvet in the master bedroom. Or to ignore the scent that had chased me awake. The warmth that lingered over my skin, even now. Despite racing miles away in the opposite direction, Revend was still in my head. Tearing me apart, piece by piece.

I woke up before dawn, restless and paranoid. I wasn't stupid enough to leave the hotel, but the room felt more suffocating by the hour. Desperate to *move*, I changed into a clean pair of sweats and headed out into the hall before I could talk myself out of exploring.

When I wandered into the lobby, a smiling receptionist took one look at my clothing and suggested I try out the gym. Almost too eagerly, I followed her directions to the basement of the building. Aside from a decent array of machines and equipment, there was a large, open space before a row of mirrors.

I huddled in the farthest corner and started to warm up. After days of inactivity, it was a struggle to regain my usual sense of flexibility. I worked hard anyway, stretching my feet out, warming my legs up, and practicing simple variations.

I cooled down for a bit before heading upstairs. My thoughts were on a long, hot shower as I opened the door and crossed the threshold.

The scent of peppermint caught me off guard. I froze and glanced up just as a pair of dark eyes settled over mine. A fearsome expression shifted before I could truly register it; the fire left his gaze, and his shoulders lowered a fraction of an inch. He was piecing together the clues in my appearance as to where I'd been.

"Good," he said finally, squaring his jaw. "You're already warmed up."

He jerked his head, and I entered the room, closing the door behind me. He held his cane today, though he promptly set it aside to push a chaise into a corner of the main room, clearing a space.

"First position," he commanded, nodding at the section of Persian carpet before him.

Without comment, I settled into first and obeyed his following command to transition into fifth. Eventually, he made me run through a minimized version of the *Giselle* variation. When I fumbled through a step, he shook his head for me to stop.

"You're tensing." His hand fell over my shoulder and shoved it into perfect alignment.

I think I tensed even more.

His heat burned through me, melting my resolve. It was insane how I felt more unbalanced beneath his touch than I did while en pointe. As if aware of that, Revend withdrew his hand and hid the abruptness of the motion by crossing both arms over his chest.

"Get dressed," he said, no longer looking in my direction. "I'll wait."

I couldn't enter the bedroom fast enough. Drowning beneath the rush of my pulse surging in my ears, I snatched an outfit from my bag and scurried into the bathroom. I didn't deny myself that hot shower but dressed quickly, settling my wet hair over my shoulders. It was only when I entered the main room that I realized I was wearing one of my mother's hand-chosen outfits. The black skirt and the navy blouse felt like the clothing of a dead girl, ripped right off her ghost, still ice cold.

Without a word to me, Revend rose from a leather chaise and headed out into the hallway. Only his body language warned me to follow. His shoulders were set, the muscles rigid—so sharp against his skin that I figured I might be able to cut myself if I touched him.

In silence, we took an elevator down to the main level, where he headed across the lobby and into a small café inside the hotel. He must have made a reservation because a waitress immediately stepped forward to lead us to a table at the very back of a nearly deserted dining room. Through a row of bay windows, we had a view of the rain lashing the city streets outside.

"Sit down," Revend said.

I was transfixed by the storm raging beyond the glass, but I sat on the chair across from him, unsure of what to do with my trembling hands. In the end, I shoved them under the table and tried to meet his gaze without flinching.

I failed. Twenty-four hours had hardened him up, like ice solidifying overnight. *Black* ice. You didn't know you were in trouble until you were slipping and it was already too late. You crashed. You fell. You smashed into pieces.

"Pick something to eat," he grunted and shoved a menu in my direction.

A smiling waitress approached our table, and I rattled off something from the menu without really registering just what I'd ordered. Revend requested coffee.

There was an uncomfortable moment of silence during the wait for our food when we just sat there, avoiding eye contact. Unable to avoid it anyway.

He stared me down for breathless seconds before turning his attention to the window behind my head. A heartbeat later, his gaze would return before I'd fully caught my breath.

Wash. Rinse. Repeat.

Our conversation hadn't progressed beyond four words— *"Pick something to eat"*—by the time the waitress returned to place an omelet in front of me and a mug of coffee before him.

We ate—or, in his case, drank—and I had just set aside my fork when he finally spoke.

"You mentioned pictures…"

I stalled by tucking a damp piece of hair behind my ear. Reality was threatening to descend. I only had a few seconds left to decide if I would let it crush me or at least attempt to roll out of the way.

"Did you send them?" I glanced up, and the world seemed to stop spinning as I waited for his answer. God, the anticipation shouldn't have hurt so much.

"No," he said gruffly. "I didn't."

A sigh of relief billowed out of me, ruffling the edge of my menu. Then dread began to set in, mingling with the remains of my omelet. If he hadn't sent the pictures, who had?

"Did you see anyone that day?" he asked.

I shook my head. "No." Though on second thought… "Just a woman with her dog, but I don't think she saw anything."

"A woman?" He frowned. "And no one else?"

"No one."

"Are you sure the photos were of…us?"

Unless I had straddled any other grown men in the front seat of a Rolls, my costar in the photo had been Revend. "Positive."

He cursed, raking a hand through his hair, and the reaction made something inside me clench.

"Your face wasn't clear," I added, my throat suddenly going dry. "No one will know it was you—"

"You think I'm worried about myself? You don't—" He broke off and nodded to my plate. "Are you finished?"

Without waiting for me to reply, he started to rise from his chair, but I didn't move. Instead, I braced my hands against the table, eyeing the polished surface while my thoughts raced.

"I'm sorry…for everything—"

"Don't apologize," he hissed. Abruptly, he sat back down, his gaze narrowed. "There was a delay, but the final round of auditions will begin on Monday. As long as you keep your focus…" He trailed off, but the unspoken words were obvious.

As long as you don't screw up, you have a shot.

"Don't worry about the room," he added in an undertone. "I'll take care of it."

"Why are you?" I wondered.

As he'd said himself, he didn't hand out charity, but he scoffed as if the answer were obvious. "I owe Victor a lot more than can be repaid with a broken window."

Remsky again.

"How do you know him?" I asked.

"That's none of your business." Only his tone kept the brush-off from seeming like an insult. He sounded more guarded than dismissive.

The same way I'd been when he had come too close to personal topics.

Fair enough.

"So, what happens now?"

The plan he laid out sounded neat and clean, at least in theory. I would stay in a hotel—on his dime—until Monday and then ace the next round of Roria auditions. Somehow, I would find a way to Europe without confronting my parents, the barbiturate elephant in the room, or the fact that I had had sex with the man sitting across from me more times in four days than with my last boyfriend over the entire span of our relationship.

It hurt to admit that, even to myself. On the other hand, it felt damn good. Only Revend could split me in half like this—drown me in conflicting emotions of shame and relief. Need and regret.

"We should leave," he said, reaching down to grasp his cane in his right hand.

I caught sight of two women who were watching us from across the café—those busybody types with permed, gray curls and smug expressions. They were huddled together, casting us furtive glances.

Once their whispers reached our table, it wasn't that hard to guess the topic of their conversation. Was Revend my father? Was he something more? Our ages alluded to the first scenario, but…we sat too close, even though we were on opposite sides of the table. My chair was angled toward him. My hand was alarmingly close to his. The flush in my cheeks wasn't usually found on most doting daughters.

"He's her father, obviously, Betsy!" one of the women stage-whispered. "I mean, really. She's a child."

"I don't know, Cynthia," Betsy whispered back. "I just don't know."

If Revend could hear them, his face didn't reveal it. But his jaw was clenched tighter than usual, and he reached for his cane again. "Let's go—"

I lunged from my chair, leaning across the table. I think, deep down, he knew what I would do—and maybe the fact that he didn't resist meant something.

Poor Cynthia was already listing out the possible reasons why he couldn't be more than a relative. Her words ended in a gasp when my mouth finally met Revend's.

And then the world disintegrated.

His lips were softer compared to the rest of him—soft, warm, and completely unyielding. It was like kissing a statue. A statue that exhaled as he cupped my chin in the palm of his hand to guide each motion of my mouth. A statue that didn't pull away.

He never pulled away.

For once, I was the one in complete control of the kiss. Of him. Drunk beneath the rush, I tilted my head to slide my tongue along the seam of his lips even though it was going too far. Even though he would never let me in. It was okay, though, because any minute, he'd break the contact. Any fucking minute…

In the end, I was the one who had to pull away and collapse back onto my chair or risk losing my balance altogether. Betsy and Cynthia were gone, their meals left half-eaten on their table. A waitress across the room was staring. My lips were wet. Revend was watching me.

He didn't say a word as I flicked my menu open and time slowed back to normal.

Then I said, "I think I want dessert."

The rest of the week passed in a blur. Every morning, Revend would meet me at the hotel, and we would rehearse either in the suite or the gym downstairs. According to him, the next stage of rehearsals would feature two variations from the first act of *Giselle*—a *pas de deux* and that infamous solo.

If I had been foolish enough to assume that the bruises and cuts on my limbs would make Revend go easy on me, I would have been sorely disappointed. If anything, he pushed me harder, until hours in the suite's jacuzzi bath couldn't erase the ache lingering in my muscles.

At least the physical pain was a distraction from everything else. My only tie to reality was my cell phone, which was charging in the corner of my room, flashing every now and again with the notice of text messages and missed calls. I wanted to feel guilty for not calling home to let my parents know I was safe. Sometimes, I came close to even dialing my father's number or apologizing to Mom for missing her Sunday brunch.

Then Revend would barge in and command me into first position, his cane at the ready to correct any defects in my posture. *Once,* I gathered the nerve to ask him about the broken window. The ruined chair. The dent in the wall. How I was going to pay him back. Rather than respond, he made me do so many arabesques in a row that I collapsed.

By Sunday, I knew better than to attempt to strike up a conversation with him. Instead, I was up by six, already wearing a baggy T-shirt and tight sweats. Revend was usually at the door by seven, but when eight rolled around, I wasn't worried.

At least not until ten, eleven, *noon.* By three o'clock, he still wasn't there, and I picked my cell phone up for the first time in days. When I started to thumb through the contacts, I realized I didn't know his number by heart. I had no way of contacting him.

And, for some reason, my fingers started to shake. It became harder and harder to breathe—an ordeal just to suck in air

—as a million thoughts raced through my mind. *What if he left you here? Sayonara.*

Or—*What if…he's hurt?*

I barely registered the text messages flashing across the screen—*Jake—call me. Dad—We're worried about you. Dad —Please call*—before the phone slid through my fingers and hit the carpet. Then I started to pace, my gaze on the gilded clock affixed to the wall.

Four.

Five.

Six…

It was nearly a quarter to seven by the time a stern knock finally rattled the door. I rushed to open it and found Revend standing on the other side. At the sight of him, something shot through my chest so fiercely that it stung. *Relief?*

But it took only two seconds to realize that something was wrong. His *eyes* were all wrong—the darkest hue of black I'd ever seen. Midnight. For the first time, the energy wafting from him felt cold rather than sweltering.

I shivered as he took a step closer, consuming every inch of space in the doorway and forcing me to stagger back.

"What happened?" I managed to croak.

His gaze honed in on mine, drilling right through me with every step he advanced. Once he'd cleared the threshold, he tossed his cane aside with a flick of his wrist, unconcerned by the sound it made as it rattled across the floor. By then, the distance between us had narrowed to a foot. Then an inch. Less...

The room was too small. He was too big. I was just a fly in danger of being smashed against the windowpane as he cupped my chin in his palm.

Up close, I noticed the other pieces that had fallen out of place. His bottom lip was swollen. There was a thin scratch around his right eye. It looked like someone had punched him.

Twice.

"W-what... What happened?" I asked again, trying and failing to keep my voice level.

God, he was too close. Closing me in. Pinning me against the glass. I shivered when his free hand slid behind my head, impatiently pulling me forward.

Our lips met. I tried to recoil, my heart threatening to hammer itself right out of my chest. "W-what are you—"

"This is what you want from me, isn't it?" His voice was gruff, sinking into my veins. "This is all you want."

Before I could think to push him off, he lunged, sealing his mouth over mine. His tongue easily pried my lips apart and plunged deep. Consuming me whole. His hands were tangling within my hair, pulling me in and forcing me onto the tips of my toes to maintain the contact.

Then he broke the kiss long enough to wrench my shirt over my head before his hands tugged at the waistband of my sweatpants, stripping me naked in front of an exposed window. Maybe another day, that fact might have induced the panic it should have. I tried to care…

But then my bra was hitting the floor, and his hands were there to replace it, kneading the flesh so roughly that his nails dug into my skin. It hurt. It burned. I didn't want him to stop. Something between a protest and encouragement tore from my lips.

His hands went to my waist, yanking me flush against him until I had no choice but to wrap my legs around his waist while clinging to his shoulders for stability. Then he was staggering into the master bedroom, and seconds later, I wound up on the mattress, staring breathlessly up at the ceiling.

My pants were off. My underwear was being yanked down my legs. Then Revend was crouching between them and his fingers…

God, his *fingers*.

He slid two deep inside me at once, forcing me to adjust to the intrusion. *Ow!* The word caught on a ragged whine— but before the discomfort became unbearable, he used his thumb to flick that part of me that made me see stars. One. Two. Then an entire galaxy speckled the ceiling. A heartbeat later, he spread both fingers apart, and I gasped out, my back arching. Everything felt hotter, more intense. This high was even higher. The crash was going to kill me.

I was vaguely aware of heat searing the insides of my thighs. His breath. Rushing in. Out. My only warning before he lowered his head and a rush of fire swamped me under was the creaking of the mattress. I squirmed, and his hands seized my hips, pinning me down as his tongue slid between my folds. Lapping…sucking. *God.*

Jake had tried this tactic once, and I couldn't even remember enough to compare him to Revend. There really wasn't anything *to* compare.

With Jake, I had been able to think. With Revend, there was only instinct. *Move. Feel. More.* Nothing but this hungry need to seek his touch out drove myself toward… something. Something incredible. Something deadly.

And he drew it out with every slow, hungry touch until I was making noises I'd never known I was capable of.

I couldn't…take…any more.

Desperate, I made the mistake of glancing down, seeking out any hint of mercy from him. His eyes were already focused on me, so fathomlessly dark. His gaze bored deeper than his searching fingers, stealing bits of me away and shattering them all like glass. With every hungry arch of my hips against his fingers, his arm jerked, straining the corded muscle. One of his hands had slipped beneath the open fly of his pants to palm the considerable bulge straining against the fabric.

God, God, God! My head fell back, my hands fisting in the sheets. My mouth opened, but I couldn't hear the sound that came out. I was too far away. Too busy falling in on myself, trying to put the pieces back together before I hit the ground.

One second.

Two…

The first thing I was aware of again was the sound of air rasping in and out of my chest. Then the mattress shifting beneath someone else's weight, followed by a different kind of heat along my inner thighs and the sound of something crinkling. Paper? Or…foil, I realized when I looked up. Revend was holding a small square of it to his mouth and tore at the corner with his teeth. It was only when he withdrew the coiled slip of rubber between his forefinger and his thumb that I realized what it was. Transfixed, I watched him slowly slip it on over his distended length. So damn slowly.

My legs were already spreading apart—it was as if my body had a mind of its own. I was powerless against this unbearable need to feel him everywhere. Inside and out. Then he was hovering above me, his mouth finding my lips as his body settled against mine and then invaded me in a single thrust.

Fire ignited in my core, building in intensity. We were closer than ever, yet the thin sheath of rubber created a distance that separated us even as we came together.

Again and again.

There was nothing left of me. Nothing left of him, just pieces shattering on top of an expensive duvet while a storm raged on around us, lashing at the windows.

Eventually, I put the pieces together and faced the obvious. Revend didn't breathe like this—heavy and erratic. He didn't move like this, either—hungry, vicious, greedy.

The man catching his breath beside me was a stranger without the perfect crystalline exterior. Something had cracked the outer shell. Pieces of him were spilling out, sweeping me away in the aftermath.

But that was all of this was. Aftermath.

"What happened?" I gazed at the ceiling, counting the tiles. I couldn't look at him. It was so much easier to face the fact that I had been used while staring at those neat squares of plaster, perfectly in place. *One. Two. Three.*

The mattress dipped, and from the corner of my eye, I could see him stand and tie the used condom off. After tossing it in the trash, he began the trek around the room in search of his clothes. A few items he tossed onto the mattress—a pair of pink panties, black pants. The last thing he grabbed was a white shirt, which he slipped over his head.

Piece by piece, he struggled to reassemble himself, and the more collected he became, the more unsteady I felt. It was like he was stealing my oxygen. I inhaled nothing and exhaled parts of myself until a million bits of Anya were floating around the room and Revend was oblivious to them all.

"What happened?" I tried one last time, my voice barely above a whisper.

He didn't say a word before he left the room, but when his shadow finally disappeared down the hallway, I thought I heard someone grunt, "Be at the theater tomorrow. This is your last chance."

ACT 3

It was almost ironic that the Christmark looked the same as it had nearly a week ago. Grand. Imposing. Mocking. It felt like the burgundy walls were taunting me—*you will never be a part of this*—as I hurried into the main studio only to find that I was the first one there.

In silence, I changed into my leotard and began to warm up in front of the mirror anyway, flexing my arms and my legs. I didn't know how much time had passed before the first dancers trickled in—not that I really noticed. Not that I saw anyone apart from my own reflection, struggling to keep up with an imaginary count. *Arabesque. Turn. Pirouette. Again.*

I didn't really understand why I stopped midturn, still balanced on pointe. Or what exactly forced me to glance over my shoulder and find someone staring me down from the center of the room, their eyes an endless black.

"First position," Revend commanded as casually as if we were standing back in the suite.

I glanced around the room, but I didn't see Rebecca or any of the other dancers who had assisted her previously. Just him wielding his cane.

"Take your place at the barre," he snapped when I didn't move fast enough.

Six other dancers were already neatly lined up at the opposite end of the room, though. My heart pounded as I raced over and took the spot at the end of the row, which just so happened to be behind Katja. Today, at least, she seemed to ignore me in favor of settling her perfectly pointed feet against the floor.

"Grand plié," Revend called from across the room.

I copied everyone else and sank low, but my gaze didn't leave him for a second. He was wearing a gray shirt paired with a darker pair of slacks. His hair was mussed, but the unkempt look made his scars stand out in stark contrast. They glowed as he paced the length of the barre, observing every dancer in his wake.

"We will start with a warm-up," he said after passing the last dancer in the row—me. "Then we will run through the final audition piece. It will be—"

"One of us is missing," someone called out from the front of the line. *Caleb?*

Whoever they were, they received a fierce glare from Revend. Though, after glancing around, I realized they were right—one of us *was* missing after all. A quick scan of the line revealed that Sarah McMahon's head of red hair was absent.

"We will run through the final audition piece," Revend continued as if he hadn't been interrupted. "A variation more commonly referred to as 'Giselle's madness.' First position."

It was the hardest rehearsal yet. Where Rebecca had been stern but patient, Revend was anything but. He scolded. He shouted. He slammed his cane against the floor, demanding harder, faster, more. However, he came short of hitting people with it—a punishment only reserved for me, it seemed.

Never, not once, did he even look at me again. It was like I wasn't even there. Like the past few days had never even happened. Once again, I was invisible amongst stronger, more graceful dancers, and in his own subtle way, Revend didn't let me forget it.

This is your last chance, Anya. His voice taunted me with every step and every harsh intake of air I took. *Don't waste my time.*

Eventually, he made everyone form two lines—one male, one female—and perform part of the variation from the first act.

"Good," he grunted as Katja flounced before him, all smiles and charm.

Even I had to admit that her every motion was flawless, displaying poise, emotion. But knowing that didn't make it any easier to ignore that word. *Good.*

I never would have thought that praise existed in Revend's vocabulary. When my turn came, he didn't offer any encouragement. In fact, I'd barely performed the first round of footwork before his cane was striking the floor near my feet, throwing me off-center.

"Again! Watch your face!"

Somehow, I managed to keep moving. Spinning. Turning.

"Your face!" Another strike against the floor. "Enough! Next dancer."

I barely managed to jump out of the way before Claire McDaniels, an elegant brunette, pirouetted across the floor. Revend watched her every motion like a hawk, observing her perfectly placed arms as they twirled in the air.

"Good," he said when she finally finished.

My feet were aching by the time he called the rehearsal off. I had to cling to the barre for balance and gulp for air while staring at my insubstantial shadow. *Get a hold of yourself, Anya.*

"Change," someone growled into my ear, their stubble scratching the side of my throat. "Then wait for me at the hotel."

I turned, but he was already marching across the room, using his cane for support. I waited until the other dancers had trickled out before I entered the dressing room and quickly changed. Darkness had descended by the time I left the theater, painting the sky black. A bitter wind tinged the air, and I huddled within my jacket as I began the trek back to the hotel.

It felt like an eternity before I approached the door of the suite. It flew open before I could even pull the keycard from my bag.

"Get in," Revend prompted with a jerk of his head.

The tension coiled in his body set every nerve in mine on edge. Taking a step over the threshold felt like jumping into the cage of a lion. An angry lion swatting its paw at whoever dared to make eye contact.

However, when my gaze did meet Revend's, I didn't find any anger—but something much worse. The worst part was that I couldn't quite name it before he turned away and stormed over to the row of windows that overlooked the city.

"Put on your pointe shoes," he ordered from over his shoulder.

I hesitated only for a second before fishing the black slippers from my bag. Then I laced them on and warily crept toward the center of the room.

"Warm up," he said next in a guttural tone that resonated in my bones.

I moved anyway, shrugging the fear off in favor of reciting those familiar steps. *Prance. Prance. Arabesque.*

"Again," he commanded before I'd even finished the final movement. "And, this time, drop the act."

I froze on the toes of my left foot. "What do you mean?"

"Show me what you showed me the other night." He turned to face me then, his eyes honing in on mine. "Show me *passion.*"

Passion. That dangerous word conjured up memories of the other day. I couldn't breathe. I couldn't think. And then, the next thing I knew, heavy footsteps were circling my position.

"You know how to move." The words preceded the warm fingers that settled over my clavicle, electrocuting me. "You know how to feel, and you seem to have no trouble portraying emotion."

I assumed he was referring to my demolition of his house.

"Stop thinking, Anya." His fingers crept up the side of my throat—making that request impossible to follow—and he tilted my head so that my chin jutted into the air. "Move."

One of his hands caught my arm and guided it above my head while the other seized my waist, his fingers fanning out along my hip bone. For two seconds, I suffocated. And then I was moving, a slave to the manipulation of his fingers.

My eyes slid shut. I lost count. The series of steps ceased to matter in the face of his touch—that uncanny way he could make me forget everything else that used to be so vital when I danced.

"Giselle," he said into the nape of my neck.

With him so close, I could only do a painfully slow version. He matched me for every step. Every turn. Every twist. My skin was glistening with sweat by the time he allowed me to finish.

"Look," he said, sliding what felt like his thumb underneath my chin.

I opened my eyes, but it was nearly a full minute before my mind processed what I was seeing. He was positioned behind me, before the sheet of glass that threw our reflection back. My mouth was twisted in that unfamiliar expression. My chest heaved erratically. I was thrown by the realization that this was that window…

"Why didn't you tell me that you would direct the final rehearsals?"

"It's not important." He turned away too quickly for me to make out the expression that transformed his face—not that I couldn't fill in the blanks. Dark eyes. Stern frown. That strange, unnamed expression.

"But what about Sarah McMahon?"

Revend snatched his cane from the couch and headed to the door.

"Be there tomorrow," was the only thing he said as the door slammed behind him, and I was left standing in a pair of black slippers, searching my reflection for any hint of what the hell I'd done wrong.

CHAPTER 24

"You look dead," Revend hissed as I collapsed to the floor of the studio. "*Prematurely.*" What felt like the toe of his boot nudged my corpse, forcing me onto my side. "Next."

My cheeks heated as I climbed to my feet and took my spot at the end of the barre. Not even a heartbeat later, someone else was already prancing across the floor in the space I'd vacated, her expression flawless.

"Good," Revend grunted as Katja spun around in mad circles, picking pretend flowers as her life crumbled around her. "Utilize your expression. Good."

Even Katja excelled at playing insane. On the second day of rehearsals, it was already apparent just who, once again, was at the bottom of the pack. At least, without me weighing him down, Caleb shined. I *tried*.

I tried to "watch my expression" and "utilize my face" to embody poor, rejected Giselle. It should have been easy considering that two feet away stood a man who seemed to have no problem fucking me only to turn around and ignore me in public.

Though why wouldn't he? I was the slut in the red dress who screwed strangers for drugs—at least that was what my parents thought.

I couldn't understand why Revend hadn't called me out. Why he wasn't demanding answers to those obvious unspoken questions. Why he kept dangling the prospect of the Roria before me like a shiny, prized carrot when we both knew I would never be able to take a bite.

"You okay?" The question was followed by a playful nudge to the shoulders—which turned out not to be playful at all once I realized that everyone else had already inched up along the bar.

"Fine," I whispered back to Caleb who raised an eyebrow and looked away.

In complete silence, Revend observed the final two dancers. Then he slammed his cane down loudly enough to send ripples throughout the line. "That's enough for today. Tomorrow will be the last day to rehearse before the last audition." After that, he turned his back to us.

That was the cue for everyone else to file out without looking back. I couldn't explain what made me linger, bending down to fiddle with the laces of my slippers. Then I sensed the air shift behind me and every ounce of oxygen caught inside my chest.

"You," he said. "You will stay behind."

I exhaled. "Okay—"

"M-me?"

The other voice shattered the illusion that Revend and I had been alone. I glanced up and found Katja halfway across the floor, frozen midstep.

"Yes, *you*," Revend snapped, jerking his finger in her direction. "You." His gaze cut over to me. "You can leave."

I managed to without making a sound. When I finally regained control of my body, I was stumbling through the lobby and rushed outside into the bitter cold.

She's the real talent, a part of me whispered as I hurried down the block in the direction of the hotel. *You were just a waste of time. A distraction. As he said, he's already had his fun…*

That thought haunted me during the rest of the trek to the suite. And I waited there for what felt like an eternity before someone finally knocked on the door, demanding entry.

"Is this the part where you tell me to quit and send me back home?" I asked.

Revend pushed his way past me and tossed his cane onto the couch. "What the hell are you talking about?"

"Or is there another reason you want to keep me around?" I added, my voice catching in my throat. "Get your fun in before you send me packing—"

"I don't have time for this." He approached the couch and snatched his cane up just as quickly.

"I'm not a whore," I blurted out when he was reaching for the doorknob. "You can't just barge in, have sex with me whenever you feel like it, and then treat me like shit—"

"And why not?" he countered, turning toward me.

I flinched back. The look in his eyes seemed to freeze everything in its path. It was that ice cold.

"You seem to have no problem doing the same. You want to be treated with respect?" he wondered while advancing on my position, step by predatory step. "Then have some of it for *yourself.* Starting with all the men you seem to enjoy stringing along."

"Like who?" I didn't know how I'd managed to keep my voice steady.

He laughed as if the answer were obvious. Then he flicked the hollow of my throat with the tip of his thumb. "Humor me this once by not trying to play innocent. Who is he?"

The skin along my neck prickled, remembering the weight of Jake's pendant. "None of your business."

For a split second, I thought Revend might let me get away with that response. I'd thought wrong. A heartbeat later his body pinned mine against the nearest wall, his face inches from mine.

"I don't know how many men you're toying with, but do not mistake me for one of them—"

"Stop *saying* that." I struggled against his grip, swatting at his chest with both hands.

Unsurprisingly, he didn't budge, and I figured that the pathetic blows hurt me more than they did him.

"I do not *toy* with people."

"Tell that to the man whose token you wore," Revend countered.

"He's my boyfriend," I said, satisfied by the flicker of shock that crossed his face. "*Ex*-boyfriend."

His eyes narrowed even further as he processed that. "Oh? As of two seconds ago?"

"As of six months ago."

When I pushed him away, he let me go, and I scurried to the other side of the room, feeling as though my heart were about to explode from my chest. The truth might have proved his accusations false, but it also brought up a different line of questioning I wasn't ready to answer. Why had I worn the necklace of a supposedly ex-boyfriend?

"Why does it matter anyway?" I demanded, beating him to the punch. "You said it yourself. Mistake. Mistake. It all meant nothing."

"That doesn't mean I enjoy being taken for a fool."

"Well, congratulations," I said, crossing my arms over my chest. "The only fool is me."

This time, he didn't have a cutting reply ready.

"Can you give me any explanation for the other day?" I asked, hating the way my voice shook. "Anything?"

His jaw tightened.

I tried again. "Why isn't Rebecca directing the auditions?"

Nothing.

"Why are you?"

He headed for the door.

"What happened to Sarah McMahon?"

"What made *you* turn to cocaine?"

A pre-prepared answer slipped out by force of habit. "I don't do that anymore."

"I don't even need to look at your face to know you're lying," Revend spat. He turned around anyway, and his gaze honed in on mine. "Sarah McMahon was poached," he said bluntly. "She was offered a job by the same company that has been stealing my dancers for years. The company that drove us to recruit on the other side of the world—"

"*Cygne Noir.*" I didn't know what the hell had made me say that name.

Revend's nostrils flared, but then he shrugged. "Apparently, you were eavesdropping after all."

"Is that the company?" I questioned. "Or…the person?"

For the longest time, he stared me down. "Sit," he said finally and jerked his head to the leather chaise between us.

I didn't move. "Was she your wife?" *Or one of them, at least.*

"Sit down." His eyes took on a cold gleam that dared me to disobey.

After a deliberate second's pause, I skirted the back of the couch and sat while he took the chaise opposite me.

"Your boyfriend," he began. "What is his name?"

"Ex-boyfriend—"

"His *name.*"

"Jake," I bit out. "Why does that matter?"

"Is he the one who supplied you with the pills?"

I winced at the reminder of the secrets he held over my head. "No."

"Then who did?"

"Someone else."

Surprisingly, he didn't challenge that answer. "You said that you began using the pills to cope with your injury."

I nodded. "Yes."

"Hmph." He cocked his head as his gaze swept over my face. "It sounds feasible enough. So then why are you lying?"

I tore my gaze from his and uneasily crossed both arms over my chest again. "Who's Camille?"

I couldn't see his expression, but in a way, I could *hear* it. The sound of his teeth clenching. A gruff exhale. Hell, I could practically hear the way his muscles coiled, lacing his body with tension.

"Was she the one who hurt you?" I added when he didn't answer. "Your face—"

"You claim that your injury was the cause of your reliance on pills," Revend said, changing the subject. "But that was a lie."

"Why does she want to steal your dancers?" I wondered, ignoring his question. Had she approached Sarah after the last audition? Had she approached anyone else? Even worse —"Was she the one who threw the stone—"

"Just tell me this," Revend said over me. "Supposedly, you had a boyfriend. You have loving parents. A good home. And yet…"

"Yet what?"

"And yet you keep coming back to me," he continued, "and I don't mean for dance."

"It doesn't mean anything, remember?"

He turned away from me. "You're right."

The next few seconds passed in silence so heavy that it felt inescapable. There was no combination of words in existence that could fill the space.

"I'm sorry if...if I crossed a line the other day," Revend finally said. It was like when a storm cloud broke. The tension released only to drench both of us in the aftermath. "It won't happen again."

"Just like all of the other times never happened—"

"Anya."

"I didn't mean it that way."

How then? He didn't say it out loud, but the question lingered in his gaze, demanding an answer.

"I'm tired," I said finally, staring past his head toward the window.

Like hell would he let me off that easily. He shifted, drawing my attention, and his gaze held mine captive before I'd even known what was happening.

"How long have you been dancing?" he asked.

"Since I was four—"

"A child," he said, cutting over me. "But when did you decide that you couldn't live without it? That ballet was in your veins. That you would risk heartache and injury to follow this path."

"I...I don't know what you mean—"

"It happened for me when I was sixteen," he said. "I grew up in a small village in Surrey. My mother was a widow. My father left her a parcel of land and enough money to support us, but she didn't understand how to raise a child, let alone a boy. When I was old enough, she shipped me off to any boarding school that would take me, and I almost made a game out of ensuring that I would be expelled from every single one."

He laughed bitterly, his gaze focused somewhere in the past. "The longest one I'd ever managed to stay enrolled in was run by a parish. In addition to harsh discipline, they believed that every boy needed an outlet. Something to... channel their energy into. One of the instructors was of Romani heritage—though he didn't broadcast that of course." A corner of his mouth quirked. It could have been a smile had it reached his eyes. "The rumor was that he was from a family of circus performers, and he taught a few skills to a chosen few."

"Acrobatics?" I asked.

He shrugged. "Not quite. A few tips for flexibility. Some strength training. Nothing refined, but enough to hone when the time came."

"How did that turn into ballet?"

"I ran away to London when I was fourteen. A fool's whim. I had only the ten pounds my mother sent me monthly and the clothes on my back. When night fell, and the extent of my folly sank in, I broke into a building and slept in the attic. It turned out to be a theater, and rather than kick me out, the curator allowed me to work as a stagehand. I think he thought that I was homeless and took pity on me, and I was too much of a coward to go back to school. I think it was a year before one of the dancers in the corps became injured and they threw me in in his place. The rest…as they say, is history."

"You became a principal?"

"I worked hard," he said. "I learned what I could… And you?"

My own story wasn't quite as dramatic. "My mother put me in dance because she liked dressing me in the costumes. I kept with it because…"

Because I liked the attention? I liked being the center of the universe for the five seconds I was on stage? I liked spinning and spinning until nothing could touch me?

"I don't really know why," I admitted. "My dad didn't really care as long as my grades were good enough. I was accepted into an academy when I was ten, and I carried all the way through, until…"

"Until your…*injury*," Revend finished for me.

I didn't miss the way he stressed that word. *Injury?*

"Yes," I said, ignoring the unspoken question.

"And yet you still pursue a career in dance?"

I swallowed hard and found myself shrugging. "It's all I know."

Though that wasn't really it… Was it?

It sounded so anticlimactic in the face of his own story. *I'm a dancer because I am.*

"It's… When I dance…I—"

"Don't tell me." He reached for my hand before I could react.

Confused, I could only follow him to the center of the room. There, he spun me around, placing both his hands directly on my hips.

"Show me. This is how you communicate with the world." The fingers of one of his hands caught my wrist and traced my swollen knuckles. "This is why you dance. Words mean nothing. Your truth lies in the *motion*."

I swallowed hard. *Motion.* It was almost ironic how my entire body seemed to be spinning while the rest of the world remained frozen in place. *Truth lies in motion…*

"This is what makes you a dancer," he told me with an assuredness that blew my mind. "*This*…not the technique."

His breath scorched my throat. His presence was overwhelming—like a freight train slamming into me. Only I was too stupid to jump out of the way. Instead, I watched the resulting chunks of me fly apart, unable to ever be reassembled.

"You have one more day to prove this to yourself," he warned me, pulling away. "One more day to prove it to me. Do not waste this chance."

He was gone before I caught my breath again. Before I gathered up the nerve to truly register the sensation of his heat still prickling over my skin.

He was gone before I remembered how to hate myself.

So I settled for hating him.

*I*t wasn't that uncommon to get a song stuck in your head, a few nonsensical lyrics that replayed over and over until you found yourself humming them out loud without really understanding why. You could get stuck on a person the same way.

Until their thoughts and words and scents filled every waking moment like a distorted melody only you could hear. When you hummed them, no one else recognized the tune—and deep down, some guilty, stupid part of you wanted to believe that you were the only person in the world who could decipher that brand of humanity.

Even though it stained your soul. Tainted it.

Even though it hurt.

Revend Marcus had scuffed my psyche beneath the blows of his cane and scribbled over the rest of it in gaping strokes that spelled out two words.

Feel something.

Yet all I could feel was him, and it was a sobering realization for someone who had never really felt connected to anyone.

Maybe I had really gone off the deep end this time, pills or not. Though it was fitting in a way—Hope Bridge would most likely wind up being my destination if I couldn't pass Revend's test.

There was no rehearsal. Only challenge after challenge that rattled even the best dancers. You think you can perform the *Giselle* variation from act one? Then try doing it fifty times in a row at twice the normal speed. You think you can die properly? Then expire a hundred times. Your face. Your body. Your tempo. Watch it all. Do it all over again. Do it *better*.

And when you'd finally struggled through a variation without making a mistake?

It just wasn't good enough.

I wasn't good enough.

By the end of the rehearsal, I was at the back of the pack, dripping sweat, shame, and regret. My "last chance" would reach its breaking point the next day, and I honestly couldn't see myself even lasting that long.

"Ten minutes," Revend grunted out before turning on his heel.

There was a collective groan from the group when he marched out into the hallway, trailing anger in his wake.

I staggered like everyone else over to the barre and tried to catch my breath—and maybe my sanity. My feet were aching, blistered, and sore. I couldn't stand upright without shaking. The core of my being had been knocked off-center and cracked beneath the thwack of his cane.

You can do this, I tried to tell myself as I curled my hands around the wooden barre. *You are good enough, Anya. You are not a failure, Anya.* But those lies sounded a lot hollower than they had when spoken by my therapist.

Around me, the remaining dancers were drinking from water bottles or massaging their aching feet. They never lost sight of the goal, never gave in to the crushing doubt—and when Revend finally returned, they weren't the ones who suffered beneath the disapproving weight of his glare.

"Back into lines," he commanded, leaning heavily on his cane. "From the beginning. This time, make me feel it."

By the time he dismissed the group, those of us who had any energy left managed to stagger into the dressing room before collapsing. I curled up on a section of the floor instead and tried to regain feeling in my limbs.

I wasn't sure when I first heard it, the cadence of a man's baritone.

"Tomorrow," he said. "Act no differently. You'll fly to Paris at the week's end."

"Okay," a woman hesitantly replied. She sounded young. Familiar. Katja? "Thank you, Mr. Marc—"

"Don't thank me." The gruff accent took on a razor's edge. "Just live up to your duty."

Duty. Performance. Paris.

I tried not to jump to conclusions as I rolled onto my side and attempted to stand. Jumping to conclusions was a dangerous game to play. Just like when my doctors, the nurses, and my parents had all overreacted when I'd accidentally (purposefully) swallowed only a few more pills than I usually took. Ten more. Fifteen. The rest of the bottle.

It had been an accident, I'd claimed to anyone who would listen. But no, they'd stuffed me full of sugar water and wheeled me into a "healing" facility, where therapist after therapist had told me in nice, neat terms why I was damaged. How they could help. The road to recovery was an easy one to follow, you see. All I had to do was stop worrying. Thinking. Crying. Caring. Hating. Wanting. Needing.

Everything.

I had to play my part. Know my lines. Dance to whatever song they wanted me to and hope that they might deem my actions "normal" enough to set me free.

I couldn't jump to conclusions.

"You're still here." Revend's voice held the hint of a questioning edge. *You're still here. Why?*

I didn't want to look at him. I didn't want to see his face. Those eyes. That frown. The salt-and-pepper stubble that coated his chin. It was so much safer if he remained intangible. A smell. A presence. This overwhelming force that had possessed me like a parasite and made me hope for things robots shouldn't need.

I didn't want to *need* Revend. But I looked anyway. He was standing near the doorway, his shoulders hunched away from me as if the sight of me were that repulsive.

When I finally opened my mouth, a series of words tumbled out. "My parents… They think I tried to kill myself."

I couldn't have pretended to guess his reaction—but a sigh wouldn't have been on the list. Or a nod.

"I know."

He knew. *Of course he knew*, a part of me echoed. Revend Marcus, the man who could gather my personal information without batting an eyelash. Of course he knew.

"Remsky?" I asked halfheartedly, too exhausted to feel betrayed.

"Yes. Victor," he said.

I wasn't sure how even Remsky knew. Maybe it was just that obvious. *Damaged Goods* must have been written across my face in permanent marker, a warning to anyone who dared to get too close.

"He didn't tell me…at first," Revend clarified, his words halting. "Not until…"

Something that could have been a laugh trickled from my mouth. "Not until I trashed your living room."

He turned away from me, hiding his expression. The shock. The remaining tendrils of anger. The pity.

"How long ago?" he asked.

I fluttered my fingers against the mirror glass as if counting out the days one by one. "Almost ten months."

"And you took pills."

It wasn't a question, but I nodded anyway. "Fifteen OxyContin." I could still remember washing each one down with a sip of water until the room had started to blur and the feelings of shame and disappointment had given way to happy, dizzy nothingness.

I don't think I had wanted to die—simply wanted the pain to stop. The fear. The doubt. The need to please everyone with a smile while screaming a silent plea inside they never seemed to hear.

"My mom found me on the bathroom floor," I heard myself say, as detached as if this were some other girl's sordid tale. Not mine. "Her husband had to give me CPR until the paramedics came."

I'd woken up, dazed and numb, to a scene of chaos unfolding in my hospital room—a barrage of people— doctors, nurses, and family—all demanding the same thing. Why? *Why?*

How could I be so selfish? So stupid? So self-absorbed? People loved me. I had a future. How could I throw it all away? Why?

Then, like the steady drip of IV fluid, the shock had turned to anger, reflected on anyone and everything within a five-mile radius.

It was my fault for being too much of a perfectionist. Mom's fault for not watching me closely enough. Dad's fault for being too happy with his new family to bother with his wayward, test-round daughter. It was the paramedic's fault for making a scene. The doctor's fault for being too honest. My fault. *My* fault.

I needed to change. Dance was too much of a focus—everyone knew I would never make it anyway. I needed a change of scenery. I needed a "father's stern hand." I needed to enroll in college and earn a degree in something. I needed to be "good" and believe the lies my parents told, that I had been hospitalized for "exhaustion" and a "flare-up" of my ankle injury.

Anya had needed to play her part and learn the role of the perfect daughter.

"You lied to your parents about continuing ballet," Revend said, his voice sounding light-years away.

I didn't speak. I managed to nod somehow, too terrified to ask how he'd learned that tidbit. In the end, I didn't have to.

"I spoke to your parents," he said. "They know you're safe."

Safe. Is that what he called it? Impromptu sex and verbal tirades? These Dr. Jekyll, Mr. Hyde, and the broken puppet games we played. It certainly wasn't the clinical, calm notion of the word my therapist had claimed I'd needed.

But all I asked was, "With you?"

"They know you're not in an alley somewhere, high on drugs," Revend clarified as if reading my mind. "But I didn't tell them where you were. Just enough so that they wouldn't go to the police."

It must have been recently, during one of his mysterious absences. "Did my dad punch you?" I asked, allowing my gaze to travel up to the bruise around his good eye.

"What will you do?" Revend asked, ignoring my question. "If you don't earn the contract. Where do you go from here?"

State your goals clearly, Anya, my therapist would say to frame that same question. *Voice them with conviction. You are capable of anything. Let's try saying it together…*

"I have to earn a contract." I turned back to the mirror, eyeing the sickly, skinny waif of a girl who was leaning her entire body against it. Her lifeless, blue eyes were glassy, pretty marbles set in her head for decoration. Poor thing, she didn't seem to realize she was already dead. "I have to dance," the ghost said. "It's the only thing that matters anymore."

"Prove it," Revend said. As if it were that easy. That simple. "You want it? Then show me your hunger tomorrow. Hold nothing back."

My hunger. Counting calories since the age of twelve had made me an expert on that sensation. How it gnawed away at the pit of your stomach, burning and burning until you couldn't think about anything else. Until the disgruntled sounds began to resemble words demanding that you eat more. Something. Anything.

I needed ballet, but when I thought of the word *hunger*, dance wasn't the first thing that came to mind. Just dark eyes. Black hair. A cold, frozen expression that could portray true emotion like molten lava seeping through the base of a dormant volcano. Hunger was an instinctive need, alerting you to a craving that was vital to fulfill.

So what did that make him? The shadow lingering just out of reach, ruthlessly scanning my sweat-coated forehead.

"Who was Camille?" I asked, my voice a tired croak.

Revend flinched. In one fell swoop, I'd turned this heart-to-heart into a tit-for-tat. I was sure he wouldn't answer. Even when he began to inch forward with the aid of his cane, his face expressionless, his jaw clenched tight.

He came close enough for me to reach out and touch him —but I didn't. And, like a specter, he quietly settled into the corner where the mirror met the opposing wall, a safe distance away.

"She was my wife," he said almost casually. "A prima ballerina for the French Royal Opera Ballet. Camille Dufont. Young. Beautiful. Flawless technique…" He trailed off, his voice full of admiration that prickled something inside me. She had been flawless. "I was her mentor. We were paired to perform *Manon*. She was nearly ten years younger and still outshone me."

"You loved her." It was the only emotion I could name to describe the slight tremor in his voice, the way his eyes turned a soft shade of charcoal. I'd never seen that look on his face before. Was that love?

"Loved." He laughed as though I'd presented the punchline to some inside joke. "I think I…*admired* her. She was—is—a brilliant dancer. But loved?" He shrugged, tapping his cane against the floor. "Women like Camille are impossible to love. They feed on the world like an insidious parasite, demanding what they want. Taking what they need. Leaving a husk of a host behind."

"So then why marry her?"

He smiled, a flash of teeth against the backdrop of two ebony eyes. "Why not?"

For the first time, I allowed myself to study his scars more carefully, tracing each jagged line. "Did she cut you?"

"No…" Revend brought a hand up to the left side of his face. His expression remained unreadable as he turned to the mirror, observing his own reflection. Then he shrugged again, allowing the hand to fall. "She had another do her dirty work for her," he said. "A lover. Our marriage was never enough for her. She wanted more. Needed more… always. Our careers were an obstacle." One of his hands absently brushed his injured leg. "Mine was…a hindrance."

So she'd ended it. He didn't have to say as much out loud. I could still remember what Remsky had said, his words filling in the blanks. *She's already taken everything…but your life.*

"She didn't go to jail?" I asked. "For hurting you?"

His lips formed another rueful smile. "There was no evidence. Just the word of a cripple too busy prancing around in tights to shower attention on his pretty, young wife. My career ended. She moved on. And when I try to move on…" He broke off. Blinked. Shook his head. I think he thought he'd said too much, and he shifted away from me in an effort to rectify that. "I accept things for what they are."

"What about your first wife?" I knew even before the words had fully left my mouth that I'd overstepped. Camille was a barely healed wound he didn't seem to like prodding. His first wife—Vika—was a decade's old incision I'd just reopened with a rusty butcher's knife.

"Victoria." He'd said her name almost as if by accident. An involuntary slip, like *ow* when someone hurts you unexpectedly.

I didn't expect him to tell me about her. A part of me didn't really want him to. It was selfish. Camille had made his eyes narrow with a mixture of nostalgia and regret. Victoria left them downcast.

"She was a decent dancer," he said softly. "No accolades to her name. No remarkable technique. No memorable performance to be discussed by socialites during their evening trips to the Opera. But when she smiled…"

His gaze was far off, in the distance. Years into the past, seeing a woman I would never meet. Never compare to. *This* was love—this pain that shaped his expression and made a corner of his mouth tremble.

"She was just a member of the corps. I don't even remember what made her stand out. She wasn't particularly beautiful. No unusual talent... But she loved ballet. She lived for it. Every pirouette and *jeté* contained a piece of her soul for the world to see—not that she danced for them anyway. She was a selfish performer, only caring to please herself over some judge."

"What happened to her?" I prompted when he went silent for what felt like hours. I knew even before he said the words that her fate hadn't been as bright as Camille's.

"I killed her," Revend said. "I snuffed out her love of dance with pointless corrections. I chased my career, leaving her alone in London, or Moscow, or Vienna while I performed. She never complained. Never gave me a single hint as to how lonely she'd been. How ill. She caught tuberculosis a year and a half into our marriage and died three months later. And I...the selfish, cowardly bastard that I was, couldn't even be bothered to attend her funeral. I performed that night in Paris. Swan Lake. Victor never forgave me for that."

My eyebrows shot up. "V-Victor? *Remsky?*"

Revend nodded. "Her brother. We all danced for the same company at some point."

I struggled to hide my shock, though it made sense. Why Victor had deferred to Revend. Why Revend had taken me on in the first place.

"I owe a debt to him," Revend clarified. "One that can never truly be repaid—even by traveling to another continent merely to audition one dancer at his behest."

I didn't say anything. Any way I read into his words led to a dangerous scenario. That audition had been for one dancer. *Some of you might learn something...*

"He said that you reminded him of her. I elected to give you an audition," he said gruffly. "I do not accept charity cases, not even from him. I gave you one chance, and within an instant, I realized he was wrong. You were nothing like Victoria. You had none of her finesse. Her strength. Her physique. Victor, growing nostalgic in his old age, had been mistaken. But then..."

"Then?" The word was a breathless whisper that formed condensation against the mirror's surface.

"You defied me," he said simply. "You resisted. You were stubborn. Not like Vika... But still." He shrugged. "I gave you another chance. And you were even more defiant. More impertinent. I could beat you down, yet you still got up."

"Why even help me at all?" I asked, trailing my gaze over his hulking frame.

He was so much taller than I was. So much bigger. Older. Stronger. But right then, with him slouched against the wall and my hip pressed against the mirror glass, we almost seemed to be on the same level. Bitter. Mistrustful. Jaded.

"You don't remind me of Victoria," Revend said finally. "You're stronger than she was."

I misheard him, obviously. Me, strong? Though I guess that was the good thing about robots. Their metal bodies certainly knew how to take a pounding.

"I'm not strong," I argued. My limp, noodle-like legs could barely support me now. I had been shattered by his rehearsal, numbed by his presence. Pathetic porcelain Anya.

"Maybe not now," Revend agreed.

Before I could react, he pulled away from the wall. Using his cane, he approached me steadily, carefully. Then he caught my chin in his palm, forcing my gaze to meet his.

"But when you dance…" There was something in his voice I'd never heard before. Something I wasn't sure I ever wanted to hear. Something dangerous. Something more addicting than any high.

"What?" I croaked.

"When you dance, you are…untouchable," he said, frowning as if the fact irritated him. "You dare the world to break you. Mold you. Even if your technique isn't flawless. I'm not sure if it is a positive trait or negative."

Definitely negative, my therapist would say. *It's not good to be stubborn, Anya. Selfish.*

"So, why train me?" I asked.

His eyes took on a blacker hue and narrowed. A corner of his mouth tightened, tilting it into a frown. In the end, he simply grunted, "Why not?"

It felt like we were at an impasse after that. With his fingers still cupping my chin, I couldn't seem to move. His gaze searched mine, peering through the old cracks and into the crevices deep down.

"What are we doing?" Revend asked almost as if he were speaking to himself rather than to me.

I wasn't in any position to answer him. In a few short days, my life had been upended. He somehow had become the focus of it, and nothing else seemed to matter anymore but the brief, brutal moments when he forced me to move and I had no choice but to listen. *Feel, Anya. Dance, Anya. Breathe, Anya!*

I wasn't quite sure what the draw was for him, though—his stern expression revealed no answers. Maybe it was the easy sex. The banter. The guilt he felt toward Remsky. I would probably never know the real answer. Thinking was against the rules in his presence anyway. I was only supposed to feel...

Heat. Fire. Guilt. Insanity.

"You need to return to the hotel," he said, each word sounding deliberately slow.

I think we both tried to distance ourselves at the same time. I tried to slip past him. He attempted to lurch in the opposite direction.

Our lips collided.

Just like that, there was no more thinking. No uneasy feeling in my gut like I was walking on a tightrope. Only heat, the firm give of his mouth against mine, and the nonsensical rush of fire that flooded my veins every time he touched me.

This is wrong, a part of me warned. It was wrong for him to tilt my body sideways and press me up against the mirror, his eager little doll. It was wrong for my hands to grasp his shoulders. Every hasty meeting of our lips defied logic. Wrong. Wrong. Wrong. We were reckless. Right there for anyone to see, multiplied into a million different couples, spread out amongst the row of mirrors. I squeezed my eyes shut, trying to ignore the images. His hands. My gasps. Our desperation...

Then, all at once, Revend pulled back, leaving me to scramble for balance.

"Mr....Mr. Marcus?"

I opened my eyes and found a woman standing in the doorway, her green eyes narrowed slightly, unsure of what she'd seen. What *had* she seen?

My lips were wet. I swayed on my feet. Revend was lumbering away from me, heading for his cane, which had rolled to the center of the floor. He wouldn't look at me.

"What do you want?" he snarled at Katja.

"N-nothing." Her gaze flickered in my direction, containing the question she didn't dare voice out loud. "Just… See you tomorrow."

Turning on her heel, she retreated down the hallway, and a part of me wanted to follow her. It felt too dangerous, staying in that room alone with him. I couldn't trust myself. I couldn't trust my robot brain not to go haywire whenever he was near.

"That's enough practice for today," Revend said gruffly, his tone carefully controlled, erasing the intimate conversation and whatever had happened after. "Tomorrow is your last chance. Don't waste it."

He left me alone to face the wall of mirrors and the stranger standing there, who I didn't even recognize.

CHAPTER 25

*J*woke up in the hotel, struggling to get my bearings the same way I wrestled to fit into a skintight leotard and sweats. I should have felt more focused. *Dance. Ballet. My future.* Those should have been the only thoughts circling my brain—nothing else. Not what might happen *after* the final performance or if I won the contract. If I didn't…

Or where I would go from there. To London? Right back to Hope Bridge and the shackles of my parents' good-daughter routine?

I tried not to care as I dutifully packed my pointe shoes and scraped my hair into a bun. Once I reached the theater, I focused on warming up. Not the other dancers or how rested they seemed, despite how exhausted I felt. Not the fact that Rebecca was once again tiredly directing the rehearsals and Revend was nowhere in sight.

All that mattered was moving—the fluid stretch of muscle, coaxing my limbs into unnatural positions, breathing—and ignoring the ache in my chest that grew once the rehearsal ended and we were ushered into the dressing rooms to change. I ignored the way I felt empty in my black leotard and tights, the only one without a costume. How some deep-seated part of me seemed to know what was coming, even before Katja muscled her way beside me at the counter of my vanity.

"Hello, Anya." With careful concentration, she traced her mouth with pink lipstick. Then she smacked her lips and smiled prettily, the beautiful expression undercutting the venom in her next words. "Did you fuck Remsky too in order to earn your spot here?"

All around us, the other pretty, perfect girls were too busy maintaining their own illusions to notice the crack in mine. Those words had fractured the calm I'd spent the entire day struggling to build. Ugly truths and lies spilled out before I could scoop them back up, tainting the air like mint and pepper.

"No," I said, forcing myself to meet my own gaze in the mirror.

That was true, wasn't it? Remsky had taken pity on me for his own reasons—I hadn't done anything to encourage him or to make him pass me onto Revend.

Or had I?

"Hmph." Katja's eyes glowed a frosty shade of emerald. They were similar to a cat's, gleaming with the same "gotcha" expression. The mouse was caught between her paws, but she was too bored to devour it.

Yet.

"I only wanted to let you know that, this time, it didn't work," she said while neatly recapping her lipstick. "Whatever you think you've done to get the part, it didn't work. I've already gotten the contract."

Gotten the contract... My robot brain didn't comprehend. *This does not compute.* "We didn't even audition yet," I said, watching in the mirror the way my eyes flickered a million different shades of blue to challenge the words coming out of my own mouth. Cerulean. Indigo. Cerulean. "You're lying."

Katja just smiled. "I've already booked my flight to London." She unfolded something coiled around her lipstick tube and held up for my benefit—a receipt for a plane ticket to London, one way.

"You could have bought that yourself."

"He told me yesterday. Mr. Marcus," Katja admitted as she gave herself one last scrutinizing look. Her costume was formed of blue chiffon, perfectly tailored. Her makeup was flawless, her posture perfect. After tucking a piece of blonde hair behind her ear, she turned on her heel and winked at me over her shoulder. "Good luck, Anya."

I inhaled as she returned to her own vanity. Exhaled. In. Out. She was lying. She had to be. She was lying…

"Five minutes," Rebecca called from the door of the dressing room. She clapped her hands once, and like trained puppies, the other dancers filed out to meet her one by one.

She's lying.

I was the last one out, cradling a pair of black pointe shoes against my chest, my hair a mess. Up ahead, Katja was the picture of grace, her golden head bobbing up and down with every confident step she took.

She's lying.

Numb, I fell into the back of the pack, fighting to keep composure. Back straight. Chin up. Face forward. Smile. Smile…

We were led to the theater again, taking turns to block each scene. Everyone was to be utilized for every audition, filling in as the background extras to ooh and aww while each male and female took their turns acting out the lead roles— the shocked villagers forced to watch Giselle's descent into madness.

Ooh, Giselle's peasant beau was actually a wealthy lord. Aww, but he lied and planned to marry someone else. Ooh, no, Giselle! Scene.

I watched on while the other dancers rehearsed their roles. It mainly consisted of agonized facial expressions and dancing out of step. No hard technique to master, nothing really worthwhile difficulty-wise. Just emotion. The portrayal of a character, which Revend claimed was more important than the dance itself.

Feeling. Believing the illusion. Crafting a lie so real that those viewing it had no choice but to get sucked into the charade.

Like the fact that a wayward dancer could ever excel. Or that a broken doll could ever be more than a convenient puppet-daughter or used for casual sex.

"Anya?"

I glanced up and found Rebecca watching me, one eyebrow raised.

"Are you ready?"

I blinked, realizing I was the only one left on my corner of the stage. It was my turn to mark the routine, my turn to mime my way through exaggerated movements I didn't really feel. My turn to scurry into the shadows when I was finished to take my place with everyone else in the wings while the lights dimmed and the judges once again made their silent appearance in the box above our heads.

I think it was only then, beneath the shadows of the gallery, that I realized that Katja hadn't been lying. I could still remember the snatches of the conversation she'd had with Revend the other day. I knew that the smugness in her gaze hadn't been all bravado. And deep down, a part of me had always known that this was how the story would really end.

No one ever believed in me.

"It's time."

As if from far away, I heard Rebecca call the first two dancers, and the rest of us followed them onto the stage, filling the gaps in the background. When the music played, we flounced about, playing our various roles. I watched poor Giselle stagger around the village square, confused and heartbroken. Figuratively. Literally. In silence, she collapsed into her lover's arms, going limp in one dramatic motion.

And scene.

From our position, the judges' expressions were obscured by the glow of the stage lights. I had no trouble imagining one judge's reaction in particular, however. He would frown, the expression alone revealing what he thought. *Unemotional. Dry. Lifeless. Dead.*

Next victim.

Rebecca complied with the silent demand, calling two more names. Two more star-crossed lovers and one more hopeless Giselle.

Their performance was too fake. The dancers pantomimed their expressions, never truly letting themselves feel.

Next.

Katja performed. Through facial expression alone, she went from joyful to confused, sad, devastated, mad, heartbroken, dead. I almost believed it as her deceitful lover shook her limp body, his face contorted by grief and guilt.

But the bodies of most heartbroken peasant girls weren't smirking in triumph.

"Our next performer," Rebecca announced, her voice echoing throughout the theater. "Anya?"

I was still standing amongst the peasants, wearing my blank smile, waiting for the organ grinder's instrument to play so that I could do my little song and dance—not that it even mattered. Some heartless critic had already ruined the ending of this play.

Still. I needed to follow the script. Act my part out. Believing that, I took a step forward, but I couldn't remember the steps. Gazing into the blinding stage lights, I couldn't even remember why I was there.

"Anya?"

Everyone was watching me. The starting position was near stage right. I needed to cross over to it, but time had slowed down, the steady thrum of my heartbeat counting the seconds. One. Two.

What are you doing, Anya? apart of me demanded, breaking through the monotony. *You didn't think you could ever really belong here, did you? You didn't really think he really gave a damn about you... Did you?*

"Anya?" Rebecca tried again, sounding light-years away.

A seat cushion squeak above the stage, followed by a thud like that of wood striking the carpeted floor of the balcony —a warning. *Don't waste my time.*

"I'm fine," I heard myself say, my voice gravelly and robotic. With stiff, deliberate motions, I moved to take my place, facing forward, smiling…always smiling. On cue, the music began to play again.

I was Giselle, pretty, youthful, and happy, performing for her village. Only the festivities quickly turned sinister when I realized that my lover, Albrecht—Caleb—was betrothed to someone else. A liar. A fraud.

That revelation was supposed to make me feel something…

"Anya?"

I noticed a flicker of motion from the corner of my eye. Once again, Rebecca was forced to make her presence known from the wings.

She took a step forward, clipboard in hand, her mouth curled into a frown. "Are you okay?"

I couldn't move, frozen in place by the sound of something steadily approaching the stage from the gallery. It didn't belong in this scene. *Thump. Thump. Thump…*

"Anya?" Caleb asked, breaking character. He looked every bit the deceitful prince in an elegant costume, but his expression didn't fit—worry and concern came a few scenes too early.

"I'm fine." I shifted to settle into the starting position again. I tried my worn smile on. The music played…

But I didn't seem capable of lurching into motion until the moment a figure finally lumbered toward the stage, shrouded in shadow. His dark gaze chased me as I rose on pointe and darted between the other villagers.

It was a simple story, *Giselle*. Cliché, really. Charming, pretty village girl rendezvoused with her secret lover, convinced they would be together forever. Her mother tried to warn her—Giselle had a bad heart, you see. So fragile was she that she needed to be coddled. Protected. But she made a stupid, fatal mistake—She trusted someone. She let someone else in. She let him sink inside her soul and taint the outside until she didn't even recognize it anymore.

Once the truth was revealed and she was finally thrown away, she did the only thing she seemed capable of doing—She danced in circles, picked imaginary flowers, and chased her dreams across the stage like invisible butterflies. It was the only way to keep the pain at bay. To keep from breaking.

But the tempo of the music became harder and harder to follow. Her dance became a disjointed mess of broken fantasy, and the moment she finally faced the truth, her heart gave out, and she died right there on the spot.

Silly Giselle. She let herself believe the lie. She let herself hope. She listened to a stranger who had claimed to know her better than she knew herself, and when the lies were ripped away to reveal the harsh reality underneath…she couldn't cope.

"You did great."

The whisper brushed my ear, though I should have been dead. My lifeless eyes were transfixed on the ceiling, my body limp in Caleb's arms. I shouldn't have been able to hear the way my heartbeat surged, beating through my skin. *Bump. Bump.*

I could hear people chattering, saying words that didn't matter. The only sound that actually registered was a sigh, deep and masculine, that somehow easily cut above the rest of the noise. That single expression alone conveyed more than any language ever could.

"And that's the last performer," Rebecca said. "Thank you... Anya?"

I managed to climb to my feet with Caleb's help, but I couldn't seem to merge with the rest of the dancers. I kept going, through the corridor that led backstage and then out into the hall.

The walls of the theater blurred into one indistinguishable shade of mahogany, and I had no clue where I was heading. Almost as if by accident, I blinked and found myself standing before a row of mirrors that threw my reflection back at me. My hair was slicked by sweat, my chest heaving. For once, my eyes weren't empty, at least. They were... blurry, overflowing with tiny, clear drops of liquid that slid down my cheeks in rapid succession.

I swiped at them with the back of my hand. Even more fell in their place.

"Was I *convincing?*" I heard myself ask as a series of unsteady footsteps approached the doorway to the studio—the same ones that had haunted me all the way from the stage.

Revend didn't answer. The mirror showed him to me, leaning on his cane, his face expressionless.

"You weren't terrible," he finally said.

"You didn't have to lie to me." The words just tumbled out, though I wasn't sure if they were true or not. Maybe he really hadn't lied. I'd just been stupid enough to read into his words, seeking out some shred of hope. "Katja told me," I added, watching my mouth move through the mirror's surface. "You gave her the contract."

"I did."

Why the hell did his admission sting so much? His honesty pierced me through the chest, slicing deep, deep down.

"Why?"

"She's a better fit," he said so casually. "Maybe one day you can try again for the corps. But you do not have what it takes to become a principal now."

He didn't try to soften it—didn't try to sprinkle any sugar onto the poison he injected into my heart—and I felt so pathetic for missing that tactful delivery. *You're a beautiful dancer, at least. You tried your hardest, at least. I didn't write you off without even bothering to see your final performance.*

"So, what now?" My voice was ice cold. My face was blank, my mask perfectly rearranged. Apart from the tears, no one would have been able to tell anything was wrong.

For some reason, that thought made me want to laugh. Cry harder. Scream.

A few seconds passed before I realized that Revend hadn't answered me. He was just standing in the doorway, blocking my path. I couldn't even leave. I flicked my gaze to the window and considered wrenching it open and climbing out. Shattering the glass. Making noise. A scene.

I couldn't. My obedient body had rehearsed this part of the act too many times—dashed dreams and broken hopes. The role of Anya wasn't as vibrant as the one of Giselle. You merely stood there, staring blankly ahead, while your own reflection shattered at your feet.

"Just…" My raspy robot voice reverberated throughout the room on a distorted echo. "Just tell me *why*."

"Your technique isn't—"

"No." A million reflected Anyas spoke in unison, daring to disobey their puppet master once again. "Not the dancing part. Not this." The fragile dolls jabbed their hands into the air as if indicating the entire theater. "*This*…" Porcelain fingers fluttered over their chests, settling against faulty wires and plastic skin—somewhere deep down beneath it all was supposed to be a heart—a busted ball of sparking circuits. *This.* What did she mean?

Revend seemed to have a grim idea, even if I didn't. I had no damn clue why pain curled in the pit of my stomach and churned through the rest of my body with each beat of my pulse.

"I…I warned you," Revend said, "not to let anything cloud your judgment."

"Judgment," I echoed.

The dead girls watching me all smiled, snickering at the absurdity of such a stupid word. *We might have fucked more than once, but don't you dare let it cloud your judgment.*

"We agreed…it meant nothing," Revend insisted in that firm instructor's voice of his.

"We *said* it meant nothing," the ghostly Anyas said.

As if it were really that simple. It struck me then that maybe it really *was* for him—the puppet master used to having the world at his beck and call. Dancers pranced at his command, contorted, strained, jumped, and twisted. Why not hearts?

Revend was the expert artisan, shaping the world in his image and not giving a damn when the creation shattered at the tips of his fingers.

Luckily for me, porcelain dolls were used to being tossed aside when unwanted and smashed to pieces. But the first crack always hurts most. It's the deepest. The most jagged. Contained within that vicious wound is all the pain from the issuing blow.

By the time you noticed the other broken pieces scattering down around you, you were already numb.

Like when mommies and daddies paid for a piece of paper to declare them divorced and decided to saw the dollhouse in half. Maybe Mommy got caught screwing her "accountant" or Daddy had been growing sick of her anyway. Regardless, the other dolly had no choice but to shuffle between them, with her painted-on smile and her charming disposition. There was a protocol for belonging to a perfect family, you see—Mistakes were never to be acknowledged. You forgot, ignored, denied, lied. Maybe the tug-of-war became too rough, or the poor doll was already defective, but when she started to crack, no one noticed until her pretty little limbs were already dashed into a million pieces.

"You don't want anything to do with this company. Are you listening to me? Anya..." A hot finger brushed my shoulder.

I jerked out of reach, swaying on my feet. "N-no," I croaked, shoving the offending arm away.

My parents had taught me well—You never cleaned the mess up yourself. You hired a broom by the name of "therapist" and a dustpan called "medication", and you used the threat of both to sweep the jagged pieces away. You *never* touched them. Why, you might prick your finger...

"Will you just listen to me, damn it?"

His nearness made my robot parts sputter into action. I was moving, slipping right past him and into the hall. I managed to keep walking, my computerized brain shutting down, focusing only on what mattered. Breathing. Blinking. Pretending.

"Anya, wait."

I walked faster, racing through a narrow corridor, focused only on the exit. Just three simple motions—Left. Right. Left.

"Anya!"

I took off, barreling through blurred, faceless people and out onto the street. A cacophony of city noise assaulted me, warping my reality. Honking car horns. Shouting people. Rushing pedestrians.

I was still wearing my leotard when I entered the hotel and took the elevator up to the suite, but I couldn't step over the threshold. Not with that smell filling up every space, sinking into my lungs. Taunting me.

I took the elevator back down. I asked the concierge to let me use a desk phone. I dialed a number without thinking, and when a wary voice answered, I almost didn't understand the barrage of words that tumbled out.

"I want to come home. Now."

CHAPTER 26

Emergency family meetings were best conducted at eight in the morning, within the office of a licensed family therapist. There, everyone took turns voicing their concerns in stern, serious tones. *I'm worried about you, Anya, because…*

Through it all, the villain of the story wore her "very sorry," contrite expression. She apologized over and over. *"I'm sorry for making you worry. I'm sorry for running away. I'm sorry. Sorry."*

Eventually, her pleas were graciously accepted with a warning to never do it again. Then, together, everyone made a "treatment" plan that would best adapt to their own schedule. Outpatient, maybe? Somewhere close by, but not *too* close. She could take the train. She could go every day for the first week, twice a week the next, and so on until all of her jagged pieces melded together perfectly.

She would sit there and nod when directed to. Smile when required. Utter her lines on cue. *Yes. No. Okay. I want to get help.*

With a fat check written for the time spent, the porcelain doll would be neatly mended with superglue and tape. *Ta-da!* The whole thing would conclude with a giant "family" hug. Mom and Dad might even look at each other for five seconds while their brand-new spouses glanced out the window or shuffled their feet.

Everyone would agree on "what was best for Anya"—without ever requiring her input—and congratulate themselves on a job well done. There was no need to ever list her sins out loud—*thief, liar, slut.* Hell, no one even had to shed a single tear.

Just like that, I was whole again. Everyone else told me so.

"We… We'll just take it slow for the first few days," Carrie assured the steering wheel once we were back in the minivan.

Dad had taken the Volvo to work—I guessed even repairing his daughter couldn't trump the need to pay the bills. Mother and her husband were off for brunch. It was just another normal day, after all.

"Your dad and I will work out a schedule for who will take you to your sessions," Carrie added, still speaking to the dashboard—though, on second thought, she seemed to direct some of those words at me—*Your dad will work out a schedule for dealing with you.* "We don't have to t-talk about anything…" She broke off, unsure about the whole mothering thing.

Her gaze strayed to the rearview mirror, where she watched Taylor fiddle with her cell phone instead. Every furtive glance contained a silent plea she thought I couldn't decipher—*Please, God…don't let defective genes be inheritable.*

"Don't worry," I said while rain mixed with clumps of snow drifted down to splatter the windshield. "I know…"

Twenty minutes later, we reached the house in silence, moving like strangers who somehow managed to share the same space. What did they call it? *Symbiosis.* The phenomenon that made it possible for a big, fat elephant to inhabit the savanna along with the beautiful, slender gazelles as long as it remembered to stay on its side of the watering hole.

"I'll make lunch," Carrie halfheartedly offered as we entered the foyer. Lunch—her way of stalling until Dad got home by keeping me in sight without having to speak. "I'll call you when it's ready."

"Okay. Great." I nodded and headed for the stairs under the guise of changing out of my pretty, starched clothes. "I'll be right down," I promised while each step weighed me down.

The pale pink headband keeping my hair in place couldn't restrain the way my pulse sped up and ached for something to slow it to a crawl. *Pills? Rejection? More therapy?* My neat, lavender sweater set was a straitjacket, constraining my body with the slightest movement, and my rebellious fingers were tugging at the sleeves before I staggered into my room.

I closed the door with one hand and reached for the poster hanging from it with the other. Anna Pavlova smiled widely as I tugged, tore, and ripped, leaving her in pieces on my floor—much the same way the past few days had left me. Sinking to my knees, I rummaged through the carnage, searching for the tiny baggie I'd taped to the back of her all of those months ago.

Puppet girls were brilliant liars, you see. Maybe they *hadn't* taken every single pill when they'd first gone off the deep end. Some might have fallen onto the floor and scattered like the pieces of her fractured, hollow self—as if they had *known* they might come in handy at some point.

I hadn't noticed until the day I'd been discharged from the hospital and sent to pack my things from my mother's house. There, they had lurked in the shadows like Gretel's morbid trail of fucked-up breadcrumbs. With my brand-new therapist's number in my pocket, I had carefully sought out every single one, wrapping them up in plastic and sticking them with Anna for safekeeping. She'd never tell.

There had been five. Five tiny promises of instant numbness. Five naughty, little secrets hidden within the dollhouse of lies.

But they weren't there now. I searched and searched but only found crumbled pieces of paper and dust. *Silly girl.*

Anna's voice cackled over the remnants of my thoughts. *You're not the only one with secrets, Anya...*

Desperate, I shifted each shred, running my fingers along the torn edges. On my third pass, I realized that one slip didn't belong with the rest—a small, roughly torn piece of notebook paper. *Use your anger; someone* had written on it in heavy, sloppy scrawl.

My anger. I fell back onto my knees, laughing out loud. Then, somehow, the laughter turned into a different, broken sound and tears were falling fast—way too many to wipe away.

My "anger" told me to fuck *his* advice; he didn't know a damn thing about me. Besides, every good plot for self-destruction always required a Plan B. I thought about Sally Elias waiting for me in that alley. Or the pills Carrie kept hidden in her dresser where she thought Dad wouldn't check—the subject of one of their many fights.

Revend wouldn't win by commandeering one little stash...

"Anya?" A sudden knock on my door reverberated through my fractured parts. "You in there?"

"Yep," I heard myself croak while my fingers crushed Revend's note into a ball as if that might be enough to obliterate the guilt. "I'm...I'm here."

Liar, Anna Pavlova taunted. *Not for long. All it takes is one little trip over the edge...*

"Can you do me a huge favor?" Carrie asked. "I forgot to mail a stupid bill." Her voice shook—*bill* was a code word for something else. Her own prescription, maybe? "I just have to run to the....post office. It should only take a second, but Taylor hates it when I interrupt her program. Can you watch her for a second? P-please?" She broke off and bit her lip. "Or maybe I could just take her anyway—"

"I'll watch her," I agreed out of habit. I clenched the fingers of my other hand tighter, crushing the remains of Anna Pavlova, smothering her laughter. "Just... Just give me a minute."

"Okay." She inhaled brokenly, likely trying to figure out a polite way to rescind her offer. "I'll be waiting downstairs," she said in the end.

Sinking my teeth into my lower lip, I began a frantic scavenger hunt around my room to toss each piece of the poster into the trash. The shredded image of Anna snickered at me from the crumbled pile, amused by my desperate attempts to ignore her. *You're losing it, Anya.*

I was. My reflection was a mocking parody spread over my bathroom mirror, gazing on as I ran a hand through my hair and pulled a tattered sweatshirt on over my neat blouse. The ghostly girl mimicked me when I tried to rub the rest of the tears out, leaving bloodshot eyes as the only clue— but the joke was on her because she wasn't whole by far. Lean in too closely, and you'd see her cracks—the way her bottom lip trembled while her fingers shook, aching for anything mind-numbing to pop into her mouth.

It was pathetic, really. But the show had to go on, even if the lead was broken.

I crept downstairs to no applause for my continued performance. Only the muted noise of the television and Taylor's babble filled the empty spaces while Carrie lingered by the front door. The moment she saw me descend the final step, she opened it, her designer boot toeing the threshold.

"Are you *sure*?" she asked, drawing the word out. "I mean, I could take her with me."

"It's okay. I don't mind," I emptily assured her, a blank smile tugging at the corners of my lips.

"Okay, then. I'll be right back," she said, though I wasn't sure if she was trying to reassure herself or me. "I'll only be a second."

"Okay."

She hesitantly inched down the driveway, not taking her eyes off the house until she entered the minivan. Then she drove off at a slow crawl up the street.

I stood in the foyer barefoot, a slip of paper I couldn't be bothered to throw away still clutched in my fist. I glanced down, reading the words written on it once again.

Use your anger.

Your anger, Anya.

Use it.

But what if you didn't have any anger left? Just… exhaustion. Sore, blistered feet and battered limbs.

Experimentally, I flexed my left foot, observing the way my toes pressed against the wooden floor. They were worn out, bleeding, and bruised—so tired of performing the same little dance. Even ballet wasn't as complex as navigating your own emotions on tiptoe, knowing which ones to avoid, so they didn't explode underfoot like a landmine. Only there was no audience or instructor waiting to judge you at the end of those performances. Just silence and your own robotic inner voice commanding you to wind yourself up again. *Do it all over.*

I would have performed Giselle's role a thousand times if the practice could have helped me compose a new invisible dance for myself. I would have worked through the aches and pains while the puppet master toyed with my strings if it all actually mattered in the end. The pills had given me a teeny bit of relief, but now, the stage was crooked, requiring too much balance to stay atop it.

Did I still even want to? A shadow stained the pristine emptiness of my imaginary theater now, spying on my inner ballet. *Use your anger, Anya,* it barked from the gallery.

As if it really were that easy.

I took a step, brutally slamming my heel down against the floor so hard that it left a tiny scarlet streak. Pain flared up, crackling along my nerves like fire, but I didn't feel anything other than that. Frowning, I took another step, entering the living room, where a million framed photographs cluttered the walls, their smiling occupants watching on in silence.

Use your anger? My mind twisted those scribbled words around. Anger—those deep-seated feelings that festered in my veins. The same ones my therapist and the entire world begged me to suppress or forget. How exactly could I use it?

With nothing more than the cheerful music of a children's program to count the beat, I fell into first position, only there were no pointe shoes to conform my toes. No leotard to flatten my stomach or keep me contained. No one shouting any commands or banging that damn cane.

Just movement.

First position.

Wood remained motionless beneath the soles of my feet as they slid across it. Air steadily entered my lungs and filled up those semi-deflated balloons. Would it be enough to lift me up? Float me away?

Second Position.

Muscle and bone contorted, blindly obeying whatever my brain commanded. Did any real emotion lurk within the robotic motions? I couldn't tell. My audience of photographs didn't seem convinced.

Third.

Fourth.

Fifth.

First.

I was transitioning into second again—still searching for that elusive anger—when I noticed someone watching me from across the room. Her eyes were blue like mine, her cheeks plump, her lips smeared with graham cracker goo and pursed in concentration while her legs flexed against the floor—a clumsy imitation of a ballet pose.

I switched into third. She copied me, holding her arms out, bouncing on her feet. "Is…is this okay?"

Technically, no. Her placement was all wrong, her lines sloppy, her balance laughable. Without realizing it, I crossed over to where she was standing by the couch and coaxed her tiny limbs into the right positions.

"First," I prompted while prodding a pink-slippered foot to turn out properly.

"Cool." A smile tugged at her mouth as she observed the placement for herself. She didn't seem to care that her technique was off or her posture was sloppy.

She didn't seem to hear the disembodied voices of a perpetually disapproving audience telling her that she was never good enough.

All that mattered was the way she *felt* performing each clumsy step. Her enormous grin proclaimed that it was as simple as that…

And I had never envied her more.

Carrie returned in exactly twenty minutes, more shocked by the sight of me interacting with Taylor than the fact that we were both still in one piece.

Maybe that therapist had been right after all? The hesitant hope diminished the lines etched into the skin around her eyes. She almost seemed human again.

"T-thank you," she stammered as she crept through the doorway, her arms laden with bags of fast food. "I thought you might be hungry, so I bought you…" She trailed off and shook a white paper bag clutched in her fist.

The awkward silence that came afterward alluded to what she couldn't say—a *sandwich*. A peace offering. Something greasier than carrot sticks yet more harmless than the elaborate meals prepared at the discretion of some smiling television personality.

"Thanks," I said.

Carrie smiled, the expression bitter and strained. We rarely progressed this far in conversations that weren't monitored by a therapist, leaving her to compile her lines on the fly.

"I'll just leave it on the counter."

I stood, trying to ignore the kid tugging on the sleeve of my sweatshirt. I wound up crossing my arms over my chest, unsure of how to manage my limbs outside the strict lines of a ballet position. Protocol dictated that I follow Carrie into the kitchen. Eat. Smile. Simper. Pretend. My muscles hummed defiantly, aching to move instead. Run. Escape.

"I think… I think I'm going to go for a run first."

Carrie froze with her hand on the handle of the front door. Her fragile smile faltered, her doll face paint cracking a little around the edges. "Oh, I don't know, Anya…"

Was it safe? Let the marionette wander off her strings so soon after her last fall? She teetered on the edge of a decision, chewing on her bottom lip. Nibble. Nibble. Almost desperately, her gaze fell to Taylor, and her green eyes took on a hopeful hue.

"Just for a few minutes?"

I nodded. "Just to loosen up."

"Well…" Her conscience was warning her that it was a bad idea.

Stick to the script, our charming family therapist had all but urged as he'd tucked Daddy's check into his pocket. Draw boundaries in crayon and spell out warnings in refrigerator magnets. Keep fragile dollies safe on their shelf.

"Okay, then," Carrie said with a sharp tilt of her chin. A nod, maybe? "We'll wait to eat until you get back."

I accepted my victory with its limitations and fished a pair of old sneakers from the hall closet. Jackets were for long runs, so I was only wearing my sweatshirt when I slipped through the front door.

"Just a few minutes," Carrie reminded, restating the terms of our hostage negotiations.

"Okay," I agreed.

But good-girl intentions had a funny way of shifting behind closed doors. Ten minutes tops. That was the goal. The plan. The promise. But, once I reached the five-minute boundary of my father's development, I kept going. And going. Running. Racing. Flying.

The snow-swept landscape was a gray smudge across my vision, the sounds of the world a muted hum, so easy to drown out if I panted loudly enough. The ache in my chest never diminished, though—no matter how hard my heels hit the pavement, how vigorously I pumped my arms at my sides, or how much I willed my mind to forget…

My destination was a Russian roulette of bad choices. That lonely bench to visit Sally Elias? A dark boulevard that led to a foreboding house on a hill? The therapist's office in search of a magic pill to mend my new cracks?

I was almost surprised when I finally came to a stop within the entryway of a darkened theater. The door slammed shut behind me, dislodging a cloud of dust and rattling the building to its crumbling core. Up ahead, the stage lights were lit, illuminating the wooden platform devoid of any scowling instructors.

Numb, I headed for it, skirting around the velvet chairs in the gallery until my chest was level with the height of the stage itself. I braced one hand flat against the solid surface, sensing the specters of hundreds of dancers and thousands of performances. How many tears, blood, and droplets of sweat had made their home deep within the grain?

In the end…did it all even matter?

I still hadn't come up with an answer by the time I became aware of the presence of someone watching me from the shadows. Not Remsky. There was no exasperated sigh of pity to accompany their shadow. The figure wasn't Revend, either. No, their scent was noticeably devoid of cigar smoke and resentment.

"Did you come back to beg for a position?" Katja wondered, her scorn echoing along with the sound of her steady footsteps.

I didn't turn to see her there. Instead, I watched loose particles of dust drift through the air, performing an endless dance for no one in particular. Around and around, they twisted and spun, seemingly destined to hit the floor, only to catch an invisible breeze seconds before they could fall.

"Remsky isn't here," Katja said. "Though Mr. Marcus hasn't left yet. Maybe, if you hurry, you could still fuck your way into the corps—"

"I'm sorry." My gaze was still on the glittering dust, my thoughts on the shattered dreams and intimate touches that should have made me feel disgusting. Not wanting. Maybe I even felt something akin to guilt.

If porcelain wind-up dolls like Katja and me shared one universal language, it was guilt. And anger. Hate. A sense of disgust so profound that you had to turn it on the outside world or it would swallow you up like pills in an endless bottle.

"I'm sorry," I repeated while her footsteps faltered a few feet behind me. "I'm sorry if you feel like…I wasn't trying to compete with you for the—"

"Compete?" The harsh sound of her laugh sent my dancing dust particles all darting in brand-new directions. "Jesus Christ, Anya. Wake up! 'Competition' implies equal footing, but from the moment you walked into this studio, you've had everything handed to you. Remsky coddled you. Even Mr. Marcus couldn't resist little Miss Perfect—"

"What are you talking about? Revend didn't even choose me."

I faced her to see how she gauged that fact, but her mouth was set in a stern line, her eyes burning fiercely enough to melt steel. A dance bag dangled from one of her hands, most likely containing whatever few belongings she'd salvaged from her locker backstage.

"Yeah. Well, thankfully that man can distinguish between true talent and the tricks of a desperate slut," she snarled. "Just tell me—How soon did you wait to seduce him? Ten minutes? A whole day?"

"I didn't seduce him." Or had I? It was so hard to rectify the bits and pieces circling my brain. *Revend. Me. Our dares. Taunts. That fateful night in his studio.* "I didn't seduce him…"

"Sure." Katja eyed me from head to toe, her gaze narrowed. "Whatever. Deny it if that's what helps you sleep at night. But just know some of us have to *earn* our place."

"I just wanted…" I didn't even know, and my words died right there on my tongue.

"I know what you *want*," Katja said. "Get over it. He chose *me*."

"So then why do you even care?" My voice echoed off the rafters, tinged with an emotion hollow girls weren't supposed to feel. Regret? Doubt? Irritation? "You're on your way to London. You've gotten the part."

"The part." Katja scoffed, shaking her head as if she were in on the joke, but I'd botched the punchline. "Yeah. But it's never really that simple, is it?"

In my world, it was that simple. She had won the contract. The end.

But Katja's mocking emerald eyes were downcast rather than blazing in triumph. *If only it were that simple…*

"Does he really think we're all that stupid?" she demanded of the rotting floorboards shrouded by threadbare carpet. "Like we didn't know." Her gaze cut up to mine. "In the end, he only ran after one dancer."

"That doesn't matter," I said, employing Revend's own logic. He had chased his broken puppet down simply to reinforce the fact that all of those lessons and demands to feel had never really mattered in the end. "Like you said. He picked you."

"Me." A corner of her mouth quirked upward into a smirk. "Congratulations, I guess. After twelve years of training, I'm a dancer in a mediocre company that hasn't opened at a major opera house in years." She cocked her head to the side. "Though who's to say you still won't sleep your way into another corps?"

"Maybe," I found myself croaking. After all, Revend had given me that same advice. *Network, Anya.* "I heard that one of the directors, Simon, has a weakness for desperate young girls…"

Katja flinched, her lips pursed. Was I joking?

Am I joking? "Troubled" dolls chased all sorts of vices to fill the void in their hollow little hearts, after all. Drugs. Alcohol. Men who taunted them with their hopes and dreams turned out to be the most addictive treats, crushing them from the inside out.

Revend hadn't been the only option on that list. There were plenty of big, bad men out there, eager to "mold" a young, desperate ballerina. They'd worsen my cracks. Chew me up and spit me out like the world's most sinister narcotic.

Those thoughts didn't lessen the ache ripping through my chest, however. They didn't silence the voice that drowned out whatever insults Katja spat at me next. *Use your anger, Anya.* Was that what this was?

Anger. It was a bit harsher than the high of oxycodone, sinking into my veins with the intensity of a million vicious words. *Stupid. Whore. Slut. Pathetic. Bad, bad, bad. Never good enough.*

"Though maybe that was the point of all of this?" Katja said, sounding a million miles away. "Maybe I'm the real idiot in all of this. For all I know, you got the real contract... I'm just his way of saving face—"

"No."

Her words threatened to rip away that protective rush of emotion that made it so much easier to stomach everything else.

"You're wrong," I told her, wrapping that denial around myself like some invisible cloak. *Wrong, wrong, wrong.*

Frayed wiring and damaged metal parts could only be bent so far—until they snapped.

Reading into Revend's intentions any further than what was displayed on the surface was only asking for the hammer's blow again. Hope was a different kind of narcotic from oxycodone, attacking the brain rather than the skeletal system. An overdose of it and there might be no coming back.

"I wonder if Remsky knows," Katja declared suddenly, her nose wrinkling. "Just how far his precious, perfect little Anya would go to win the crown? Shall we tell him?"

It was a pathetic bluff. For all I knew, Remsky could be on the other side of the world by now. Even so, taking the bait was impossible to resist. If Katja left, there would be no one there to stop crazy little Anya from finding another dark rabbit hole to jump down. Sally Elias was still on that bench...

"Katja, wait." I chased her across the darkened theater and out onto the street without really knowing why.

She was too fast anyway, her blonde head darting around a corner when I cleared the doorway. I lunged onto the tips of my toes, intending to follow her, when a sound pierced the hum of midday traffic like a knife, slicing into my eardrums. Too loud. Too real. *A scream?*

"Katja?" I took a step, the nerves in my spine tensing in warning as another muffled cry battled with a car horn. "Katja?"

I never received an answer.

Step by step, I crept to the corner of the theater to where an alley formed in the gap between it and the office building next door. Some of Remsky's students would gather there for a smoking break after lessons. There was a dumpster at one end, and on rehearsal days, the music drifted through the walls like a distorted melody.

Today, the only sound was a resounding thud that echoed off the brick walls.

A second later, something rolled across the pavement in my direction. Slender. Round. Almost like a cane but not as straight—this object swelled from a narrow base, rounding toward a blunt end.

"Shit." A man was standing a few feet away, shrouded by a gray hoodie, his body half crouched over something lying at his feet. Something that moaned, its blonde hair spilling out over cigarette buds and loose garbage.

Each quick breath brought a new piece of the puzzle before me into clarity. Katja was lying on her side, her face contorted in pain. She wasn't screaming anymore, her mouth opening and closing before she could even get the words out. Then her eyes found mine, and she managed to choke out one coherent plea.

"Help!"

"Fuck." The hooded figure turned and saw me, his face a swatch of shadow hidden beneath the hood.

Before I could react, he lunged for his discarded weapon, and I finally realized what it was—a baseball bat. The motion brought him too close. I wasn't prepared when his arm lashed out, shoving me against the wall and out of his way. Reflex controlled my fingers, making them curl around a fistful of gray cotton. I tugged, and the hood fell back, revealing a flash of light-colored hair. *Blond?*

I couldn't tell before he swung his arm again, bringing something too quickly in my direction to dodge. It made a sound like draining water from a bathtub, and I saw stars. The world exploded into a million vibrant pieces, but surprisingly, my head didn't shatter like glass.

It merely floated, disconnected from the rest of my body like a wayward balloon still tethered to it by some fragile bit of string. Consciousness came in snippets resembling some artistic thriller movie that made no sense. Disembodied words narrated blurry images formed of finger-painted light and shadow.

What happened?

Miss, can you hear me?

Someone call an ambulance!

Blue and red. The colors invaded, flickering over the walls of the alley and closing in while even more voices joined the fray. *Can you hear me? Can you blink? Talk? Move? Feel this? Feel that?*

I saw a white light, shined directly into my eyes, but I wasn't dead. I'd passed that abyss before, and there was only silence and darkness, no dramatic stories of "Heaven" to tell. There wasn't any pain there, either, churning sluggishly beneath my skin. Or this ache that traveled down my spine with every hammering blow of my pulse.

I wasn't dead, though I wasn't quite sure when I regained control of my senses. Maybe it was somewhere between the ride in the ambulance and the arrival at the emergency room, where they stripped my shirt off and bundled me up in a little paper gown. When a doctor with a worried expression asked me how many fingers he was holding up, I could finally talk again.

"Two," I said.

He nodded and rattled off a series of orders. CT scan. X-ray. Neuro checks. *One, two, three* needles pierced my skin and dripped liquid into my veins because too much was leaking from my head.

Nurses murmured reassuringly while I was led from test to test. Eventually, I wound up in a little, white room with beeping machines and plain, clinical walls.

Another doctor came in and read off a list of defects from a strip of white paper. *Laceration on the back of the skull. Five stitches. Minor concussion, but nothing major.* After perhaps another hour of observation, I might be able to go home. Did I want to call anyone?

When I didn't answer, he shoved a paper cup of water in my face and scurried out while a different nurse rushed in to check my circuits and test me with a barrage of questions just to make sure I wasn't broken.

Maybe it was the medication they'd given me once they'd deduced my brain hadn't exploded. My blood churned too slowly; my thoughts were too heavy to lift. The world kept spinning, but I felt rooted in place, trapped within my own invisible snow globe.

Maybe it was better that way…

At least until someone new came into the room and ruthlessly shook it up, sending a thousand bits of Anya scattering in every direction.

"Are you her father?" my nurse asked the newcomer from the station in the hallway.

"Yes," a man replied.

I stiffened. While Andrew DeSotto's work may have taken him around the world on business trips, he didn't possess an accent. He certainly didn't use a cane, which clattered against the linoleum flooring with every step "my father" took.

"The doctor thinks she'll be fine," my nurse insisted, appearing at the intruder's shoulder near the cusp of my room. "Though he might want her to stay overnight for evaluation…"

"No." My throat ached beneath the word, and my isolative snow globe fractured. "I'm not staying."

Revend said nothing. He was wearing his heavy black coat—my proverbial Grim Reaper again. His expression certainly looked stern enough. Black eyes trapped me beneath their scrutiny, peeling layers of thickened skin back to reveal the fragile shell hidden underneath.

Ready to die, Anya?

Caught in the crossfire, my nurse nodded and darted back into the hallway, clutching her clipboard.

"What are you doing here?" robot Anya croaked, sounding sufficiently detached. The beeping machines hooked up to her undermined that strength, however. Her pulse was too fast, her blood pressure creeping up, up, up…

"Do your parents know where you are?" Apparently, Revend was the puppet master once again. Cold, his gaze trailed me from head to toe, sensing the secrets lurking beneath my flimsy hospital gown.

"No," I admitted.

He wasn't the only one who could evade the obvious.

My parents didn't need to know where I was. If I was lucky, they had forgotten all about this morning's therapy session, and Dad was discussing his day at work over some ridiculous dinner. No one needed to know that the dolly had taken another whopping.

"Oh?" His expression shifted into something unfamiliar— any passing stranger might have mistaken that frown for concern.

Why do you care? That's what I'd meant to ask. Demand. In reality, I was only capable of shaking my head while nodding. *Yes. No.*

"Do you know what happened?" he asked.

"Someone hit me," I said, though he didn't deserve to know a damn thing. It felt strange acknowledging it out loud, regardless. *Someone hit me.*

"Oh." Once again, his reaction seemed all wrong. He didn't appear shocked. Not by what I'd said or by the gauze sealing my broken skull shut. It was as if he'd skipped ahead and already read the next lines in the script; he knew what I would say next before the words even left my mouth.

"Yeah. It was near the theater… I think Katja got hurt. She…" I swallowed a lump in my throat, finally able to think about someone other than myself. *Katja.* I had no idea if she was okay.

"She's fine," Revend said as if reading my mind. Uninvited, he crossed over the threshold of my tiny room, swallowing every inch of space. "Well, she's alive," he rephrased.

Alive. "How... How do you know?"

"Her right leg is broken, however," Revend went on as if I hadn't spoken. "She won't be dancing on it anytime soon."

Leg. Broken. Dancing.

I think he meant the blunt delivery to be a courtesy, sparing me the dance of eggshells I was so used to. But, at that moment, the honesty made it harder to focus, harder to give in to the pain medication and count floor tiles.

His nearness made it impossible to float.

So I sank right back down, ricocheting off the walls and the plastic mattress. It was a violent crash, worse than any overdose of a narcotic.

Yesterday, Katja had been hired by a prominent ballet company. In one fell swoop, her career was over. But I suspected that it wasn't that simple—nothing in Revend's world ever was.

"Someone hit her," I heard myself say, arranging the phrases like pieces of an elaborate jigsaw puzzle. "With a baseball bat..."

There were so many more questions aching to be plugged into the right spots. The assailant had known exactly when to pounce. Who to attack. When. How. What thief went right for their victim's legs?

And the fact that Revend was there spoke volumes to another theory…

"I know." He was even closer now, creeping alongside the bed toward one of the plastic chairs against the wall. Unwanted. Unable to be repelled.

I held my breath when he sat down, my gaze on the clear tube snaking out of my wrist while an ominous feeling took root in my stomach.

He knew.

"Someone hit her on purpose," I realized, blurting out the terrible realization as it formed in my head. "They knew where she was. They aimed for her legs."

The average thug wouldn't be so thorough in injuring an aspiring dancer. Then again, the average dancer hadn't just been accepted into Revend Marcus' company. And Revend Marcus certainly didn't own the average ballet company.

"They wanted her out of the Roria," I said, tasting the theory on my tongue.

Revend made no sign of acknowledgment. No nod. No frown. Just a stern expression that remained fixated on the screen displaying those numbers that reassured everyone I was still alive. A red indicator flashed beside the number counting my pulse, however. *One-oh-five. One ten. One fifteen.*

"They aimed for her legs..."

"Everything okay in here?" The nurse reappeared just as an alarm blared from the monitor.

She made a show of checking my parts to make sure they were all still attached. My heart rate was a tad too fast, but everything else seemed normal. I should try to relax and she would page the doctor, and all would be well.

"You knew this would happen." The words scorched the air once the nurse had left, directed at Revend, who withstood the heat like a statue. "Katja... You *knew.*"

His gaze was on the wall across from him, finding fault in the hygienic posters and cupboards of medical supplies. He could make even a hospital feel unsafe—just another stage to perform on.

Right now, he was my "father." My scowling, British, crippled father who didn't even have the decency to play along with my lies the same way I acted out his.

"You used her," I croaked.

A part of me didn't want to believe it. It was too cold. Too calculated, even for Revend, I thought. But, then again, hadn't he warned me as to how far he was willing to go to get his way?

"You used Katja. You set her up."

He didn't answer. He didn't have to. It was the plot twist, after all—The artist had never had confidence in his creations, knowing all along they were doomed anyway.

"Why?" I wondered, flicking through every word he'd ever said to me. *Dance, Anya. Feel, Anya. This is your last chance.* "D-did you enjoy getting her hopes up—"

"But you forget," Revend interjected coldly. "I'm not the one who benefits from her downfall."

The one who benefits... Guilt raced the IV fluid rushing through my veins while his insinuation sank in. One person stood to gain everything if Katja was out of the running. One dancer. One hopeful, desperate ballerina.

"I...I didn't want this," I insisted even as my throat tightened as if threatening to close up around the protest. *Liar.* "I didn't want *this.*"

"I never intended for you to be accepted into the Roria," Revend said, finally admitting as much out loud. "Not at first."

"Why?" I demanded.

He merely shrugged, but a devious whisper at the back of my mind filled in what he was too cowardly to. *Camille.* The same woman who might have thrown a rock through his window simply to intimidate him, poached Sarah McMahon, and driven Revend to carry a gun wherever he went. The woman behind the company Revend's own executives had warned me about.

"Heed my words, miss. When the Cygne *comes calling, it's better not to refuse…"*

"Your wife," I somehow managed to choke out. "She did this."

Revend sighed, his knuckles growing white as he clutched his cane. "Listen to me…"

The words began a sordid fairy tale I wasn't sure I wanted to hear unfold. Porcelain Anya and the hammer named Revend. Which one would survive without being smashed in the end?

"I always intended to convince some other company to take you on once I'd deemed your talent worth the risk." He didn't mention if the Cygne Noir was one of those "other" companies, and I wasn't brave enough to mention it myself.

I held my breath instead, hoping to wake up from the nightmare he was painting around me with every word.

"I would uphold my duty to Victor. That was it…" He trailed off.

"Until what? Until you started to screw me," I said, filling in the blanks he was too polite to. "Until I got you off. Until—"

"Everything okay?" someone asked from the hallway, my raised voice having caught their notice.

"Everything's fine," Revend replied, sounding infuriatingly in control.

Once the concerned Samaritan retreated down the hall, his scowl returned, tugging on his mouth.

"My intentions didn't change until you truly began to *perform*," he snapped, reluctantly picking the thread of the story up again. "And I started to believe that maybe you were destined for more than being shoved into the back of some corps for the rest of your life."

"Even if Katja had to suffer," I surmised. "Camille only targets your best dancers. You knew that. You knew that whoever won the contract… Whoever… She…"

"I didn't." His jaw tightened, his teeth snapping shut. "I…I wasn't sure how far she would go," he spat out after a terse second's silence.

"Don't lie." My fingers twitched, aching to smother my ears to shut him out. I curled them around the tube snaking out of my wrist instead. "Don't lie."

"It's the truth," he said simply. He didn't even have the decency to look ashamed or guilty—those naughty emotions my therapist had implored me to stop feeling.

God, I needed to feel them *now*. I needed to hate. Vomit. Scream. Shout.

I needed to cut off this selfish part of me that chose to ignore the callousness in his actions in favor of repeating a few stupid words. *I started to believe…*

"Katja had talent too," I pointed out. To myself or to him? I wasn't sure. "What makes me any different?" I twisted the plastic tube around my fingers as if it held the answers, tugging, ripping. "She wouldn't screw you, maybe? Therefore, she deserved to have her legs smashed to pieces—"

"Stop it."

"And you were too much of a coward to even call the police—"

"Anya."

"Not even when she threw a rock through your window!"

"Stop it."

"What next?"

"Stop—"

"Or maybe Katja was just another casualty. Like *Victoria*."

A sharp intake of air was my only warning that I'd crossed a line. Maybe one day, I'd actually regret sinking to his level.

"Just get out," I said before he could retaliate. "Leave me alone. Like you said, none of it fucking matters anyway."

Without warning, his hand crossed the unspoken barrier between us, settling over my wrist. I stared down at the callused fingers, hating the warmth they breathed into my skin.

"Anya—"

"Get out!" I tried to wrench my arm away, but he held tight. "Let go of me—"

"I never meant to hurt you," he growled over me. "If I did—"

"*If?*"

The implications of that stung as he finally released his grip. *I'm sorry if I hurt you, Anya. I'm sorry if I used you, Anya. I'm sorry if I saw you, Anya.*

The tears were falling again, stinging my skin like acid. Were any of them even for Katja? Or just for myself?

I almost wished he'd simply chosen Katja over me— anything but this, using her as a pawn to outsmart his deranged ex-wife because he was too much of a coward to declare checkmate himself.

"Did any of it even mean anything?" The words spilled out like blood from a wound, too fast to stop. I slapped a hand over my mouth—a flimsy Band-Aid—but it was too late.

He didn't answer anyway, his silence delaying the poison even he was too tactful to inject into my soul this time. *No.*

Was I really so pathetic that his rejection stung worse than the fact that he'd used someone's life as a chess pawn, guiding it ruthlessly across a board-like stage?

Seconds ticked by, but I couldn't come up with an answer. Relentless, I tightened my grip over the IV tubing until... *Pop!* A burning pain shot through my wrist a heartbeat later.

Red liquid was suddenly everywhere, splattering the pristine linoleum floor and splashing all over the front of my white hospital gown when I tried to stand up. The machines were beeping again, drowning out a man's shouts and rushing footsteps.

"Anya!"

I attempted to walk forward, teetering worse than Taylor. I had to brace one hand against the wall, grappling for balance, as something wet and warm slicked the surface of it like oil.

"Whoa, honey!" My nurse returned, her gaze fixated on my dripping left arm. "What happened?"

Muttering under her breath, she ushered me back to the bed and bundled my bloody wrist up in gauze. By the time she finally managed to stop the bleeding, my "father" was gone, having left just as abruptly as he'd appeared.

Had he ever really been there at all?

My brain hurt too much to decide if it had conjured him or not. Eventually, the machines monitoring my vitals beeped reassuringly as they deduced I wasn't in danger of dying anymore and the doctor returned to perform yet another assessment.

He made me count my fingers and my toes and recite the letters of the alphabet. Then he held a mirror up so that I could see the jagged crack in the back of my skull, stitched together and covered with a square bandage.

"You shouldn't go to sleep for at least a few more hours," he warned. My "father" should check on me every half hour to make sure my batteries didn't die. If we noticed any "change in mental status," I was to return to the ER right away.

I nodded, smiled, and promised to obey the instructions to the T. As he left, I'd almost gathered up the nerve to consider how I'd really get home. A cab? Jake?

A shadow fell over the foot of my bed and made the decision for me, almost as if on cue.

"Anya?"

That voice cut through the icy numbness that encased my spine, cracking my outer shell with a therapeutic dose of reality. I glanced up and found a stranger standing over me, his face drawn tight with exhaustion, his work tie partially undone.

"D-dad."

My real father didn't possess the cool reaction of Revend. He went pale at the sight of his daughter sporting a visible crack. He shouted at the doctors and the nurses, demanding answers. *How? How? Why?*

He glowered when they unhooked my IV, grumbling to no one in particular. "It's been five fucking minutes since therapy and already…"

He trailed off, but my conscience had no trouble filling in the blanks for him.

It's been five fucking minutes, and already you've fallen down again.

When the nurse returned with the release paperwork, he read my discharge instructions with a frown and grumbled something into his cell phone to my mother, which sounded like. "She's at the hospital. Yeah, I'm here now. One of the doctors called me—"

Something told me that "doctor" had a British accent and an uncanny knack for gathering any information he wanted. I peered out into the hallway, searching for a mysterious figure sporting a cane, but found nothing but a sea of medical personnel in multicolored scrubs.

"I'll take her home tonight," my dad said. "But tomorrow…"

Tomorrow, I'd be shipped right back to Hope Bridge, the resting place for naughty dolls too broken to salvage.

Some part of me wanted to resist that plan. Get Angry. Rebel.

Instead, I meekly got dressed and followed my dad out into the hallway while he snarled expletives at my mother through the phone—quietly enough so that the people walking past us wouldn't hear, of course.

This is your fault…

The only time he spoke to me directly was to gruffly order me to, "Wait here," before stalking off toward the parking lot. Not even a second later, I noticed a black car idling near the curb, and maybe it was only then when my head injury took full effect, that I started to hallucinate.

The sleek vehicle wasn't my father's Volvo. The driver palmed the steering wheel, eyeing the cluttered stretch of the parking lot behind my head. He finally put the engine into drive as I approached the passenger's side door.

Too late. I snagged the handle, pulling it open, and tumbled onto the seat.

"You called my dad," I said to the dashboard, the accusation almost resembling a whine. *Tattletale.*

He didn't answer.

In silence, I scanned the row of parked cars while yanking the door shut before I could understand why. Was that a sports car drifting toward the hospital's main entrance? It drove past us, its headlights spilling across the pavement like searchlights.

"I don't want to go home," I heard myself admit the moment that shiny car slowed before the curb, searching for someone who wasn't there.

"You have a concussion," Revend said, his voice weighed down by those logical concerns I was too tired to worry about. Though, for all I knew, he was just an "illusion" born out of blood loss and a head injury.

"I can't go home...yet," I told him while I tried to remember how to reassemble myself. *Get dressed. Forget. Pretend.* Or was I supposed to suppress *then* pretend? Why was it so hard to remember the correct order?

Why was it so hard to remember that I should hate him? I couldn't go home like this, where I'd creep up to my room unnoticed while everyone else worked out a "plan of action" without me.

Hope Bridge.

Therapy.

Hope Bridge.

Therapy.

Places where trained professionals would ask me to spell out how I felt in poems and journal entries only to stuff them inside a desk when I was done and tell me to think positively. *Have a positive outlook, Anya. You are capable of anything.*

No one there would smack me with the truth and then have the audacity to demand that I do something with it. *Use it.*

Through the shadows that painted the car's interior, I studied Revend, sensing all the hollow cracks I'd been blind to before. All of this time, he'd wanted me to feel *something* —but even "anger" only had substance around him. I only ever felt *anything* around him. Not exactly the right emotions—shame, hate, disgust—but they churned through my veins, more addicting than anything else, and I couldn't withdraw from it.

Not yet.

"Please…"

Revend slammed his foot on the gas pedal, and the sensation of the car jolting forward hit me like another blow. I was dizzy and silent as he drove through the streets, his jaw clenched as if he were wrestling with his decision every inch of the way. When the car came to a stop, it was before his lonely house on the hill, and I didn't resist when he led me inside, where he made me lie on the bare-bones couch in the sitting room, a threadbare pillow tucked beneath my head. Above us, a lopsided chandelier cast orange light that illuminated the room in bits and pieces like a smokeless flame.

"Don't sleep," he warned, scanning me from head to toe. "Maybe you should have stayed at the hospital for evaluation." A threat was hidden among those words, but I was too tired to react to it properly.

"Don't pretend like you give a damn about me."

He didn't, of course. Not even when he left me alone long enough to creep upstairs, returning minutes later with an oversized gray shirt. A quick glance down at my own sweatshirt revealed why—It was speckled with crusty patches of dried blood.

Aware of him watching, I stripped my sweatshirt and my blouse off, shivering beneath more than just the room's frigid temperature. Dark irises caressed my skin, leaving a searing trail. Under the pretense of "monitoring" me, he didn't even pretend to look away.

Gritting my teeth, I pulled on his button-down shirt. It became a game, trying to decipher what thoughts were reality and what might have been the result of my bruised brain. Revend's hand on my shoulder when I attempted to stand—that was real, too firm to be shaken off.

"Lie down." He sat too close, at the other end of the couch, forcing me to bend my knees to keep my toes from touching him.

Time ticked by, drip-dropping like the melting snow. It was thirty minutes later, on the dot, when he finally spoke.

"Say something."

"You stole my pills," I said, my tongue heavy. "My *other* pills."

Ignoring me was his first instinct, but he couldn't for long. *Doctor's orders.* "Yes," he finally grunted. "I did. And you would only know that if you went *looking* for them."

"Why?" The question echoed off the peeling wallpaper. *Why? Why? Why?*

He sighed and shifted around to face me. His scars caught the light, reflecting off the darkness in his eyes. Was it just my imagination, or were they even blacker than before? Endless.

"I... How many fingers am I holding up?"

I squinted. "Three. No, four…selfish, cowardly fingers."

He frowned, unsatisfied. "What day is it?"

A hoarse sound caught in my throat. "The day Katja's career ended." I hated saying that out loud. God, it sounded so final. So dramatic. One bad crack and the wind-up doll was ruined forever. I turned my head, burying my face into the musty surface of the pillow, but the action didn't shut out the memories of Katja. Her face. Her pain. "Just admit that you picked her on purpose…"

He didn't deny it. Didn't admit it, either. He merely sighed. "I didn't know it would go that far, Anya."

"Liar."

"I am," he said.

I peeked through a fringe of my tangled hair as he lifted his shoulders in an expression that might have passed for a shrug.

"I am…lying," he said. "I didn't mean for her to be injured, but…"

But. "There's always a *but*," I said as I slid my eyes closed for a moment to dispel the blurriness in my vision.

That one word held the lethality of poison, worse than any casting director's rejection. *But I didn't care. But someone had to "win." Someone had to lose. But, Anya. But.*

"You're selfish," I told him as I opened my eyes again and sought his out in accusation. "You're a coward. It's why

Victoria died. That's why Camille hates you. You're a selfish, asshole coward."

He nodded once, disrupting his shadow on the opposing wall.

"*I* hate you."

"How many fingers?"

I clenched my jaw shut rather than answer, but he nodded again, seemingly less worried than before. Then he studied the clock again. Thirty-five minutes later, he spoke.

"I never lied to you," he said almost too softly for me to hear. Maybe I didn't *want* to. "For what it's worth. I never lied to you."

I couldn't muster up a response. I merely counted the seconds until the doctor's deadline passed and I could sleep without being in danger of never waking up—not that I could.

"How many fingers?" Revend asked after I'd squeezed my eyes shut.

The question preceded the moment warmth grazed the side of my calf, leeching through the denim of my jeans. I didn't dare look. I was hallucinating, succumbing to my concussion. Defiantly, I counted my own heartbeat while my hallucination continued to travel up my thigh, eventually reaching the hand I had outstretched at my side.

I jerked my fingers away, curling them up tight. That persistent heat sought them out anyway, encasing my wrist

—lightly enough that I could break the grip if I wanted to. But I didn't.

I'm hallucinating.

Either way, I reluctantly let him weave yet another illusion —this one way too intricate to ever be erased.

CHAPTER 27

I woke up freezing. Icy air nibbled at my skin while murmuring voices lingered over the silence like frost.

Real?

Imagined?

My head throbbed too badly to even tell.

"Did you receive my present?" a woman asked somewhere nearby, her rich voice tainted by a musical accent. "I went through so much trouble."

"Get the hell out," a man growled in response. *Revend?*

Confused, I peeled my eyes open to a gray ceiling and tried to remember which nerves controlled what limbs. My arms seemed to be on different wavelengths, and my legs refused to cooperate. A million blaring sounds and sensations clashed inside my sore brain, demanding to be identified all at once—pain, exhaustion, that same woman's voice again.

"Now, now, Revend. No need to be rude; I only came to talk."

"We have nothing to discuss. Now, leave," Revend snapped.

"Oh, but I think we do. Did you really think I wouldn't figure it out?" that woman asked, her voice seeming to come from every location. "Who your real toy was?"

"I said leave—"

"She's a special one, that *Anya*," the woman continued, easily overpowering Revend. "It wasn't hard to see why she caught your eye. So fragile. So selfish. So needy. And it's been so very long since you've been *needed*. Hasn't it?"

Revend stayed silent.

"What?" she questioned innocently. "Oh, come now, Revend. You didn't honestly think you had fooled me, did you? The blonde and the redhead were convincing decoys, I will admit. But neither of them had that *spark*. That desperate little gleam in their eye that promised they would do anything for not only a part but attention. Affection. Some tiny hint that someone might give a damn about them—even if it's only when her clothes are off—"

"You leave her out of this."

"Oh," the woman purred. "So protective. But I'll let you in on a little secret." She paused, allowing the silence to build for dramatic effect. I pictured a cat bouncing a captured mouse from paw to paw, delaying the moment it took a bite. "I was never going to hurt her. Not Anya," she said finally. "Oh, don't look so surprised. It's true. I never would have laid a finger on her. Do you want to know why, *Mon Cher?* Girls like that have no problem with destroying themselves. Whether in the depths of a bottle of liquor or with pills or razor blades. They chase their own demise. One only need watch. An overdose today? Tomorrow? It doesn't really matter. It is a shame about that blonde, though. Her career, gone in a *poof.* I could have sworn I told my lad to aim for her pretty face—"

"Hm. Your *lad?* What poor, besotted fool do you have doing your dirty work now?" Revend asked, his voice grating on both rage and fear. I'd never heard that emotion in him before yesterday—the way his tone lowered a broken octave and how his eyes flashed obsidian.

"Besotted? No," the woman clarified. "As for fool… Well, he's one of yours, actually. I only had to promise him a spot in my company, and he eagerly jumped to do my bidding. The irony is rich, no?"

"Who?" Revend grunted, his tone promising retribution against whoever had dared to play this little game for the other team.

"I think his name is Kyle? Caleb? He's certainly performed his tasks better than expected, wouldn't you agree? I especially admire his way with a camera…"

"Why do it?" Revend snarled, echoing the question circling my own brain. *Caleb...why?* "If you knew Katja was a *'decoy'*, why even go after her in the first place?"

God, I wished I were dreaming. Hallucinating. Revend's world was a two-faced nightmare woven from deceit and deception—so vastly different from my dusty, stale dollhouse. I almost craved the mind-numbing monotony of being tucked safely on my shelf.

"Why?" The woman made a sound between another giggle and a sigh. "Why not? I was merely playing my part in our game. You knew that. Always. I watch. I wait while you scamper around, collecting your game pieces. You made it too easy, though," she added, sounding almost disappointed. "You've never tried to outsmart me before, Revend."

"Get the hell out. Now—"

"Do put that thing away," the woman taunted. "You'll hurt yourself, *Cher*."

"Or maybe I'll do what I should have done all those years ago," he suggested, allowing the threat to linger in the air.

"Maybe," the woman agreed. "But we both know that you won't. You *can't*."

"Can't I? I have nothing left to lose. I've already sold my share in the Roria, if that's what you're here about. Simon owns everything now. You can continue to sabotage it from the shadows, but it no longer matters. I've washed my hands of every stock—"

"And what about Anya?"

For a moment, Revend said nothing, while my delirious brain took that statement and ran with it. What about *Anya? Anya? Anya…*

"She was a fun diversion," he said as if the woman he spoke of was nothing more than an afterthought. "Nothing more."

"Oh, I'm sure she was—"

"I've informed the police about what I know of the attack on the Sorenson girl," Revend added, cutting over her. "I won't play complicit for you this time. Though I'm sure you'll be in France before they can question you."

"Perhaps. And what about *you*, my dear Revend?"

"That's none of your damn concern," he said coldly. "Make no mistake—Without a company tied to my name, I have nothing left to lose. Nothing to stop me from—"

"What? What are you going to do, Revend?" the woman wondered. "You don't think you really have it in you to kill me, do you?"

A numbing silence stretched on in the wake of her words, freezing everything in its path.

"Let's not pretend," someone murmured, their voice too soft to be identified. "Without this game, you have nothing to live for…"

I chased the words, fighting to regain control of my body. My fingers twitched, humming with sensation again. After what felt like an eternity, I managed to lurch upright, shrugging off a heavy material that felt like wool. One of my wooden legs jerked to life and hit the floor just as someone shoved me right back down.

"Lie down," a masculine voice commanded. "You're dreaming."

Dreaming? My emotions were rarely this sharp in reality, let alone in my dreams. Electricity raced up and down my spine, coiled with a million different sensations. *Fear. Pain. Confusion. More fear…*

My tongue was a rudder, grappling for control through the tempest. "Camille. That was her, wasn't it—"

"You're dreaming," Revend insisted, withdrawing his hand as if the lack of sensation might help enforce the lie.

Or maybe this really *was* a dream? A nightmare. Shadows painted the walls, moving and twisting as heavy footsteps circled my position—my very own boogeyman.

"Th-the police. We need to call the—"

"Go to sleep," Revend said, his expression harsher than chiseled stone.

This is a nightmare, a part of me whispered while my gaze drifted to the gun he was trying to shove into the waistband of his pants.

"You need…to call the police," I heard myself repeat.

"Why?" He crossed his arms over his chest.

"Why? Why? She was here. She admitted to attacking Katja and me. They need to know that."

"What do you think they'll do?" He shrugged. "Nothing. Go back to sleep, Anya. You're delirious—"

"So, what happens when I wake up?" I huddled in on myself, pulling my aching legs up to tuck both knees beneath my chin as if that might tether me to this fragile reality. A shudder ran through me while I dug my toes into the worn upholstery of the couch, waiting…waiting.

"I'm sure you'll find your place in another company."

"Another company," I echoed. As if it were really that simple. As if my career was all that mattered. Maybe, in Revend's reality, everything had such a clear outcome— mine was a little vaguer than that. "And another instructor?" I wondered, risking everything to glance at his face.

I found nothing in his eyes. No recognition. No hint that he knew what I *really* meant.

Old, awake Anya would have torn her gaze away in defeat after only a few seconds. Tired, delirious, concussed Anya was bolder. She stared on blankly and caught the flicker that crossed each black iris before the puppet master could squash the emotion, whatever it was. In the end, he looked away first, his hands clenching into fists.

"It…" I trailed off, licking my lips. What was it he'd said? *Stop resisting. Use this emotion. Give me something. Feel!* "It always meant something…to me."

"No, Anya." He shook his head, his eyes glinting darkly. "You don't know what you're saying. You're—"

"Delirious?" I finished for him. Maybe I was. My head hurt. The world was spinning too quickly. Fear mingled with the remains of dread, but for some reason, it had nothing to do with the woman who'd lurked on his doorstep or the conversation they'd had.

Selfish, little Anya. She only ever gave a damn about herself. Her feelings. Her emotions. Her pain.

"You sold the Roria," I said, switching topics. Slowly, I reached for the blanket discarded at my feet—a brown, knitted afghan—and pulled it around my shoulders like a cape. "Why?"

"It doesn't matter why," Revend hissed before beginning to pace. Each step was heavy, unsteady, and he wasn't using his cane. "All that matters is…"

"What?"

For the longest time, he didn't answer. He traveled the path beside the couch over and over, wearing away at the floor. When I thought he'd finally storm off and leave me to "dream" in peace, he turned on his heel and approached me.

"Tell me why you dance," he said while reaching down to cradle my chin in his palm.

God, I tried to smother the shiver that ran through me— really, I did. It felt so wrong. So needy. So desperate. Was that gleam in my eye really there? I couldn't tell, and Revend's expression didn't reveal any answers.

"The real reason," he barked. "Say it."

"I… It was the only time I didn't have to feel."

"Feel what?" he said, searching for the one word in particular he'd dragged out of me once before.

"Anything," I rasped.

"And that…" He inhaled sharply and cleared his throat as his fingertips dug more firmly into the underside of my chin. "*That* is why I needed to sell the Roria. Why I continued to run it in the first place, long after I'd last felt any real joy in it. I needed a distraction from the world. From the shell of who I used to be. The dreams I used to chase. I needed…"

Pills? I wondered without guessing out loud. *Drugs? Oblivion? Sex?* Something even stronger to help smother the pain and chase the self-doubt away?

"Do you really want to know why I was willing to sacrifice that girl? *You?* I think you've figured it out already. So go ahead and say it." His grip tightened, forcing my chin higher. His gaze was impossible to escape now, boring deep down into those fragile bits of me only he was strong enough to prod. "I'm a coward," he declared before I could say the magic word myself. "It was easier to hide within the remains of a dream than face the harsher truth. Don't be like me. Don't…"

He trailed off, though a part of me readily filled in the blanks. *Don't seek safety in the shell of an illusion. Feel. Use the emotion. Turn it into something.*

"So, what now?" I croaked, my voice breaking on a pathetic, desperate note. *Tell me. Tell me.*

"Now?" Revend grunted and withdrew his fingers while plunging his other hand into his pocket. Slowly, as if to make sure I couldn't miss a single detail, he removed two wads of plastic and threw them onto the cushion next to me. "Make your choice. I won't stop you."

I inhaled sharply, chewing on my lower lip until I tasted blood. This wasn't the route my therapist would have recommended. My fingers shook while I eyed the floor rather than look. I wouldn't look…

"What… What are you doing?"

"It's the release you crave," he said. "Isn't it? I may have succeeded in elevating you more than I'd ever assumed possible in dance…but I can't fix you, Anya. No one can. So here. Take them. All of them. I won't stop you."

"But—"

"I'm sure there's enough there for an overdose," Revend said, cutting over me.

I did the math in my head and realized he was right. Five plus ten. Fifteen. The same dose of poison the dolly had swallowed last time.

I hated the way my skin itched, and my body ached for the high. That numbness. That freedom. Even if it killed me.

He really wouldn't stop me. I could see it in the way he hobbled over to the door.

"Take them or don't," he said, his back to me. "It doesn't matter either way. All that does is that you finally stop pretending. Stop suppressing. Allow yourself to feel…or don't."

I hated the hoarse note in his voice; it wasn't supposed to be there. God, the unfeeling, asshole Revend who used people for his own gain—*he* would have been easy to obey. But I didn't recognize the stranger walking away to linger on the cusp of the entryway. Or maybe, deep down, I did. The same man who'd taunted me day in and day out, forcing me to feel, only to cringe when I did.

Camille was right—All I wanted was to drown within one little pill.

Do it, Anya.

Without looking, I slid my hand out in search of plastic and greedily latched on to the flimsy surface. One tug. Two. It was in my hand, full of promises of relief and another chance to fill the void even ballet couldn't.

It would be so easy…

I toyed with the plastic baggie, eagerly finding the opening and slipping my fingers inside. Something small and round nudged my pinkie as if anxious to be swallowed.

"Take it," Revend barked from the doorway.

My gaze drifted over to him, finding nothing but emptiness in those black eyes as they met mine over his shoulder. With a nod, I obeyed, fishing one tiny pill out and popping it on my tongue. My throat jerked, but for some reason, I couldn't bring myself to actually swallow. I gagged while it sat there, bitter and melting into a puddle of high-inducing, heart-stopping chemicals.

"Swallow it, Anya," Revend prompted, but his mask flickered around the edges

I swallowed, gagged again. The pill flew out and landed on my lap, encased in saliva.

No worries, though. I could always try again. I fisted my hand inside the plastic bag, capturing two pills. Then I slapped that hand over my mouth, throwing them inside as if to catapult them down my throat. But they got stuck somewhere between the roof of my mouth and my tongue, refusing to go any farther than that. I swallowed and swallowed, but my naughty throat wouldn't accept its latest dose of medicine. It made me cough and gag until those pills slithered out and dribbled down my chin.

I tried again.

On the fourth try, my stomach had had enough, and I threw up a foul-smelling pile at the base of the couch. In an instant, heavy footsteps approached, and warm fingers batted the hair from my eyes.

"Look at me."

I did, my watering gaze tracing the wrinkles that lined a pair of fathomless eyes that contained secrets I'd never learn and motives that made me shiver. I don't know how long we stayed like that, his thumb propped beneath my chin, forcing me to hold his gaze. He didn't move again until—whether on purpose or by accident—my grip on the baggie loosened, allowing it to bounce off the couch and hit the floor.

In silence, Revend encircled my wrist in one of his hands before I could reach for it and pulled me to my feet. I shuddered when he stepped in close, his scent burning my lungs from the inside out. One of his hands skirted my waist before the fingers ghosted up…and settled over my shoulder. The other traveled from my wrist to my hand, lacing with the frozen, trembling fingers.

"First position," he prompted, nudging my body into the correct placement. "Second," he said next when I'd robotically complied.

Then third. Fourth.

I performed each step at his command, my eyes drifting shut while I tried to search for some elusive emotion. It was ironic how everything had come so easily to Taylor, but I felt like a wooden puppet brought to life without consent and forced to describe the differences in one single word.

Feel.

With Revend's breath on my shoulder, I just felt heat. His fingers imparted more warmth, dancing along my skin as he put me through the basic paces. *Fifth position. First again.*

Somewhere in the transition to third, I realized that nothing else was registering. Not the pain pounding away at my skull, the suffocating sensation of being locked in my own skin, or the oxycodone residue dripping down my chin.

Just silence. *This.* The motion.

Maybe I really was dreaming. Maybe I was only hallucinating. Maybe the real drug was behind me, delivering a lethal overdose with every touch.

"Breathe." The grunted word grazed my neck.

As if it really were that easy. I inhaled anyway, feeling the air warily go into my lungs and drift back out.

Feel.

I shifted my feet against the floor, the wood creaking beneath my weight. Without really knowing why, I lifted one foot and reached down to strip my sock off before doing the same to the second. Harsh bits of wood nipped at my heels, attempting to break my outer shell. But Revend had already succeeded in that endeavor the moment he'd seized the hem of my shirt, tugging on the cotton.

I fluttered my fingers to the buttons of my shirt before he could command me to take it off. I undid them slowly, registering my own body's reaction to the cold air that kissed every inch of bare skin.

Feel, Anya.

I rose up on tiptoe while my eyes drifted shut again. The impatient fingers on my shoulders disappeared. All I felt was…

Muscle and bone bending and twisting. Moving. Aching.

The clumsy series of steps I found myself performing weren't from *Giselle* or *Romeo and Juliet*. Just the tragic ballet of Anya the fractured doll. Was it possible for her to ever be mended?

She moved her fragile parts, desperate to become human again. Her stage was a rickety foundation of old wood and stone. Her audience was a mixture of peeling wallpaper and worn furniture. The spotlight was formed from the puppet master's watchful, black gaze, which chased her across the room.

There was no real technique—it was a disjointed dance, more abstract than even *Giselle's* mad scene. Just a broken doll finally tumbling off her pedestal.

When she finally stopped spinning in circles, had she convinced anyone?

I didn't know, and the specter behind me didn't supply any answers as he gently coaxed me back onto the couch.

Someone was knocking, the sound ricocheting like gunshots through my throbbing head.

I opened my eyes, blinking rapidly. The world was a soup of white walls and gray shadows. Where was I? Clarity returned in stingy snatches as I took my surroundings in. I was lying on a couch—Revend's couch. Someone had draped my body with a thick, brown blanket, and my bloody clothes littered the floor like discarded toys.

Gray daylight spilled in through the windows. My head felt like someone had stuffed the inside of it with cotton, and taunting words danced across the inside of my skull. I wasn't sure if the conversation they depicted had been real or merely a dream.

"Anya?" The voice sounded muffled from yards of distance and a wooden door, but recognition sank into my sleepy limbs, urging them into motion. "Anya, are you in there?"

Bang, bang, bang!

Revend was nowhere in sight, and I knew even as I warily approached the front door that he wasn't on the other side of it.

"Anya, *finally*," my dad exclaimed the moment I undid the lock and twisted the rusting handle. "Are you all right?"

Worry distorted his features. We looked more alike than ever. Same dazed expression. Same marble-like eyes struggling to convey what their body truly felt. He must have been malfunctioning when he touched me, breaking one of his own unspoken rules to trail a trembling hand along my porcelain cheek before pulling me in for a wooden hug.

"Are you okay?"

Okay?

I scanned the driveway beyond his shoulder. It was empty, devoid of that lurking black car.

"Anya?"

"I…" The words wouldn't come. I had nothing prepared. Our script had been torn to pieces in my search for drugs. I had to compile the words on my own. "Yeah, I think so…"

Was I really? My robot brain was struggling to reconcile my broken doll parts.

"I think I'm okay. I think so…"

Dad pulled away and ushered me out of the towering, empty house and toward Carrie's minivan, which was parked in the driveway. He didn't explain how he had known where to find me, or what the unknown whistleblower had told him to make him so anxious, all threats of Hope Bridge tossed aside.

He didn't say anything.

And, for the first time in months—years, maybe—I felt like he was trying to listen.

CHAPTER 28

I stood on the train platform, counting the minutes I had left until the clock struck nine. My first day of "Saving Anya 2.0" and I was late already. Supposedly, Dad would be waiting for me at the therapist's office. Supposedly, we would finally talk. Supposedly, things would change.

Did I truly believe they would?

Without my trusty script, it was harder to tell. The rest of this play was unwritten, the ending left up to the actors' discretion.

Through the intercom, an announcer proclaimed that the next train would arrive in five minutes. I fingered the strap of my bag, struggling to keep up with the press of people jockeying for a position closest to the platform's edge.

How many of them were like me? Forced to keep "important" appointments. Sit. Roll over. Beg.

I was shivering in my jacket when the train rolled into the station, billowing steam. My destination was two stops away, roughly ten minutes. I had only seven to spare.

In the end, I spent twenty, including a backtrack toward a desolate hill. Then I took another eight minutes walking down a lonely boulevard, toward an enormous house that looked like it should have been condemned months ago.

The front door was closed, but no hint of life drifted from behind it. Just silence. There, on the doormat, was a white box devoid of a name.

Once I gathered the nerve to wrestle the lid off, I found a pair of lavender pointe shoes inside. On top of them was a folded slip of paper that contained a few hastily scribbled words. The same phrase had been partially written and then crossed out again.

Remember to use your anger.

TWO YEARS LATER...

My mother would hate the cafés in Europe. They were louder than the whisper-soft ones in Buckley, filled to the brim with people who aren't afraid to laugh, talk, or lie at the tops of their lungs while sipping tea from chipped saucers. *Real* tea.

It was the ideal place to pour over a dog-eared ballet program while simultaneously contemplating the reality of being alone and abroad with nothing more than a hasty Google search of a single name to guide me.

Positive thinking was all about the mindset, according to my new therapist. You sought out the best aspects of the situation and highlighted them while still acknowledging the bad. At least the "positive" in this case was easy to see once I left the café and trudged up ten blocks to reach an old, distinguished theater that towered over everything else. A gleaming marquee above the entrance displayed the current production—*Swan Lake – The Roria Ballet Company.*

The tides had turned in two years, apparently. A crowd of well-dressed Londoners streamed inside, eager to fill their seats. Wearing the same sweats I'd arrived in the country in, I stuck out. And not in a good way.

An usher frowned as he scanned my ticket. "DeSotto?" he asked, reading my name off the slip of paper. "Your seat was moved. This way."

My heart pounded as I followed him through a dimly lit hallway and then up a flight of stairs before being led into a private box with a bird's-eye view of the stage.

"I think there's been some kind of mistake," I blurted, eyeing the row of red velvet chairs.

"No mistake," the usher insisted. "Enjoy the show."

I sat warily. Unease bubbled up in my stomach, but I swallowed it right back down. Instead, I fished the program out of my bag and skimmed through it for the millionth time. I didn't recognize any of the names peppered throughout the brochure, not even under the producer's heading. Beside the Roria's name, only one owner was listed —Simon Guilles.

When the lights dimmed, no one had come to kick me out of the booth, even as the rest of the theater filled to the brim. The stage curtains rose, the hush of murmuring voices died down, and the ballet began.

There was something painfully beautiful about watching other people dance. I envied their graceful movements and apparent freedom at the same time I held my breath through even the tiniest mistakes. I knew what it was like.

To float on the tips of my toes.

To fall flat on my face.

To falter. To feel…

Dancers feed on applause. It's the only sustenance capable of satisfying the craving in our souls. Nothing else can even scratch that spot. We eke out a living as a slave to the stage, putting our bodies through the wringer, contorting our limbs into unnatural, violent positions…

But one sound can make all of that pain worth it in an instant.

Clap.

Clap…

Whether a slow trickle or a deafening roar, those few seconds soothe the years of struggle and grueling rehearsals that preceded them. For five minutes at a time, we're utterly alone, warm, wanted, respected.

That cherished sound flooded the theater as the last act before intermission drew to a close. The lights returned to their full brilliance, leaving me to wonder exactly what I was doing there. Two years was a long time to still chase something, even after you've "cleaned" up and moved on, having ticked every box on a therapeutic checklist.

I wasn't the star prima of some prestigious ballet or still clawing my way through a company. I wasn't using any crutch I could to get by. I wasn't still waiting…

Regardless, I couldn't name exactly what had driven me halfway across the world to see *this* one show for *this* one night in *this* city. Maybe it was part of that all-important healing process my therapist touted. Facing the past, saying goodbye to it once and for all.

Admittedly, this place wasn't a terrible venue to close that chapter of my life. The theater itself dripped with history and elegance. The performance was breathtaking, everything I'd expect an international company to put on. I even had private seats to view it from. Or at least they *had been* private…

"Can I join you?" The voice came from a shadow lurking around the mouth of the box. Deep. Accented.

When my chin jerked into a nod, the figure crept closer, allowing the light to wash over his features. He looked older, unsurprisingly, with more silver streaking his hair than before. As cold as always, still wearing that perpetual frown.

He took the seat beside me, resting a wooden cane against his knee. In an instant, the charming box was transformed into a narrow realm of shadow and peppermint.

Revend eyed the audience beneath us as they rushed to and from the auditorium in an effort to grab refreshments before the next act. Then he inhaled raggedly. Paused. Exhaled. Inhaled again.

"You look well," he said finally.

"Th-thanks." I guessed that was a compliment, all things considered. I looked different too—less fake smiles, more slight wrinkles around my eyes. My hair was still long. I was still too short. Still stubby. Still Anya.

"You look…" I peeked at him from the corner of my eye, watching his fingers clench at his sides, his posture stiff in the elegant chair. "Like you," I finished softly.

A corner of his mouth twitched. "Do you still dance?" It was a dangerous question, which he uttered almost gently. Warily.

He didn't mean literally—a dancer always danced.

"Not professionally," I admitted. Surprisingly, it didn't hurt, telling him that much. "I teach now. Ages eight to twelve, intermediate level." A smile tugged at my mouth, though I think he had already known.

No, the way he quickly turned away proved it. He *had* known.

About a month after he'd left, I'd received a mysterious transfer to my bank account—an amount that I figured was similar to what an international ballet company might be worth. Part of it went to classes—real ones—for business management, while the other went toward a small local studio to teach basic ballet. Not long after our first recital, my dancers received anonymous donations of costumes, slippers, or flowers after performances.

At least, now, I had definitive proof. He knew.

"What about you?" I asked rather than mention any of it.

He shrugged and cast me an unreadable glance. "Enjoying my retirement."

He seemed to mull over his next statement before making it. "Are you ready for me now?"

I nodded once, providing my answer just as the lights dimmed again. The curtains drew back to reveal the next set dressing, and the ballet continued as if nothing had ever changed.

A WORD FROM THE AUTHOR

Hey there!

Thank you so much for reading! If you enjoyed the story, please leave a review and recommend the book to any friend you think would love this twisted world. You'd have my eternal gratitude. Even a short sentence goes a long way!

Then, come join the rest of us dark romance lovers in my Facebook Group where you can get snippets, sneak peeks of upcoming books and even help vote on aspects of future novels.

Come to the dark side:

https://www.facebook.com/groups/lanasbeautifulmonsters/

WANT MORE STUFF TO READ?

Join my newsletter and get a **free book**! Plus, you get to stay updated with any new releases, random giveaways and exclusive sneak peeks!

https://www.lanaskybooks.com/newsletter

Other Novels: https://lanaskybooks.com/

Lana Sky is a reclusive writer in the United States who spends most of her time daydreaming about complex male characters and parenting her Cockapoo Joey. She writes dark, twisted romance across several genres. Her titles include everything from mafia romance to vampires.

www.ingramcontent.com/pod-product-compliance
Lightning Source LLC
Chambersburg PA
CBHW071424190726
48292CB00001B/103